W9-BBI-708

# REMNANTS
## OF THE
# FIRST EARTH

Also by Ray A. Young Bear:

Winter of the Salamander
The Invisible Musician
Black Eagle Child: The Facepaint Narratives

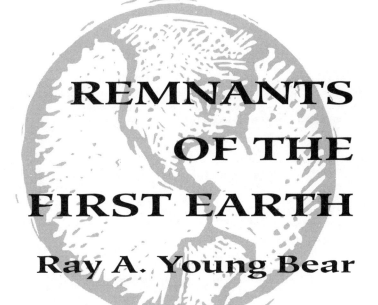

# REMNANTS
# OF THE
# FIRST EARTH

## Ray A. Young Bear

**Grove Press**
**New York**

FIRST EDITION
*Published simultaneously in Canada*
*Printed in the United States of America*


Library of Congress Cataloging-in-Publication Data
Young Bear, Ray A.
    Remnants of the first earth / Ray A. Young Bear. — 1st ed.
      p.      cm.
    ISBN 0-8021-1581-0
    1. Indians of North America—Iowa—Fiction. 2. Boys—Iowa—
Fiction. I. Title.
    PS3575.O865R46   1996
    813'.54—dc20     96–1444


DESIGN BY LAURA HAMMOND HOUGH

Grove Press
841 Broadway
New York, NY 10003

10 9 8 7 6 5 4 3 2 1

*For Todd Dana Young Bear, August 1960–January 1992*

# Acknowledgments

This novel would not have been possible without the unwavering encouragement offered by the following people in my "word-collecting" endeavor: my parents, Leonard and Chloe Young Bear; Stella Lasley Young Bear, my wife; and the many supportive family members of the Meskwaki, People of the Red Earth, Nation of Central Iowa.

The same adulation goes to my editor, Anton Mueller, at Grove Press; Peter Basch, literary agent; and to the vast support I received from the beginning of my career to the present, via Bill Beyer, Wesley Abbott, Robert Bly, John Strong, Robert Gish, Elizabeth Cook-Lynn, and Leslie Silko.

I also give my deepest thanks to those cherished influences who have gone West to the Meskwaki Hereafter: Jack and Ada Old Bear; Todd Dana Young Bear; Irene Young Bear Bernadino; Kenneth Young Bear; and Curtis Young Bear. Their warm, smiling spirits have recently surfaced in my thoughts, making it seem like they never really left, helping me and everyone still.

Lastly, and the Creator knows this, I respectfully acknowledge my great-great-grandfather, Ma mi nwa ni ke, the Sacred Chieftain who initiated the purchase of our tribal land in 1856. His monumental accomplishments remain unparalleled. Without him, the Meskwaki Settlement would not be in existence.

—*Ray A. Young Bear*

# Contents

# Preface

## The Wish That Bear King Had

At daybreak, the Black Eagle Child Settlement—home for fifteen hundred tribal members—protrudes as a geographic anomaly against the flat, rural horizon of central Iowa. When seen from the west several miles out, especially along Runner's Bluff, the Settlement resembles a tree-covered island encircled by monotonous vistas of cornfields, pastures, and grazing livestock. If it weren't for the gray, rounded hills that rise slightly above the drifting layers of fog from the Swanroot and Iowa Rivers, we would be indistinguishable. Literally.

In these few hours before the fiery orange sun ascends the wooded terrain, replacing the foggy shroud with clear daylight, it seems as if this place, my home, is momentarily surrounded by the wide, sweeping waters of an invisible ocean called eventuality. If you look down further into the drifting fog and think deeply about dreams that make you prepare to leave for an unknown destiny, an inner sense of fear never fails to conjure a serpentlike image of a Supernatural seeming to pause in its wondrous swim before flicking its massive tail. In the boil and wake created by the mythical sentinel, treacherous waves crash noisily along the shores of our borders. On occasion, the "shadows," or souls, of certain individuals lose their footing here and tumble headfirst into the surf. You wouldn't think it, but the consequences of a single loss upon our clan-based society is devastating. More so when we are few to begin with.

Yet, this metaphorical earth-island is where three generations of my grandparents—*wa wi ta wi*, on either side—flourished in order that we would have a chance at some undesignated point to carry on where they left off, performing errorfree ceremonies to guide believers through the murkiness of the Cosmic Earthlodge. This, according to my limited knowledge, was the original wish of Bear King, the Settlement's founder: to find a sanctuary where generation upon generation would flourish and maintain the customs that would forever identify them as Black Eagle Child.

What makes our tribal homeland distinct is the fact that a small Algonquian dialect-speaking world has been in existence here, legally, for the past 140 years. As startling as it may seem to some, my great-great-grandfather, through his status as a living divinity, secured the initial purchase of property from the state of Iowa in 1856.

That's where the "legally" comes in.

After centuries of warfare with the European newcomers in which our predecessors barely pieced themselves back together, my grandfather, who was a young *O ki ma*, or Sacred Chieftain, provided the answer by implementing his exclusive birthright to obtain acreage in our former dominion. Since a government-enforced order of exile had to be defied to facilitate a return to a region that was once the source of fierce territorial contention, solidifying the destiny of the Black Eagle Child people was not easy. But after persecution by different-colored flags that would have made others succumb, splinter, or simply vanish altogether, our acquisition of real estate was the only logical solution. And this could come about—and it did—only through the wish and actions of a single but blessed person by the name of Bear King, *Ma kwi O ki ma*. That was his exclusive role as a savior: to rescue us from suffering and ensure our survival.

If it was provincial isolation that Bear King sought, he and his grandfather could not have picked a more desolate midwestern hinterland—the middle of Iowa—to conduct the ongoing affairs of a tribe. It is said my two grandfathers based the Settlement's location on a story, *a ji mo ni*, told by an ancient hunter who was once approached by two underworld goddesses informing him that people would one day make their homes on these hills. Declining the goddesses' offer of immortality, the hunter returned to the winter Mississippi River encampment and conveyed with astonishment what the Supernaturals had said.

Long before any name was bestowed to this fertile country, back when the soil was black, moist, and untainted, our grandparents many times previous were well acquainted with the trees and saplings that stood here in abundance. They were also aware of water transparent and sweet to the taste. As the strong summer wind rushed enchantingly over the adjoining prairies, making peaceful sounds, they remembered the ancient hunter's story, which they then gave to their grandchildren's grandchildren and beyond until it reached the ears of Bear King's grandfather.

It was on the northwestern tip of Runner's Bluff that Bear King's emissaries, after a long arduous journey from Kansas, camped before setting out for the state capitol in Iowa City. They carried with them a written message asking the state legislature permission "for Bear King, the Boy Chieftain, and his followers to acquire land and reside peacefully in Tama County." In a historic turnaround of the attitudes of the era, the Boy Chieftain's request was granted in 1856.

While it is generally a rarity—even today—for a tribe to become property owners in the United States, Bear King, whose name is remembered today only in the prayer-breath expelled by elders of the Earthlodge clans, was futuristic: He raised the necessary cash and made the authorized proposition to the government higher-ups; he was then given a deed to said property. On the surface, the transaction probably sounded acceptable, but it was also an outright capitulation of ancient customs and beliefs. Yet, for what was ultimately received, it was a momentary acquiescence of values. Without much intrusion from the Newcomers, the Black Eagle Child Nation was guaranteed at least a chance to thrive on its own.

Beginning with the revelation given by the goddesses to the living divinity status of my grandfather, spiritually interwoven factors brought us out from the nightmarish exile of the Kansas prairies.

Through our stories we were brought back to an area familiar to our predecessors. For the Boy Chieftain, Bear King, figuring out the intricacies of a farming enterprise replete with barns, silos, machinery, and knowledge of grain and hog prices was the furthest thing from his thoughts and intentions.

My maternal grandmother used to say it was crucial we have a place of our own. Listening intently, I learned that our lives were dependent upon a plethora of animistic factors immersed in ethereal realities.

Basically, she instructed that the very ground on which we all stood, Grandmother Earth, was the embodiment of a former Supernatural being. She was all of nature, this Grandmother: She was the foundation for rivers, lakes, fields and forests; she provided homes and sustenance for insects, birds, reptiles, fish, animals, and human beings. She held everything together, including the clouds, stars, sun, and moon.

Our sole obligation, my grandmother instructed, in having been created in the first place by the Holy Grandfather, is to maintain the Principal Religion of the Earthlodge clans. It was agreed eons and eons ago that if these ceremonies were not performed, the world would no longer be held together, the elements of wind and ice would whirl together and splinter us apart. Our forgetfulness, in other words, would become part of a chain of natural and man-made catastrophes—flag wars and ecological suffocation—leading to the end of the earth. And the people who so connivingly and viciously sought to make us forget ourselves by subjugating us, the Euro-Americans, would be the root cause.

It is therefore prophesied that by making us forget who we are, they inevitably kill themselves. . . .

*Edgar Bearchild*

# Part
# One

# The Year of the Weeping Willow Day School

On the playgrounds of the Weeping Willow Elementary School, six Black Eagle Child Indian boys sat on a creaky motionless merry-go-round with their legs dangling over the bluish gray pebbles. Within the octagon-shaped ride, two empty places separated the two sets of third- and fourth-grade boys. Calmly and deliberately they addressed one another in a mixture of English and their tribal language.

The topic, it was somehow decided, was their father's occupations. It somehow seemed important to talk about employment, the vehicle of their clothes, food, and shelter. Included in the first responses were the names of distant Iowa cities, like Cedar Rapids, Waterloo, Des Moines, and Iowa City. Even though they had all gone on a school field trip to Minneapolis a month previous on a train, none of them had been to these cities. Incomprehensibly, each father seemed to be a welder, a factory employee, or a construction worker in the cities. Money amounts were discussed.

Everything about the conversation was going well until the group asked Edgar Principal Bear what his father did for a living. Sensing five sets of eyes on him, the light-brown, round-faced boy lifted his glasses to his flat, chubby nose with his finger and looked downward at his scuzzy brown shoes. He was reacting as if he hadn't heard a word said.

"Edgar, *ki na we na-ke i sha wi ya-ko se ma?* Edgar, what does your father do?" the group asked again pointedly. "*A kwi me ko-ke ko-i no we ya ni ni.* You haven't said anything." Edgar's head involuntarily jerked upward and a tuft of black hair broke free from the oiled-down Elvis Presley hairdo, dangling upright in the breeze of an intense afternoon sun and curling.

The group, consisting of Pat Red Hat, Kensington Muscatine, Horatio Plain Brown Bear, Theodore Facepaint, and Hayward Muscatine, couldn't understand why Edgar was unusually quiet. Typically he was talkative and jovial. Now he only made them curious.

The question startled Edgar, rendering him dry-mouthed.

Finally, after shrugging his shoulders and straightening his hair, Edgar offered that he didn't know. It was obvious he was not comfortable. He fidgeted and kicked some pebbles to the center of the merry-go-round before continuing. "But my uncle works at Whitmore's Sawmill in town. My mother works at the chicken factory, and my grandmother at the Why Cheer Laundry and Dry Cleaners. *Tte na-ne tti se e ma-mi ke je wi wa*—Whitmore's Sawmill—*o te we ne ki. Ne ki ya-wi na*—chicken factory—*mi ke je wi ya ka o ni-no ko me se ma-a i me ki*—Why Cheer Laundry and Dry Cleaners."

From the movements of the shadows cast in stark detail over the gravel, Edgar ascertained the boys had all looked at one another. He had dodged the subject of fathers. Again. There was a brief but strained pause in the conversation. They sat still and listened to the chain fasteners of the whipping flag and looked toward the empty swings. As they did this, Edgar took out a comb and fixed the curl. When they returned to him, he looked down at his brown scuzzy shoes. Again.

No one had noticed before but the warm breeze that pressed their shirts against their upper torsos outlined either their ribs or the tiny ridges of their backbones. Above them, at the end of a tall clinking metal pole, the American flag whipped loudly. In precise moments it undulated and ended up with a sharp snap. The chain fasteners tapped steadily against the pole. There was something about colored cloth that hung in the air, responding vigorously to the warm spring breeze. Nearby, lonely swings swung without riders. In the air, the smell of fresh dandelions and apple tree blossoms.

Today, for no apparent reason, a subtle change was taking place in their six young bodies. As a group they had decided to skip a game of softball. Was it maturity? They couldn't even begin to know. Whatever the source or cause, they found certain comfort in taking a break from the norm to converse like adults.

After all, they had been together as students hopelessly immersed in school, yet they hardly knew anything about one another's families. They had listened to each other read and do arithmetic badly. No one had the edge on grades. Not even the girls. They were all equally illiterate. Yet they were Black Eagle Child, held together and separated.

All at once, like the warm sensory breeze rippling over their tight shirts, a sense of maturing generated thoughts on the purpose of life itself through this discussion of their fathers' employment in the daylight air.

Wanting to continue the conversation, the group turned to another classmate, the one who sat to Edgar's right, Theodore Facepaint. "Ted, what does yours do? *Ki na wa na-ka tti-i tti te wa?*" But Ted was just as dumbstruck. He could barely lift his head from the metal handlebar, and he blinked repeatedly as if intending to speak. His parched thin lips were curled inward, and quick audible gulps of air were taken. Under his thick black glasses was a slightly pale and pockmarked face with a wide, flat nose that looked broken. Under his long brown-tipped hair was a set of puffy, trembling eyes.

Ted, in a halting voice, explained that his father was a construction worker. He worked on buildings in Iowa City. There was a reference to "u . . . ni . . . ver . . . siti . . . ha . . . spi . . . toes."

It was a warm, sunny 1960 spring afternoon, a recess period in which everyone else had gone to the other side of Weeping Willow, frolicking over the large grassy lawn in a much-needed game of softball. Teaching and learning was hard for both the Bureau of Tribal Affairs staff and students; hostilities had somehow ceased temporarily. There was a semblance of amicability.

No one would be chased after, scolded, roughed up, and sent inside. On this occasion, the yellow-jacket wasps were doing the chasing—with each other. They seemed to shoot through the blue sky openings in the high fluffy clouds that were unevenly smeared across the green wooded horizon. Upon seeing the boys, the wasps hovered for a moment between the gray tubular merry-go-round bars before buzzing toward the concrete haze around the school building.

Pat Red Hat, who was a portly, big-boned boy, sat with his sleeves rolled up past his forearms. His tattooed knuckles gripped the bar tightly as he stretched backward, basking his little face and hooked nose in the sun's rays. Never one to be afraid to look directly at the sun, his eyes were halfway open. It had something to do with an ancient story about how mischievous children had once tied up the sun with cordage on its daily crossing. "Are you really afraid of children?" he would shout upward at the fiery sphere before throwing rocks at it. With his large exposed rump hanging over the wooden seat, Pat started singing songs from the annual tribal celebration, breaking the awkward stillness. The first was a pipe dance song that was made with a country and western singer's name.

*Ya-a ho John-ny Cash, Ya-a ho Johnny Cash.*
*Ya ho Johnny Cash, Ya ho Johnny Cash . . .*

The second pipe dance song, he related, was the same except that it mocked a dancer's oddly placed regalia pieces—the white Angora goat leggings.

*A sa mi-a kwi tti i-ke bi se ka-ke mi . . . tti-ka ta ka na ni.*
You are wearing your fu . . . ur-r-r leggings much too high.

While Pat was chanting away on his improvised lyrics, Horatio Plain Brown Bear shot his arms and legs out, holding them rigid when the verse stopped. As another verse was winding up, in the dance part where the drum was rumbled, Horatio began to gyrate as if in a rigorous pipe dance. At the part where the "fur" mention was over-emphasized and elongated, Horatio, taking a few good sniffs to clear his perpetually runny nose, scooped up some rocks and placed them inside an empty milk carton. On the next verse, near the "fur" part, he shook the milk carton like a rattle.

Everyone had a good hearty laugh, but the song that alluded to "fur," or hair, also made them nervous. All at once they realized there could be implications in acknowledging the song's message. They eyed one another quickly before looking away as if they were being blinded by the afternoon sun. It was an excuse to look stupid and act uninterested, the way they had taught one another to do in class: instant mutes, avoiding participation.

Of course, the threat of being deprived of recess for not participating made the strongest among them quiver like a nauseated rabbit. They all knew how to read, Pat had said, because the white teachers had drilled holes into their skulls and with a funnel poured in the liquid sustenance known as the English language, the real "alphabet soup." In dejection they had all read from the musty-smelling textbooks aloud, enunciating and uttering words that were essentially meaningless. *Magellan. Magna Carta. Michelangelo.* Before, Pat related, we were like wild reptile babies that refused to eat during captivity, forcing Euro-American owners to ram potent doses of civilization down their throats with sticks in order that they might live. And twice a week they were stripped of their grimy clothes, herded to the bathroom showers like war prisoners, and lathered with bulk Lysol-smelling soap before Mr. Mateechna, the Indian janitor, scrubbed them down with a hard bristle brush.

They may well exhibit signs of knowing how to read vowels and syllables, the Weeping Willow staff commented at lunch, but words like *skyscraper* and *museum* are meaningless unless these places are introduced to them. Therefore, beginning in the 1950s, field trips were taken twice a year.

Yet, even on short excursions to the Tama County courthouse to look at World War I memorabilia donated by the Potato cousins, the Black Eagle Child version of Audie Murphy twice over, Pat Red Hat, was closely monitored. Besides being a singer who was forced since infancy to drum with adults, Pat was unusually body-oriented. "Maybe I got this way from the old men," he'd begin, before sharing wicked stories in Black Eagle Child with his diminutive classmates. This master held them spellbound with adult storytelling.

As Pat amused Horatio with his improvised pipe dance lyrics, the other boys, not wanting to acknowledge the song's allusion to intimate body hair, joined Edgar Bearchild as he stared downward.

\*    \*    \*

For Edgar, there was an incredible sense of relief, and he welcomed Pat for being a timely distraction. The question about his father's occupation was unnerving. He couldn't even begin to guess what his father looked like, much less where he worked or if he even did. There was a slight chance he might have actually seen him the summer previous, walking at a brisk pace down a brick street in cowboy boots, but he wasn't sure. Pondering a father who was virtually nonexistent was a strain, but no one would press the issue.

As Pat sang on, the boys sat like baby pheasants, frozen and listening. They could see Horatio's shadow over the bluish gray pebbles. He was oblivious, and his antics were unabated. No one quite knew what to make of the silly dance business.

Did Horatio even know, or was it part of a gag?

The fact was, in 1960, rural midwestern Indian boys—or girls— were told absolutely nothing about themselves, thanks to America's mind-set back then. Therefore, the phrases that came forth from Pat Red Hat were strange things they didn't recognize. Nevertheless, they acted as if they did for fear of embarrassment. The boys were wholly dependent upon Pat's tremendous knowledge of human anatomy, knowing no one could possibly make up such bizarre but enlightening stuff. Pat was born and raised in a traditional family whose stories were infused with what most people might consider sexually explicit themes. Sexuality wasn't anything novel and it wasn't anything to be secretive about. At school, however, it was drastically different.

"Come on now, Pat Red Hat! Don't fight us!" was a familiar teachers' yell heard in the pale green sterile hallways of Weeping Willow Elementary. Everyone would know Pat was being physically restrained, and someone would actually attempt to stick a bar of lathered soap into Pat's tightly clenched mouth. Washing his "dirty mouth" had little effect.

Once in third grade Pat was unduly punished for using the word "but" in the wrong context. It began with Pat being asked by the teacher to spell "Mississippi" on the chalkboard. Properly trained to write in Black Eagle Child, Pat waddled up to the front of the classroom. There he turned around, looked at the shiny waxed floors, and said in broken English that he could spell it in "Indin." Somewhere along the way the teacher thought she was being called a "big butt." What Pat had meant to say was that he couldn't spell what the teacher wanted *but* could instead spell *"Me tti Ne bi si,* or Big or Great River" in "Indin." The teacher went into a fit, with all the other teachers joining in, squawking like chickens about to lay eggs and pecking away at the closest students available. Eavesdropping from their classrooms, the other students were frightened by the sounds of holocaust as Pat was dragged into the bathroom. He went down to the floor with his arms wrapped around two heads, but his effort was useless. The students understood perfectly what he had tried to say. From that day forth, based on their observations of teachers' examining each other's rears, they learned "but" also meant a person's rear. Add "big" before that, and there was trouble.

"Okay, me no sure!" Pat cried from the bathroom. "Okay? Big, big way! Know my way! Ow! Know only . . . spell my way only! Ow!"

It took five teachers to wrestle and tie him down with canvas straps. They stopped when Pat's gums began to bleed and when one of them realized that Pat was right about the "big but," that it was given as a preface to an apology for not knowing how to spell "Mississippi" as requested. Embarrassed, the teachers marched back to the classrooms smelling like cheap bulk soap. Such commotion would be a predictable highlight of a day at Weeping Willow.

When Edgar Bearchild finally lifted his head from the gray merry-go-round bars, he looked directly at Horatio Plain Brown Bear. Light-complexioned and clownish, Horatio implored Hayward and Kensington Muscatine, who sat on either side of him, to engage in the same pipe dance mimicry. All attention to that point had been directed to Pat, who did the singing, and Horatio, who did the dancing. And now the Muscatines were desirous of the same attention. They joined in, shaking their imaginary pipes and gourd-rattles in a frenzy—only to become part of the joke. Pat had inserted their clan-given names in the song and they didn't even know.

"And look at these monkeys, looking like they're scratching their privates instead of dancing," said Horatio. With a sneering grin, he pointed to their stiff curled hands over their slouched bodies.

Realizing how weird they must have looked, Hayward and Kensington stopped their frenetic gyrations. Although the Muscatines shared the same last name, they weren't really related. Physically, they were exact opposites: Hayward was tall and lanky for his age and good at basketball; Kensington was short and oriental-looking and good-for-nothing. When Hayward laughed he brought the back of one hand to cover his mouth and leaned backward on one bent leg like a girl; when Kensington laughed his oriental-looking eyes bulged out of his wide, well-developed forehead, and his gaping pink mouth could be seen with stunning clarity. Especially around younger female classmates.

Somewhere two to three generations back, they sometimes said, they must have been related. For whatever reason, the Muscatines hung around Horatio like servants, taking abuse. Horatio constantly persuaded them to do stupid things, like planning a group depantsing of a female student or humping one another for kicks. Today they were duped into performing a dance that alluded to the dreaded arrival of pubescence.

Humiliated by what they had just done, the Muscatines hunched their shoulders, dropped their jaws, and pretended to laugh at themselves. Along with Horatio Plain Brown Bear they sat on the octagon-shaped ride, facing the south, toward the midafternoon sun and the school; the other three boys—with Edgar sitting between Ted Facepaint and Pat Red Hat—were facing the northern hills of the Black Eagle Child Settlement.

When the singing, drumming, rattling, and laughing settled down, the sounds of a whipping flag and clinking chains returned. With his little face still bent backward toward the sun, Pat, with nostrils flaring in his hooked nose, asked what everyone was doing after school. The Muscatines were thus spared further humiliation.

"In case you're not doing anything, would you like to go see those hills above Liquid Lake? People say some kind of spaceships are landing there."

"Oh yeah, I heard my grandfather talk about it," said Horatio, after he chucked the milk carton to the weeds. "Didn't they have a feast for them last year?"

"That's right!" answered Edgar, surprising the group. They all looked at him as he turned around and pointed his left arm to the southwest. "I think they took food and offerings to the last ridge over there. You can barely see it, though. My grandmother went. She said tiny people were seen walking through the underbrush, coming from . . . over there. Look. That way."

The boys all looked toward the precipice of pine trees on O'Ryan's Hill. Edgar asked if anyone thought they could find the spaceships. The Muscatines looked around, hoping someone would carry the discussion further.

"Of course we can," replied Pat assuredly, as he gently rocked the playground ride with his bulky weight. "We just have to wait until nightfall. I guess that's when the lights in the sky begin moving. Some spaceships are supposed to be the size of quarters, with black smoke trailing behind and sounding like ten trains."

"What I hear," interjected Horatio, after wiping his nose on the cuff of his shirt, "was that these spaceships are the Supernaturals who have come to check on us, to see how we are doing."

"But-ta . . . but-ta . . . what-ta if-f-f they're not?" asked Theodore through an intermittent breath of inhaled and exhaled words. "What-ta . . . if-f . . . they're fr-from ou-outer space? Or-or fr-from the stars? My-my aunt Louise . . . Stabs Back . . . sa-says th-they're . . . th-the . . . they br-brought us Star Me-Medicine."

"What are you talking about, Ted?" inquired Pat. "Star-Medicine? On whose back? What-ta what-ta do you mean?"

Quick to imitate, Horatio followed with another question. "And-da and-da who-who a-are you staying with since your fa-fa-father is working in Iowa City?" On the side the Muscatines covered their mouths, and their beady eyes gleamed as they giggled.

Theodore's eyes began to shift at the mockery, and then he suddenly clammed up. When the recess bell was manually rung, Horatio got up and proposed a camp-out at Liquid Lake over the weekend, to which Hayward and Kensington quickly agreed. They looked at each other and smiled. As everyone started to get up, stretching arms and legs, the Muscatine duo volunteered in an excited tone to bring "the weenies." The rest of the group, led by Pat, took that as innuendo, saying "Wee-h!" with a basslike emphasis. The short but pronounced verbal utterance was a turnaround, the reference to "weenies" being taken as a literal delivery of their privates.

At further expense of the Muscatines, the group's giggling ac-
celerated as they entered the school building. Once inside, Pat and
Horatio said to the teachers aloud, "Hey! The Muscatines are bringing weenies to the camp-out!"

"That's good," said the teachers who stood in front of their classroom doors. "I'm sure they'll taste scrumptious over the fire," they
said. "Mmmm—mm-mmm, yum-yum," said one of them, rubbing her
belly and rolling her wet tongue over the top lipstick-covered lip.

"Wee-h!" cried the group in an exaggerated manly intonation
before breaking into a more pronounced laugh. Upon hearing this
and without knowing what the joke was about, other tribal students
began squealing uncontrollably as they stood in the water line. "The
Muscatines, they're bringing weenies!"

When the teachers indicated the Muscatines might have to
"bring lots of them, in boxes," the entire school erupted into throes
of maniacal giggling. When Mr. Mateechna, the janitor, was summoned by the teachers to figure out what was so funny, he simply
told the students in question to stop talking.

"Quit talking! Quit talking nasty! *Bo na na ke to ne mo ko! Bo
ni-wa ne ska-a to to ne mo ko!*" the janitor warned. "You are going to
get these others blamed. They will wash everyone's mouth with soap.
*Ki me tti ta wi a ba ke i-ma a ki-ko ta ka ki. Ke ki me si ke i-ki ko ka be
to ne o ko ki-si bya i ka ni.*"

Mr. Mateechna tried unsuccessfully to stop the addictive giggling. It only increased. More so when Horatio shared a story of a
previous camp-out in which Hayward Muscatine threw an uncooked
weenie in the fire because he wanted to go home. As the weenie was
being described in broken English, picking up "bits of dirt" and ash
on its roll to the fire, the janitor's stoicism broke. His yellow, chewing tobacco–stained teeth were bared as he emitted a hearty chuckle.

"Oh? The weenie got grubby?" asked one of the teachers.

The boys, pumped up to a frenzy, all pointed at the red-faced
Hayward and screamed out his new name, "Grubby!"

If not for the spectacular weather, Pat would have gone home
with bruised gums. The janitor covered up for the boys by saying the
word "weenie" just sounded funny. To the teachers he explained,
"You'd have to be Indian to understand. The word, if it ended with

'na,' would mean him or her: *wi na.*" Satisfied with Mr. Mateechna's explanation, the teachers stood in front of their blackboards and proclaimed their adoration for "weenies" by saying, "*Wi na* and all of us like weenies! Right?"

And that really did it: the foundations of the aged school shook from the stomping feet of its students. Which wasn't good because the building had been condemned for years. But Pat, who was an expert at making sexual innuendo all-inclusive, made everyone near him aware of such stuff. In particular, Horatio. Any word spoken was an invitation for lewd associations or imaginary predicaments. Horatio made a spark into a roaring flame. If you were conveying a story of how big an object was or how delicious lunch dessert was, it became something else in an instant with a low vocal exhalation. "Wee-h!" In spite of its unoriginal obviousness, the Bureau of Tribal Affairs teaching staff never caught on. In their suspicions, they simply became frustrated, and a federal psychiatrist was summoned to Weeping Willow when mouth-washing failed.

After the doctor offered his evaluation to the staff, a perpetually embittered teacher, Mrs. O'Toole, came into the classroom, shaking her red-painted fingernail angrily and saying, "Dirty. Dirty. Dirty Red Hat!" From that day forward, like Hayward with his new name "Grubby," Pat was known as Pat "Dirty" Red Hat. Credited with defaming an Indian student's family name, Mrs. O'Toole was eventually forced to resign from Weeping Willow.

The federal psychiatrist had been one of a kind. After researching the myths of the Black Eagle Child tribe, he had simply determined that sexual-related themes were introduced early on to tribal youth, and nothing out of the ordinary had taken place.

# In the First
# Memory of My Life

On November 12, 1951, I was born in my maternal grandparent's two-room house on the Black Eagle Child Settlement. Today, this house stands a quarter of a mile from where Selene Buffalo Husband, my wife, and I presently live. Back then it was an unpainted house where my mother, Clotelde, and her two younger brothers, Winston and Severt, and their mother and father, Ada and Jack Principal Bear, shared the small rooms. My father, Tony Bearchild, would by choice remain aloof from our lives for another decade. When I was a child, this small, unpainted house and the people within, as well as the surrounding hills, comprised my total worldly realm.

The house was equipped with two woodstoves, one of which was used for cooking and the other for heating; the smoky brown interior was illuminated by either daylight or the wicks of two kerosene lamps. The floor consisted of well-worn, shiny, smooth slabs of wood. Above, the cardboard panels on the smoke-darkened ceiling provided a perfect artistic medium: My two young uncles, using safety pins, carved and scribbled what must have been the first pictographs and names I saw in elaborate longhand.

Today from afar I can only look at the house and ponder in amazement: This is where memories and a personal and family history were developed. What the house gave me, you could say, was the basic knowledge I would need on this largely enigmatic "Journey

of Words." For that I am grateful, but it isn't quite enough. There
are many things I don't yet understand, and it's highly unlikely that
I ever will.

That much I already know. . . .


In 1954, before my younger brother Alan was born in the same unpainted house, my grandfather Jack Principal Bear passed away from
complications of failing health. Of the four earliest childhood memories I have, three deal with events that involve my grandfather and
what occurred within and outside the four walls: The first was his
encouraging me to walk to him; the second was three young men
supporting him as he stepped off the porch; and the third involved
the solemn ceremonies surrounding his inexplicable disappearance.

In the first memory of my life my grandfather went on to sweep
me off the sunlit floor and place me on his knees; I can still visualize
his face and his large brown hands on my infant arms. In the second
memory of my life he stood precariously over a well-trodden path;
his two sons, my uncles, and their cousin stood under his weak arms
as they walked into the thickets. In the third memory of my life he
was suddenly made to be no longer, and another person, a living
person, was chosen to stand as his replacement.

And in the fourth memory of my life, wearing imitation cow-
boy-type clothing, I stood on a dusty path where grandfather had stood
and watched a shooting star explode right over the house and the yard.
As the glittering sparks floated down into the green, whispering garden, I saw myself in them. Bits of meteor. Black discarded pieces of
charcoal that first had to be nurtured and brought into total being.
This I can now see resulted from the love of four women: my mother,
my grandmother, my wife, Selene, and Grandmother Earth herself.


With such a strong tether to both personal and family history, there
should be an utter sense of regard for this house now clad with white
aluminum siding. In a way there is. Regrettably, it isn't enough to
compel me to take action, to serve its present occupants a notice to
vacate. Were it not for the fact that the house still provides shelter,

I'd make an effort to declare it a house of historic significance, for it truly is. For me at least. But I can only look and ponder from afar. I remember everything. . . .

On hot sunny days you could clearly see and feel with your open hand the elaborate texturing of the yellow knots on the wooden siding. And if per chance the box elder bugs didn't surface from underneath the slabs, disturbing the scene, I perceived the knots as an odd assortment of reflections of the sun preserved in gray, cracking wood. These you could look at without hurting the eyes.

Ghostly sensory images from the 1950s are stirred up in research like sediment in a translucent creek. As the muddy clouds billow and expand underwater, a return is facilitated to my first years at the Weeping Willow Elementary School: how I whimpered in protest at the staff feeding me a horrid mudlike substance called "chocolate pudding" on top of the nauseating purple liquid of "beets," how I sat later that evening on the hardened dirt floor of a priest's lodge with giant wedges of sturgeon fish in fresh green bean soup, relishing the moment, the invitation to eat.

If knocking memory ajar proves to be difficult, I rely on a musty-smelling collection of visual aids. Old photographs and newspaper clippings. On occasion, along with listening to early rock and roll music, the family photograph album is inspirational. Without pause or objection the mind agrees to play back certain events by way of the sun's color and intensity.

In remembrance of experiences with modernity itself, aside from elementary school, there was a dark blue 1932 Ford we had that transported us to the Why Cheer Theater. This was another historic place where I first rubbed elbows with Selene Buffalo Husband, my wife-to-be. From popular Mattel toy firearms and Daisy Red Ryder BB guns, I advanced to a Remington bolt-action tube-fed .22 caliber rifle with a peep sight. And Log Cabin, the maple syrup that came in a tin container shaped and painted like a miniature log cabin, was a delight but a mess at the family table. There was also a 35 mm camera my uncles borrowed from Howard Courting, their cousin. In terms of electricity we were the last family to get hooked up in 1957. For one summer, through a boy who was about to be orphaned, we had a black-and-white television set. The person who owned the TV was the boy's uncle, Billy "Cracker" Jack. Witnessing Saturday morning cartoons for the first time was to relive visually the myths told by Grandmother. As a result perhaps of watching my two young uncles scratch pictographs on the darkened ceiling, like twin Michelangelos, I found anything visual important. Later, this transcended into a penchant for art forms that included wood carving, painting in mixed media, photography, and filmmaking. The color photographs I took in 1967 with Uncle Severt's Petri camera, the 35 mm model he brought back from South Vietnam, bear astonishing witness to this interest. I was sixteen.

In Bureau of Tribal Affairs birth and medical records I am listed as "Edgar Principal Bear" via my mother Clotelde's maiden name. My father, Tony Bearchild, was nonexistent then. Evidently, due to differing political beliefs, there was disapproval of their Montague and Capulet–like romance from both sides of the family.

At least that's what I have been told.

In any case, there is something Shakespearean-intriguing about how I was born into a Principal Bear family as opposed to being written legitimately into existence as a Bearchild. It has never bothered me per se. Yet the subject has managed to surface in matters that pertain to family, clan, and tribal obligation via religion. As on that day on the octagon-shaped merry-go-round at Weeping Willow Elementary when the question of my father's occupation was posed, it throws me into an abyss. Every time. Of course, there's a possibility Romeo was used far too much as an excuse. My father's absence was just exactly that. Whatever reasoning he went by, it pointed to something having gone askew. In not being there he was simply un-missed. There was no basis on which to base an emotion. Does that make sense? *No basis on which to base an emotion?* Selene who is listening from her beadworking studio as I read this section aloud says that's a harsh indictment. It isn't meant to be. My father, Tony, and I are merely two different people. I could never be like him as a Bear clan leader nor could he ever be like me as a writer. Influenced and guided by opposing factors, we remain two different people in two different worlds. He will always be my mother's love, however. For me, he remains the man who came after me at the small unpainted house one afternoon. Together, in his Mercury Coupe, we went to the Heijen Medical Center to await the birth of Dan, my second younger brother. Afterward, I stayed with him while he went out drinking at the tribal fairgrounds. Along with his friends and relatives, with a twelve-pack of beer each among them, we sat high atop the bleachers, whooping war cries and gossiping in the clear blue moonlight. That morning we went to his home and fed the geese. . . .

But like I said, there was this phase in which I subscribed to the belief that being fatherless was the sole reason why I was remiss with the Earthlodge clan ceremonies. Today I am inclined to believe that's not the case, for others without fathers or tribal enrollment status have aptly demonstrated that anyone can become a clan priest apprentice. Which ostensibly weakens my defense. It has to be a question of priorities, then.

And what about the fatherless, unenrolled mixed-bloods who excel in roles full-bloods should have followed? There's no humiliation quite like the kind religious mixed-bloods serve, outshining us cop-outs with copious amounts of ceremonial bedazzlement. Their presence in Black Eagle Child society has prophetic dimensions; I am in awe of such talent. Yet, at the same time, I theorize that their religious commitment is based in part on a desire to become "accepted" as tribal members.

So a question arises: What would prevent the mixed-bloods from becoming just as remiss as me after being accepted? In their being where they presently are, "in limbo," not accepted as legitimate tribal members but crucial to the Principal Religion's continuation, aren't the life-years of the earthlodge ceremonies indirectly extended?

Above all this, though, is the proverbial comeback for anyone who thinks he can detach himself from involvement: What is my purpose as a Black Eagle Child tribal member? What have I done to prolong life-years of a tribal religion? While there probably ain't a damned thing wrong with me, I always end up asking halfheartedly: Have I been irresponsible? What are my priorities? Centuries of history could be blamed, but it's simpler to plead guilty. In the Cosmic Earthlodge Tribunal I would not contest the charge of forgetfulness. My rationale is, it is merely a part of "eventuality."

Ironically, in an indirect way my being aloof probably began with the Six Grandfathers' Journals. My introduction to Black Eagle Child society and the general workings of the greater world itself came by way of my grandmother dictating her entries to these journals. Beside the kerosene lamp, with my small elbows on the kitchen table, I wrote down her thoughts and ideas replete with politics, religion, family, and our social condition. I became so adept at taking notes that I began jotting down my own observations that had nothing to do with our impoverished plight, like "drinking the orange skylight" from a Ne-Hi pop bottle.

In addition to this star-crossed genesis—I can only postulate—there were two beliefs that led to my becoming a "word-collector": From my mother's side were the conservatives, and from my father's side were the progressives. It is an ongoing tale of a bitter entanglement between two families, within the same Bear clan, and how they contributed to or impeded the destiny of the tribe itself.

It was in 1856 that my maternal great-great-grandfather, who was a Sacred Chieftain named Bear King, or Principal Bear, orchestrated the Black Eagle Child tribe's return and subsequent purchase of the first acreages in central Iowa. When the famous chief died in 1890, the untimely rape and murder of a young woman named Dorothy Black Heron interrupted the proper transference of the chieftainship to his son. Simultaneously, the Earthlodge clan elders in an unprecedented decision felt Bear King's son was too young to assume the hereditary reign as a bloodline leader. Which was odd because Bear King himself was but a boy when he brought the tribe to Iowa.

What had really been at stake was the direction of the Black Eagle Child Nation. Should we go forward or back? was the question asked. Sensing an opening through our confusion, the white politicians of Why Cheer and Gladwood contrived a ploy that would irreversibly assimilate the tribe deeper into the American mainstream. When they learned Dorothy Black Heron's murder had been committed allegedly by my paternal great-great-grandfather, Bearchild's elderly father, history was forever changed: They blackmailed Bearchild, a noted translator, into becoming a "federally recognized chief." Alcohol, you could say, brought education onto our land and right into our lodges. Although Bearchild was not a traditional bloodline chief, the shrewd white politicians made him into one. There was little choice, and even less so when his father vomited a night's worth of homemade wine at the dreadful crime scene: his moccasin tracks matched the ones left at the sandy thickets.

In exchange for his father's freedom, Bearchild, as an unauthorized tribal representative, signed education into law. And alcohol was the root problem. This wasn't anything new. Since white man immemorial, alcohol has been hazardous for all tribal groups on the North American continent. In fact, there wouldn't be a state of Iowa if it hadn't been for intoxicants. They were used to coerce two lost Black Eagle Child hunters, who were made out to be our leaders, into signing away territorial rights to Illinois and Iowa. It was easier for everyone to ignore that Dorothy Black Heron had been raped and murdered—had ever existed—like a possession that is irretrievable.

Bearchild saw some benefits to his role as a federally appointed chief. For one, and the most obvious, there was his elderly father's life. Would you squeal on your own father? Probably not. Second, a fancy-sounding title was more appealing than the translator job Bearchild had held with the tribe, reading documents that only a lawyer should have read. Third, five hundred dollars a year for allowing the government to establish a school on tribal land probably didn't seem like a bad deal. This "cultural disfiguring" would have happened, anyway, so say our mixed-blood tribal historians. But Luciano Bearchild, my first cousin, used to say that being educated meant one was nursed with misinformation and therefore history-blind, implying that "our self-proclaimed historians were accessories" in the cover-up of the "Heron, Dorothy Black" atrocity. Her suffocation made the dormant creature named Education breathe its revolting breath. . . .


From the twisted carnage of the Principal Bear and Bearchild family histories, in which political betrayal permeated and dictated the lives of all concerned, there arose "Edgar Principal Bear," who later became "Edgar Bearchild." Up until seventh grade at Doetingham Junior High School in Suntour, Iowa, I signed my last name "Principal Bear." When my mother and father began living together in 1961, I was told to change my last name to "Bearchild." Upon the arrival of a younger brother, Dan, the Bearchild name was consecrated for Alan and myself.

Mrs. O'Toole, the former Weeping Willow teacher who followed me shadowlike to junior high, called me "Ed P. Bear" with certain delight during student roll call.

"You mean Bearchild," I said after she made the daily put-down.

"No, I mean you, Ed P. Bear!" Mrs. O'Toole returned with a snap.

"That's not my name anymore," I returned, standing my ground. The heads of the students who sat around me dropped at my stupidity.

"This sheet lists all of the students' names!" she shouted. "Today and for eternity it says you're—"

"Bearchild!" I interjected. "That's my name now, Mrs. O'Toole. The paper and what it says, that can be changed. The same way you changed Principal Bear to 'P. Bear.'"

Mrs. O'Toole, who still harbored feelings of resentment for being fired from Weeping Willow, marched down the aisle like a high-goose-stepping Nazi soldier. In her long gray apparel and a helmetlike hairdo, she stood over me with a blunt little staff. Looking up I saw that her left eye twitched and she was biting the inside of her lower lip raw. "No! That cannot be changed!" she protested. "Simply because you say so, you impertinent little—"

"Excuse me, sir!" said Luciano Bearchild, my first cousin, from the hallway. In his pinstriped pants, vest, and white shirt, Luciano leaned against the inside door, giving a James Deanesque pose. An unlit cigarette wobbled from his mouth as he spoke again. "Sir, I don't mean to intrude, really, but could you tell me where the men's room is?"

Mrs. O'Toole, looking more inflamed, spun on her toes and looked directly at the unexpected and well-dressed visitor. Luciano, in an effort to provoke a response, slung his suit coat over his shoulder and took two steps into the classroom. He stood in an area where the morning sun reflected off his jewelry, blinding us.

"For your information, young man, my name is Mrs. O'Toole. Mrs. Can you hear? It's Mrs. And what are you doing here?"

"Well, oh . . . that's my mistake, thinking you were a man. My apologies. But with regard to the young man there, he told you his name is Bearchild. Respect his wish. As for my visit, it has to do with my inquiry. Good day."

Whatever the reason, Mrs. O'Toole partially respected my wish for a last-name change. Later on that month, when she learned I had been selected by mistake to submit a piece to the *Twintowns Chronicle's* student writers' section, she saw to it that my first poem was published under the "Child Edgar Bear" name.

In eighth grade, when white classmates began to know who I was, they recalled how I was "Ed P. Bear" one month and then "Child Edgar Bear" the next. They also recalled Luciano Bearchild with his sparkling jewelry and his unbuttoned shirt, but when I told them he was my cousin, no one believed me. Anyone who switched names in one day was suspect, they explained. But like the Black Eagle Child boys at Weeping Willow Elementary who didn't harass me with regard to my father's occupation, the whites never pressed the name-switching issue. In one day's time I became someone else. . . .


On my father's side of the family there were two sisters, Lydia and Agnes; their father, Thomas; and three brothers, Henry, Alfred, and William, the latter being a half brother. They all had families, large ones. Coming into their family ten years too late, I didn't know anyone with the exception of Luciano Bearchild, my first cousin, and William Listener, my father's half brother who was a respected Earthlodge clan leader.

Right up until the fifth grade at Weeping Willow I thought the only cousins I had were from my mother's half brother, Clifford Water Runner, a diligent railroad worker and part-time farmer. They were Mae Lynn, Sue Lynn, Lynn Lynn, and Mateo. Their cheerful mother was Grace. In their pink 1954 Ford Victoria convertible they would visit Grandmother on weekends, or else we'd accompany them to town. Packed into a stylish-looking car we'd cruise into Why Cheer with the top down. Brown, smiling faces in a pink car rumbling down Main Street of a small farming town wasn't an everyday occurrence. For years I didn't know the convertible was only a test-drive situation, from a white car dealer who was a close friend of Clifford's.

Anyway, Luciano Bearchild proved the most captivating of my Bearchild relations. That day at Doetingham Junior High in 1964 when a well-dressed angel from the surreal hinterland came into Mrs.

O'Toole's homeroom and intervened on my behalf was the second time we met. Strange, I never knew what Luciano was doing there or whether he found the rest room. Our first meeting took place four years previous in the starlit hills above Liquid Lake. He rescued everyone—six boys in all—who were on an all night camp-out. My mother's brother, Severt Principal Bear, published a memorable account of this event, "Unearthly Manifestations," in the *Black Eagle Child Quarterly*. That summer Luciano took me on a powwow trip to Montana near the Rocky Mountains.

After Luciano Bearchild, the most intriguing of my Bearchild family was my father's half brother, William Listener; he could invoke invisible deities through the remnant soup in wooden bowls that held the sacrament. Both of these people—Luciano and William—made me realize that there were things far greater than my capacity for understanding. If Luciano hadn't disappeared, taking food offerings and material goods to the hills as instructed above Liquid Lake in 1966, he most certainly would have become like our half uncle, blessed and powerful.

# The Black Eagle
# Child Settlement

The Black Eagle Child Settlement, with a twelve hundred–plus populace, is located near the small rural communities of Why Cheer and
Gladwood, Iowa. When people ask me where I am from, I usually
say Why Cheer. Which is sometimes unsettling because a majority
of people either will have no idea where I'm from or will think I'm
making up the name of the town as a joke. Sometimes I really can't
help but chuckle along. It's an unusual name—and rightly so.

The fact is, Why Cheer is a small white town—five miles to our
east—where we frequently shop for groceries, household goods, and
clothes. Remarkably, some of us graduated from high school there.
It also happens to be our postal mailing address. But neither the tribe
nor myself, with the exception perhaps of four or five tribal-affiliated
families, live in Why Cheer. Since the town has no unique identity
of its own other than supposedly being the "BIRTHPLACE OF THE RE-
PUBLICAN PARTY," Why Cheer and its white citizens are viciously jealous of the Black Eagle Child Settlement's notoriety. Out of curiosity,
academic or otherwise, visitors in multitudes are drawn by our ancient Woodlands tribal culture. As a result, our white neighbors feel
excluded. That's why they deliberately misinform visitors by refer-
ring to the Settlement as the "Why Cheer Indian Reservation." Sometimes they will even give wrong directions, and our potential friends
never find us.

This is an insult.

But for years the Twintowns (Why Cheer and Gladwood) Chamber of Commerce printed "HOME OF THE WHY CHEER INDIANS" on postcards they made, sold, and distributed. It was extremely embarrassing. The subjects photographed were not even Black Eagle Child. They were local whites in hideous black braided wigs, potato sack dresses, and scraggly chicken feathers, resembling Hollywood extras.

What purpose this served no one quite knows.

Was it simply an ignorant marketing practice or was it mockery? There are war paint suspicions. The irony is, these controversial postcards first issued in 1928 have since become collector's pieces. And so it surprises people, Iowans generally, when I explain that whoever first called our tribal homeland a "reservation" made an unforgivable mistake. When people realize they are accessories to an error, they listen. Of course, in making these corrections, I take every opportunity to plug several facts: (1) that we own the land; (2) that it wasn't allotted by the government; (3) that Why Cheer "depends on the Settlement's reputation"; and (4) that if Why Cheer had any worth, the tribe would buy the town just for the sake of changing its name.

Why Cheer. If nothing else, it's my mailing address.


The lone gravel road of the Black Eagle Child Settlement, "Rural Route 2," winds through the main valley, where 126 tribal families reside. In the summertime this is an immaculate woodland jungle, with green shimmering leaves, the echo of children's laughter, and the scent of wild purple flowers everywhere; in the winter elegant frost hangs on the dark, skeletal outline of trees, and your breath, as you exhale, drifts skyward to join breakaway pieces of clouds that dash across the glistening prairies.

At night the sounds are plentiful. If it isn't crickets, distant whippoorwills, or barking neighborhood dogs, it is the mournful cry of a wintry blast of wind piercing the clattering pine trees. Of course, at two precise hours at sunup and sundown, the vehicular traffic on the main gravel road comes alive as the Black Eagle Child Casino workers head for the complex whose doors never close.

The houses, as has always been the case, sit a quarter of a mile or more from each other. There is no overwhelming evidence to signify that an economic boom is taking place. In Why Cheer and Gladwood, however, the white business types have helped themselves to loans from the banks stocked with tribal monies to bring new hotels and restaurants to the area. Those who have hated us in the Twintowns hate us even more now in thinking we are rich.

You would think that remarkable projects to benefit the tribal community, backed by casino coffers, might have taken root, spewing forth dozens of marvelous structures—houses, a fire and police station, a library or a museum, a tribal hospital, or even a school with a professional, competent staff.

But that isn't the case.

The houses here are merely functional. Some structures that were built in the early 1900s are still occupied by families who are loyal to houses they grew to adulthood in. Only recently, in the last twenty-five years, have new units been built under federal housing programs. To accommodate water lines and sewer drainages, the tribe began clustering these new houses into residential zones. "Candlestick Park" was the first such zone. It was so named due to faulty wire installation; whenever thunderstorms rolled over the Black Eagle Child Settlement, these poorly constructed houses were the first to sit in darkness, lit only by candles. They were intended only to meet the temporary needs of a tribe; it wasn't long before they became useless. Water lines froze and foundations under the bathrooms molded and gave way. Some houses had to be totally rebuilt.

Today, depending on who you are in the community—it's better to be a family, clan member, or friend—you can apply for a new house. If you are not a political adversary, you will probably receive one. The only trouble being, quick large-scale prefab housing solutions become old recurring problems. Your house is guaranteed to rot in twenty-five years. People say we are fast becoming a part of modern society, but we have yet to learn about housing contracts and substandard building materials.

Although there are twenty gambling enterprises within the state, the Black Eagle Child Tribal Council has made a stupid business decision to expand the casino, pumping thirty to sixty million dollars into a new gigantic structure on top of the ten million dollars already invested. All in an effort to "stay competitive."

Corruption has haunted the casino from the start. The strange thing about this is that some of the tribal leaders involved in the casino trade serve as clan priest apprentices. Black Eagle Child prophecy warns against money. And they should know this. Yet they act like money-hungry piranhas on a wild feeding foray. In the shredded frog-skin cloud, the quarterly per capita remains are doled out to the tribe "like table scraps intended for mutts." Betrayed and aware these illegalities can lead to more trouble, the elders hoard money. Their pillows and mattresses have secret seams for huge wedges of multi-denominational currency. There is a real fear this is only the beginning of what surely has to be the end.

The fact that interaction with the greater American public is required for the casino to operate runs counter to the isolationist objectives espoused by our founding grandfathers. The reason they chose isolation from the Outside World was so that the Principal Religion would be practiced by each succeeding generation without fail. But today the very people who wave the banners of religion are the very people who don't consult the Earthlodge clan elders on critical issues that pertain to the welfare and future of the tribe. Novelties, like gambling, are introduced without tribal consensus, without the input of the elders. In the skies, in the water, and under the earth, so say these cast-aside elders, there is dissension—because of this act of forgetfulness—among the Supernaturals who control all earthly matters.

Because of its tightly enclosed valleys, evening begins early on the Black Eagle Child Settlement. Conversely, after the sun has illuminated the surrounding countryside, darkness also lingers a bit longer here in the morning. Because of this factor, traditional-minded parents are quick to warn children sternly of the risks of remaining or going outside during these intervals. There's a long-established belief that witches make use of the concavities of darkness just before sunup or just after sundown, even with the pervasive casino traffic, to render their animal or bird disguises more believable.

The landscape is thus used as part of a subterfuge.

If there is turmoil seething among the people, their disruptive situation is exploited by the opportunistic witches as a means to enact their practice. During the smallpox outbreak of the late 1800s, for instance, witches were said to gather en masse like hunchback buzzards near the geodesic dome–shaped lodges to await death.

It is no different today, say the Earthlodge clan elders. A century later witches continue to strengthen their own immortality by preying on Black Eagle Child victims of the casino enterprise. There is turmoil through political infighting for monetary control. In another sphere, among the lifelong alcoholics, the quarterly per capita payments from casino profits merely hasten the rot of livers. Among youth and restless adults there is a craving for a thimble-full of crystalized substance that keeps them awake and delusional for two weeks at a stretch.

The casino money that flows like a strong creek, cascading through the hands and bodies of those who are near it, causes a sickness called greed. In this sickness our spiritual and physical defense against tangible and intangible forces is compromised. From the sky or water or underground, a message is forthcoming.


Just as the history of this tribal homeland is different, the Black Eagle Child people themselves are supposedly "entrenched" in what self-annointed scholars call "beliefs that are detrimental to their overall community progress." If you could include in that judgment an animistic worldview that prophesies an earthly demise upon the loss of our identity due to the white-complexioned people, obliterating forever the compact we made with the Well-Known Twin Brother, then there would be room for plausibility. Native Americans possess a blood-borne knack for understanding the machinations of unexplained phenomena. It is an ancient form of knowledge left behind by the Supernaturals to remind us of a dualistic existence. Accordingly, there is daylight or darkness, sunshine or moonlight.

From high along the sandy ridges of Rolling Head Valley, Ridge Road, Cottonwood and O'Ryan's Hills, including Liquid Lake, to the farthest fence line of the tribal South Farm, with Lone Ranger, Half

Moon Beach, and Onion Creek nestled somewhere in between, this land strives to provide a sanctuary. Its geographical face has not changed much, but the generations of people who came and left took with them parts of our god-given thoughts, practices, and beliefs. In losing these we became vulnerable. Among the believers and nonbelievers of the Principal Religion there were sorcerers who thrived on turmoil as a means of unleashing their destruction. The cross fire between fate and sorcery of the Black Eagle Child Settlement, if it could be seen, would resemble a night sky lit up with tracer fire from antiaircraft artillery.

I refer to the Black Eagle Child Settlement as an "earth-island." We are its passengers, the only ones, and we are on a perilous journey. Yet, depending on a variety of factors, like microdegrees of assimilation, some of us are truly aware of destination, while others are totally oblivious. Some of us, thinking we have successfully straddled religion and modern tribal bureaucracy, end up being ultrahypocrites. Major transgressions in real life are committed openly against tribal precepts, business ethics, and religion itself. When you are more of a danger to our future than an asset, something is wrong. We are told this sanctuary was founded through divine means; we are also reminded that if we are not careful, we can lose it. Even those who seem well-intentioned do not realize they, too—perhaps more than the nonbelievers—are responsible for directing culturally debilitating fire to the tribe itself. Crippled and set ablaze by these disarming forces from within, all of us are responsible for the piecemeal deterioration of the Black Eagle Child Nation. It is a wonder that this bird aegis, this scuttled, smoldering "earth-island," has been left alone high atop a cottonwood perch, sewing its wounds back together and mending itself. The biggest question now is, How long before we falter—and do ourselves in?

From any of the cardinal points, the hills of the Settlement seem to form a single geographic edifice. In all, though, there are eight elongated hills that form the basic layout of our heavily wooded tribal homeland. They generally lie in a southeast-to-northwest configuration, snaking along the Iowa River and quitting at the confluence where the Iowa merges with the Swanroot River. When seen from the south the flat riverbottoms of the Settlement begin where the hills

end, stretching westward until the first ridge of Runner's Bluff begins. Going toward the east the last hill abruptly stops and gently evens
out on a long sloping hill where Why Cheer sits. Toward the north
the two uppermost ridges of four hills and their valleys stand out
against the open sky. From a landmark there known as Sand Hill, all
that can be seen when one faces south is Runner's Bluff disappearing in the distance past the valley of two rivers.

Because of these two rivers, the Swanroot and the Iowa, a good
portion of the Settlement lies over the grassy prairies and thickets of
floodplains. For half a century, before the infamous U.S. Corps of
Engineers alighted on the scene, the Earthlodge clans constructed
their respective longhouses beside the rivers near areas that were
believed to be the mystical doorways to the realm of the underworld.

Recalling these special places, if only by threads of memory,
through songs, dances, and prayers was crucial. Long ago the clans
had access to the Supernaturals, and they even made visits to gain
their wisdom and advice. No one knows who made the last visit, but
those who knew about the doorways kept it a secret. Everyone knew
the Supernaturals used the hillside springs as doorways, and others
burrowed beside or under where the two rivers came together on the
southeasterly tip of the Black Eagle Child Settlement. At sundown
they would emerge from the tree-silhouetted horizon like shooting
stars, crisscrossing the sky.

Unfortunately, somewhere along the way, whatever knowledge
of the doorways remained slipped away in the clouded memories of
our clan elders, the secret-keepers. In time the sons of the secret-
keepers would rationalize in the course of their sermons to their believers that "exact locations are not important." What mattered was
the overall intent for communion. "As long as we are in the general
vicinity of the doorways," the sons would say upon delivery of offerings to nonsites, "the Supernaturals will know. . . ."

No one, of course, disagreed.

What is one to say when told a major transgression has already
occurred? What is one to say when told we have already begun to
forget? We were told that losing the doorways would be only one
among the many transgressions forthcoming. It was a simple eventuality, a sign of a greater nonhuman spirit at work, the elders conveyed.

They knew this earth-carrying knowledge was fast disappearing; they also felt our chances at salvation were next to nil if there was no one present to listen and to learn. Thus our piety was measured.

It was blatantly evident.

Through the polity that subjugated us, we had splintered apart into factions. Political groups who had nothing but good intentions for the tribe became self-defeating entities. As we fought with tribal members and our families over control of the tribe's future, young people were struck down around us like innocent passersby in a gangland-style shoot-out. Sparks in the night sent real lead bullets, and witchcraft spells turned into trains, plowing into unsuspecting lives.

From this tragic series of events storytellers and their stories were made. Each succeeding Black Eagle Child generation for hundreds of years encountered different obstacles. Modernity came to us in different forms; the early versions brought forth war, disease, famine, and undreamt-of atrocities. Invariably, our plights became our legacy. In instances where survival was the outcome, songs and ceremonies were said to come from the Creator Himself. Stories were retained for the purpose of instructing others. Through the retelling of our suffering, it was hoped lessons could be learned.

Among the most notable tribal storytellers was Carson Two Red Foot, my grandmother's adopted brother. He wasn't much of a drinker, but a bottle of sweet Ambrose wine was "helpful" he'd say in dislodging all that he had experienced. "That is, if you want to hear it," he'd always remind his visitors. Born in 1896, Carson was said to be the last person who knew where the Supernaturals' doorways were located along the mossy riverfronts.

From 1971 to 1975, three to four times a year, I would take a fifth of Ambrose in a brown paper bag to Carson. Sometimes I took cigarettes too. His stories were of great interest to me. Blessed in the sense that he possessed an astonishing memory, Carson was long thought to be the person who knew the secret of tribal immortality. But my sole purpose was to ask him about the One Most Afraid. I was fascinated by this story of a young enchantress who stole Carson's father from his family in 1908, a story replete with romance, witchcraft, and an unsolved murder. Years later my grandmother would reflect that Carson's mother was thought to be the person responsible for the One Most Afraid's death.

Carson Two Red Foot told stories the old way. Meaning you didn't realize until a day or even a week later the meaningful revelations he had shared with you. He knew stories told by his grandparent's grandparents, and he recited them as if they had occurred only the day before. In an epoch where others barely remembered their histories, he could relive past lives and events. His recollections were numerous and unparalleled. Unmarried, Carson Two Red Foot lived by himself in a one-room house on stilts along the desolate riverbottoms. Attired in a skull-snug New York Yankees baseball cap, dark green khaki pants, a wool shirt, and a large baggy sweater, Carson always welcomed his visitors with wide, quick smiles, excessive handshaking, and a Charlie Chaplinish gait. If he knew you were there exclusively for his stories, he would start touching his dark brown face until he felt the blue-green mole with his left hand. He had a small, gentle face, and so the mole stood out over his lower left cheek beside his pudgy nose. Out of habit he'd touch it once or twice as if to confirm the intent, to send an electrical message to the story's light source somewhere behind his wrinkled but sparkling eyes. Before his discourse on our family histories or on the reason why he would never divulge the doorways' location, he'd raise a speckled coffee cup to his thin mouth. After a long, audible drink, he'd pull the brim of the baseball cap downward and begin thinking. Then he'd hold his frail, sweater-covered arms together, trembling slightly from the gathering cold.

"When I was young my grandparents told me not to talk too much," he'd say with wine-moistened lips. "That's how I was raised, to not be so talkative." He'd explain that words were powerful, citing instances where invisible spirits were awakened and angered. "That we don't want to cause, but many people around here seek to know what the past was like. Without me, no one would know. Still, I have to be careful in what I say. People listen. Those we can't see, like ghosts and spirits, are listening as well. They are aware of every movement you make, every word you say. They are here in all sizes, you see, standing and swirling around us. . . ."

With that, he'd take four Marlboro cigarettes, breaking three of them in half, and sprinkling their tobacco over the tile floor of his house. A fourth cigarette, an unbroken one, was then lit and left outside on the ground next to the lower porch step.

"This last cigarette we leave for the invisible spirits who may have followed you here or are simply wandering around. My grandparents believed they are mostly up to no good, looking for trouble. This lit cigarette is also an offering to our relatives, those who lived long ago, for we will talk about them. May this smoke drift to their shadows and appease them. . . ."

Carson was renowned for speaking to things other people couldn't see. And because seemingly inanimate objects, like rocks, benches, cups, bowls, and spoons came to life by either rocking or moving at his presence or command, he wasn't thought of as a lunatic. On the contrary, he was a well-respected community member, on occasion feared. Because of his abilities, there was solace as well as trepidation in the knowledge that many forces, "all sizes," perpetually swirled around us en masse, watching.

Once, on a spearfishing expedition with Winston Principal Bear and Dwayne Afraid, some friends and I came upon Carson as he was praying and waving his right hand over a stringer of huge flathead catfish, *tte kwa me kwa*. Although he was mumbling we could hear his words clearly over the river ice. At the point where he asked for confirmation that the subjects had readily given of themselves, the bloody catfish arched their punctured heads upward and shook. It was uncanny. They quit moving as soon as Carson spotted us. We learned they had been given to him by some spearfishing farmers for no reason.

On the way back home, empty-handed Winston and Dwayne said Carson was regarded by the Iowa and Swanroot Rivers as an ally. He knew where the Supernaturals kept their doorways; in return for keeping this a secret, they gave him gifts. When most Black Eagle Childs asked for safe passage in life through prayers, Carson was literally bestowed with gifts. The invisible spirits gave instead of taking. In appreciation for his stories, people, white or Indian, walked up to his porch and left canned goods, flour, coffee, and canned triangles of ham. In that way, Carson became envied, but within his own Earthlodge clan, many resented his storytelling status. While he was liberal with some of his stories, he was criticized for insensitively hoarding Black Eagle Child life itself.

Although there were ceremonies designed specifically to communicate with the Holy Grandfather, His Twin Sons, and Grandmother Earth, the mystical doorways remained sealed forever and as elusive as Carson. Everyone knew the doorways could reverse our ignorance. What nobody could fathom was why Carson Two Red Foot, a mere mortal, had unconscionably deprived the tribe of the future. As he got older, we lost a little piece of ourselves in his clouded memories until there was suddenly nothing. . . .

When the Corps of Engineers built a dam on the Iowa River in the early 1900s, it only confirmed the realization that we were bound—regardless of whatever precautions we took—to lose. Every decision or event that was aimed at loosening our firm grip on the old ways only underscored the obvious. When the gallant plan to diminish flood levels backfired, causing huge floods, it was no surprise. When the Swanroot River joined the fiasco, three cities and one hundred farms downriver suffered. No matter how many times the dikes and levees were rechanneled or reinforced, the overflow caused incredible mayhem throughout the countryside. Because of the experimental landscaping of the government, the two rivers made the *Why Cheer News-Herald* headlines: "TAMA COUNTY UNDERWATER!"

Everyone in Tama County suffered. Although the tribal elders had been informed that such a structure would "reduce damage to the business and residential zones downriver," it never happened. Instead, the tall prairie grass that once stood beside the clan earthlodges disappeared under the muddy rivers. Flood level records were broken and new ones made in astonishing succession. As expected, the dam builders attributed blame to "inclement weather" and the flooding was not a result of a suspected flaw in the design of the Indian Dam itself.

There was something unusual about this occurrence because it affected all of what happened thereafter. The width and spread of these floods was like a giant mirror, *ke tti-wa ba mo ni*. In the reflection the people saw themselves, fleeing. Victimization. In clan gatherings the elders were reluctant to convey in their prayers that everything might have been predetermined, that the doorways to the underworld realm had been replaced by doorways that led instead to the loss of our culture. What our neighbor, Carson Two Red Foot, talked about before is here, said the elders. Loss of language, despondent youth amid unimaginable poverty, and the blurred face of modernity are the signals. When the people looked around they saw much of what the old stories revealed—a gradual darkening of tribal society in the future.

"Yes," they nodded among themselves, "this is what was said about how we would start to lose ourselves." Even without Carson's stories no one could avoid the signs. Eventually, the verbal means to send prayers to the Holy Grandfather would be lost, proving the linguistic demise of an ancient religion was a sure portent for extinction.

Carson, knowing they would ridicule and blame him in their sermons, rarely attended the earthlodge ceremonies. Blame didn't reside with Carson alone. Blame among the tribal people was rampant; it made a full circle, assuming different guises and forms. Many felt they were still being punished for the past and present sales of religious longhouse property, like gourd-rattles, stone effigies of the Supernaturals, and even songs. It made sense. Lightning scarred Cottonwood Hill with regularity, and railroad tracks became final pillows for drunken relatives. Others felt it was the transgressions of youth. Or women engendered the chaos. There were suspects; no one was excluded. Many blamed the religious influentials themselves, including those who befriended academics. Whichever explanation you heard and believed, Grandmother used to recollect, the rains fell in unprecedented amounts and did not cease until the families packed their belongings and headed for the safety of high ground. Some of the young men were asked to retrieve the sacred altar mats from the dangerous debris-filled waters. When the families looked back down from where they came, the waters were said to shimmer eerily as far as the eye could see, reminding many of earth's beginning.

Today, perhaps for this very reason, most of the tribal households are situated atop four prominent interconnected hills that overlook the riverbottoms and adjoining prairies.

# Unearthly
# Manifestations

*Recently, on a spring evening in 1960, six Black Eagle Child Indian boys—all Weeping Willow Elementary School classmates—reported seeing "tiny unknown beings" in beaded finery, clasping their tiny hands together as they traversed the railroad tracks. As the tribal elders spoke to them about the incident, the boys collectively recalled with amazement how their tiny moccasined feet leapt over the large purple rocks and the iron railings that lay atop splintered wooden ties. Held motionless by their power, the boys could only observe as their tiny moccasined feet crystallized. Suddenly, a bluish light from within set them all ablaze, reducing them in size. Next, the small round blue lights separated and hovered in wait as a train came barreling down the winding river valley. As soon as a boxcar became available, with metal screeching wheels and all, the blue lights, like some kind of supertransients, hopped onto a railroad boxcar, using it as a means of propulsion for a quick ascension to the stars. Showing off.*

*Among the boys who witnessed this manifestation was Edgar Principal Bear, my sister Clotelde's son. The other boys' names are as follows: Theodore Facepaint; Hayward and Kensington Muscatine; Horatio Plain Brown Bear; and Pat Red Hat.*

*At a predesignated point near Liquid Lake, the group of boys met for an all-night camp-out. Each had agreed to bring food, water, fishing line, sinkers, and hooks, as well as matches, small axes, flashlights, and blankets. These supplies were then stuffed into blue jeans, which were worn over the lower back, making them look like backpacks or parachutes. From Boy Scout meetings they had learned the legs of blue jeans could be tied as the straps. This is how my nephew, Edgar Principal Bear, began his account of what transpired that night, feeling as if he had just cartwheeled from the sky and landed behind enemy lines.*

           —from Severt Principal Bear's Diary\*

Edgar Principal Bear, with hardly a breath expelled, sat on the largest sandy beach of Liquid Lake, on the north side. With both legs crossed, he leaned against a homemade backpack and peered into the hill looming above. To the west, through the condensation on his glasses, he could see the last strong sunlight reflecting off the oak leaves of Rolling Head Valley. In the mild breeze he could smell the oiled railroad ties. To the east was nightfall itself. With the sun's glow gradually fading over the darkening waters of Liquid Lake, Edgar began wondering how much time he'd have for a mad dash home in case no one else made the rendezvous. He had been warned by his grandmother repeatedly that the moments before night and day were the most dangerous. Realizing this, Edgar began to breathe rapidly, and his heart thumped loudly underneath his boney chest. He had been here before with his uncle Winston and his friends on a spearfishing expedition. In fact, this was close to the place where they had spotted Carson Two Red Foot holding a conversation with a stringer of resurrected flathead catfish. But it was daylight then, and the only fear was thin ice.

Were there similarities between breaking ice, earth's darkness, and what lurked within? he asked himself. Spying into the fish's realm, underwater, was an experience he'd treasure for years. Driven by the pounding of logs over the ice, catfish in multitudes would travel under

---

\*It should be noted that Edgar's story was changed for a creative writing class at Parsons College in Fairfield, Iowa. It was first published in the *Scarlett O'Hara,* a college literary magazine, in 1962. Four years later, in 1966, upon the mysterious disappearance of a young prominent tribal member, an accomplished singer of religious songs, the piece was republished in the *Black Eagle Child Quarterly.*

the half-submerged mossy green trees. Edgar with a long six-pronged spear in his frozen hand would lie by a hole in the ice beside his uncle with a blanket over his head, blocking out daylight. In an effort to calm himself down, Edgar began thinking how this large body of stone-encased water provided good fishing and swimming.

He inhaled the cool fishy odor of the thriving backwaters of the Iowa and Swanroot Rivers and then scared himself with a thought pertaining to Carson Two Red Foot and the secret he possessed: If the Iowa and Swanroot Rivers were forced to reroute themselves, could the doorways of the Supernaturals shift in the landscape and arrive here? Could this also be the reason for the sightings of lights and tiny people?

Edgar thought about the town whites who called this place a "quarry," which was an error because no one ever dug rocks here for commercial purposes. Amid his racing thoughts of his grandmother's admonitions against coming out and being alone in the woods, he saw a figure roll out unexpectedly from the overhanging maple branches.

"Hey, hey! Who's there? *We ne a tta-i na i-ki wi ta ta?*" yelled out Edgar in a quavering voice.

"Ed-Edgar, is-s-s that you? *Ki-na a na?*" came a stuttered reply. Twigs were being raked and snapped from the limbs. In the sunset-reflecting water, bullfrogs began their loud bellowing, scaring Edgar ever more.

"Ted, is that you? *Ki na a na?*" cried out Edgar in despair.

"Yes, ha-ha-have you see-seen the others? *E a i, ke ki tti-ne wa wa ki-ko ta ka ki?*"

The figure of Theodore Facepaint that had been crawling toward Edgar stopped mysteriously halfway up the beach and bunched up. Edgar twisted his neck in every direction to look around. Seeing and hearing nothing, he answered Ted's questions. "No. I haven't seen anyone. Hey, how come you're not coming over? *Akwi-me i-ne wa ki ni-ko wi ye a.* Hey, *ke te tta wi-e ba wi-bya wa ni?*"

"Sh-h-h-h-h . . . I hear something. Listen. Sh-h-h-h-h . . . *Ke ko-ne ka ske ta. Be tte tte no.*"

As the two quieted down a short distance from each other, the bullfrogs in the pond did the same. Cranes and herons, their large wing-spans in silhouette, glided across the blue and orange iridescent waters of Liquid Lake, landing with minimal noise on the willow branches. To the south, from as far away as the Stonehouse on old Lincoln Highway 30, cackling owls could be heard flying toward them.

"Ther-there's thr-three of-of them. *Ne so wi-ta tti wa ki,*" said Ted in a fearful voice that began to stutter less. "It-it also seems as-as if they're getting closer. Or is someone talking? *Me to tti-ke e i ki-ke tti ni-bye wa ki. I tti ke-ko i ye a-ka na wi ya?*"

The dark hunchback-shaped mound that was Ted scuttled across the white sand sideways like a crab. Its pincers were held outward, aiming at the silhouette of Edgar, who was by then standing up, having gathered his parachute-looking apparatus, breathing more heavily. Every time the three owls cackled, the crab stopped its jerky travel and spun its shell-body in a quick circle, like an armed turret with twin machine guns, making sure nothing was thinking of taking advantage.

From the east, along the railroad tracks, the sound of shoes grinding the huge rocks against each other could be heard. Next came the illumination of three bobbing flashlights—and voices! Edgar and Ted held their breath and looked upward toward the elevated tracks, hoping. Gradually, the talking got closer and more distinct. It was Horatio Plain Brown Bear, Hayward Muscatine, and Kensington Muscatine, jabbering away. They were noisy and totally unaware of the three owls who were getting closer.

Edgar and Ted called out to their friends. Above, on the railroad tracks, the three flashlights froze. Just when Horatio was about to shout a question, an explosion shot up from somewhere over the water. *Whh-h-oommmp!* It sounded like a huge boulder had been lobbed over them from the hills. Around them, the cool water spray fell in huge drops.

"Have you seen Pat?" asked Horatio, while directing a dim beam of light down toward the beach and into cowering Edgar and Ted's eyes. Hayward and Kensington did the same until strange bubbling sounds echoed over the water. Together the trio swung their flashlight beams across the top of Liquid Lake, searching. Under their combined lights, strong waves were visible. Horatio, this time in a tone of worry, said, "Maybe a beaver, huh?"

"Geez, I don't know," answered Hayward, whose flashlight was edging toward Horatio's. "Maybe a family of beavers or a catfish the size of a man or even a seal, the one named Dam Monster?"

"Whatever, there's something out there," said Horatio, as he slid down the railroad tracks and onto the sand. "How come you guys are so quiet?" he asked of Edgar and Ted.

"The owls," they both replied, pointing downriver.

"What's this owl business? Don't you know something just blew up?"

Cautiously, Horatio walked across the pale beach, going past Edgar and Ted. Near the shoreline he knelt on one knee. "But it isn't what you say, Hayward," he resumed. "Look, everybody, the waves are building up again!" Horatio, along with Edgar and Ted, trotted to the bottom of the tracks; they then readied themselves to climb back up.

Hayward, who was rarely apart from Horatio, began to panic. "But . . . hey, you guys . . . don't get scared," he said in a spurt. With his skinny rear in the air, Hayward slid backward down the embankment, scraping his knuckles.

"Get back to where you were!" commanded Horatio, lighting up Hayward's butt, but it was too late.

"Ow! Watch it!" cried Hayward upon impact with Horatio's flashlight.

"Well, geez, be quiet then," warned Horatio, pushing Hayward away. With that, they lost balance over the discarded railroad ties and fell into some tall thistles. After they picked themselves up, an argument was about to ensue when Kensington began shouting. "Look at the water! Look at the water!" Sure enough, when they redirected their dim flashlight beams, there was another disturbance in the water. This time they saw it. *Wh-h-h-oommp!* Like the "Old Faithful" geyser they had seen in classroom films, the water shot straight upward and high. And shortly afterward bigger plops of rain fell around them and onto the nearby trees. With that, they all climbed onto the tracks, scurrying away like wary crabs.

As they stood huddled together on the tracks, Kensington whispered in a deep, excited breath and the others listened. "It could also be a bunch of geese! They're here all the time. They nest on the stone columns where the first Settlement bridge used to be."

"Hey, that's where my grandfather captured a witch," said Edgar.

"Now what's this witch business?" asked Horatio, complaining. "First, you said there are owls. Which is it? Make up your mind."

Ted, who was standing next to Edgar, asked in a clear unwavering voice how far the old bridge was. Kensington, with one hand groping and handling something inside his backpack, reiterated that it might be geese.

"The bridge? It isn't far," answered Edgar, adjusting his parachute and keeping a cautious eye toward Liquid Lake. "It's that way."

Without a single word being stuttered, Ted delivered another swift sentence. "This has to be the same place where Dark Swirling Cloud received the Star-Medicine."

"Hey, come on now," implored Horatio to Edgar, "don't start scaring us!"

Suddenly, behind them, deep in the woods, they heard leaves being parted and twigs being broken. There was movement behind the tall cottontail grass.

"Another noise!" remarked Edgar.

"Yeah, we heard it," snapped Horatio. "So what?"

"First, the three owls; second, the water; and now this! But my grandmother says that if you don't dwell on strange occurrences, you decrease their presence."

"Yeah, there's a lot of noise here. And if what your grandmother says is true, we should think about something else entirely. Ted, don't make this any worse by your strange talk. OK? We're here to look for spaceships. Remember?"

Sounding agitated, Ted defended himself without the slightest misinflection. "No, I'm not talking strange. That's what my aunt Louise Stabs Back told me. This place is supernatural."

Kensington, who was standing behind Horatio and Hayward, clutched his backpack like a hand puppet, holding it beside his wide face. He was still convinced it was geese diving from the stone columns, playing around.

In the middle of their discussion, another voice joined in from the darkness. "Geese don't throw themselves like bombs into the water, you savages!" Startled, the boys jerked their flashlights toward the voice's direction. It was Pat Red Hat, emerging from the swampy portion of the woods.

"Bombs?" whimpered Hayward. "What are you talking about, Pat?"

"Those spaceships," Pat said, pointing toward the hillside, "I think they're doing this, warning us to stay away."

Pat ambled up to them and told them to turn off the flashlights, saving their batteries for later. Over the starlit railroad tracks the group of boys sat down—three facing south on one rail and three facing north on another, listening.

"Don't you get it?" Pat said, "we're not supposed to be here."

"How many times has the water exploded?" asked Edgar.

Before anyone answered that it was two times, Liquid Lake exploded again. Twice in succession. They could feel vibrations of the natural stone basin undulating under the soles of their shoes.


On their subsequent ascent of the shadowy hills above Liquid Lake the boys were convinced by what Pat Red Hat had said: that whatever force didn't want them in the area made the water explode. But there were limitations. There had to be. Stuff like that, being harmed through actual interaction with Supernaturals, just didn't happen. The most they could logically expect was a fearful apparition.

As they got higher up the hill their courage grew. On their first break halfway up they passed around a jar of tea and everyone took long swigs. "Ah, that's good tasting," each proclaimed after a healthy sampling. Wiping the excess onto their shirtsleeves, they all sat down, not far from each other. Each of them gazed upward past the thick forest canopy, trying not to think about what had just transpired. They noticed the stars were becoming increasingly brighter and more distinct. Beside them, in the underbrush, even the sounds of small animals or birds became more audible. And then out of nowhere a cool, nearly undetectable breeze materialized; it swirled over their warm, perspiring skin, bouncing from one boy to another, until one of them felt something poking him.

"Hey, did you touch me a little while ago?" someone asked.

"No, did someone touch you?" someone answered from the shadowy foliage. They could hear the capricious breeze swirling around in the brush, making small murmuring sounds, but they ignored it. They had no choice. They had to concentrate on something else. Edgar started talking about how delicious tea tasted after a breakfast of scrambled eggs, fried mushrooms, sticky rice, and frybread. After Pat said he could almost smell the food, inhaling the night air, he talked about how he'd try to outstare the fiery morning sun as it came through the treetops. Hayward said something about not liking being jabbed in the ass with such a hard flashlight. Kensington cradled the backpack and gently rocked it as if it were a child, and Horatio babbled on about tree-gnawing beavers. They were speaking this gibberish until the mysterious hand began touching them.

"Hey, did you touch me again?" someone asked.

"No, did you touch me? Wait. Who is nearest to me?"

"I am," someone replied.

"No," someone said from behind a tree's silhouette, "I'm the closest."

Only for someone else to say, "Hey, someone just touched me!"

From the foliage, as the boys spoke their nonsense to no avail, the lights of a dozen fireflies began to assemble and flicker. Like the crickets they, too, were coming out, lighting up the fine stalks and leaves of ground-level plants. With that, the boys sprang to their feet. Once the weight of the backpacks over their boney shoulders was secured, they were ready to continue their climb. Beside them the fireflies began making an elaborate kaleidoscope-shaped design with their flickering green and yellow body-lights. Without a word the boys took a few steps up the incline and then paused to listen, looking backward. Far below, Liquid Lake was a shrill cacophony of frogs, and to the east and west toward O'Ryan's Cemetery and Rolling Head Valley, the whippoorwills were calling. Before, except for the watery explosions and an occasional mosquito or two, it had been disturbingly quiet. It was now different under a deluge of pleasant night sounds.

As the boys started walking up the terrain, the fireflies broke from their geometric design, following closely behind. When the boys stopped for a breather, the fireflies stopped also, lifting and then dropping repeatedly in one spot with their slow but intermittent body-lights. The boys began to realize this particular batch of fireflies had probably been with them—two fireflies per person—from the time each of them entered the wooded domain at sundown. Everyone was aware of that fact but no one wanted to point it out, for fear of triggering another mystery. No one dared to look. Again, out of fear, they had no choice but to ignore the pestiferous fireflies.

Upon reaching the top of the pine-tree-covered hill, the boys began tramping down the weeds and underbrush. They made a big circle and spoke little, gathering dry twigs and branches for the campfire. By then the twelve original fireflies had multiplied into dozens more. On each occasion when they suddenly dropped and flickered their lights in flight, other identical fireflies would appear. In turn, the new fireflies would generate others until the boys, who were sitting around the gathered firewood, were surrounded by a large circular mass that was a bright hazy green in color and pulsating.

"Start the fire," Pat said in a weak voice. "Who's got the matches?"

"I do." Ted's hands shook violently as he attempted to open the paper box of matches. The matchsticks could be heard as they were being rattled. To help him out, the flashlights were turned on again. With all eyes and concentration on Ted's hands, his shaking calmed down. He struck a single match and lit the crumpled *Why Cheer News-Herald*, which set everything else ablaze under the iron grill. The dry twigs crackled and hissed as the flames rose to the cool night air.

In the orange-red firelight they could see each other. Mostly they saw frightened faces. Behind them, aligned horizontally with their ears, was the circle of green light. They saw they were connected in this blinding, luminescent configuration. They couldn't ignore it; it was there pulsating and growing brighter.

Horatio, as he sat on bent feet, shot his hands upward, covered his face, and began sniffing. His partners, Hayward and Kensington, both wearing frowns that made them look like fish, kneeled beside him, wide-eyed and struggling to breathe. And Ted was still holding on to the box of matches and couldn't let go; he shook them like a ceremonial rattle. Pat, with his eyes staring fearlessly at the green circle, stood up, shaking his fists. Edgar, near tears, reached over with a branch and stoked the fire. Sparks from the campfire leapt out to the treetops, stopped, and then floated back down. Soon the boys found themselves encompassed by a fiery green waterfall. Pat began singing, or he tried to, before a clogged nasal system shut him up.

When the boys regained their sight, there were two overlapping beams of light, green and red, being projected by a tiny yellow light that was itself connected with shiny threads to a giant silver craft. By some mechanism the spaceship was being lifted from the sandy earth. The fine grains of sand could be heard scraping against the metallic surface.

Suspended in the air between the packed trees, the silver disk-shaped craft and its occupants, small in size, could be seen silhouetted against the opaque windows, moving about. The boys sensed collectively that these occupants were seeing to it that whatever had to be done was accomplished in precise order. A whirring sound then erupted in their ears, and just when they were about to be levitated toward the ascending spaceship, a leather pouch belonging to Luciano Bearchild was thrown into the campfire. It burned rapidly and the contents began to boil as if something was about to be deep-fried in grease. As the red, glowing coals came into contact with the antiwitch compound of cedar, wool, and fine boughs of tender clusterberries, the blue smoke rose in the boys' place and traveled to the spaceship's designated point of entry. Suddenly, the green, burning waterfall reverted back to normal fireflies until all that remained was a phantom domelike impression in the boys' vision.

# Birthplace of the Republican Party

In the latter 1950s, between the ages of seven and ten, I became aware there was another existence altogether to our east, and a strong curiosity developed. With the exception of bimonthly trips to Why Cheer and Gladwood for groceries and clothes, I really didn't know anything of these white neighbors who—as I've mentioned—pegged their area as "BIRTHPLACE OF THE REPUBLICAN PARTY." Although most Black Eagle Child households were dependent on their canned meats and sweets, I never gave their origin much thought. Mixed with our homegrown vegetables or with fish and wild game year-round, the food was fatty, sweet, delicious—and maybe in the long run dangerous to our health.

For Grandmother the Twintowns meant employment. There she worked as a laundry and dry cleaners helper. Every day by cab or her feet she left for work. Sometimes, depending on the season, my mother, Clotelde, also worked at the chicken hatchery or window frame factory. While Severt, my uncle, was away at Parsons College, Winston, my other uncle, dropped out of school to work at Whitmore's Sawmill. Everyone tried to help out. Later, I would learn that my grandfather, Jack Principal Bear, had toiled for years as a railroad laborer. Philosophically and politically, any contact with "the Outside World" was forbidden, especially among the Sacred Chieftain heirs. But by then everyone was aware that keeping a family fed was a basic necessity. Fiercely conservative on all issues pertaining to tribal progress, the Principal Bear family had a staunch work ethic embed in their conscience.

On occasion, when Grandmother worked on Saturdays, my brother Alan and I were treated to the movies. The Why Cheer Theater was right next door to the Laundry and Dry Cleaners. We didn't mind waiting three hours for the doors to open, and watching the shows twice over was common. By the time we got out, it was a short wait before Grandmother got through with work.

We became familiar with the theater, *ne ne ki sa i ka ni;* it was a dimly lit place where my younger brother grew to idolize James Dean and the one-eyed Cyclops in *Sinbad and the Seventh Voyage.* The theater's flashing lightbulbs and the tantalizing aroma of popcorn beckoned us. Inside, over the red carpeted floor, we marveled at all the candies under glass. On both sides of the wall, past the concession stand and the restrooms, movie posters of *Giant* and *I Was a Teenage Werewolf* were illuminated. Entering the unlit area itself was spellbinding and dizzying because the floor was built at a downward angle. The music would be on, vibrating off the high ceilings as we came out of the archway. We'd stumble around until we found the very first two empty seats.

The movies, *ne ne ki sa a ni,* were an ingenious way to see and experience the lives of other people in what was otherwise a faraway, inaccessible world. As the curtains were drawn, monolithic life-forms moved rapidly on the white screen in an array of plots and scenes. Hearing amplified speakers for the first time made our eardrums tickle. Overall we didn't understand the dialogue, for the English language was new. Even the Westerns seemed harmless back then.

The Why Cheer Theater was also a comical place where Grandmother once walked down the aisle believing she was actually with the characters on the screen: grimy but sultry World War II nurses escaping from a Japanese prison camp. She was so caught up that she got tired from the wild adventure. Her intent, she would often muse, was merely to go to the side of the jungle and "rest."

On another theater outing, an infant-child by the name of Brook, Rose Grassleggings's youngest daughter, got her hands caught between the backrest and the chair seat. It was shocking to know how this sweet, soft-spoken thing could bellow like a man. Little did I know that Brook, hermaphrodite that she/he was, would later enter the lives of Ted Facepaint and Junior Pipestar.

The theater was also a place where I sat next to a young girl who would go on to impact *my* life and career. Were it not for the fact that what you are about to read came about through an erotic dream I had as a young man, I would be extremely reluctant to discuss this matter. Had this happened in real life, in other words, I might have gotten into serious trouble: She was _____ years old back then, and I was _____. Because of the crowd in attendance for *What's New Pussycat?* she and her _____ ended up sitting next to me. I had seen her before and thought she was quite attractive, as Settlement girls go. After sitting beside her and intentionally rubbing my elbow against hers, I dreamt of her. For several years, once or twice a month, the nightly scene repeated itself: With no regard whatsoever for lawful conduct, singing along with Tom Jones, I suddenly found myself back in the theater. *"Pussycat, pussycat, I love you, yes, I do . . .."* In the dream I would slowly hoist her limp dress up with my left hand, jamming it gently between her warm, moist thighs. Before she could react and resist I slid backhanded through the loose elastic band of her towel-textured underwear and over the smoothness of her skin. As her chubby hips arched upward in surprise I went deeper, widening the way with my sensitive fingers, all in an effort to touch the softest, most private portion of her body. In waking up, however, there was a stupefying guilt for having such insatiable, obsessive thoughts. For that, a burning sensual desire behind my belly button, I had no control.

Little did I know that this young, lovely girl who was rudely subjected to my nocturnal pubescent urges would become a future beloved companion. Seriously. Eventually, the dreams stopped and I forgot about her. I wouldn't see her up close until a softball game four years later. But for a while there I couldn't help but wonder what influence, if any, heaven forbid, Kensington Muscatine had upon these idiosyncratic musings. Sometimes childhood acquaintances can have an unsettling influence. That time at Liquid Lake, for instance, when the fireflies transformed into a burning waterfall, the sight of Kensington's left hand protruding through the blue jean backpack, clutching an undressed doll with its plastic nippleless breasts exposed to the strobelike flashes of the Supernaturals, became memorable.

Pat Red Hat often joked that from that night on when he espied a bare-chested "Sandra Dee," he was forced to wear sunglasses. "Sandra Dee, not the flying saucer, blinded me," he'd say in mawkish rhyme, and we'd all laugh. "Sandra Dee, Hollywood actress, stripped of her dress, excited me" was another quip. The sad fact was, Pat's retinas had been burned by the Supernaturals' manifestations and the "Sandra Dee" doll was only the beginning of an unnatural penchant for "Kensey."

For an hour or so movies at the Why Cheer Theater transported us to unimaginable places. Sometimes Alan and I were the last of the matinee crowd to leave. We hung on to our seats, knowing the projectionist would rewind the film. Bedazzled by the fast, reverse motions on the screen we made our twenty cents' admission go a long ways. But when the burly, silver-haired white man waddled down the aisle with his flashlight, the fantasy promptly ended.

Outside, under the dusty lightbulbs of the marquee, Alan and I inhaled the warm summer air mixed with the odor of automobile and tractor exhaust, buttered popcorn, and steam from the dry cleaners where Grandmother worked. We stood over the warm concrete sidewalk, waiting for Grandmother and Joe Gadger's taxi. Destination: the Black Eagle Child Settlement.

In less than twenty minutes we'd be home.

Once Grandmother paid the talkative taxi driver, we'd cross a small, clear creek, using the three wooden planks as a bridge. If the planks floated away in a flood, they were easily replaced by finding others. Situated in the shadows of trees and thickets, the creek had a pungent smell of mud. Here, the dragonflies flitted at our presence and the light green frogs leapt deep into the sandy pools. Correspondingly, in a flurry of silt and chunky particles, large minnows and chubs propelled themselves to safety underneath the willow roots, chasing out crawdads in the process. Past the makeshift bridge, we'd climb the clay-hardened steps that were carved into the ravine. Like swimmers emerging from a river, we'd come up onto the large, well-kept lawn.

This was where we lived.

The small unpainted house was all lit up by the hot afternoon sun, standing out against the hills of the thick, green forest. Caught between two worlds, this home was where we were taught there was nothing of value worth learning from white people, not even their language. Oh, we could work for a living and enjoy their cinematic forms of entertainment, but anything else meant contaminating one-self. Grandmother said so. Granted, using their food, clothes, and shelter is unavoidable, she would say, yet it is imperative in the religious and cultural sense we remain Black Eagle Child. Because education in the white world, through the martyrdom of Dorothy Black Heron in 1890, was a legal requirement, these critical factors were not easily retained.

For the Principal Bears, the family in which I was born and raised, the enactment of a law designed "to hasten the transition of the primitive heathen to Christian citizen" was the birth of the tribe's discordance and remoteness. The Sacred Chieftains felt there was more at stake than mere subjugation. It isn't so much a test of our susceptibility, the Six Grandfathers conveyed, as it is an effort to keep prophecies from reaching fruition.

With the advent of education came unwanted experiences. The Six Grandfathers wrote about it. Extensively. Over a period of sixty years a startling, collective revelation materialized through the gradual loss of traditional practices and values. Democracy, or a crude replica thereof, was eventually shoved down our grandparents' gullets in the 1930s. In confirmation of our fears a bread factory was built near the railroad tracks. Next came a small grocery store that was also a barber shop and pool hall.

There was even a school, the Weeping Willow Day School a.k.a. Weeping Willow Elementary. Built from government blueprints for an "Indian Reservation Sanatorium, Class B," the school was the first and last tribal school. As student enrollment grew, rooms were simply merged or divided to accommodate the six grade levels. In 1935 the seventh, eighth, and ninth grades were added. In Iowa history books, the school earned status as an "institutional landmark." In 1950, however, federal safety officers had the school condemned as a fire hazard. Undeterred, and taking the threatened closing as a government ploy to integrate tribal youth into the Why Cheer community school system, the tribe successfully fought to keep the classes going.

It was an unprecedented twist of events. What was once a transgression *against* us became a permissible form of acquiescence *by* us. In a tribe that had formerly opposed outside education, a consensus indicated there could be immeasurable benefits in children attending school on the Settlement. Embroiled in nonending controversy, Weeping Willow withstood multiple arson attempts, hordes of termites, and indecent exposure charges against its Bureau of Tribal Affairs principals and regional officers in command. These allegations led to the tribe gaining total control of the school.

Troubles were both internal and external.

Neighboring whites felt it was their god-given duty to "remind the skinjins of their rightful place." In 1920, the Why Cheer Women's Preservation Club, with state endorsement, acquired property adjacent to the Black Eagle Child Settlement, near the tribal school. Like the club, the two highways and the two sets of railroad tracks that came afterward, running parallel through the Settlement's geographical heart, reminded us daily of eventuality. The lonely whistles of trains passing each other each afternoon became familiar. And on the trip toward town everyone would pass the Red Barn Premises. Behind the high, barbed-wired fence stood the three fire engine red–colored barns where tribal youth in 1890 were "culturally disfigured," as Pat Red Hat used to say.

Once a year, during the Saturday and Sunday of the annual Black Eagle Child Field Days and Chautauqua, the Red Barn Premises were open to the public. Black Eagle Childs included. Grandmother, Alan, and I would make the long trek by foot from the tribal fairgrounds to what we later came to know as a museum. The Red Barn was historic. In 1890 some of our grandparents were brought back after their failed escape; here they were stripped of their clothes, given haircuts, and bathed in preparation for mandatory schooling. Our young grandparents, outfitted in dark uniforms, fresh from the wilds, sat rigid and expressionless for group photographs. Their capitulation was well documented. Grandmother would point every summer at her relatives encased in glass. While commenting on their sallow eyes and disheveled body posture, she recalled their clan-given names and how we were related to them. Watching them from the sides in the photos were the mustached federal truant officers who had cattle-herded them through the barns.

Needless to say, the Red Barn Premises were monuments. Technically, these were the first government-designated schoolgrounds for the tribe. Beside the barns, on the same property, were log cabins that housed the first teachers and their classrooms. The white visitors who were there for the tribal Field Days and Chautauqua streamed through the antiquated structures, buying imitation beadwork and hand-decorated postcards celebrating the "HOME OF THE WHY CHEER INDIANS." Through the iron windows of the cabins we could view the three-room structures where the teachers lived; some were prettier and furnished better than most Settlement homes. Goose-down pillows and intricate quilts graced the brass beds; on elegantly carved nightstands were open Bibles and stacks of fat books with gold lettering. There were fancy lamps and chandeliers on the walls and ceiling of the dining room and kitchen. In the sink there was even a hand-operated, short-handled water pump. Around the lace-draped round table set for three, the chairs were richly stained and varnished. Inside the cast-iron woodstove glowed a red lightbulb.

Eventually, the white Preservation Club women, along with the Combined Christians of Iowa, built a church to rescue "the lost souls of heathendom." During summer weekends or national holidays, the women and their out-of-town guests would arrive in an automobile convoy, unlock the locks of the barbed-wire fence, and indulge in old atrocities. Like the trains, the carloads of umbrella and picnic basket–toting women became familiar annoyances.

For a long time after Weeping Willow Elementary was opened, I detested the transparent-skinned teachers who brought strange-smelling books and papers, along with nauseating foods like beets and chocolate pudding; later, I would also find their sports games with spherical objects abhorrent. As was done for the predecessors of the Weeping Willow teachers, the Bureau of Tribal Affairs constructed Donna Reed American faculty housing. Like the log cabins, the whitewashed houses were surrounded with high barbed-wire fences.

When I first met the Weeping Willow teachers and their families, they were impatient and jittery. To communicate with me they had to improvise; they sign-languaged. Simple doglike commands: stay, go, sit, lie down, and so forth. On more than one occasion, they requested and received visits from Clotelde, my mother. In her presence, they compared me to "a contagion"; I defeated their purposes by making "my peers converse in Indian."

Whatever it was they accused me of, Mr. Mateechna, the school janitor, would be summoned. Kneeling beside my desk, he'd whisper in a refreshing breath of Juicy Fruit gum, "If you don't keep quiet, your friends and relatives will be unduly punished." But it was too late. Since no one had explained English and the need to speak it to me, each member of the class suffered a red, ruler-sized welt on the forearm every day for weeks.

In both of my years in fourth grade I went with different classes on train rides to Minneapolis and Chicago. It was during the repeat year that I met and made friends with Ted Facepaint, Pat Red Hat, Horatio Plain Brown Bear, Hayward and Kensington Muscatine. I was the only student to repeat a grade. There were advantages: I initiated all reminiscences; I'd been there. It was pleasurable and an honor of sorts until I realized something was not right. When I asked my mother why I flunked fourth grade, she said, "The teachers think that physically you're too small." For a while I accepted that as an explanation.

Who could help it? I thought to myself; I was made this way.

It soon began to dawn on me that being deprived of promotion to the next grade had nothing to do with size. My questions escalated into theories of conspiracy, that it was all a payback for being fluent in Black Eagle Child.

Whatever the reasoning, these were memorable days when some of the older female teachers wore blotches of cherry red paint on their lips, while the unmarried ones wore skirts so tight that company logos of their girdles showed up over their thighs. The outlines, it was reported by Pat Red Hat, felt interesting to the touch.

On one particular field trip there was a voluptuous Negro woman who became so involved with her monitor duties that several students crawled under her skirt and looked heavenward between her stocky, muscular calves at the mysterious constellations. Moving secretly like a bull snake under the seats of the rumbling school bus without drawing the attention of the teachers was done for amusement. With the exception of Pat Red Hat, nobody knew what to look for. But compared to other educational seediness offered at Weeping Willow, African astronomy was kid stuff. For example, from the sewer drains, especially in a quick, spring thaw with rain, white balloons that the older students said the principal wore on his "peeno" slid out into the swamps.

They would be brought out like uncaged circus animals, dangling from the tips of long, crooked sticks. Everyone ran in ignorant terror. Even when Pat Red Hat, an erudite but slow-running classmate, tried to explain their function, I was befuddled by the commotion caused by the wet balloons. I was told to visualize that they had been used by the only man-occupant of the faculty housing, the principal. With whom? Nobody knows, Pat whispered. Maybe the principal's invalid wife or the Bureau of Tribal Affairs secretary? The juvenile delinquent, John Louis, made illustrations of this provocative affair, which were then traded for cigarettes or bullets. Highly valued, they were shared among the classes. We feasted on the side cutaway profiles of two intertwined people. An arrow pointed to the necktied man's protrusions where the balloon might be placed; another arrow pointed to a groin close-up, showing internal compartments where the "chicken soup" might be made; another arrow showed the upside-down Y bodily contortion of the would-be woman partner; and the final arrow pointed to a woman asleep and alone in her wheelchair beside the bed.

From the year I was able to speak and gesture with my stumpy hands, imitating the mannerisms of noted storyteller Carson Two Red Foot, I composed and recited tales on the spot for my proud mother and grandmother amid throngs of ogling playmates. At family get-togethers, there were constant requests for "Ki sko, the Beastly Tongue Man" or "To ka ni, the Witch's Brown Club." Even before I accepted invitations to perform these one–child actor skits, I would make a crowd chuckle as I impersonated the Indian Katzenjammer Kids. Without fail my characters could generate an appreciative audience.

As further proof of precociousness, and long before I heard of chapbooks or comics, I made gifts of my tales through illustrated, hand-sewn booklets. When I was three years old, my mother said I peppered people with words fresh to my vocabulary. In one famous incident, I kept saying "So?" for an entire day to anyone unfortunate enough to be within hearing range. With each white or Indian word acquired, provided it didn't backfire, I grew. This word-collecting talent led my grandmother to believe that I should be the caretaker of the Six Grandfathers' Journals.

During the first years at Weeping Willow Elementary a group of older classmates became frustrated by my vocal talent, judged to be insolence. They pointed directly at my round, chicken pox–scarred face and yelled, "Don't you know you have an ugly face? *A kwi we na-ke ke ne ta ma ni ni-e ne tti wi na ko si wa ni?*" This was the ultimate put-down in 1957. Still the smart alec, in defense of my scars, I retaliated, "Yes, I do grimace . . . when I am toileting on your face!"

In what was perhaps reprisal for being quick-witted and tongue-talented, I was also ambushed by five lunch-table leaders who then proceeded to depants me beside the orange school bus with onlookers around. I can still recall the incredible surges of humiliation as I bucked and wrenched about helplessly over the wet concrete. There were strong, boney grips over my husky legs, arms, and shoulders, and a flurry among females unlike any I had ever seen. Their dresses sprouted large, grotesque wings that flew around me like metal spears, prodding me into submission.

Lying on my back over the wet sidewalk I could see the rain-clouds from another angle, a view I had rarely experienced. In multitudes the watery specks grew larger shortly before they landed, stinging my terrorized, tear-filled eyes. As the zipper to my crotch was unfastened notch by notch the girls displayed sneers along with looks of profound satisfaction. As my baggy shorts were peeled down shamelessly around my chapped thighs and ankles, they kept chanting, "Do you know what revenge means, you stupid little kid?" In an act of futility and to keep from crying aloud, I tried to spell this unfamiliar, mean-sounding word, REE-VENN-GEE, in my damaged psyche. "How do you spell it?" I moaned under the strong, perspiring bodies.

I fought the lunch-table leaders so hard that several had to use their developing chests to subdue the thrashing elbows and knees.

In the ensuing ruckus my uncircumcised penis fossilized itself with blood. Usually it awoke during wrestling matches with weak females or upon sight of colorful Christmas decorations. On this particular occasion I was caught off guard. There was a wrestling match, yes, but I was the one being pinned under the tall, bushy pine tree with leftover Christmas decorations and tinsel. Like a startled snake roused from its den by unannounced visitors, it uncoiled and rose to the challenge, engorging itself with stone liquid. On their hands and knees the lunch-table leaders looked at one another in disbelief at the young male erection that tottered menacingly in the rain. The grotesque metal spears folded in midflight and shot back to the side panel of the dresses.

"Do you like eating corn mush? *Ke wi ka ta ba-ka ni mi na bo wi?*" I asked in a brave but quivering voice. Because of bedwetting, my penis had been jokingly named "Corn Mush" by my uncles, Winston and Severt Principal Bear, when I was four years old. "What do you say when someone you don't know comes to your aid?" I cried out again in defiance to the braided gargoyles who were panting heavily in their training bras. "Corn Mush!" I answered myself, pointing. "He is looking at you with one eye!" The lunch-table leaders scrambled to their feet and walked away from me backward and open-mouthed.

From the back of the bus, John Louis, the juvenile delinquent who drew the "chicken soup" diagram—the principal's male reproductive system—classified the failed ambush as "a case of the nearly raped visually raping the would-be rapists." Neither I nor my classmates understood what he said. We appealed to the grown-up wisdom of Pat Red Hat, but it didn't matter. Everyone cracked up uncontrollably as I pulled the wet shirt from my back, giving it space to air-dry. They had seen everything; showing my bare chest and stomach was nothing. For a riotous hour the orange school bus shook from laughter en route to the Colonial Bread Factory in Cedar Rapids, Iowa.

# The Great Flood
## of the
## Iowa River

In 1920, almost thirty years to the day her older sister, Dorothy Black Heron, was raped and murdered by my paternal grandfather, the One Most Afraid, aged twenty-two, met her own tragic end. Like the sister she never knew but had heard a great deal about, the One Most Afraid would perish on the western edge of the Black Eagle Child Settlement under bizarre circumstances.

This was the one story I asked Carson Two Red Foot to tell in detail. There were historic implications and a flagrant abuse of justice. Evidently, according to Carson, the One Most Afraid had been waiting in the late evening hours for a young man who supposedly summoned her by note through a female intermediary. She was advised to wait at a particular fallen tree. As she sat near this designated area, however, three people who had been waiting snuck up from behind and clubbed her lifeless with blunt objects. The assailants' tracks were followed by the authorities to the Iowa River, where they became lost. Eight to ten miles up- or downriver, no swimmers had emerged. "By all appearances," wrote the Tama County authorities, "the female Indian subject was about to commit infidelity but someone caught her and punished her swiftly as required by ancient tribal custom."

On Weeping Willow Elementary School field trips to the Tama County courthouse, I would lean my face against the glass case that held the plaster footprints of the One Most Afraid's killers. There were three *of them. While their footprints have long been removed from the exhibit, I now believe that whoever assaulted the One Most Afraid dove from the dirt cliffs of the river and changed into the three owls who have for centuries decimated our own through witchcraft.*

*Three times in my own lifetime the three owls would make their presence known: once at Liquid Lake; second, at the Iowa River bottoms; and third, through the voice of Junior Pipestar, medicine man extraordinaire. The fourth time, I suspect there will be more than a trivial light-and-sound display. The next time they will be coming after me. Judging by the frequency of their appearance, they will arrive a lot sooner than I expect.*

*For Dorothy Black Heron and the One Most Afraid, there was a short but remarkable life. Their stories intrigued me for a number of reasons. Of utmost importance, obviously, was the older sister's murder: Dorothy forever altered the course of the tribe.*

*With regard to the One Most Afraid, who was set up by her own friend and confidant, there were tales of her extraordinary beauty and the tragedy it brought. In 1908, the One Most Afraid, at fourteen, was sought after by many suitors, including my grandmother's adopted brother, Carson Two Red Foot's father, John. Carson's father was so smitten that he left his wife, Mary, and five children.*

*In my research of events surrounding the deaths of these two well-known sisters, I once came upon an old photograph taken of the One Most Afraid.*

*Looking into her alluring, slanted eyes, held in suspension back in the summer of 1919, I saw that everything they said about her was true. For hours in the public library I gazed into this woman's face, wondering how she could be so perfect. To this day the One Most Afraid still inspires lively talk among the elders. They bemoan the fact that this incredibly beautiful young woman's murder, like many others, remains unsolved.*

*I recalled the first time I asked Carson Two Red Foot to talk about her: Among the many to be captivated by her looks, Carson recounted certain events involving the One Most Afraid and his beloved sister, Bent Tree. Their fates, he would say, were hopelessly intertwined.*

*In 1913, as a result of his mother's marital frustrations and the failure of their self-imposed exile from the Black Eagle Child Settlement,*

*Bent Tree committed suicide. Seven years later, still devastated that the One Most Afraid had stolen her husband, Carson's mother sought the services of a witch, the one who was captured while crossing the Iowa River bridge by Jack Principal Bear and Alfred Pretty-Boy-in-the-Woods. Against the One Most Afraid, the strongest night-enemy medicine was unleashed: a trio of cackling owls who had the ability to control the behavior of vulnerable human beings. The three owls, for as long as it is necessary, wear the minds of people who are not mentally in control to accomplish their heinous deeds or requests.*

### Carson Two Red Foot (as Told to Edgar Bearchild):

One winter day while spearfishing for catfish, *tte qwa me qwa ki*, with my sisters and brothers at the confluence of the two Settlement rivers, my oldest sister Wa ki me te kwi, Bent Tree, confided a terrible secret. The knowledge was so powerful that I will always remember that particular day: *e tti ya ki-i ni na i-ka o ni-e tti be ma te si ya ni i ni na i*, the way the weather was and the way I was feeling then.

Bad memories can stand out like formidable enemies. In adversity of this sort you see everything clearly. It is unsettling. You remember tiny details around you, like the cold, gray sky dotted with swirling snowflakes. Your eyes seem to remember and you conjure the colors, like the pale edges of frozen mud along the river's edge, the tan barkless tree covered with frost, and the indented burrowings of insects.

We were on our fifth year of independence, fending for ourselves without Father. This wasn't too long after the winter in which Mother set out in the blizzard to search for stranded livestock.

You remember that story, don't you?

How we left because of Ma tti qwe ta tti ta, the One Most Afraid, and Father's obsession with her? The One Most Afraid was the younger sister that Dorothy Black Heron never knew.

Don't you remember how we almost starved until the blizzard came as a blessing?

The silhouette I saw of Mother?

There she was in a woolen shawl raising a giant meat cleaver with both arms, hacking away at the half-frozen pigs who were piled along the fence line in the tall snowdrifts. Had it not been for the pigs who huddled and climbed atop one another for protection from the historic snowstorm, we would have either frozen or starved. The boars and sows ended up crushing each other senseless.

Toward spring thaw, numerous bodies of frozen animals and birds covered the forest and prairie floor. The hollow-eyed, sparsely fleshed pig skulls proved the most disturbing.

I recall thinking: This could have been us.

As we approached these areas of devastation where the deer, fox, and rabbits last congregated before dying, the scavengers ran or flew away in a flurry as if they had just committed an atrocious crime. It wasn't their fault; they were only being what they were.

For months afterward I had nightmares about mice and crows expertly scraping their way into our rigid bodies. Tunnels of our once-life melting. Of course, I now know these dreams were premonitions, the volatile beginnings of a family tragedy. I sometimes feel death has overpaid me.


For the first time since we had made a reluctant return to the central encampment of relatives in Tama County, I was feeling good. In spite of the flood of the Iowa River, we had survived four harsh seasons, and we were on the verge of knowing better how to take care of ourselves. But I never anticipated being enveloped by my sister's private secret. And I never expected to be troubled by a beloved person's twisted direction. The direction Mother took.

How I wish I could go backward! There are many things I would have changed. . . .

Before the flood we were doing perfectly that fifth year at the Amana Colonies: We traded corn and beans we grew in the summer for sausage and ham in the fall. The red-cheeked European farmers were eager to obtain our crops. They were astonished at how much longer our garden varieties lasted and how well they tasted. To hasten the trade, we learned German words like *"ke to ben,* potato" or *"schwi ben,* onion."

But all that came to an abrupt standstill when the torrential rains started, rains that caused uncontrolled emotion to inundate the heart of a woman with malice for her beloved daughter. Mother and Bent

Tree, they were entangled in the leftover webbing of love medicine spells that took our father. Unexpected visits and written notes from the One Most Afraid proved the most potent. An alluring young girl and a family of suspected sorcerers who desired their daughter and niece have a bountiful life, free from want.

John Two Red Foot, our father, was thus seen as an ample provider; an ideal mate. What cost was it to his wife and family but humiliation? they must have said as the first mirror shots were sent from the woods into the door of his lodge. Directing the sunlight to the area where he kept his bed they must have spoken into the mirror in a breath of "persuasion" plants.

Throughout our existence, there are bound to be periods when tragic situations spring up from the calm. If these tragedies are missing, the elders used to say, a person will be overwhelmed with melancholy when it strikes that "lives can be taken." And it is strange. A family that cares for each other can also die from loneliness for each other.

Back then, of course, we were more susceptible to diseases. Many varieties, as many as our garden held. The loss of a single youth or parent could cause the loss of other family members. Even if disease didn't inhabit all our defenseless bodies, the deaths of people close to us had similar devastating capabilities.

The "shadows," or ghostly presence, of deceased loved ones would return in dreams and guide us by hand and familiar voice to where they resided—the Afterlife. Even when we had abided by the rules of not naming their names in daily conversation, their faces and bodies came to us as if they had never left for the West, never died.

Had I known the course of upcoming events then, I would have confronted Mother. But I sought to remove myself from Bent Tree, my sister, as she whispered those awful descriptions. It was an intimate subject best understood by women. Their anatomical physicality, the differences. Traditionally, even as siblings, we the boys were separated from the girls, and fathers were not allowed to change or bathe their own daughters. That's just the way things were. I didn't know Mother's anger and suspicions would become evil.

Just as there are bound to be moments of personal disaster, there will also be moments of helplessness. This is how I reacted that day by the river: I was rendered speechless, and I prayed it would go away. It didn't. It was like waking up to find a smoky-shaped trespasser, a night-enemy, beside the bed, inhaling at will your breath, causing paralysis. I was unable to move or say anything.

Of course, I knew instantly what Mother was doing was wrong, but I didn't know how to resolve it. I had no words to give to my sister or mother; I felt bad, for they should have been given in either consolation or complaint. I was aware Bent Tree had reached womanhood, which often made it necessary for her to sleep, eat, and hide in a *mi ya no te wi ka ni,* menstruation lodge; I just never expected to know beyond the obvious what young girls must endure to become women. *I ni ye to ki-ke te na e tti ke ki? ne te tti te.* Is this the way it really is? I thought to myself.

"I don't like this at all," Bent Tree said in a quavery voice. "And I am bothered every day by her suspicions. She tells this to the women who visit. They probably go home and tell everyone of my supposed wrongdoings. With who? I don't even know any men other than you two, my brothers! She checks me physically for signs of sexual activity!"

Even though I found her secret unbelievable I began to realize that strange events had indeed transpired between Mother and Bent Tree. For no apparent reason we were sometimes told to do chores. Of course, we obeyed, thinking there was a good reason why they had to be alone. Whatever it was, it didn't sound pleasant from a distance. When we got our work done, we went on long meditative walks. Maybe we didn't want to hear their words. By evening the long quiet spells before falling asleep somehow became increasingly bothersome. It went beyond being respectful for the occasion of family sleep. There was trouble.

In the shade of the cottonwoods that lined the four riverbanks I began to shiver. With two rivers, there was twice the wind, twice the cold. Presumably, twice the fish. Consumed by thoughts of confusion, I lost all interest in spearfishing; I didn't want to look for the watery shapes of dark catfish lumbering and hiding beneath the unwanted fish. The half-submerged spear began collecting layers of ice.

I soon began to fear that my eyes would freeze as well, for I had begun to weep. Unknowingly. In a fleeting thought I knew then our lives would somehow go awry. It was as if an entire railroad bridge had lifted upright, levitated, and settled itself slowly on one sharp corner over my boney chest. The weight of the bridge, *ko ka i ka ni*, was more than the frail rib cage could tolerate. It splintered and sliced into an already saddened heart. I could either thrash about or lie still like a speared fish. In either case there was sure death.

As the clouds and the sun began creating varying levels of intermittent daylight, I couldn't think of anything appropriate to say. Over the crusty ice, shadows made from our combined breath raced in the cold wind, circling my other sister and two younger brothers. The rectangular opening over the frozen river where we had seen fish in multitudes became a portal to a dark, dark earth. Death reached out its long fingers and prepared to trip Bent Tree. She would fall and never see anything again.

With exposed fingers I leaned forward slightly against the spear and listened to the barbed tines grind and sink into the sandy riverbottom. We had been taught that frank discussions about our bodies was taboo. More so between a brother and his sister. It was inappropriate. Mother had taught us that. As we matured we were forbidden to do many things together; the point being, the less we interacted, the less the possibility of incest. Because of the difficulties we faced as a fatherless family, working together and being close was virtually impossible. Yet there was never any intent on either side of exploring each other, not even out of curiosity. We cared for each other too much.

"Mother thinks I am seeing a man," confessed Bent Tree. "She also thinks an admirer is stalking me and I am encouraging him by allowing him to touch my private parts. 'You are probably too shocked or so full of evil that you can't tell the truth,' she accuses me."

As she started to tell me when and how long ago Mother began inspecting her for alleged sexual misconduct, I purposely drowned her out with my own thoughts, remembering: I caught them once, surprised them by returning too early. I had dismissed the event as being normal. Things only women and women-to-be knew about. Something beyond the realm of a young man's life. Something not easily understood, like childbirth or "being outside" monthly in the personal lodge.

Finally, as my eyes began to get clearer on that long-ago wintry day, large catfish shapes began to emerge from under the hundreds of suspended fish. I hovered the spear close over the sandy, stone-lit bottom and waited for the largest. Like a clear blue sky that has a uniqueness of its own, I remember everything from that day when Bent Tree divulged her ugly secret on the confluence of the Iowa and Swanroot Rivers. The white rocks we had thrown to the riverbottom to serve as a light background shimmered before they darkened with finned and barbed silhouettes. Looking up I saw the fish-drivers, my siblings, lifting the wooden posts and pounding them to the ice, driving the packed fish out from the deep greenish waters. There were vibrations on the soles of my worn-out boots. Bent Tree, looking distraught, kneeled down, scooping away the icy slush from the rectangular opening with a perforated tin dipper. When she stood back up, she vowed Mother would never touch her again. High above the willow saplings the double echo of wooden posts slamming against the exposed branches of huge submerged trees resonated between the two rivers.

It was hard to dismiss the picture she had drawn in my mind of a hideous belt made of male genitals, the one Mother accused Bent Tree of wearing as proof of her sexual conquests. It wasn't true, but Mother had convinced herself the old story about an unfaithful woman was happening to Bent Tree.


Shortly after our return to Tama County, Mother's condition worsened. She did what she could to fight the doldrums, though. She began talking to Bent Tree more. She was still deeply embittered about being abandoned by our father, John Two Red Foot. Bent Tree, as it turned out, took the brunt of this pent-up anger. Mother eventually became suspicious of everything she did, questioning her movements around the house—and the Settlement. Whatever semblance of mental clarity Mother had fought so hard to regain at our Amana Colonies camp crumbled when the torrential rains began, ruining our home and the gardens we had subsisted on.

During one endless week of pounding rain in the month of July, *Be na wi ki tti swa,* anyone who lived anywhere within a mile or two of the Iowa River—for one hundred miles in either direction—was forced to high ground for a three-week period. The flood was unlike any experienced in history.

Near Gerslossen, where we lived, a family of farmers died when the man refused to leave his cherished home to the rising debris-filled waters. They were all found weeks later with bullet holes in their decomposed skulls. Mass suicide was preferred over drowning.

Forty miles upriver, on tribal lowlands, news came to us that strong young men had been sent into the muddy brown waters to retrieve sacred mattings from the earthlodges. In the rush for high-ground safety, the mats were inadvertently forgotten. There was panic, for if the mats were drenched in the slightest, new thunderstorms would materialize. Another calamity.

All along the circumference of the flood the religious but fearful elders paced. It was rumored that the sale of a sacred mat to a Belgium museum by a man named Francis Marie led to the angry retribution of the Thunderstorm Gods. When they spoke, lightning bolts shot forth from their mouths and set fire to tall cottonwoods. Under the branches was where sorcerers took shelter and congregated. There were many.

Standing behind the elders were the young swimmers' parents. Everyone peered in a worrisome manner toward the swollen lowlands. Above the river valleys were long streams of smoke, marking places where cottonwoods fell. Dozens upon dozens. The sun couldn't be seen due to the smoke-darkened sky.

As the swimmers came to view and emerged, everyone was told what happened. After being confronted by large snapping turtles who blocked the smoke portals of the longhouses, the swimmers were able to dive and open the submerged doorways of the earthlodges. They then broke through the roofs, kept the mats dry by tying them to staffs, holding them above water, and taking turns.

This was the closest the Well-Known Twin Brother had brought us to earth's untimely demise. The unrelenting torrential rains brought defiant turtles who saw a chance to revert to the monsters they originally were in the First Earth. They were still upset by the Well-Known

Twin Brother posing as a woman momentarily to steal back his sacred mat. (Maybe this was the very mat that Francis Marie sold, speculated the people.)

The flood hung on, and all that remained of our home and the three gardens in Gerslossen was shiny black mud and bare trees. Everywhere was the putrid odor of rotting fish and livestock. Mud-covered shapes of pregnant horses, some with their insides ripped apart, glistened ominously under the blue sky.

The scene reminded us of another season. If it wasn't a blanket of head-high snowdrifts, then it was a vast sludge-ridden grave. Surviving scavengers with wings and paws deflated the gaseous carrion systematically with their beaks and sharp teeth before the feast.

After Mother saw our lodge poles under a valley of oily mud, including the surrounding countryside, she abandoned any thought of staying. All the clothes, dishes, kettles, and traps we had accumulated in trade and purchase were swept away. We waded knee-deep and found nothing salvageable. We consoled one another and said we were fortunate to have gotten out with clothes and dry food satchels. Had it not been for the sound of sizzling embers in the cooking fire being engulfed by the initial floodwaters, we would not have awoken.

If given the chance again, Mother would have preferred drowning rather than going back. We remained in the hills over our valley for as long as the supplies lasted. At the central encampment we were looked upon with intrigue, like people who had ventured far away, failed in their exile, and then straggled back. We must have been a spectacle: shameless adolescents in ragged clothes and moccasins indistinguishable from soil. The children we once played with had all grown. They were told to keep away but couldn't.

After we were taken in by relatives who were both worried about our health and embarrassed by our appearance, it was nice, catching up on news. Listening to dreamlike voices other than our own was the best part of our reunion.

Through the generosity of Mother's cousins we were allowed to stay in a house with a smooth wooden floor, glass windows, and one creaky door. The only trouble was, Mother would by habit stay in the house all day and never come out until well after sunset, *e ki tti-*

*ni ki tti-ki tte swa.* Mother didn't want to meet up with our father, *no se na na,* John Two Red Foot. There was a good chance he was somewhere in the community, traveling by buggy and horse with his seventeen-year-old wife and two infants, our half siblings, without a hint of disgrace. On occasion, he would attempt to converse with us but it came out awkward and insincere. He tried and we denied.

If we happened to be within hearing distance with Mother, he would mimic banter and carry on like a zestful but pathetic man. With me alone, however, he reacted differently: He would stare, nod faintly, and smile without wanting or meaning to. It was the way adult men exhibited resentment. This was the way it was then, *i ni tta-e tti ke ki-i yo i ni na i.*

There was excitement amid the despair. One day we were tricked into going to Weeping Willow Elementary. We felt like the early runaways on their way to the infamous "barns." Once the school officials understood we were "irreversibly illiterate," we were led back to the wagon and given a quick but polite good-bye. Personally, I was relieved, but the others were somewhat dejected; they wanted to display their speaking skills in German.

As young people are apt to socialize within our own age group, we would frequently leave Mother alone at home. This didn't seem harmful then, but our absence was probably hard on her. And for Bent Tree, my sister.

"I find the daylight annoying here," Mother would say to us every time day's end arrived. "It is an unusual red and yellow glare." She would therefore wait for sunset. Only then with the curtains fully opened did the warm, stale air rush out. "There! You see what I mean," she would assert. "The sun is still that reddish tinge."

In spite of her peculiarities, the evenings at the Black Eagle Child Settlement were beautiful as we all sat in the small room of the crude government-built house. Mother would sew and bead in the shadows. On weekends we were sent to Why Cheer, *o te we na ki,* to set up a roadside crafts display. She could still support us with her diligent work. But something lingered and it festered in her thoughts.

At night she was restless and couldn't sleep. In order not to disturb us she would leave for long walks, no matter how cold or rainy.

She'd return around midnight, *e na wi te bi ki ki*, or early in the morning, *ma ma wi ke ki tte e ba*.

Once during our deepest sleep we began dreaming to the babylike wail of a screech owl. Suddenly, the cry changed into her words. Upon waking, we saw her there in the middle of the room, talking to herself about Bent Tree. She eventually woke her up and began addressing her like a stranger on a mature subject.

"Don't think about men," she hissed. "You persist in visiting all over. 'She likes to visit for the purpose of giggling in front of men' is what they will say about you. Everyone no doubt believes you are destined to wear a belt of men's private parts around your waist, a loathsome belt that will accompany you to the Afterlife, for all to take note of your promiscuity."

We grew dry-mouthed as we listened from our beds on the floor.

"This is what will happen to the One Most Afraid, the girl your father lives with. They talk about her. My aunts. She sees other men, collecting still new prizes on her belt. She will wear it into her death and beyond. Do you aspire to be like her? *I ni e tti-a ka wa ta ma ni-ni i na te si wa ni?* Tell me! *A tti mo i no!*"

With eyes wide open, I lay still and smelled the air, hoping to detect the faint sweetness of homemade wine in her breath. There was none. Intoxication, *ke skwe bya a te si we ni*, would have accounted for her strange behavior.

At the oddest hour Bent Tree would be told a story about the hideous belt of male genitals, of the brother who punished and killed his married but promiscuous sister for the honor of the family.

## The Wife That Was Slain with a Club by Her Brother

*In the distant past there was once a woman who was promiscuous with men. It was in the summertime, when the people of the tribe were gathered in a single village. It was then that this particular woman had arranged a sexual union with a man who cut a hole in the wall of a bark lodge in order to carry on their secret but dangerous affair. This woman used a cutout piece of bark to cover the hole in the wall so as not to arouse her benevolent husband's suspicions.*

But before long, the husband somehow found out that his own lodge provided access to his beloved wife. So one night he made a casual suggestion to his wife:

"I think I am going to sleep next to the wall tonight."

As expected, the woman was not in the least willing to exchange places, and she eventually became so distraught, tears streamed down her cheeks, which gave the husband an idea. He decided to stop talking to her in a persuasive manner. After she fell asleep, he carefully lifted and moved her body from the place in question. Finally, he was next to the wall. After a short while, he, too, fell asleep.

Pretty soon he was nudged by something on his rear. As he was groping in that direction, he took hold of a rather large penis. It was protruding from the hole in the wall. Without forethought he turned around and whacked off the penis in one swing with his knife.

"I-I-I!" screamed a manly voice on the other side of the bark-lined wall. The husband then proceeded to cut a hole in the penis, and he fastened a string of sinew through it, which was then tied to his sleeping wife's belt.

Early in the morning he innocently said to his wife, "Wake up, you should be cooking."

Without realizing which side of the bed she awoke on, the woman rose groggily and stoked the cooking fire for the meal. At the same time her elderly father-in-law stirred and sat up in a half daze. The old man edged closer to the warm fire and began smoking tobacco. While she was cooking and sweeping, the old man noticed an object dangling from the woman's belt.

"Oh, daughter-in-law," commented the old man, "there is something unusual about your knife case."

At that precise moment the woman's eyes fell upon the so-called "knife case." She promptly screamed out in horror and disbelief. She raced out of the lodge to dispose of the detached penis.

Elsewhere that morning a lifeless man was discovered. He was sprawled out on the doorway of his lodge. He had died on account of having his penis cut off. A path of blood was trailed back to the exact place where the man had met his ghastly fate.

And when the woman's brother heard of the astounding news, he set out to confront her for the shame she had brought to the family and clan. From outside her husband's lodge the brother asked his sister to *join him. As soon as she came outside and into the clearing, she was beaten to death with a club by her brother. After the brother did what was expected of him as the closest kin, he went home and told his little sister to go sweep the bed of their former sister's abode.*

*"After you have finished," the brother added, "I want you to stay there. Permanently. Do not return here ever again."*

*The young girl then went and swept the sleeping place of her older but deceased sister. After she finished, she sat down as commanded by her brother and took the man that had been her sister's husband for her own. For as long as they lived she had him for a husband, even until his death, which was after he had become an old man.*

*And as for her, she was held in fond affection, even when she had become an old woman. Everyone knew she and her husband cared deeply for each other. In no way whatsoever did they ill-treat each other, nor was there any talk of the original circumstances that brought them together. Because of his love for his wife, the man never had aspirations to be unfaithful. All this during the full course of their happy lives.*

This is a revised version of an excerpt from *Fox Texts* by William Jones.

# Remnants of the
# First Earth

On the outskirts of town one day, on old Lincoln Highway 30, a bill-board sign that was repainted yearly became readable at long last for Alan and myself. In huge frontier-style lettering, next to a side-profile silhouette of a big-nosed Indian man, the sign read "WHY CHEER: HOME OF THE WHY CHEER INDIANS." Thanks to Weeping Willow, we had some-how learned to read English. We rarely spoke it, though, for there was a lesson after all from Pat "Dirty" Red Hat's famous misinterpreta-tion of the word "but." And Hayward Muscatine's becoming "Grubby" forever due to a soiled wiener was another fateful lesson. Mistakes would be made, and they inadvertently became fodder for stories.

Over the table our uncles would enjoy retelling the story of Mateo Water Runner, our ingenuous cousin, who told a Weeping Willow Elementary teacher he had accidentally swallowed the gum when asked to spit it out.

"Mateo, what are you chewing?" the teacher had demanded.

"Teacher, *ne be tti-ko-o ma-a-a-a,* I accidentally swallo-o-wed i-i-it," Mateo had replied in Indian, emphasizing and elongating the last two syllables in an English-type pronunciation. The vocal elon-gation of the last syllable, my uncles theorized, was the sound the wad of gum made on its way down Mateo's throat.

There was adventure, humor, risk, and fear of humiliation through verbal usage of the English language. Grandmother, like most

Weeping Willow students, knew enough English to get by. She had to because of her Why Cheer Laundry and Dry Cleaners employment. Enunciating the language made her uncomfortable, but she could deliver words in a fake cheerful voice if she went to a restaurant for lunch or to the bank. "Hello-o-o, good-bye, th-h-hank you" were the easiest. Ordering food wasn't too bad either, provided she had one of three memorized choices: eggs, bacon, and coffee; hamburger with pickles and coffee; or hot beef sandwich with mashed potatoes. At the bank downtown, where before she had gesticulated and made facial expressions if an idea wasn't communicated, she knew how to say: "Can I cash this check? Here? Me work. Dry Cleaners! Wash and iron clothes every day. Oh, than-n-nk you ve-ry much, my good frien-n-nd!"

Having recorded Grandmother's entries in the Six Grandfathers' Journals since childhood, I knew she was embittered by all that she witnessed transpiring around her. At the most importune time when she was peeling potatoes in the kitchen or cutting out floral designs from brown grocery bag paper with scissors, she broke down suddenly and wept for all the difficulties humanity had undergone. Her emotional surges came down from the hills, like invisible whirlwinds, demolishing the small house's tranquility. If I wasn't hiding behind the door, I stood beside her, not understanding what depressed her so.

At the Why Cheer Laundry and Dry Cleaners, though, with her small arm swinging down the huge, padded steam press, she was calm and detached. Being so involved with the operation of the hissing machines, ironing the slacks, sheets, and shirts of the white people, maybe she didn't think about these extraordinary changes. In giant vats the detergent bubbled and churned eight hours a day while the pulleys on the second floor squeaked under the bouncing load of suits and dresses on hangers. It was a bustling business; for the few minutes I visited, the burnt-smelling steam would cling to my nostrils for hours. Eventually I became inured to its flurry of sights and sounds. It was always a thrill to push or pull a laundry trolley for Grandmother from the back room to the front. At her station she'd wipe the sweat from her eyebrows with a bandana and begin the tedious task of sorting the mountain of clothing.

"If you want to make something of yourself, Grandson," she'd say at home over supper, "you will need to find better things to do than this. Don't do like what I am doing." She would talk about my grandfather, Jack Principal Bear, and the commitment he gave the railroad. "Whatever the weather condition he worked in order so that we would have food, clothes, and a place to live. But he never forgot about the Sacred Chieftain blood that coursed through his physicality." She would emphasize that Grandfather, a good provider, felt the tribe had been irreversibly swayed by the white man's novelties and way of life. "Everything starts over again," she'd say, "for this, all this we see outside the window stretched before us, is the Second Earth." I looked past the frosted glass and beyond the silhouetted trees on the hilly horizon, peering into the rose-spotted clouds. In the proper frame of mind, I saw the First Earth as a fireball and then a vast ocean previous to the Black Eagle Child Creation. "Anything that we do here," she continued, "our successes and failures, have all been done before by the Supernaturals." I came to understand that in emulating their previous lives, through the instructions given in the Principal Religion, the Black Eagle Child people were reenacting Remnants of the First Earth. In this reenactment was found a continuation, a strengthening in a largely unpredictable cosmos.

There was good here, just as there was bad.

From Grandmother I learned that Jack Principal, my grandfather, accepted fate, but in his prayers he asked the Well-Known Twin Brother to keep the worst imaginable catastrophes away from the Settlement. Undaunted by the inner and external forces that had excluded his own grandfather from leadership, he donned his spiked shoes on the iciest mornings and punched in for work. In open Chicago-Northwestern boxcars he sat with grubby-looking white men, traveling noisily down the lonely tracks in search of a passenger train caught in a snowdrift.

"That's the example you must follow," Grandmother urged. "To keep on improving your life, no matter how horrible the circumstances." She also taught me to see and remember the past and how it should reflect as clearly as a mirror in the present and future. Through her teachings and the Six Grandfathers' Journals I learned about the hereditary chieftainship of my uncles, Winston and Severt Principal Bear. For whatever purpose and not being conscious yet that they were family members, I memorized the names of Earthlodge clan people who had prevented them from reclaiming their divine Black Eagle Child decision-making roles.

"We are looking for prophecy in its early stages," Grandmother would forewarn. "It is all around us. The people themselves, those who reside here with us, are the initial messengers. By their actions we are witnessing the beginnings of what had been said would happen by our grandparents and theirs before. . . ."

From fourth grade on, I heard Grandmother say I had been selected to be the next caretaker, *e ka wa ba ta ka,* of the historic but badly tattered documents called the Six Grandfathers' Journals. It wasn't even a revelation. From serious and encouraging looks received at the family dining table I was aware steps had been taken to strengthen my Black Eagle Child language and writing skills. For the most part, I was probably too young to comprehend the enormity of what Grandmother told me to write or read.

Among the twenty-two dusty notebooks, ledgers, and deerhide boxes of rolled parchment kept by six of my maternal Sacred Chieftain grandfathers, my own entry writing, beginning in 1958, consisted mostly of Grandmother's thoughts on the state of tribal affairs. Even if I didn't fully embrace what she was dictating, my sole purpose was to listen, break down the separate vowels, and transcribe the sounds heard. Utilizing the English alphabet, as we had been taught by early French explorers in the 1600s around the Green Bay (Wisconsin) area, we wrote the entries in the Six Grandfathers' Journals phonetically.

While the Black Eagle Child people used oral tradition as the main vehicle for keeping our stories, prayers, and philosophies intact, our forefathers made extensive use of quill, ink, and writing material. This "word-collecting" task, due to its precarious nature, was relegated to the *O ki ma wa ki,* or Sacred Chieftains. Since writing was deemed too powerful for most people, my grandfathers— through their living divinity status—were the primary word-collectors, *ma ji to ji ki-ka na wi ye ni.* Crucial history-altering information that would have otherwise been dismissed as inconsequential was recorded forever on ribbon-held rolls of parchment. In some ways the rolls resembled the sacred mats of the Earthlodge clans that were inscribed with pictographs. Beside some of the elaborate black and red line paintings on the boxes are the names of my grandfathers, going back through time: 1832. 1801. 1787. 1754.

No ko me se ma meant (my) Grandmother, and Ne me tto e ma, (my) Grandfather. Ne bi for water. A sko te wi for fire. A ki for the ground or earth. Wi ske no for bird. Ne me sa for fish. Ma ka te Ke ti wa A be no, or Black Eagle Child proper, which was my fifth grandfather's name, became our tribal namesake. This was a popular second or third name for the Brown-Spotted and Black-Bobtailed Bear clans. Both of my grandfathers, on my mother's and father's side, owned this name, the reason being that when they were infants their families sensed they were dissatisfied with the one name they were given at birth. In tribal society, infants who have not yet walked or talked are considered to be attuned to their surroundings. If there was a family matter they disagreed with, the infants had the means to make their feelings known. Overall, though, multiple names meant the person was destined for notoriety—or unyielding rancor. In the case of both grandfathers, the issuing of additional names seemed warranted.


Undeniably, I often felt insecure about being the journals' caretaker, e ka ba wa ba ta ka, but these feelings would subside whenever I recalled that throughout childhood I was told that my life had been prearranged. "Yes, it is true, E he i, ke te na me ko," lectured the family repeatedly, "your life is prearranged, ki tti se ta te wi-ki ya wi."

At Weeping Willow Elementary, however, my classmates got a kick out of my stubbornness in completing assignments. They also took delight in my ability to share personal stuff about my family. Trying to be like Pat Red Hat got me in trouble; I finally had to curb my speeches and was forced to apologize with my mother present to the teachers for speaking in Black Eagle Child. By then this gift for stories, which was nurtured in playacting, learning words, and just living, had become uncontrollable. An unwanted, overcooked stew. Given my childhood passion for wild, artistic expressions, I resorted to developing imaginary characters when I couldn't discuss what was most accessible, my own family's antics. Imitating the storytellers I had heard and seen, I would also unfurl the anecdotes written in tribal syllabics and read them aloud, once the teachers left the classroom. That's the point where the meteors collided.

Being a child prevented me from fully understanding what my Six Grandfathers wrote, for the most part. All that was required of me back then was that I read their works aloud or write new words. Today, at midlife, I still cannot grasp the minutiae of what they discussed and pondered without going back to the actual manuscripts themselves.

Contained in the withered pages of the twenty-two manuscripts are insights and commentary on a vast array of subjects, including military tactics, how a village should be constructed and fortified with timber, and the ordering of the respective clans, their warriors, as they protected the sanctuary. There are also references to lists in other journals of which types of food can be stored the longest, as well as what could be harvested from the wild in times of war, like roots, berries, and nuts for nourishment and medicine. Detailed in the page margins are the plants and trees themselves and where they grow along the Great Lakes and the Mississippi River. There are also thorough explanations for each decision the Sacred Chieftains made with regard to whether or not to declare war on our adversaries, who carried different-colored flags. Also included are the accompanying Earth-lodge clan wartime ceremonies and their specific songs. In earlier journals the various battles of victory and defeat are chronicled. The passages that most intrigued Grandmother—and later myself—were those that confirmed how we would succumb to the vices of the greater world around us. Instructions were given to the Sacred Chieftains on how to prevent this cultural atrophy. But Grandmother would emphasize after each reading that prophecy in its rawest form was fatalistic, that whatever was slated would indeed transpire as the manifestation of undeniable truth.

Weeping Willow Elementary was a perfect example. By law it existed. "That about said it all!" as Carson Two Red Foot used to conclude his wide-ranging stories. Unchallenged acceptance of white culture would be another. Even before we were born we were hopelessly ensnared in a web comprised of dazzling beams of history-bending light.

Before long I was truly convinced I possessed an innate talent to communicate. Grandmother reinforced this interest by taking my writing to a mimeographed community newsletter. In the summer of 1960, my first work, after being edited and finalized in English, was published by the *Black Eagle Child Quarterly*.

## Grandmother

*If I were to see*
*her shape from a mile away*
*I'd know so quickly*
*that it would be her.*
*The purple scarf*
*and the plastic*
*shopping bag.*
*If I felt*
*hands on my head*
*I'd know that those*
*were her hands*
*warm and damp*
*with the smell*
*of roots.*
*If I heard*
*a voice*
*coming from*
*a rock*
*I'd know*
*and her words*
*would flow inside me*
*like the light*
*of someone*
*stirring ashes*
*from a sleeping fire*
*at night.*

# Part Two

# Journals of the
# Six Grandfathers

In the fall of 1964, which was my first year at Doetingham Junior High and my first year away from Weeping Willow Elementary—a time I recorded as "The Autumn I Was Instructed alongside the Caucasians"—I rediscovered the process of writing poetry. This was in seventh grade, thirty years ago. Since then I've often thought that if there's external guidance to our destinies, I would have to say mine— the Well-Known Twin Brother's cosmic hands—reached through the autumn air and twisted events so abruptly that all appeared natural.

Of course, to have an illiterate Indian boy stumble over another language was perhaps part of the divine plan all along. Likewise, with Mrs. O'Toole, ex–Weeping Willow teacher. You see, this is what I visualize happened:

At meteoric speed my Black Eagle Child and Christian name must have appeared on the Twin Brother's secretary's monitor:

Ka ka to a.k.a Edgar Bearchild, formerly Edgar Principal Bear.

*This*—He or they must have assessed—*is an archaic Bear clan name whose meaning fell long ago from the unrelenting European encroachment—and the life-taking modernity that followed. These people, some of them, possess forgotten names with forgotten meanings.*

*Take special note of this one, the ochre, seal-eyed word-collector, seeking absolution through his name. Ka ka to, he says, is a verb-based noun: a person with inordinate talent to instill in others a will, an influence that persists until an insurmountable task is completed. In being who he is, a word-arranger, this inflated explanation of his name is all he can offer the question-askers, those deprived of themselves, of identity, victims of progress. He is clearly attempting to make a meaning for himself—and for them, those who know more or less than he.*

*Please forgive this lie, he whispers through his sniffles. He walks away, unfulfilled. Sooner or later, he will forget, ni wa ni ke wa, for that is the way he has been taught by those who value forgetfulness.*

*The Newcomers. Five centuries of unparalleled genocide—seventy to ninety million dead Indians in North and South America—equals in supernatural time a mere breath expended by God, our Father.*

And just as quickly as a falling star falls—President John F. Kennedy was assassinated the year previous—a decision must have been circulated among the multitudes on that fateful autumn years ago.

> *Bless Ka ka to with a meager life*
> *as a collector and arranger*
> *of words and let half or more*
> *belong to another language*
> *that which entangles*
> *confuses*
> *and let this existence surface*
> *in tenuous daylight*
> *only*
> *when prophecies of Earth's End*
> *will only confirm what*
> *was known all along*
> *and complicate further*
> *this life*
> *with imagined grief and wild humor*
> *which shall be the essence of truth—*
> *in the end*
> *let ALL OF THIS occur*
> *in the midst of learning a god-given language.*

Divine intervention aside, it's also possible that Mrs. O'Toole, a white, middle-aged female teacher, simply unleashed her bigotry and altered my life forever. That part doesn't need visualization. What was, in my opinion, an average essay entitled "A Day in My Life" made Mrs. O'Toole whisper coarse-sounding words in my ear, stating I had not "fulfilled the assignment" but had instead written "a poem."

What the hell? I asked myself as my sensitive blowholes attempted to shut tight against her gruesome spit-spray. It was useless. As the youngest in the pod I lagged behind and ended up swimming alongside the very vessel that was hunting us. With her harpoon-laced breath, she came on like a vociferous sorceress. The only other person ever to douse me with her misty breath was Ada Principal Bear, my grandmother. But that had to do with traditional healing, annointed breath, and a wish to drive the green Spanish galleon's mass back through the kerosene-darkened cardboard ceiling.

At home, Grandmother reduced my fevers; at school, Mrs. O'Toole ignited a literary spark in the dimly lit hollowness of my immature being. Granted, with the family's help, I had already published poemlike work in the tribal newsletter called the *Black Eagle Child Quarterly*. But for years I didn't have the vaguest idea what I was doing.

Had it not been for the *Quarterly*'s editor, Billy "Cracker" Jack, who was renowned for making disparaging comments to children, I might have kept going. Nineteen sixty was not only my debut year as a child-poet but also the year of my first literary-related downfall. Before he left the Settlement in search of "relocation" adventure, "Cracker" Jack went on this extreme W. C. Field's kick, which corroborated his greatest disrespect for young people. All children, except his own, were subjected mercilessly to his petty admonitions. With some children he began by making fun of their physical characteristics. If there wasn't any flaw, he would create one and persist until the child became self-conscious and convinced something was terribly wrong. With me, he attacked my words. On the one hand I am indebted to him for encouraging Grandmother and Uncle Severt to submit my work to the *Quarterly*. But as it turned out, "Cracker" Jack started belittling my "proud indin" themes in public. He was quoted as saying "my voice wasn't real," that my "ideas were implanted by Liquid Lake Martians."

There was more to this than a child-poet worth picking on.

If memory doesn't fail me, there was a vicious tug-of-war in court over the custody of an abandoned child, the one who brought a monstrous television set for one glorious summer to Grandmother's house. I can still see in my imagination the kid being tied between the two opposing team-families over the green lawn. The father, "Cracker" Jack's brother, was dead, and the mother couldn't claim the orphan due to another marriage. Before the tug-of-war countdown ended, both of his limbs in a false start were ripped off by sympathetic family members—and everyone fell. Like a beheaded chicken, the orphan's torso lost its equilibrium and flopped aimlessly on the ground, spilling his suffering.

Or at least that's how the disorder caused by the social services seemed to end up. Incidentally, both families lost the fight, and when the orphan left for the adoption agency, my brother Alan and I were deprived of television for three long years. Its presence in my life was significant because the Saturday morning cartoons verified what I had seen with my own pre-TV mind through Grandmother's stories. My thoughts had been set aglow with pictures of talking animals and supernatural deities who transformed themselves into whatever they desired. We had seen movies, obviously, but tribal mythology animated by amusing creatures completed our perception that another realm, the Supernatural, existed all around us.

Anyway, because of "Cracker" Jack's animosity engendered indirectly by my work, I lost four valuable years. Yet, it was at this juncture that Grandmother, after seeing my work translated into English, began to hint there was probably an invisible force at work. "Maybe there's a sentinel spirit, guiding you and your words," she'd say. "Maybe there's nothing wrong with you learning a little bit of English. But your work with your Six Grandfathers' Journals has to continue."

I would not see the orphan with the large television set for fourteen years or "Cracker" Jack for twenty-four years. The former became a Navy Seabee, while the latter went west and came back with "a deck of cards." Meaning the shady gambling trade.

*   *   *

Somewhere within the trillion Milky Way stars the Well-Known Twin Brother's secretary must have typed out a crucial question: Is the life of Ka ka to a.k.a. Edgar Bearchild-to-be one to be led or misled? With regard to who I presently am, I have a feeling the cosmic computer had a major malfunction when Mrs. O'Toole's acidic food particles drew a Goyalike etching throughout my anatomy, verifying suspicions white people could not shake their murderous mode of operation.

*We were herded into an alley with our arms raised, trembling from the ultimate act of submission. The well-dressed militia cocked their rifles, took aim at our peasant hearts, and braced themselves forward against the impending recoil. On a cobblestone street that was illuminated like a theater stage—with fluorescent lights under our feet—we were painted with our own blood and done away with. Our arms fell limp, and whoever didn't die right away ate glistening bayonets for dessert. . . .*

A metaphorical death by firing squad is exactly what my grandmother, Ada Principal Bear, had feared about Weeping Willow Elementary. Whether in a classroom or a bloody floor-lit alley, education coincided with colonial subjugation.

"These white people will destroy everything and they will cause the demise of humankind and Grandmother Earth," she warned at the onset as we awaited the orange school bus beside the frosty gravel road.

(I would later indict Mrs. O'Toole of Doetingham—*Doo-tin-hem*—Junior High School as a conspirator. An agent of the Red Pedagogical Army. From her coffee- and nicotine-stained dentures a message was spewed out. Propaganda.)

I am blessed with a mission, I recited aboard the orange school bus, to be the harbinger of prophecy, the angel of Earth's End . . . ally of the Northern Lights . . . me, an ochre, seal-eyed poet in a tight flannel shirt, hole-ridden jeans, and Presbyterian Church–donated shoes.

That autumn at Doetingham Junior High, through classroom assignments, I rediscovered poetry. If I listened to Grandmother and

wrote what she said, I adduced, certainly I could do the same with
my own thoughts, employing the English language. I had done it
before. After "Cracker" Jack's infamous attack on my first poemlike
work, Grandmother opined that if the tribe was oblivious to the
Sacred Chieftains, then it was not inappropriate to use every opportunity that presented itself to apprise the greater American public of
a disrupted Black Eagle Child dynasty.

With a radio in the household, the Why Cheer Theater, Weeping Willow Elementary, and Grandmother working at the Laundry
and Dry Cleaners, the English language proved omnipresent. In the
kitchen, even as Grandmother narrated for the Journals, the radio or
the phonograph would be playing in the background. Every day and
most of the night we gorged ourselves on the airwaves.

Listening to "oldies but goldies" radio stations today, I can still
recall songs from 1956 like Guy Mitchell's "Singing the Blues" and
Fats Domino's "Blueberry Hill." From 1957 I really liked "Young
Love," but whether the artist was Tab Hunter or Sonny James, I'm
not positive. By 1958 I was swept up by "Twenty-Six Miles" by the
Four Preps and "Twilight Time" by the Platters. The same with "Poor
Little Fool" by Ricky Nelson and "It's All in the Game" by Tommy
Edwards. For 1959 and 1960, there isn't a single song that stands out
as being influential. Which is understandable, considering what disc
jockeys were playing: "Charlie Brown" by the Coasters; "Alvin's
Harmonica" by David Seville and the Chipmunks; "Running Bear"
by Johnny Preston; "Alley-Oop" by the Hollywood Argyles and "Mr.
Custer" by Larry Verne. Oh, Elvis was around, as were Roy Orbison,
Sam Cooke, Bobby Darin, Neil Sedaka, Chubby Checker, and, last
but not least, Dion. These were high-caliber music makers! Jesus,
where was I? In 1964 my ears finally perked up to the tunes of the
Beatles, the Kinks, and the Animals. Music and movies—like 1955's
Oscar winner, *Marty,* with Ernest Borgnine, or 1957's winner, *The
Bridge over the River Kwai,* with Alec Guinness and William Holden—
I now theorize, were instrumental in subconsciously reinforcing the
English taught at Weeping Willow Elementary.

But nothing could have prepared me for junior high. Having Mrs.
O'Toole for a teacher again and sitting beside cream-colored classmates proved a riveting experience. Sensing that my brother Alan and

I were metabolically deficient, Mother made us familiar with vita-
min supplements long before they became popular. I may not have
been a plump, healthy child, but whatever horrid-tasting chemistry I
ingested made my sight less transfixed.


Being a child-poet and "word-collector" wasn't novel, but a boat tips
over if the rider is unfamiliar with its balance and means of propulsion
—right? Especially when the boat was shaky to begin with. Simply
put, I was like the baby Moses in *The Ten Commandments* movie,
cast off and set adrift down the Nile River in a small waterproof basket.

No one with the exception of the Well-Known Twin Brother
could have possibly conceived what was in the offing. For each succeeding generation that my Six Grandfathers lived in, there were
different priorities. Unfailingly, each grandfather faced the same
obstacle, but unbeknownst to them, each was a faded duplicate of
the First Grandfather. Grandmother taught that the world was a
wicked amalgamation of modernity, eventuality, and social change.
In listening to her observations as the Principal Bear matriarch, I
began to construct a scene over which we had little or no control,
our self-destruction.

Guided by these vast influences, I began to formulate a life plan
of sorts. Part of my time would consist of updating my grandfather's
journals; the other part would be spent on my own writings. Being a
"word-collector," being able to write and think in both languages, was
a rarity. I resolved to ignore the "Cracker" Jacks and Mrs. O'Tooles
of this convoluted society.

Almost effortlessly I started to feel the strength and weaknesses
of words. In both languages, thoughts and opinions could divide,
anger, or injure people but could also become a vehicle for empathy.

In an earthly realm where the forces of nature are infinitely more
powerful than human beings, personal and collective insignificance
is a given. In our relatively compact tribal society, there was equal
standing among everyone other than the chieftain hierarchy. In the
ancien régime our people hunted, fished, gathered food, planted
seeds, and harvested crops together, making everyone interdependent.

This philosophical stance of insignificance was reflected in the journals. Preceding each passage my grandfathers wrote were such disclaimers: "Now, at this very moment, I will be forthright and say that I do not know much, that I am not exceedingly knowledgeable, but this is what I have been told: whatever you see, you will document that fact, for it will serve as a point from which present and future Black Eagle Childs will have an unobstructed view of our life. This I have done in the same way my other grandfathers did. . . ."

With that as a catapult, and with zero apologies to Shakespeare and Popeye, I write what I see and therefore and therein I am. Not unlike the aspirations of many a would-be writer.

> Where the rivers of existence
> do not come together
> is the only
> geography cherished
> by my Six Grandfathers
> Where the rivers do not come together
> is a geography known only
> to the Six Grandfathers

Among the trillion stars traveling through the earthlodge cosmos I was destined to have a collision with a supernova. And this is what I saw: Other than the brown-tinted skin that encompassed our bodies and minds, nothing impacted our lives more than the food we ingested, as well as the breath we inhaled and expelled within a particular existential moment and place. This earthly existence made for our exclusive use came with socioeconomic and physio-biological divisions.

It began with the organic spaces each of us occupied. The air, for instance, where Jane Ribbon—that fabled "Dam Monster"—snipped pages from C. M. Marshall's catalogs emitted a faint but pervasive scent of riverwater and boiled roots. Admittedly, the shadowy space inside her small two-room house, where the arts of pearl diving and medicinal healing were venerated, was markedly different from the air held inside a distant farmhouse inhabited by whites. Further, the air inside the black limousine, the one I saw parked on Uncle Clifford Water Runner's road in the summer of 1967, was extremely different. Behind the tinted windows breathed Jean Seberg, the Iowa-born Hollywood actress. (Up until her unfortunate passing in 1974, she had wanted to meet me, but "Cracker" Jack at a West Coast screening for *Paint Your Wagon* advised her my family had "perpetrated a cruel nonexistent child-poet hoax" to people like her who were interested in "saving us from our plight." Jean Seberg, on that long-ago summer day, bought Crawdad, our beagle puppy. Uncle Clifford, ever the schemer, made the unauthorized twenty-dollar sale and didn't even split it. Years later when I told Grandmother about Jean Seberg's suicide in Paris, she commented that my brother and I were fortunate in that she took nothing else with her. Maybe the puppy took both of your places in death, she would say instead.)

These experiences of the air we breathe, the food we eat, and the spaces in which we are contained are interrelated in the sense that they involve human beings, yet there are pervasive divisions that make us inimitable. The space we occupied in rural or wooded earth-light was experienced firsthand, organically.

From our pain we have gained energy; from our losses we have barely recovered. Do-nothing academic types tout us as "the tribe that miraculously reemerged from several remnant groups." They are swift to compile reams of new and old information about our religion, mythology, and current political beliefs. Books about us with hyped-up phraseology and absurd anthropological theories are published.

We know ourselves more than they do. So much so there's no need to incite arguments. Three times the Well-Known Twin Brother's blessing—escaping the enemy in a flag war with the summoned aid of inclement weather—saved us. The sad thing is, even luck has limitations; resilience is costly. We became adept, you could say, in hiding and making up for most of what we lost. The lives and events that somehow slipped through the protective netting and fell into the wide, sweeping waters of an invisible ocean called eventuality were an additional expenditure.

Lulled into believing we were highly spiritual, we perpetrated a major transgression by making our prophecies less important, condoning laxness and setting aside ancient forecasts. Maybe there were too many *a te so ta ka na ni,* winter stories, and *a ji mo na ni,* stories, to keep track of. Once armed with a strength that made us rush about like fervent summer wind, bending the highest cottonwood trees, we lost our momentum, and our children fell into a chasm of imminent change.

In this fatalistic consciousness, religion faltered, and some of our Earthlodge clan leaders took on the oddball persona of television evangelists. They sinned and forgave themselves in public until their followers were inured to the abuse. And our culture, that amazing matrix of ideas and self-worth, curled up over the cool concrete floor and never woke.

Enter the mixed-blood tribal historians.

"When mixed-bloods, *a be ta we si a ki,* begin misinterpreting history and forget they are visitors," say the Six Grandfathers' Journals, "they are an indelible part of genocide itself." Our history, according to their library research, wandered out from the green majestic forest and walked onto the hazy road only to be struck down by traffic. Dumbstruck by portent and mystified still by this once-noble, brain-fat animal, we were doomed travelers from day one, so to speak. According to them, we stood in awe of this overturned carcass, inhaling its utter lifelessness until our mouths dried and so forth.

That perception is wrong, though. So state the Six Grandfathers. Our history on occasion has had the eminence to wear a shiny coat of black feathers and soft white plumes, having absolutely no need for historians who don't even know or dare to ask their mothers the names of their fathers.

Unfortunately, as the strength of mythology and history diminished in the summer wind, membership in the Principal Religion, *Ni ka ni-Ma ma to mo we ni,* dwindled. For each person indoctrinated into the Earthlodge clans, three to four others reneged. Everyone felt no individual was accountable for the life expectancy of a tribe, a strength that once toppled the highest cottonwoods. Well, *mon ami,* hinterland rainbows are synonymous with black hummingbirds.

# The Blinking Child
# Traditional Dancer

Luciano Bearchild *ne ke ki no a ma kwa-ni ne wa ki-ne na wa ka si a-na i na ki na wi a we te-me to se ne ni wa. Ma ni-a be i yo-e si tti: Na i na-e tte tto o wa tti-o na te wi no wa-a ne ta-e se se se si wa tti-tti ke-e mwe mwe ske i wa tti-a sa mi-a si tti-o ski tte kwa-tte tto o wa ki. Na i na tta i-ei-e ki ta ko se wa tti-me to se ne ni wa-ki tti tti bi ne kwa so wa ki.*

*I no ki tta-na i na-be no tti-e ki we ska wa ni-mi ya tti-me go-ta ta ki-ne ta ka a ba ma wa ki-ki ji bi bi kwa so tti ki. Mo tti-me ko-a be no a ki. Ne ta be tti ko tti-me kwe ne ta-e se bo tte ska tti-e ta tti ke ke ne na ke tti-ne ko ta-kwi wi se e a-mi tta tti ta ta:*

*Ne ko te wi-1960-ne wi te ma-e kwi se i ya ni-e me ki ki we ska tti. Me na ni-me ko o ni-ne ta tti i tti te a be-e ma wi ki e ska ya ke-i ni na. Ne ke te ma ke si be na ke wi ni-tte na-na a wi ya be-i yo-i ni ya-tto ni ya a-ni me ka wa tti. I tti me ko-na i we si kwe ni. Ne bwe ka kwe ni-ke e i ki. Ke te na ma ni-ke ko-na o be na to kwe ni-me tti meko-e ka wa ta mo kwe ni. No ko me se ma-ke te me na we si-i ne wa-a be. E ye ba wi-na o se tti-ta kwa ba bi wa-be tti to a i-a ma ma to mo wi na ka mo ni tti.*

*(Luciano Bearchild taught me to identify night-enemy sorcerers when they visit people. This is what he used to say to me: When they paint their medicines, some, because of being in a rush or being awkward, apply the paint too close to their eyes. When they walk among people, their eyes are perpetually blinking.*

*Now when I travel afar, I watch out for blinking-eyed people. Even children. For I always remember the little boy in a dance costume who deflated as we held him.*

*Once in 1960 I traveled with him. That's intriguing, I sometimes reflect, for us to have been traveling back then. For we were poor, but he used to be good at finding money. Through natural means he was talented. And he was also intelligent. Undeniably, he succeeded in whatever he set out out to do, whatever he wanted. My grandmother used to say he was blessed. Before he could walk he sat with the old men as they sang religious songs.)*

I was nine years old at the time I accompanied my well-dressed cousin Luciano Bearchild on a summer powwow trip to a snow-besieged, mountainous place called Browning, Montana. This was four years before he came into the Doetingham Junior High class-room. Using a light brown 1949 Ford, it took us a total of four days, *nwe wi-o ko ni*, to get there, sleeping and camping along the way at roadside stops.

On a July morning we found ourselves near the Blackfeet Tribal Celebration grounds. *E ki tti-na ka ni-te be kwi-e be me ka wa ki-we bi-me bo wi.* After traveling all night, it snowed. Styrofoam-type snow fell hypnotically from the sky, covering the rolling plains, and noth-ing moved except the smoking portals of the tipis. Through the cracked-open automobile window we could smell the distinct odor of burning wood, and our senses became disoriented.

Where was summer? Were we somewhere unreal? Which high-way sign was it that we didn't see, foretelling this mystic geography?

Later, around eleven o'clock, the PA system crackled as it was turned on.

"Tet-ting. Tet-ting. One. Two. Tet-ting. Mike tet."

The announcer who announced himself as "Nine-Ball" told the powwow committee and their families to go home and retrieve their shovels.

"Bwing wots of 'em and yo gwoves," he said.

By noon most of the snow was scooped to the side of the dance arena, and it melted, creating large, sparkling pools where dark, un-combed Indian boys in ragged blue jeans sailed handmade boats.

Together they surveyed the distant mountaintops. With one hand shielding the sun from their eyes, they swept away the last remaining clouds with the other.

While the Blackfeet dug themselves out, we sat in the Ford astounded by the untimely snowfall. Imprinted still in our minds was the large bear, *ke tti-ma kwa*, who waved us down on the highway the night previous. He stood up in the middle of the road and stared at the headlights before walking up the mountainside on two legs. Suddenly, in a surreal, mechanical fashion, our namesake dropped on all fours, going up the mountainside like a wobbly locomotive in apparent distress. The Bear Machine chugged and creaked over the rock-strewn valley. Through the chimney mounted behind its neck, black smoke was expelled. Small breakaway pieces of smoke and sparks rolled up the mountainside and came back down as an onslaught of spellbinding winter snow. That was our night.

The Blackfeet made ample use of the shovels before the hot sun, *ke tte swa*, encompassed everything. Trucks drove through the last snowdrifts and towed automobiles out of the meltwater; and the cloud-moving Indian boys were called in for lunch by their mothers.

Elsewhere, octagon-shaped drums, *te we i ka na ki*, that sounded like cardboard when their owners first test-pounded them, *e ko twe we wa ji*, began to stretch, cracking the leather intersecting ties. In less than an hour the solar-heated drums acquired the perfect resonant, hollow tone that echoed throughout the sloping hillside. Hearing this, beautiful women, *we we ne si tti ki-i kwe wa ki*, came out of the painted lodges with young helpers to bask in their elk-teeth-adorned or fully beaded buckskin dresses. Hand mirrors, *wa ba mo na ni*, decorated with dangling eagle plumes and small tin cones, flashed as the women directed the braiding of their long black hair. Their perfumes, *se swa o na ni*, mingled in our mongrel noses and we sneezed. Knowing we were ignorant of the tingling freshness of woman, we nonetheless eagerly caught their sweet air with our scroungy senses.

"Don't look at the mirrors," commanded Luciano.

I froze and shifted my reddened eyes to either side, *wa wi ta wi*.

He reached over and pulled down the car's sun visor, blocking flashes of light I hadn't noticed before. "There are women who take part in 'mirror-shooting.' With breath laced with good or bad medicine they know how to direct sunlight. On sunny days novices will practice for the hell of it. Be wary of women who pretend to unwrap a stick of gum, for the gum may not be one hundred percent gum."

He then took out a square brass mirror that he kept in his flannel shirt pocket, the one strategically placed over his precious heart. He held it up to his face, blew on it, and said: "The way the mirror fogs up. Look, the right amount. Half mirror, half fog. Womanly ingredients, their breath and saliva, stirred in with romantic expectations and the accomplice-roots from the grassy foothills, equals . . . equals . . . *ahem!*"

Overcome with fear I looked straight ahead and saw the quandary we were in. The sun was to our south and the women to the three other directions. Love medicine zipping by in beams of harsh sunlight. Cross fire.

"Equals what, Ed?" asked Luciano, scaring me out of my trance on medicine-toting women. "You believe me?"

Almost imperceptibly, the bitterly cold winds had given way to a spring breeze and then to a tolerable summer heat in the span of half a day. After the grey slanted clouds moved the blizzard wonderland eastward into another valley, the breeze bore the scent of distant wildflowers. In the automobile we lifted off ourselves the few blankets we'd brought. From sniffles to sweat—we held the snow-spewing Bear Machine accountable. The beautiful women in buckskin dresses ended the laser medicine show. Everywhere people began putting on their regalia, and somewhere over the ridge a drum began to beat.

Rousing ourselves from sleep, we pitched a small military-issue tent beside the car, took sponge baths, and were about to tour the traditional encampment when the emcee, "Nine-Ball" McRoy, made an announcement minus the Elmer Fudd imitation: "Singers and dancers, the committee says that the powwow will start as scheduled. One P.M. sharp. As for beef rations and bread, if you got snowshoes, waddle your chunky selves over to the cookshack for beef. We've got a full day ahead of us, dear people. Many fine singers from the United States and Canada are here. Let's make this right for everyone. Be on time and on your bell-shaking feet!"

"Ed, go get the reel-to-reel tape recorder," said Luciano in a rush.

"But the singing doesn't start for another hour," I said, walking backward toward the car anyway.

He shook his head side to side and explained.

"I want to record Blackfeet. Have you ever heard of the people we lost hundreds of years ago as we stole secretly through the night, eluding the enemy? Hands were clasped together in the darkness, and someone accidentally let go, severing half of a tribe forever? We were Houdinis, good at escaping, especially under the cover of a rainy night, fog, or blizzard, but we were lousy at keeping the tribe together. Anyway, you never know. Wouldn't it be wonderful if the Blackfeet had a similar story? And that they're looking for us? So, the question is, Who finds who? Is there ever a find? Pathetic, isn't it? All tribes searching in vain for their mythic halves . . ."

"Huh?" I asked.

"Nothing, Ed. Go get the damn tape recorder."

As I was half-dragging the tape recorder back, "Nine-Ball's" voice crackled through the PA again: "What was Kool-Aid yesterday is being hacksawed by the cooks and will be doled out as Popsicles to the dancers during intermission. By golly, talk 'bout Injun-nuity!"

"*Jesus*, is that right?" I asked Luciano in further disorientation.

He pulled down the flaps of his Korean army winter hat and continued the discourse.

"Another thing, Ed. Their sacred bundles resemble ours. Hey, amigo, do you understand?"

I nodded an unconvincing "yes" as he waded quietly over the icy green puddles of snow with the cumbersome Norelco tape recorder in his arms.

I didn't see him again, and then just glimpses, until the dancers filed into the wet arena, dancing to the blaring, amplified music of the White Spotted Shirts drum group. Watery explosions erupted as beaded moccasins hit the dark green grass. Bits of yellow mud splattered on my black thick-rimmed glasses. Blinded, I had to wrestle my way through the crowd that had enviously gathered around the drum. It didn't seem fair, the four excruciating days it took to get here. We wanted this long-awaited event to be a perfect live recording. Everything was a blur. Through a tiny untouched spot on my muddy glasses, I saw Luciano kneeling beside the strong-voiced wailing of the middle-aged men. In the chaos the glasses got worse as I tried to clean them with chunks of dirty snow, and I lost sight of him. My fingers with reckless abandon pressed the buttons on the tape recorder and I held the microphone above my head. Through the resonating din I could hear Luciano, blending in with flawless vocals to a song unknown. I held still to keep from being jostled about between the elbows and beverages of admiring listeners and waited. There was only one thing I could see past the crust and ruination: The pin of the Red Star on his fur-lined hat kept in rhythm to the steady but forceful drumming.

In the singular block of daylight that came through the sweeping clouds of Montana, we were propelled past the high, jagged mountains and their glaciers, zigzagging through the rocky narrows aboard a 1949 light brown Ford.

*Ne me nwe ne ta tta-me kwe ne ta ka ni-i ni ko tti-tte ski e to ya kwi-na i na-i yo-e be ma te si wa tti-tti ne we ma kwi ki.* I like memory, for that is all we have from when our relatives were alive. *I ni ko tti-e i ki-we tti-a be tti-a to ta te ki-ni me kwe ne me tti-ki tti-a yo-ki tti-be me ka tti ki-ki tti ke ne na kwi.* That is also why it is always discussed, to remember (through ceremony) those who have walked here, those who have raised us. *A kwi wi na-ke te na me-tti-be ko kwe wa ni-tte na-na i na-e ma ki wa tta o wa ni-tti ki a sko te ki-e tti ka-ji ki me te ko ki-ne ta to be na-wi se ni we ni-ka o ni-se ma wa-ne ke ka wa wa ki-e tti so wa tti-ne me tto e ma ki-no ko me sa ki-wa wi ta i-ka on ni-ma ma wi na kwa tti ki-ji na we ne ma ki.* It's true that I have not had a ghost feast, but when I cook large meals, whether placed by the fire or by a tree, I offer food and sacred tobacco, announcing their names—my grandfathers, my grandmothers—on either side, and my relatives who left prematurely. Luciano *ta ta ki.* Like Luciano.

By four o'clock the bells of the old-time Blackfeet dancers made us forget the surreal night and the foul morning weather. The Norelco was full of songs from the six local but exemplary drum groups and the visiting confederacy drums from Standoff and Gleichen, Alberta. In a brief break to acknowledge the powwow committee and the volunteers with their shovels, Luciano signaled—from a chair this time—for a blank audio reel, food, and a soda.

The dancers and singers simultaneously rose from the chairs and benches and headed toward the two arena entrances. Making my way through the crowd, saying "Excuse me, excuse me, thanks," on either side, *wa wi ta wi*, I felt a strong tug on my back right hip and it wouldn't let go. I looked back, a Charlie Brown cartoon face exhibiting disgust, but saw no one except male dancers in feathers idly smoking cigarettes. Feeling somewhat stupid, I turned around to resume my exit. In midstep I felt another, stronger tug drag me backward.

"Hey, what's going on?" I cried, not wanting to turn completely around, for fear of tripping and being trampled by cowboy boots and cowbells.

"Nine-Ball" seemed to chuckle at my goings-on; I could hear him snorting too close to the microphone from the speaker stand.

"Look at him. Right here, ladies and gentlemen. Please. *Say?* . . . *hey*, let's give him room, people. *Hey!!* Thanks. He-e-e-e's come a lo-o-ong ways to be with us he-e-e-re on the Bla-a-a-ckfeet Reser-*vation*."

The male Indian dancers stopped chatting, turned around, and made way.

In a state of near panic I reached backward to at least feel what caught me. The first cold touch sent a picture to my confused mind of a giant chicken, a red rooster, that attacked for an ungodly reason. Wrong territory entered? What infraction? What's OK?

"Let's gi-i-i-ve this person, the one who traveled the far-r-r-thest," squealed "Nine-Ball," "some generous applause. C'mon *people!*"

When the sporadic ovation began, the ruffled feathers brushed my wrist as the creature's large beak clamped down on my blue jeans in a vigorous, twisting motion.

That was the same move employed by the female lunch-table leaders at the tribal elementary school—I reflected in horror—when they hooked their fingers through my belt loop, preventing my escape from a public depantsing.

Jesus! Spell REE-VENN-GEE again?

The mysterious assault triggered more thoughts on the red rooster's victorious day: Near a gurgling creek one summer, to an appreciative audience of stationary dragonflies, jittery water spiders, snakes, and frogs, I laid on my stomach being pecked mercilessly about the neck and head by a rooster that had ambushed me near the outhouse. It jumped down from the intoxicating-berry trees and cackled a volley of Humphrey Bogart–sounding words, "OK, now. OK, now . . . " That surprise, more than anything, buckled my knees, and so when the cantankerous rooster spurred the backs of my legs, delivering swift, effective kicks, I fell face-first on the sandy path according to plan.

*Wa ni kya ye ke ni-ni ba ki se na ke tti-se ma wa-na i na-ye ma-e bye ya ki.* We had forgotten to release sacred tobacco when we got over there. *E a sa mi-mi tta te na mo wa ki-me me tti ki-we tti-be ne ne te ma ki-no ma ke i.* The fact that we were elated was probably why we momentarily lost our mental senses. *Na i na-ke wi na yo-ke tti-ma kwa-e a ski-ne wa ke tti-ba ki se ni ye ka ke si.* At that moment, back then, when we first saw the large bear, we should have released it. *I ni wa-tta-a be-i yo-na i-ne ne ke ne ta ma-a ni.* "Ki sa ko tti-ba ne ne ta mo wa kwe ni," i no we ya be Luciano. Ke ma kwi so be na-ko tti-tta ta ki.* That is why I would think about this event. "How greatly we must have forgotten," Luciano used to say. "For we supposedly are Bear clan–named." *A si me i-a i te ne ta ma ke ni-ni pa wa i ya ki. Ke ke ne ta ka ke sa-ke wi na yo.* We were too preoccupied with powwowing. We should have known then (what to do). *Me te ne ta kwi-ke wi na-ki sa ko tti-be ki ni ke nwi-e tti ya ki-ka on i-e na ba ta ni ki-a ma ma kwa ki wi ki.* It was obvious how great the difference was in the weather and the way the landscape was mountainous. *Wa na to ka-ne ta bi-ki wa ba ta ba na-e ne tti ya ki wi.* We simply went and looked at how great it was.

"Excuse me, I think we're caught," said the child traditional dancer who wore an eagle head in the center of the circle of feathers mounted on his lower back.

When I looked behind, I saw the open beak of a stuffed eagle's head stuck in my belt loop. In the crowd we had somehow backed into each other. It was a relief to see this kid and his eagle feather bustle instead of a giant red rooster. I became less tense, knowing I would not relive a spur kicking that led to the nickname "Ed Chickenback" bestowed years ago by my uncles, Winston and Severt Principal Bear.

For fear of breaking the delicate feathers, I backed up carefully and unhooked the stationary beak. It was odd, this unfastening of a stuffed eagle head. For a second I thought its eyes blinked at a certain angle in the sunlight. The young boy dancer was humored by my spontaneous comment, as were the dancers who surrounded us. We all sort of chuckled and went on our ways.

Later, as the war dances started up again, I saw the same young boy standing directly across from Luciano at the White Spotted Shirts drum, staring. No longer a youth, his whole demeanor had altered to a hideous state. More than before, I took attention of his appearance: Half of his face was painted bright yellow, and it came up right to his eyelids—maybe even stinging him, for he blinked. Constantly.

The kid stood as if in a near trance, watching every movement we made. His shiny eyeballs stood out behind the yellow paint. When he caught us looking back, he would break into a wicked, broad smile, baring his teeth like a ferocious animal.

This demonstration of supernaturalism nearly scared the shit out of me. Literally. After the long travel and strange-smelling food, and minus the luxury of real toilet paper at most rest areas, my stomach churned at the bizarre spectacle. (Linda Blair, the cinematic child demon in *The Exorcist,* would be virginal compared to the metamorphosis we beheld.) As we observed, our muscles shook involuntarily from fright mixed with sheer exhaustion.

Whatever compelled us, Luciano and I each went in the opposite direction around the drum, walking toward the child-entity, stalking him. I must have thought about my witch-capturing grandfather in wait under the first concrete river bridge of the Settlement. The big difference with us was that this encounter was in full daylight, with the sun and clouds hovering high above and songs resonating in the brisk glacier-cooled air.

Before we reached him, the child-entity made a physical gesture, like the kind a long-distance runner makes as the starter pistol is raised into the air. He held that half-crouching, about-to-leap motionless pose and then zipped away through the unsuspecting crowd at hummingbird speed. His legs did not move, however.

The people never took notice as he made abrupt right angles, zigzagging through them. The back view of the eagle's head and the feathers resembled an actual eagle, hopping away backward from something unknown. Its beak opened and closed as if gasping in excitement.

(That same year at a well-to-do Indian family's party I recoiled at first glance of toy football players who held that same motionless runner's starting pose. Witches in teams and uniforms skated across the tin field that hummed loudly from the electrical power. I stood back and looked around the room.)

We ran after the young boy through the unsuspecting crowd before he disappeared into a row of distant pine trees. Far from the celebration, large black birds with long tail feathers squawked at the intrusion and fluttered frantically from limb to limb. Their fluttering wings made the pines seem alive. We circled each tree amid crow protestations until we cornered the child-witch between two of the largest trees.

In our presence the lifelike sheen and texture of the child's skin began to harden in the cool breeze. At the point we grabbed his arms, he began to deflate like the rubber inner tube of a tire that had been punctured with a dull penknife. In our hands the small human disguise collected and then became brittle. In the silence we stood with our arms and palms extended in the air, hold nothing but bits of a memory that we thought was alive there. . . .


*Ne kwi no ma-a be i-na i na-e we bi-ta ne ne ma ki-ne tti se e ma.* I long for my older brother (Luciano) whenever I begin to think about him. *Ke te na me ko-te we bwe wa*—Leslie Silko—*e na tti mo tti-ne tti: na e bye i ke wa ni-ne tti ka ki na-ki ma tti ma wa ki-ki tti be ma te si tti ki.* It is true what Leslie Silko says: that if you know how to write, you inevitably deal with those who once lived—by yourself.

A human presence is forever. Even Luciano's. Even if he didn't quite die. Whether in the act of storytelling or fond remembrances. The mere virtue of being alive, permeable and free, rang throughout the physical totality of the person who was Luciano Bearchild. He sought and was able to experience new ways to see things, to live them and not be complacent. While we were startled by the Blackfeets and their mystic landscape, we realized that earth and humanity were immense. Both of us were also aware of inexplicable phenomena.

In thinking back, I realize it may all have been a dream. Maybe. For me, ever since the supernatural manifestation at Liquid Lake, I didn't look boldly toward the galaxies nor did I sit listening for unusual night sounds. They were there. All kinds of forces, like the whirlwinds of lost souls or shadows, whipped across the plains and prairies. Some were mischievous, others demanding. For Luciano, they came down from the stars, wrapped him in a brilliant shroud of light, and abducted him. Forever . . .

# Braided Strips
# of Medicine
# and Paper Bullets

*Through the watchful, transforming fireflies of Liquid Lake to the night-*
*marish experience with the supernatural disguised as a child traditional*
*dancer, and through the animistic personification of all living, moving*
*and unmoving, seen and unseen, known and unknown entities through*
*my grandmother's stories, I began to develop an inordinate, premature*
*sense of regard for air, water, fire, the four seasons, plant growth, and*
*wildlife.*

*From a star I had seen explode above me as I stood in my plastic*
*imitation cowboy chaps and boots with tin spurs, teeter-tottering on a*
*small mound on the path where I thought I saw my late grandfather*
*change into a winged being, along with my two uncles and their cousin,*
*I equated myself to the sparks that slowly fell to earth. Parts of me were*
*therefore scattered over the forest floor that was covered with a glisten-*
*ing blanket of umbrella-shaped plants.*

Being afraid and cautious of nonordinary things and happen-
ings was a natural part of being Black Eagle Child. Realizing this took
a long time, though. I was consumed for the most with naïveté, my
euphemism for having no direction. It was only when I saw these
supernatural manifestations in person that I began paying attention.
The strength that could make household furniture gasp and come to
life or the strength to make fireflies fly in **V** formation before expand-

ing into a bus-sized fluorescent craft was an ancient night-enemy secret. That or something else entirely.

It was Grandmother who brought this awareness about early on. Clothed in a tight flannel shirt, perforated jeans, and church-donated shoes, my cherubic innocence did not sit well with Grandmother. Through the Six Grandfathers' Journals she wanted to expedite the maturing process. Through something no normal human could fathom, she introduced me to invisible forces. I was so young, though, that a bulk of her wisdom and wizardry—real or imagined—went unappreciated.

Because of the enormity of what I was expected to digest, compromises were made. There are indications, even now in adulthood, that I was spoiled. But that in itself, in a variety of ways, was to my advantage. I could at least look forward to gifts in the form of candies, toys, movies, and trips to the local carnival and circus. The downside was that if I had tirelessly recorded Grandmother's entries for half a day and my overtures for a movie were not taken kindly, I had tantrums.

But even they were made into lessons.

Without anyone really saying point-blank that my Grandmother was responsible, tree branches at night were made to whip about by themselves, making my demanded walk to the Why Cheer Theater more frightening. At first sign of a tree's tremors I learned to bow my head unflinchingly toward the gravel. But about a mile from home, as we sat on the bridge by the Barber Shop and Pool Hall, my small, shivering legs convinced me the cinema and the enchanting fragrance of popcorn wasn't to be. (Later I learned how to prevent the unnerving "whipping tree branch" phenomena from taking hold. It was a matter of herbal "persuasion" concoctions—and mental control.)

While the image of swaying eerie van Gogh–like trees silhouetted by the stars is easily revisited, the undetected presence of upper-level wind and a wild, unbounded imagination deserve equal consideration. Nevertheless, without answer or reason, unusual things would occur in my childhood, like the green ball of fire that danced in the yard one evening at the height of a fever: in my delirium I was told that the same person who had touched my infant face, leaving a trail of chicken pox scars, was responsible. Anything that was glowing green at night was a sign of evil. Somehow I understood that the dancing ball of fire had manipulated the Spanish galleon's green mass to pass right through the kerosene-darkened cardboard ceiling. Inundated with gravity, the scratched-in image of a sad-faced baseball player and the name "EMILY" came down, forcing my liquified meal out into a bucket.

The women who had been summoned to my aid—all of them knowledgeable in good medicine—took alarm, but that was it. My symptoms were accepted as a sign that either I had broken free of the spell or the worst was forthcoming. My mother and grandmother were present that night. Like doting mother hummingbirds they flitted in and out and in between the cluster of helpers—their neighborhood friends and their daughters: Betty and Sarah Anne Red Boy, Sophia Ribbon and Rose Grassleggings, Mary Ellen MacAloon and Alice August. Nothing could be done with the green dancing light except to keep it at bay with the cedar incense that was being sprinkled over the red-hot embers inside the iron skillet.

Rendered speechless, I saw the sails and flags of the galleon dissipate amid the gentle-smelling wisps of purifying smoke. The anchor at last broke free from my chest. No longer was I being dragged along the rim of a bottomless chasm where tunnels had been bored in the side by the shiny tan pincers of giant crabs.

I was relieved but I still couldn't communicate. I lapsed into a half dream.

*On the exact grassy spot in the yard where a light green ball of fire danced the night previously . . .*

With the window curtains closed, the women were back in their chairs. Without anyone saying it, there was a sense of resignation that extraneous factors were involved and nothing could be done. When they say I "almost died," I believe it wholeheartedly. Foremost in my recollections were the washcloths presoaked in boiled herbs being wrung over my palpitating belly. After that, this:

*On the exact grassy spot in the yard where a light green ball of fire had danced the night previously—an omen of imminent death—I saw the shape of a large, muscular man standing absolutely still in the shadow*

*of a thick thorn tree. At first, he appeared very normal as he came for-
ward along the clothesline, walking a few steps whenever the wind
whipped the colorful clothes into the air. But when he got to a distance
where I could see his face, I saw a grotesque being who was part-human
and part-fish. He came out into the bright windy daylight and returned
my gaze with shiny demon eyes. Without a neck of any kind, the fish-
headed being in a dark gray suit, vest, and slacks was a grotesque rendering of someone's nightmare.*

*"Has your illness subsided any?" questioned the suited demon.*

*I elected to close my unbelieving eyes and . . .*

*"Did you hear my question?" repeated the demon more loudly.*

*I kept my eyelids shut but almost opened them when I heard slosh-
ing footsteps come to the moldy edge of the window. My own cries for
help through clenched teeth were drowned out by the women and their
daughters who chatted idly over coffee and day-old sweet rolls in the
next room.*

*"Listen to me, then," he said. "That Spanish galleon, that loathsome
ship that hovers above you like a buzzard is more of a threat than me."*

*The mere thought of this wooden ship, especially its compressed
night-enemy power and mass, floating just below the ceiling, caused
nausea. It could roar like a revved-up tractor engine, and the black smoky
afterburn clogged my nostrils.*

*Upon my opening of one crusty eye, the physical enigma that stood
near the window shook my body with such intensity that my once-limp
arms flopped about and accidentally spilled the two basins of boiled
medicine extract onto the blankets and floor.*

*The chatting of the woman and their daughters stopped.*

*"I have nothing to do with the galleon," stated the demon in a
necktie hanging askew. "Nor do I have anything to do with the green,
dancing light."*

*My tongue watered and the putrid odor of a long night's worth of
throwing up made my stomach muscles cramp in pain. I was able to
grab and dam up my mouth before it filled with bitter-tasting fluid. As
I adjusted my rigid body over the bed's edge, I emptied myself of the
galleon's strength.*

*"I'm not the one to blame for its choice to be with you," continued
the demon.*

*When my stomach and mind finally had no more to give, I sat up-*
*right and groped desperately under the mattress for my knife. It was the*
*knife I had received as a prize at the carnival downtown. Surely, I thought,*
*such a balanced sharp blade will whistle and find its mark through the*
*slimy gills of the demon-fish. But shortly after I released the knife from*
*my fingers, I saw my uncle Winston dodge the airborne weapon. He had*
*been there at the foot of the bed all the time. And my weapon, a spoon,*
*careened off the woodstove and exited through the door's window. Ex-*
*hilarated, I could feel the small house's stale air rush out. As I laid back*
*down, I sensed the departure of an unwanted boat and an inquisitive fish-*
*faced being. My uncle, with a smirk on his large brown face, swept up*
*the fine pieces of glass with a broom and dustpan. . . .*

Long before I saw oceanic vessels on film, I dreamt about them.
The Spanish galleon, in spite of its horrific overtones, along with
Grandmother's stories and awesome demonstrations, established in me
a clear understanding of animism. I could see the intricate and subtle
interrelationships of the prairie and woodland life-forms as they materialized from a pool of clear water. Underneath the sky was the wintry
earth and its long blades of dry grass, pale twigs, and smooth pieces of
multicolored stone. Held still as if in a photograph, this was the serene reflection of Grandmother Earth herself, the universal microcosm
of the person I loved the most. "She was the earth herself. . . . "

With a five-foot, three-inch frame, Ada Principal Bear was a small
Black Eagle Child woman. Her attire consisted of loose blouses and
long skirts she made by hand or with an antique Singer sewing machine. Her color preferences were simple: black, dark green, and
purple. She also wore scarves around her neck or over her head. Black
ones. Silk in the summer and wool in the winter. For Earthlodge clan
ceremonies or the tribal field days, she was adorned with German
silver jewelry on her thin wrists and fingers, including her neck and
earlobes. For these special occasions she wore traditional-style skirts
and blouses that were designed with beadwork or ribbon appliqué in
floral patterns. These would come out from storage in suitcases and
trunks. Here, the colors were dazzling and loud. We knew when a

dance was in the offing by the regalia that swung from the clothes-line. On windless days we walked up to them and studied their traditional Woodlands designs. Depicted on the skirt panels were medicinal plants and their stems, vines, and leaf formations; these were meticulously outlined with either beads or silk material in a liberal array of colors.

When I became conscious of my surroundings, at around five to seven years of age, Grandmother, No ko me sa, was nearing her sixties. Accustomed to walking, she would leave early in the morning for work downtown. In color and black-and-white 35 mm photographs I took between the ages of ten and sixteen, Grandmother is often shown squinting through her glasses. On the picnic table in front of her is a plastic dish containing beads, and her hands are caught in midair as they prepare to scoop up the beads one by one. Matching her physique was her small wrinkled face with friendly eyes and a faint smile.

And she loved to talk and reminisce. She recited stories that made one think of what lurked outside the house at nightfall. Sorcery cannot exist without human suffering, Grandmother used to say. Enemies with "daylight-seeing vision at night" were summoned and they took their evil services seriously. Just as a vulture spots a potential meal, the gradual dying of someone could be seen from afar, and the methodical wait and timing of a nourishing, life-prolonging meal became an art. Among the abilities and assets of these enemies were night-seeing, flying through thick brush with short wings, and prying open windows with their sharp talons.

Ancient accipiters?

The fact that the practice could thrive for centuries without depleting the entire pool of potential victims was never contemplated.

Was the life-taking craft ever expertly controlled, like the taking of bounty?

Was there a quota for the number of people who could be executed from a rival clan or family?

Was there a silent agreement, a code, a course taken that determined a boundary?

Was it four avenged deaths from the beloved family of a rival sorcerer in a lifetime, or was it anyone from the namesake?

If the spell ricocheted and came back to its source, did the spellshooter know his or her family was in jeopardy?

Did a self-destructive shot bring remorse?

Or were lives taken in vengeance without care and emotion?


"Listen to this, No tti se ma, Grandson," Grandmother once said to me. "I want to tell you a story. This is about apparel used and worn by *ne nyi ka si a ki,* sorcerers: Once when your grandfather, Jack Principal Bear, was walking home along the Sandhill Road, above the Indian Dam, he met an old woman and a young girl. If it had not been too late, like sundown, it would have been a chance meeting like any other. People anxious to get home before nightfall. Except at that particular time, as he had spent much of the night fishing, it wasn't right for such a couple to travel on a desolate moonlit road. As soon as they realized he was right in front of them, close enough to hear their conversation about 'travel made easy,' they stopped with emotionless faces before turning around in a levitating manner to flee. The old woman, who was wrapped in a dark, long-fringed shawl, grabbed the girl's hand. Apparently, he surprised them, for they took off in the opposite direction. Your grandfather, sensing the two were not ordinary people, ran after them. He never knew what prompted him to do so. At the point where he thought he was almost upon them, they bolted and disappeared from the forest road. Until that mystical act occurred, he had been unaware that their legs had been motionless. Instead of an outright run they floated and skimmed over the rounded contours of the landscape in amazing hummingbird speed. He never forgot how they seemed to skate down and above the hill. Effortlessly."

Grandmother indicated there had been a series of sightings of this old woman and her long-fringed shawl. My grandfather suspected the young girl was a night-enemy apprentice, for there was absolutely no way a human could keep up with the old woman's speed. Had she been a regular girl, she would have been dragged along violently over the cinder rocks and tree stumps.

Because young people liked to venture out at night, seeking to romance each other, more sightings were soon reported. Everyone who saw the fleeting shawl rarely went out alone into the warm nights thereafter. Night-enemies were responsible for amputation and even death.

The story continued.

From the village located near the confluence of the Iowa and Swanroot River bottoms, where ceremonial feasts were held, word came that the old woman often made a predawn crossing of what was then the first steel and concrete bridge.

"Through his curiosity and lack of fear as a young man, your grandfather spoke to a close friend, A se no ta ka (the One Who Understands Stone's Talk, or Alfred Pretty-Boy-in-the-Woods in English), about this and proceeded to make plans to intercept her. That night they sat hidden on the western side over the railing and they chewed bits of root, *mi ka ti a sqwi,* a medicine that repels the paralysis effect sorcerers emanated in their outings. If your senses heard, saw, felt, and smelled a sorcerer, you were rendered helpless. Especially if you were in the condition of being most vulnerable—in half sleep or ill health or even after an overdose of alcohol. Several nights passed without seeing her, but they were suspicious of anyone who crossed the bridge moments before sunrise. On the fourth morning, they spotted a hunchback figure draped in the dark shawl. Your grandfather gave the signal. Inhaling air through almost-closed lips and over the top row of his teeth, he made short, mouse-squeaking noises. Pretty-Boy-in-the-Woods knew this was it. She stood for a while on the other side, checking, before making the flight across. She had traveled down along the Iowa River, coming from the north, hidden by tall grass. A swooshing sound, like that of a small, dusty whirlwind, gathered at the end of the bridge. She floated across with the long fringes of her shawl waving. Just when she was parallel with their positions, they leapt out, surprising her to the point that she forgot to accelerate. They held her with their combined might. Twice, because of her power, she almost escaped. *'Ba ki se ni ko, ba ki se ni ko! Ke be tta wi ba ma!* Let me go, let me go! You have made a mistake!' she implored. After a while they began to think this could turn out to be an embarrassing mistake, holding a respectable woman by force. They equated her with a child who had been caught stealing and took pity. Were it not for the Earthlodge clan warrior songs they sang, she might have prevailed. As the sun began to rise through the cottonwood trees, she slowly sank back to the ground. The counter-attacking medicine they chewed weakened the barriers, yes, but the blessings given them through their fasting made them invincible. Stunned, the old woman could not readily transform into an owl, wolf, or panther."

Knowing it took a spirit-ally, ethnobotany, and fasting-blessings to subdue evil in its purest form, I could never be like my grandfather. (In one of the most memorable encounters with the paranormal, Selene Buffalo Husband and I were chased away from our river-bottoms residence by an entity we call the "Supernatural Strobe Light." It wore many masks: that of three owls, fireflies flying in **V** formation like distant military jets, a floating ball of pale light, a red fluorescent rectangular mass the size of a school bus, and, of course, the strobe light that became a small, pulsating star. Education left me wounded back then and thus vulnerable. . . .)

With a refilled cup of coffee and a plate of cinnamon rolls next to her, Grandmother took the artificial sweetener and stared at it as if the pink paper package was nonhuman.

We were back on the bridge.

"When the subject at last straightened up and looked directly at your grandfather and his associate, they promptly recognized her. The 'old woman' was not really old at all; in fact, she was outgoing and middle-aged. She was active in nearly every aspect of Settlement life—cooking for feasts, dancing, and doing elaborate floral ribbon-work on dresses. Why she should even carry on with this evil subter-fuge annoyed Jack. He released his grip and shoved her away. 'There!' he said, while pointing accusingly to her face. 'We know who you are. You won't be able to do as you've been doing.' The woman stared at her excited captors, swung her shawl back over her head, and strolled nonchalantly into the sleeping village. Shortly after this epi-sode, the woman had a strange affliction on her right leg. The tips of her toes deteriorated from rot. Her foot and ankle had to be surgically amputated. Which most residents believed was payment for her floating carelessness."

From then on, as Grandmother explained, she was greatly feared. Yet there were a few who dared to entrust their needs with her, for she was skilled with both good and bad medicine—the kind that healed and the kind that made others commit suicide or murder. It depended largely upon one's needs, the amount and nature of compensation. Any gratuity certainly helped.

Grandmother also said one had to be in good standing.

"Life, as you will undoubtedly come to realize, is that way: a delicate and unpredictable balance between what is humanly good and what is sinister. It's much like one ancient force gaining an upper hand, laying down the rules by which people should live on earth. According to this foundation, and by that alone, we are here. This existence is a privilege. Watching over us are elements of nature who took their respective places as sky, water, fire, thunder eons ago with some reluctance. Those underground, underwater, and above, we venerate them as we venerate the Creator and His Twin Sons. They have been appointed to relay our prayers. . . ."

Our main purpose, the way I finally perceived it, aside from maintaining ceremonies, was to keep prophecies of world demise from occurring or at least make note of them. But it all became so damned obvious. The sparks of distant wars on the bottom side of a cooking skillet kept us well informed. The Northern Lights appeared to warn us of pending flag wars. We kept a vigil one year when President Kennedy had a showdown with Cuba. Fortunately, the Northern Lights didn't reach the southern horizon. If they had, the horizon would have been bloodred.

We were here, after all, as a reflection of other events and past lives. We merely reenacted this constant battle of right and wrong, a promise kept and transgressions committed. We who are but Remnants of the First Earth.

Grandmother's discourse resumed.

"When the woman finally came to the point where she was debilitated by old age, she was near the family. My family. There was no house where she was welcome; she was without relatives. Of course, she was also quite feeble. It is strange how a person deemed evil and dangerous could interact with people who feared her the most. Years and years after her capture on the bridge, when she could no longer support herself and her elderly companion, they lived with us. This was before I met your grandfather. On occasion we'd all sell beadwork on Lincoln Highway 30. I recall making her last days peaceful by providing her with canned fruit and crushed sausage. These were hard items to come by then, you see. During the days when she was blamed for the birth of crippled infants, missing female adulterers, and a scorching drought, I chose not to say anything because I didn't see anything that made me believe she was involved. Youngsters here, you know this yourself, are taught not to say anything to anyone. *Ka ta-na na tti-ke ko-i tti ye ka ni-ko wi ye a.* Ever. That is not your place, we are told. Since her involvement couldn't be proven, other than the time she was pinned against a metal bridge railing 'by mistake,' she took advantage of her alleged innocence and socialized with the tribal community as much as her debilitation would allow. Once she and her elderly companion came up to me and whispered, '*Bya na yo. Ne ta ka wa ta be na-ni ke ki no a mo na ki-ni o te te na ma wa ni-me tti me ko na ta we ne ta mo wa na ni.* Come here. We want to teach you ways for you to obtain anything you want.'"

Grandmother expressed she was interested in their proposal. She followed them into the earthlodge where the two women burned cedar incense to purify the potent medicines that were spread out over the long table-bench on a yellowish deerhide. She then described in lucid detail what her eyes beheld: the hide itself was set on top of a long-fringed shawl. The brilliant rays of the sun hanging directly overhead stabbed through the smoky interiors and accented the red and black stone figurines holding miniature pipes—six of them. They were held in the center by four wreathlike displays. The braided strips of medicine had been arranged to appear in a swirling circular motion, a frozen moment in a catastrophic event. With blankets and tablecloth they had also taken careful measures to block out the daylight that usually came through the spacing between the boards of the summer earthlodge.

"*Be ki ma me ko-ke me nwi to ta wi be na-e bi ti ka tti ya ki-e o wi ki wa ni.* You have treated us extremely well by allowing us into your home," she was told. "*I ni ke-ma ni-e bya mi ka ta ki-ke tti ki we ni.*

*Ma ma ka tti ke nwi tta-ki na-ni o te te na ma ni-mi ska wi ke ki-na ta wi no ni.* Old age is presently upon us. It is important that you receive this potent medicine."

In remembering that particular event, Grandmother meditated out loud: "What they wanted me to keep and pass on was the dreaded knowledge of the medicine called *bi na i ka ni,* or love medicine. I looked at the various kinds of roots and I knew from having seen my own grandmother's handiwork that what they spoke about was truth. In the smoke-filled interior, the legless woman and her elderly companion were anxious for me to accept and keep the male and female stems and roots of their *wa be ski bi na i ka ni,* white swanroot, which was also the English name of the river nearby. While I initially agreed to care for it, not once have I utilized it for myself or others as it was originally intended—to steal and hurt hearts, to separate and destroy families. If used without caution, I was warned, the person-target can become so overcome with lovesickness that suicide is a serious consideration. Romance can take a frightful turn. I eventually learned that if the medicine was kept in a sealed glass jar away from the main family room, it served as protection against ill-fated travels, malicious thoughts, and night-enemies.

"Of course, I was cognizant then as I am now that the people who employed this root for evil means spent an eternity on their hands and knees along the road to the Black Eagle Child Hereafter digging for a nonexistent root. Never once did I think of pursuing the contrary. My own grandmother said the trees and plants belonged to the Creator's Grandmother, and that the very ground we walk on was the top of her head. Her medicinal gifts originate from strands of her lovely hair. Gifts that were meant to help. To employ them solely for the sake of harm is to ask for eternal punishment.

"There is something more you should know. Upon the footless woman's celebrated death, as her personal belongings were collected in sacks and boxes to be given away to the funeral helpers, a necklace of dried infant fingernails was found. Many believed these fingernails were the token remains of night-enemy victims. It, along with all the morbid items in the small, antique trunk, was buried along the sandy valley of what is today called Lone Ranger Drive.

"Strangely, her death did not mean she was absolutely gone. The

knowledge of the black, long-fringed shawl was transferred to someone else. A young female person, perhaps kin. So I would be cautious; she is still here. These carriers ultimately require human lives
to extend their own depravity. It is known they can change any object into a bullet or pellet. If a letter is written and personally delivered to you, let's say, and if it has been annointed with some medicine
and 'spoken to,' the paper will actually act as the bullet itself, traveling through your bones, heart, and into your fragile consciousness.

"And you will perform as it has been wished. . . ."

# The Grandfather
# of All Dream

*William Listener, a master plumber and former chair of the Tribal
Council, made a significant impression upon me at Jake Sacred
Hammer's winter funeral in 1970. As a clan elder, William often had
the difficult task of speaking the "Final Words to the Deceased before
Their Journey West." These words worked in tandem with those from
the shadow-releasers.*

    *It was during these grim circumstances at O'Ryan's Cemetery that I
first became aware of William's oratorical skills. Whether in English or
Black Eagle Child they were poetically embellished. Fundamental and
ancient, the Final Words became a doorway to the Hereafter. Gaining
passage, of course, was an entirely different matter. More than a few
tribal members were willing to say in public that Jake—who spent half
his life riling up Black Eagle Child people with his candor and
insensivity to the Earthlodge clan ceremonies—was not deserving of these
Final Words.*

    *From the early 1930s to the late 1950s, Jake contributed volumi-
nous information on the tribe's religious infrastructure to academicians
from Illinois, Washington, D.C., and Belgium. Jake Sacred Hammer
was a paid cultural informant. Everyone in the Settlement knew that,
but no one questioned his transgressions. Tribal members, as a tradition, were taught not to impose their personal views or actions upon
other people.*

*William Listener, who was also taught one shouldn't judge others, recited the eulogy in a tone that was at once forgiving and respectful. In addition to being a person who assisted "shadows" and their bereaved families, William was, to quote Luciano Bearchild, "a living songbook." When he wasn't praying, he was singing and drumming. When he wasn't running a complicated earthlodge ceremony, he was reading minutes at the Black Eagle Child Tribal Council meeting or installing plumbing in town. William was the first person to aptly demonstrate that one could educate himself in both worlds by first having a thorough command of their diverse languages. Possessing a shrewd, analytical but traditional outlook was also helpful.*

William Listener was an older half brother of my father, Tony Bearchild. Although it could be said, judging by exterior appearances, that William and I were relatively close, we were rarely—for as small as the Black Eagle Child Settlement is—at the same places. That my parents didn't live together until my tenth year was obviously a factor. Another reason, I must assume, was the division of the progressive and conservative factions in our families. In a sense, the question of who had the ultimate right to make decisions on the beleaguered tribe's behalf kept us apart. Politically star-crossed, one could say.

As I mentioned before, Clotelde, my mother—who was raised in a traditional Bear King, or Principal Bear, family—was a Capulet of sorts; and from the Montagues, there was my father, Tony, a descendant of the Bearchild patriarch who long ago, under blackmail from white politicians, got himself recognized as chief and thus brought education to the tribe. Somewhere therein my supposed illegitimacy excluded me from the Bearchild family portrait.

Politics, like money, divides people. Who was it that said tribal nations would be destroyed by four things? Handsome Lake. In a speech made in 1799, he indicated the dangers were alcohol, the Bible, the culture around us, and a deck of cards. Handsome Lake, way back then, was absolutely correct. But he omitted a fifth: money.

William Listener was articulate when it came to being a progressive. He firmly upheld only those values that were dependent on religiousness. Since very few operated successfully within that margin, he was able to look upon all modern factors with a mirthful grin.

"We can tolerate the whites," he'd explain to his younger half brothers. "We'll never get anywhere if we don't make an effort—no matter how shameful or futile—to use them." Before the advent of the gambling enterprise, he would expound on where we should be going. Through his toothless mouth, he'd discuss the future. "We've got to do better than the grocery store, barber shop, pool hall, and bread factory we now have."

William Listener moved stealthily between the two worlds, in a more dignified way than Jake Sacred Hammer, to achieve his goals. Being a religious leader, master plumber, and tribal chair required both diplomacy and outright usurpation of authority. In Why Cheer he had lawyer friends who wrote up grants for tribal housing needs in return for subcontracting jobs for their own relatives.

Maybe this is why we rarely met. He was many things to many people.

On the occasions we happened to be in the same place, however, like funerals and the few ceremonies I attended, I perceived myself as a blurred movement, an indiscernible face that somehow stood out in the Bearchild family portrait as a flaw.

William was the exact opposite. He was the Earthlodge clan's exclusive connection to the Creator and the Holy Grandfather. Without the slightest pause he would accept all requests to perform ceremonies. He sang, drummed, and recited prayers for each clan that called him. In that way was his presence powerful. Whenever he presided over these functions, something dramatic always occurred. Subtle but awe-inspiring manifestations were witnessed and experienced by all. Some unfolded elsewhere, like parking lots in faraway cities. In keeping with tribal humor these manifestations were referred to as gifts from spirits on a "need not be present" basis. Once my grandmother saw the eye of a crane wink as its lifeless hide was being unraveled. She stated the crushed feathers and fluffs expanded and trembled like prairie flowers in the wind as the crane appeared to come alive. Others reported hearing nonhuman voices that accompanied the men singing. And then there were the neighbors who saw sparks from the earthlodge fire shoot upward past the smoke portal, changing into balls of fiery light, lifting into the night sky like meteors in reverse.

Small but testimonial stuff like that made William credible as a spiritual leader. We were all affected in different ways. Sometimes it would even be extremely physical. Being pushed and rolled down a rocky hill by William at the clan feasts was a good but embarrassing thing, people would later attest. The shove prompted their sobriety. As for the gravel-stippled skin, it never healed. And then there was a case of how an alcoholic's deceased aunt appeared in clothing other than what the original "dressers of the deceased" had chosen and used. These manifestations took place during words, songs, and prayers given by William, "the grandfather of all dream," as I once poeticized.

> . . . it wasn't unusual for him to look out
> his window and see families bringing him
> whiskey, bright-colored blankets, assorted
> towels, canned triangles of ham. His trunks
> were full of the people's gratitude. Through
> the summer and fall he named babies, led
> clan feasts, and he never refused whenever
> families asked him to speak to the charred
> mouths of young bodies that had died
> drunk. He was always puzzled to see
> their life seeping through the bandages,
> the fresh oil of their black hair, the distorted
> and confused shadows struggling to catch up
> to their deaths. He spoke to suicides just as
> he would to anyone who died peacefully.
> He knew it was wrong to ask them to go on,
> but he couldn't refuse lives that were already
> lost. Everyone counted on him. Each knew that
> if they died within his time, he would be the one
> to hand them their last dream.

Jake Sacred Hammer, a distant cousin of William Listener and the Bearchild family, saw the last daylight that winter while he was sleeping. Actually, no one knew he was gone until they found him a week afterward. The cold weather was said to have helped. His small-framed single room house acted like an icebox. The community said it was as if he had known all along, judging from the premortuary customs taken.

From the attic he had pulled down antique trunks containing items collected over a lifetime. On new blankets over the wooden floor he had laid out the traditional-style clothing and *mi tta te si ye ni,* beaded finery he would wear in the pinebox casket. Standing against a wall was an open suitcase with clothes his living replacement would wear at the Adoption Ceremony. Multicolored plastic hand mirrors, expensive Sioux-made tobacco bags, and extrawide yarn belts made his family belatedly grateful for how smooth everything would go.

Nearly every item used in the four-day mourning period had been personally preselected. Groceries in dry-good form and loads of firewood had been already bought and stored. Letters addressed to friends and relatives had been written and sealed. In a large glass jar beside the bed was a set of instructions for the funeral and five hundred dollars in twenty-dollar bills to pay for it. The instructions ended with a postscript: "There is more money in the bank and more will follow to my relatives for years to come. The institutions owe me. See attorney Samuel S. Plakoda for how it will be divided. It is yours, to use and to keep."

Jake Sacred Hammer wanted his departure quick and trouble-free, the way it had been for centuries. Very little was known about Jake and his activities. When he wasn't cavorting with non-Indian visitors, he led them as they flitted from house to house on the Settlement, flaunting their leather shoulder bags that contained notebooks, pencils, and agreements for payment in return for information on the social and religious structures of the clans. What they wanted was known, but according to tribal precept it wasn't shared on a whim to strangers nor was it for sale.

However, all that secrecy changed one day.

From the earthlodge sanctums, rumors arose that someone had been providing numbingly detailed diagrams and descriptions of our ceremonies, prayers, songs, and stories. The recipients? Those aforementioned flies from academia. Thus was paved another inroad. Ironically, this purported transgression was discovered by a handful of Black Eagle Child academic types. While the elders generally had a low regard for educated Black Eagle Childs, calling them "degreed good-for-nothings," they had decided to listen to them. Somewhere, they reported, were tens of thousands of pages collected at three cents a page in the late 1880s that had yet to be translated into English. Their nameless grandfathers were the main informants. In the 1930s another generation of informants, their sons, came onto the scene. These epic archival contributions rekindled the ancient fires of prophecy.

Jake Sacred Hammer, for being more than an endeared academic acquaintance, was suspected as the ringleader. Jake, along with a number of other notable clan informants, committed a major affront to the Holy Grandfather—and the tribe. Everything on the informant's end was tranquil until someone figured out the rationalization of keeping food on the table for a family was also a foreboding sign that money could sway a person's mind and values.

Finally, in 1962, the Tribal Council was forced to intervene when Jake began offering excursions to Cottonwood Hill for profit. Every four years in a miraculous cycle stretching back to 1911, lightning had struck the giant cottonwoods. They were not completely destroyed, but they always bore astounding burn scars, and branch splinters were embedded in the ground. 1911. That was the year Francis Marie, Jake's fellow informant, allegedly sold a sacred mat, bringing the vengeful rains—and the historic flood of the Iowa River. Jake, along with an entourage of well-dressed whites lugging picnic baskets, cameras, and umbrellas, became a familiar sight. The trash, however, was a gut-wrenching eyesore. After thirty years of his profiting off the tribe's name, a clear, indirect message was sent by the Tribal Council to Jake Sacred Hammer.

For over half his life Jake had served as an unofficial Settlement guide. His self-serving actions epitomized the coming-to-fruition of the Black Eagle Child apocalypse. To counter that overt threat, "NO TRESPASSING" signs were posted on the Settlement's two thoroughfares. Everywhere the visitors had been taken, traipsing through the dark green valleys, frolicking over the golden prairies and along the sandy riverbottoms, huge gaudy signs hugged the path-riddled landscape.

Thanks to Jake the sixties proved to be a decade in which the traditional ethic of respect began to diminish. From the second generation of informants were born the first cases of public dissension

and verbal confrontation in a tribal society that once thought of itself as invincible.

In retrospect it's funny how we had nearly been inured by these so-
called "demonstrations of neighborly interest." That's the term Jake
Sacred Hammer used in his written reply in the *Black Eagle Child
Quarterly* to justify the guided tours. It was addressed "To Whom It
May Concern." Meeting hordes of whites on a Sunday afternoon was
pretty common. Like the noisy white fishermen who gathered at the
Indian Dam on weekends to camp out or the nervy women from the
Why Cheer Preservation Club, tourists could be expected.

As youngsters, some of us eagerly took part in posing for tourist
photographs at twenty-five cents a flashbulb shot: Wearing a Cleve-
land Indians Chief Wahoo mascot-type rubber mask at the annual
Cherry Hill Mansion Halloween Ball, I once made seventy-five cents
and later got photos by mail of myself in long johns and a black breechcloth. Another time I was Joseph, clutching the pink plastic doll
known as the baby Jesus Christ, for which I made three dollars. All
this cash on our trek by foot to town. "Don't be like Jake, Edgarsky
Sacred Ham!" my uncles would taunt.

All along the hilly crowns of the Settlement, there were foot-
paths that led to hallowed and forbidden areas. When the spring and
summer clan ceremonies were in session, the paths were congested
with gleeful, unrestrained tourist chatter. If Jake was unavailable,
white people slipped money under the door of his house for the pamphlets that were stacked on the rocking chair. The mimeographed
pamphlets mapped out trails and shortcuts to places that were thought
to be blessed—or cursed. And sure enough, you'd meet them with
maps in hand bypassing the new housing areas and spying down upon
the earthlodges from the hilltops. As the pamphlet instructed on the
"Watching Indians," they tried to "be as still as whitetail deer."

Without fail we were rattled into remembering our local landmark
every four years by a thunderous electrical display. The giant lightning-
shredded cottonwoods stood smoldering under the black rainclouds.

Precisely one week before the cataclysmic weather ensued, the tourists wound their way unaccompanied through the Settlement trails. Like the lightning that sent children under the table with hands covering their ears, they always arrived on schedule and Jake couldn't keep up with the demand.

We always knew when to avoid Cottonwood Hill: whenever the nightly cattle bellowing began on nearby farm pastures. Rumbling and crackling over the valley, the thunderstorms held a stationary position over the valley until the fires were set. In school you always knew which classmates had been lightning-frightened by strands of copper beads they wore on their wrists.

Regardless of how many pleas were made through the Principal Religion ceremonies, the Well-Known Twin Brother kept sending earth-pounding thunderstorms. Among the elders it was believed sorcerers still held a victory dance for the sacred mat that once belonged to Me si kwi-Ne ni wa, Ice Deity. This mat was the one on display in an overseas museum in Belgium. Along the walls of the earthlodges the other sacred mats could be heard weeping for their "younger brother."

According to our Creation myth, after the War of the Supernatural Beings obliterated the First Earth, Me si kwi-Ne ni wa, Ice Deity, had agreed to put away the icy storms in a sacred mat. In the form of water his words were blended with a dark red herbal dye and drawn out as a picture. This was then rolled up, tied together with sinew in elaborate star patterns, and set aside for the Black Eagle Child people as evidence of their tenuous earthly standing. In it was a symbol of trust. As long as Ice Deity's pictures were kept warm and dry by its earthlodge keepers, they would never know the wrath of earth-splintering hail and bolts of cottonwood-seeking lightning.

But even the grandest plans fail.

From a faraway, dingy, chandelier-illuminated Hall of the Aboriginal Collections of North America in Belgium, the Ice Deity began sending well-timed electrical storms—Tama County's meteorological quirk.


Jake Sacred Hammer did not think these paid tours to Cottonwood Hill were harmful or intrusive. His stance, as he wrote in the *Black*

*Eagle Child Quarterly,* was that if the tribe could tolerate the fenced-in memorial of the "cultural disfiguring barns," where the 1890 runaways were jailed as a first step to ensure education, then he had every right, like the Why Cheer Women's Preservation Club, to commemorate the past. "If the whites risk electrocution on Cottonwood Hill, then by golly let them do it!" was how he concluded the "RE: In Defense of Guided Tours" published letter.

The tourists came from all regions of the globe. Through their European connections they gloated over the pathetic history in old buildings and delighted in artifacts, like mossy-covered bridges, Indians, and things that went "moo" or "oink" while fouling the air, earth, and ourselves. This was prompted by the management of the Red Barn Premises the Why Cheer Women's Preservation Club. In their homage to the virtuous past, they recognized their membership and dues could grow if they—the idea repulsed them—contacted every tourist who came to "see the Indians." This started in 1928 with promotion of "HOME OF THE WHY CHEER INDIANS" via their absurd postcards, the ones that are now highly sought after as collector's pieces.

The Preservation Club consisted of the wives of small-rural-community, middle-class society types who met once a month for tea and biscuits at Kling Kower's Restaurant. They were one-half of whatever made Why Cheer and Gladwood function—law enforcement, the courts, medicine, schools, church, and properties. The wives' husbands peered from the background, whispering on occasion guarded but fruitful instructions into their wives' netted ears. In their straw hats, suspenders, and sunglasses, the influential men lagged behind their womenfolk and their guests on a hike to Cottonwood Hill. The sheriff walking like Barney Fife of Mayberry, with hands on hips near the revolver loaded with a single bullet. Behind him marched the county judge and attorney, doctors, teachers, school administrators, bankers, preachers, barbers, merchants, and a bevy of semisuccessful farmers. In addition to advising their wives, they cleaned the cabins and stalls of the Red Barn Premises, where haircuts, clothes, Jesus, A-B-C-D-Z, and Christ were introduced to our grandparents' parents.

When Jake was laid to rest that winter at O'Ryan's Cemetery, only then did the Settlement trails become noticeably quiet. Eight years had passed since the "NO TRESPASSING" signs were posted by the Tribal Council. Unimpressed by the signs and feisty, Jake continued his motley intercourse with outsiders by going underground and doing lectures in neighboring towns. Right up to his graveside Jake Sacred Hammer referred to his ill-intentioned admirers as people who intended only to "demonstrate neighborly interest."

Around this period I became fascinated with stories Jake Sacred Hammer had helped collect years before. In terms of bolstering my interest in mythological intricacies, Jake was influential. At the University of Iowa, shortly after my return from Pomona College, I met a graduate student who was doing a dissertation on these "legends and folktales." Naturally, since Grandmother had recited some in my youth, I could tell where changes had been made to hide the mysteries lurking within the words themselves. Even Jake was tribal law— abiding enough to reveal only the basic and not the whole. But no one knew that. Not even the expert team of linguistically trained ethnologists.

In a way, by being a "word-collector" I had subconsciously followed the same diplomacy by choosing less intimate symbols for my poetry. Even in my naïveté I knew enough to incorporate misleading themes.

(Later, literary critics and experts would classify my cryptic work as the "most puzzling" among the pantheon of emerging or established tribal-affiliated writers. It would bother me that these self-appointed critics of Native American literature would overlook circumspection as the light source that refracted, rearranged, and hid me for reasons pertaining to safety. Essays were published to that regard: that I was one confusing mother. Ironically, flocking to my defense were writers whose claims to Indian blood later became questionable. There was never a doubt in my mind they were who they said they were, figuring there was a sense of honor in being Indian, never thinking people would go to deceitful means to claim my ancestors as theirs. Because of this duplicity I equated both critics and imposters as part of the master mouse-catching cat race that sadistically maimed its aboriginal prey for entertainment. Perverted romanticism, if you will, before decapitation.)

Anyway, the graduate student published his commendable but unsuccessful efforts in a book entitled *Wolf That I Iz*. In an era when Black Eagle Child society was perhaps in a semipristine state, a good portion of what was held most sacred had already been documented by academic flies. Like my own verse, it was cryptic. Once the codes were laboriously deciphered, I was thoroughly amazed at the fearlessness shown by the informants. For such acts of sacrilege, "there should have been repercussions—to self and the immediate family," I noted in my journal. Except for Francis Marie, the person held accountable for selling the Ice Deity mat and whose children committed a string of mystifying suicides, there were none evident. Nor was there a succession of disappearances. No reports of vengeance. Enough for me to contemplate working with the graduate student to revise and update the old stories.

As the "maybe" answer edged closer to becoming an affirmation, my grandmother said, "*Me tte na-ka ta-a se mi i ye ka ni nay. Ni ba wi ta ki-ke ko-i tta wi ya ni.* You just as well not help him. So nothing will happen to you."

She sensed my disappointment and right away gave examples of what had befallen informants. Something horrific happened to each family. In the past before I was born. There were different, often inconspicuous levels of retribution, advised Grandmother. Stray bullets fell from the sky, finding their mark in the unsuspecting eyes of spouses. Cars unbraked themselves and rolled over playing infants. People who were last seen mildly intoxicated were found hours later in unrecognizable mangled pieces strewn across the railroad tracks, packs of hungry canines defending mangled pieces of their flesh.

It was enough to make me reconsider my role as research assistant. I told Grandmother that I wouldn't pursue the idea. Undeterred, I continued to read the Sacred Hammer translations. When I should have been painting for my neurotic art professor, I dove into the musty book stalls and read. Whenever possible, I would double-check the credibility of the contents with my grandmother and parents. More times than not the contributions bore a semblance of truth. When

the art professor cussed me out for the few pieces I had completed,
I didn't mind it one bit, knowing his class time had been used wisely.


Jake Sacred Hammer, a self-confessed Christian, scooped up ceremonial secrets freely with the spoons of our ancestors, feeding himself
and his relatives. His expertise provided transportation between the
white and red worlds. But when the "living archives" came to a standstill that day at O'Ryan's Cemetery in the chilly November wind, there
were feelings of ambivalence. A question was asked among the Black
Eagle Childs: What would the greater powers do with him for selling
all those secrets to the whites? Some elderly priests seized the opportunity to pronounce him guilty on behalf of the Holy Grandfather and sentenced him to an eternity of floating nothingness. Others,
like my uncle William, treated Jake's shadow no differently. He had
been asked—over the telephone—by Jake's kin to address their
father's brother. "The Final Words to the Deceased before Their Journey West" were instructions, a verbal mapping, on how to get to the
Black Eagle Child Afterlife. As if existence itself had been easy, there
were yet more trials replete with questions of faithfulness and compassion for humanity and nature.

It was during William's eulogy that a long-legged, bald white reporter for the *Why Cheer News-Herald* began snapping photographs of
Jake in ceremonial clothing and repose. Although many probably found
the act objectionable, no one stepped forward, for this was a white-
intermingling pattern Jake had already established. It seemed fitting.

William, however, grew annoyed at the reporter in the green turtle-
neck and safari-type jacket. Like a large buzzing fly homing in on the
sweet cemetery fragrance, the reporter measured light, calculated distance, and adjusted the camera's knobs and dials. In a flurry of motions the baldheaded fly prepared to take pictures. Suddenly, the wings
slowed down and he quietly knelt beside Jake's moccasined feet.

At the most importune moments the large camera's shutter
clicked noisily.

*So you can have a restful journey . . .*

Click! went the shutter. Buzz-z-z went the baldheaded fly.

*Your family seeks only the good for you. . . .*

Click! The fly's intrusive positioning began to grate William's patience.

*Don't think about returning if they accidentally say your clan name.* . . .

Click! Click!

*You will never feel this way again; it will never be like this again.* . . .

Click! Click! went the shutter. Buzz-z-z went the baldheaded fly.

In retrospect I now theorize that the reporter was subconsciously reacting to the eloquence and rhythmic timing of the solemn but stirring words offered. As William's frustration peaked, however, the pauses between the sentences became protracted, as did the camera shutter clicking. Composure regained, William switched into the English language. Where there had once been a serene message, a set of crucial instructions for the deceased, the situation now drastically changed.

"Must there be a perpetual infringement of our lives? Can we not have the ultimate final moment of privacy?" he questioned, with his hand pointing furiously to the baldheaded fly.

William continued angrily, and in the bitterly cold wind the numb ears of the white entourage tuned in. "For those of you non-Indians in attendance who are friends of the deceased and who do not understand our language, I have just delivered a prayer for our dearly departed. In accordance to our ways this is a time of bereavement and deep sorrow. . . ."

The reporter finally slowed down, froze in his prickly fly tracks, and listened with his bald head shining in the winter sun.

"We are not here to judge what he may or may not have done. That aspect rests with the Almighty God. It irritates me more than you can possibly imagine to have a represenative of the news media taking pictures as if this were a Women's Preservation Club picnic, a circus, or a small-town Republican caucus!"

Inside I asked myself, *Republican caucus?*

Suddenly aware he was the subject of these words, the reporter slowly lowered the Yashica camera, forwarded the film by habit, and stepped back from the coffin in an effort to hide in the crowd, but no one gave room.

"This to me is the most flagrant form of disrespect! We do not take pictures of such in our society! If you are absolutely driven to take them, then please take them as we are breathing and conscious!"

After these words, which were delivered without the slightest pause or slur, an attorney who represented the tribe in state and federal courts made his way to the circle of bereaved relatives and viciously yanked the camera from the reporter's neck. He then proceeded to pop the film out, unrolling it carefully in the sunlight. As if it could be read only when placed before light, he held it from end to end vertically toward the sky like a sacred miniature scroll. The long-legged reporter stood there in utter dejection with bloodred ears, looking down at the exposed frames curling up over the cold, hard ground.

I remember thinking as I saw this scene: "A small but symbolic victory over a newspaper that has been a disease upon our lives. One giant leap for Black Eagle Child kind." The equation of an astronaut's quote as he set his foot on the lunar landscape with the reprimand William had just delivered to the reporter was a caprice. Yet it seemed appropriate and righteous when the history of the American mass media's treatment of the First People was considered.

William stood with his oversized woolen shirt and gray khaki work pants. Sensing all was back to normal, he squinted his puffy eyes. His small-boned frame tottered slightly as he regained his footing over the casket. William resumed exactly where he had left off in the same low monotone of the instruction.

*No matter how strong the loneliness of your journey, make it easy for those who remain here. . . .*

It was difficult to perceive him as a man of tribal letters, but he was a consummate orator. With his soaring height, like the eagle, he was the closest any human could ever get to the Well-Known Twin-Brother, the Creator.


After the incident at O'Ryan's Cemetery, I looked at William Listener differently. He represented a clan leader who was also self-educated. Of greater importance was the fact that he was bilingual. Aside from being on the Tribal Council and being a successful plumbing con-

tractor, he was a drum-carrier for the Red Swan Society. The multitudes of prayers he knew and the songs he sang made young people
like myself envious. Some even said he radiated when he sang.

Of course, there were certain individuals who could never duplicate or equal his talents, especially those who judged him on the
basis of his politics. They had nothing good to say. About anything!
From the day I was told by my playmates—Ted, Pat, Horatio, and
the Muscatines—that "his wallet was fattened with money from the
sale of maps to the lightning-struck hillside," I made it a point not to
visit their houses no matter how lonely I got; I knew their parents
would make me carry back petty messages. For reasons of comfort I
avoided these people like the woods when night first begins. Maybe
this was the phase when I distanced myself. Maybe it wasn't far
enough. On long walks during my adolescent growth I rehearsed arguments with myself—before facing my friends—that William was far
removed from the offensive antics of Jake Sacred Hammer. What
William did on the outside was irrelevant, I surmised. Knowledge was
the real issue, knowledge needed by the next generation to facilitate
their spiritual passage. This was the real priority, not rumors of financial improprieties committed while he was chairman of the Tribal
Council. Abuse of social service funds wasn't a heinous crime, after
all, not when criminals lived undetected in our neighborhoods. It
mattered little to me if he told those assisted with food and fuel oil
by the state not to deal with the grocery store where his wife's check
bounced. There were murderers and rapists whose acts couldn't be
proven in a courtroom, but everyone knew they were guilty. The parents of these criminals were quick to provide alibis. They maintained
their innocence, and they remained silent accomplices right up to
the end. Their conspiracies were the fiercest kind imaginable, the
kind that vanished forever: a stabbing, a shooting, a beating somewhere in the dark before dawn, where all the participants through
their claims of innocence break apart and drift away in an oblivion of
eternal nothingness. . . .

Yet, in spite of this lawless vortex, charges were made that William had misused food and fuel oil orders. The Why Cheer business
people complained, as did tribal members. His vendetta unnecessarily
involved the tribe, it was reported. There was also talk of carpenters

and plumbers being paid in outright cash. News of his exploits came to the supper table in succession.

Mostly, I came away not wishing to understand the function of a seven-man tribal government. It seemed a bad rendering of democracy, a mutation of a small-town Euro-American council system.

And so we ate the boiled squirrel in corn meal and pondered.

Would we ever be like William? Luciano Bearchild, my cousin—before he disappeared in 1966—used to ask when discussing our obligation-ridden futures. Despite having sung his way to prominence through the Earthlodge clans since childhood, Luciano was intimidated by William. Having no response to his own remarkable abilities, Luciano would tighten his necktie and shuffle across the concrete floor like James Brown. Regrettably, Luciano vanished near Liquid Lake, and no one since has known and worn hand-tailored suits, white silk scarves, Italian shoes, and perforated fingerless gloves.

It seemed impossible in my twentieth winter to shuffle away. For the most part, I felt that in the split second the Bearchild family portrait was taken, I was already a blurred movement. *You can't make him out too clear but that's Edgar Bearchild, esteemed member of the SRS—the Society of Repressed Storytellers—or another reason why the elite literary world is very much like the Immigration and Naturalization Service a.k.a. "the good old boy network," in departmental exclusion of un-Americans.*

In my total lifetime, if a miracle somehow changed my attitudes, I could be only one-sixteenth—maybe the part that belittled the white photographer—of whoever William Listener was.

Since William was not an ordinary person, I am inclined to believe his detached hand—or a phantasm thereof—made overtures to communicate with Selene Buffalo Husband and myself in 1979. In actuality, William was lying comatose at the Heijen Medical Center in Sherifftown fifteen miles away.

From this extraordinary event was born the story called "The Incorporeal Hand," where the mystery guest signed itself in as *"The Messenger of . . ."* on the TV game show *What's My Line?* Panelists Henry Morgan and Dorothy Killgallen, with oversized blindfolds, smirked as the excess lizard skin of their aristocratic throats rippled in the cold green light. . . .

# The Stick-Shooting
# Escapade at
# Horned Serpent Lake

*Several years following Jake Sacred Hammer's funeral and after much
coaxing by my parents, I sat and sang with William Listener and the
other prominent elders of the Red Swans. This secret society consisted
solely of firstborns from the Tree-Raking or Claw-Marking Bear clans.
My first real experience with the Red Swans came a decade previous
when I accompanied my father, mother, grandmother, and William, the
Grandfather of All Dream, to a major spiritual gathering in Canada.*

In the spring of 1961, almost one year from the time I accompanied Luciano Bearchild to Browning, Montana, for the North American Indian Days celebration, my brother Alan and I took a trip with
my father, mother, grandmother, and William to a major spiritual
gathering in Canada.

Through the long travel by automobile that spring to Horned
Serpent Lake, I got to know William, my half uncle. Sort of. Likewise for my father, Tony. William and my father had been invited by
a religious group of Canadian Indians, the Ontarios. Through the "lost
tribe" theory my father felt the pilgrimage would lead to an exchange
and comparison of rituals.

Even though great distances separated our homelands, our dia-
lects were strikingly similar with this particular Northern tribe. Further, the secret societies of the tribes believed in the same mystical

bird, whose transparent and outstretched wings covered the landscape with the color of an amber sunset.

The two-day ride in a dark blue 1949 Mercury Club Coupe to Horned Serpent Lake would have been an incredible waste of a ten-year-old boy's time were it not for the Red Swan stick-shooting ceremony. In the first fiery light of dawn, we watched the all-night dancers emerge from the longhouse, to later dance and then fall to the tall prairie grass in convulsions and paralysis after "being struck" by obsidian bullets that came from sticks.

It was fascinating and scary at the same time. But before all that stuff happened, we got lost in the most isolated area of the lake, *real* Indian country. For miles there were no gas stations, nor were homes visible anywhere. Adding to the confusion were the roads. A single gravel road would split apart in three directions. With only a tattered handwritten map and a Mercury Coupe choking on mossy lake water, we were headed for disaster. Suddenly, at the last desperate moment when we were ready to turn around, the glass reflection of a rusted truck signaled us. Father and William then walked to the fence-enclosed pasture and siphoned the precious remaining fluid from the truck's undamaged radiator. Grandmother used to say our lives were probably saved that day by kind spirits who were busy watching us from behind a steering wheel of a ghost truck.


We were welcomed to Canada by an old medicine man, *ne a bi a*, by the name of Jack Frost who offered us a supper of sweet potatoes, wild rice, biscuits, and warm tea before heading out to the longhouse. Before my father explained we had had radiator problems in addition to being lost, old man Frost began making witty analogies to his own internal ailments and the Mercury's mechanical problems.

"Maybe Mercury and me sick same time?" he half-chuckled in English.

Touching and gently massaging the wool shirt over his chest, old man Frost saw himself as an overheated Mercury Coupe. I am sure I didn't understand as much of the Ontario language as the adults, but I listened closely.

He had awoken that morning with unusual chest pains. The dried blisters of his palms caught the shirt, making rasping noises before he inquired in a toothless wily smile: "When radiator get hot? Maybe same time I put medicine in tea?" Making motions as if he was turning the steering wheel of a car, he added, "Me. Car. The same."

He said our troubles must have gone away as soon as he drank the medicinal tea. "Same time you give coolant, right?"

Through the laughter induced by the Mercury Coupe medicine man, we calmed down and the fatigue went away. That was the point. To humor us and throw us off track from his prescience. (But years later my father and William really didn't know how long we had driven without coolant. Maybe most of the morning, as soon as we got off the main highway? they would question over the supper table. They conceded it had to have been a long while. Clotelde, my mother, with her daughters—my sisters Sherilyn and Toni—clinging to her skirt, had the question that made them ask no more: How did Jack Frost know what was wrong with the car? Grandmother later indicated there may have been a real connection, a godlike affinity, between the old man's chest pains and the bothersome radiator.)

By nightfall we were parked with several other cars beside a bark longhouse located in the grassy center of a large but narrow meadow. For all that was expected to take place, I was upset no one had bothered to clear the area of shrubbery and tall prairie grass. Back home, with whites for close neighbors and because of frequent trips into their community, we tended to our lawns with diligence. The tall grass swayed in the breeze and against the car. Before the car doors were opened, we were scolded. "If one sat down here in the grass, a driver would not see you and would run you over. Stay close, it's dark."

Taking their hand drums from the trunk, William and my father strolled gingerly across the meadow and stepped inside the longhouse. Immediately after the blanket-door was sealed, the raspy-throated voice of old man Frost rose and then wavered slightly before creating a roller coaster–like effect with the convocation, the calling of the guardians of the doorways from the four cardinal points.

There was a certain rhythm to his words; it was as if there were short, individual parts of music interspersed throughout the prayer. The drumming and the singing didn't quit until the next morning. The last thing I remember of the cool evening was the fiery orange thunderhead forming over a distant shore. I marveled at its electrical display. Bolts of lightning shot up to the sky and arced back down into the reddish, sunset-reflecting clouds.

Before closing my weary eyes I wondered if the thunderheads were capable of injuring themselves. Among the deities I envisioned an immature deity, someone unlearned like myself, stealing into the nearby patch of dry brush with a box of wooden matches. "Johnny Angel" sets the hillside on fire, and the pot of water brought to extinguish the flames has a hole in it. Adults from the neighborhood fight the fire for hours. . . .

When the thunder's rumbling could not be differentiated from the drumming or the wave swells crashing onto the rocky shore, my body muscles twitched. There was still a lingering taste of sweet potatoes and tea in my mouth. And the Mercury that had been the source of so much worry hissed to itself. Somewhere inside its gears I thought I heard the steady tapping of metal against metal, a mechanic among the little people.

At daybreak, a gentle tapping on my shoulder woke me up. It was Grandmother whispering in excitement.

"*Ki sko, ki sko! Ba se kwi no! I ni ke-e ka ta wi-no we ka wa tti-na ka ni-te be ki-ni mi tti ki!* Kis ko, kis ko! Get up! It is almost time for the people who have danced all night to come out—in dance!"

Looking out through the fogged-up window, I could see it was a dark, blustery morning with a drizzly mist in the cold wind. It looked like the dramatic end of an autumn day, the evening before the first snow flurries. Except for the occasional clattering of tree branches, the hypnotic singing that had lulled us to sleep had apparently stopped. I looked toward the longhouse and saw only spirals of blue smoke dissipating in the loud, rushing wind over the pine-encircled meadow. A cool and harsh season had been regenerated throughout the woodland expanse by this Red Swan gathering.

The only signs of activity were young people bundled up tightly in dull gray and green blankets, walking from their cars to the outhouses. Others seemed to arrive from the opposite direction and appeared as if they hadn't slept. They held their cigarettes loosely over their red lips and bid each other good-bye.

Among them I noticed a teenage girl who could have been an older identical twin of a Black Eagle Child girl back home. Although this one was dark-complexioned, she was very attractive. She must have been very popular, if one judged by the number of friends who strolled alongside, chatting and giggling.

"*Wa ba mi-Ko ko-me to tti-ma na-e skwe se a-Dolores Fox King.* Look, Grandmother, this girl looks like Dolores Fox King," I said.

"*Ka tti-be ki-ko me ko-me to tti.* Why, this seems to be right," answered Grandmother, who kept trying to roll down the window to get a better look. We listened to their lively garbled talk and watched the group disappear into taller grass.

With the cold wind biting through our blankets, Grandmother began straightening herself by combing her long white hair. Together, we spotted Clotelde, my mother, her daughter, emerge from the cookshack with a small, steaming cardboard box. Around us, packs of people had converged quietly with chairs, cameras, and blankets to await the dance exit and the "stick-shooting."

"*To ki-ke si me e mo. Ni wa ba me wa-ma a i-me to se ne ni wa.* Wake up your little brother. Let him look at these people."

From one nudge Alan was awake. Clotelde, who had been invited earlier to help cook, brought over boiled eggs, cinnamon rolls, and hot tea. As we huddled in our seats with breakfast balanced between our legs, a single wailing voice lifted into the cloudy sky. It was followed by the loud simultaneous cry of the participants inside the longhouse, whose blanket door had been untied and removed. A young man emerged with a shovel that was smoking.

"*I ni ke-me kwe-e ke tti wa tti. Na a wi-se ki tti i a ta ki.* I think this is the moment they come out. Now let us go outside."

We took our food and drink to the car hood and finished peeling the hot eggs. Alan shivered and rolled himself into a blanket ball with only his mouth and eyes showing. I sat next to him with my back resting on the windshield.

Above, breakaway pieces of clouds shot toward the east, following different flocks of birds. Strange ones like seagulls, birds we rarely saw back home.


The first person to come out from the longhouse was a young, lanky-built man they called "Bragi." He had the responsibility of purifying the dance area. Wearing faded blue jeans, partially beaded moccasins with fur lining, and a tan and maroon high school sports coat, Bragi paced near the entrance, waiting for instructions. In his arms he held a short snow shovel, containing flickering red-hot embers and a clump of cedar twigs. Fanned by the capricious wind, the blue smoke whipped and almost caught fire. Bragi dropped to his knees and physically muffled the flames with his gloved hands. Upon instructions being given from inside, he stood up and nodded, then began to make the four oblong circles around the longhouse, being extra sure the smoke was controlled and steady.

Grandmother described what had happened while we were soundly asleep.

"Before sunup, a young man was appointed to walk up to the longhouse fire, kneel down before it, and scoop out the heart of the all-night fire with a shovel. He then dances with this twelve times around the longhouse, and at every third passing he stokes the fire, replacing the coals and the cedar. If he is overwhelmed by searing heat, the whole affair is weakened. For him there will be lengthy ridicule, and his mentors' judgment will be questioned."

From top to bottom—a feat that acquired agility and upper torso strength—the lanky attendant carefully traced the outline of the entrance with the extended shovel. Through his facial grimaces it was obvious he was having a hard time writing with the monster pencil that gagged the delicate lungs with the billowing plumage of the Red Swan's wings.

Then, from inside, a new set of instructions was shouted out. A song was sung without the aid of a drum or rattle. With a whimsical shrug of his hunched shoulders, the attendant began to mimic a dance. He was embarrassed as he turned and faced the crowd but he continued dancing. In certain places in the drumless song, he cradled and pointed the shovel like a loaded rifle to the audience, to the cars and to the four directions, before he began trotting lightly around the longhouse clockwise, making a large, growing circle that wove through the women cooks, the spectators, and their vehicles.

As his circles got wider on the third or fourth round, he eventually ran beside our open car window, waving the monstrous smoke-writing pencil in a particular way to its imaginary occupants. By ignoring us, we were being acknowledged and blessed. Blessings for the outsiders, in other words, and their transportation. Blessings to their radiator.

Blessings, I added, for wherever in hell we had come to.

With the wind blowing just right, the cedar smoke wafted directly into the front grille of the Mercury Coupe, where it was dearly needed. Bragi's shovel drew the right messages. Old man Frost wouldn't have to rescue us again. He would keep his twinkling eye from becoming the sun's reflection on the rusted truck's window.

The sweet cedar aroma blew into the car and followed the smooth contour of the gray padded interior. It swirled once inside, peppering us with graceful touches, and then went on through. Something odd occurred when I inhaled the cedar: I was instantly reminded of the childhood sickness I once had. The cedar, I had always thought, cured me. But there were instances when its penetrating aroma conjured frightful mental images of a green Spanish galleon.

From the way Bragi was bent over from the weight of the shovel and with beads of perspiration streaming down his brow, I sensed the shovel was getting heavier. Heavy messages came with heavy responsibility. As Bragi, the attendant, took a pause, I associated his glistening sweat with the cool water that was squeezed out from the washrags and onto my small-boned, fever-ravaged body. I could see the neighborhood women still standing protectively around my bed, listening to my erratic congested breathing. I was disoriented, and hallucinations were born about the fish-headed demon in a suit.

Coming back to consciousness I saw how imperative it was for Bragi to direct the purifying smoke to everyone. Whether the cedar originated from a toy shovel or a large snow scoop, I was confident it would cleanse whoever was in its presence. In my childhood it changed into a hurricane of regurgitation and reversed the direction of the Spanish galleon. For Bragi, the task at hand was to convince Jack Frost that the area was safe. Once that was accomplished, the exit from the longhouse began. Next would come the critical part, the "shooting" ceremony.

In the quiet that followed the singing and dancing, Bragi stood erect and breathed deeply with limp arms. His apparel, especially the large 11 on his sports coat, seemed incongruous. Like the tall unkempt grass, it didn't seem appropriate for so serious an occasion.

Clothes aside, he was much too young. My thoughts were confirmed when he laid the shovel down and took out a silver comb from his back pocket to groom his slick hair, reminding me of the "Kookie, Kookie (Lend Me Your Comb)" song.

Several minutes went by before the dancers came out one by one with squinting eyes. Some attempted in vain to shield their eyes from the cloudless gray sky. Others were prepared. They reached into their shirt pockets or purses for their sunglasses. Some women donned scarves and tied them tight, while others nervously lit up and puffed on cigarettes. The older men wore faded flannel shirts and loose overalls, which still held the bulging imprints of their knees from sitting all night, while their women companions wore dark print dresses with minimally sequined shawls wrapped around their waists. The dancers were all doing something as they were filing out, tying their belts or checking their watches. Next, they cautiously followed one another around the longhouse until the beginning and end of the dance circle met, where old man Frost stood behind the young attendant, Bragi.

Of all the dancers, old man Frost, our host, was the most impressive. It was expected. On his feet were a white pair of Sioux-style moccasins; a striped woolen blanket was wrapped below his waist and over his legs; and crisscrossed across his red silk shirt were twin beaded bandolier bags in swirling floral designs.

Tucked safely under the left arms of all the dancers—"near the heart," as Grandmother explained—were four arm-length sections of freshly peeled branches. Everyone had these, held in different ways. The older ones had theirs decorated minimally with new yarn, leather, and eagle plumes. After a short prayer was rendered by Bragi, these peeled sticks were transferred to both hands and then rotated simultaneously. The sound made was like the first gentle drops of rain on a corrugated tin roof. With rhythmic precision the white rattling sticks were swung from side to side, horizontally, like firearms.

"The sticks, they're looking for someone to test their acquired medicinal powers on," whispered Grandmother in anticipation, with bits of egg yolk on her lips. I absorbed her words and observed intensely, but I failed to see how the rifle and ammunition analogy fit with the sticks.

"No one is excluded. Everyone, sooner or later, is bound to be shot. Just the slightest touch of the sticks on the shoulders—of whoever is dancing in front of the shooter—will cause disabling or paralysis. However, if the quarry isn't knocked to the side and their place taken in the dance line, the power of the attempted shooting itself is absorbed or is transferred to the dance leader, old man Frost. The more misshootings, the stronger the dance leader. It will continue until it is voluntarily stopped or until the leader is disabled somehow."

When she said that, I remembered the lightning I had seen the night previous, blazing toward the stars, to the ground, or to the side, and then back into itself. Bundled into a blanket, I watched a thundercloud as it quietly flashed. No one else was looking at it for miles. When the rumbling of the thunderstorm grew into the automobile's metal body, I wondered if electrical force could hurt itself or feel pain. I compared the Red Swan carriers in the longhouse before me to the thundercloud above. If electrical force grew as a result of others' losses, I adduced, then pain had to be involved. I was suddenly fearful for my father and his half brother. Like the cottonwoods on Cottonwood Hill back home, they were aligned to be struck by lightning. As I looked with a careful eye at the dancers who stood in pairs, the motion of Zippo lighters, Dutch bandanas, and black shawls took on a strange, disheartening appearance. At first glance I thought these Ontarios were no different from us. We shared the same materialistically sparse life. In knowing we came from this background of having less, I could hardly maintain the suspense created by the fact that the stick-shooting ceremony was a rarity.

As old man Frost walked bowlegged over the trampled grass, shouting out instructions to the fidgety dancers, the tin cones that graced the tips of his breechcloth jingled before he let out a loud war whoop. The drumming and singing by the longhouse musicians within the four walls picked up and the dancing commenced.

"On the fourth round," said Grandmother, "the shooting will start." And on the fourth evolution there were indeed about a dozen people who fell inexplicably from the dancing circle after they had been touched on their shoulders with the peeled sticks. Their respective places were quickly taken over by "strong-medicined" dancers whose victorious cries and spurts of wild dance filled the smoky air.

I couldn't get over what I had witnessed: Before Bragi even had a chance to consider "shooting," old man Frost, crouched in dance behind the doorway, shot him from behind where his heart, *o te i,* is located, and caused him to fall sideways, falling face-first into the moist, freshly trampled grass. There was a loud gasp from the audience as the sports coat–clad body hit the ground like petrified timber.

"They will wait one round before trying to shoot someone else again. Look, the dancers will rotate their sticks and take aim before lunging to someone's vulnerable shoulders. Over there on the side are the ones who deflected shots."

With all attention on Bragi, I didn't see the six to eight other dancers who stood outside of the circle in a half-bent position. They stood by themselves, "trying to shake off the effect of the medicine-bullets." On the ground the young and "weak-medicined" middle-aged people were scattered, some going into violent convulsions.

As the dance intensified in song and drumbeat, other dancers shot each other. Those shot broke from the circle, staggered like drunks, and then dropped to their knees, trying to recuperate. Behind each victim would be a retreating stick-shooter who was blowing short breaths of air to the base and tip of the four rattling sticks. These were the older "strong-medicined" ones, who simply slumped over for a few seconds when they were shot, and promptly got back in line.

At the conclusion of the chaotic free-for-all, my father and William were surprisingly among the six remaining dancers. I couldn't believe they had made it through. I had seen them earlier, but lost sight of them. It was as if they had disappeared into the spaces between the dancers, eluding the older and more powerful stick-shooters.

Downed dancers were spread out over the shiny grass near the cars. Concerned relatives and friends walked out and revived them with a gentle shake, words, or cold water. There were a few, like Bragi, who had to be lifted up and supported until he fully regained his balance.

In extreme cases where the trance couldn't be broken, old man Frost was called upon. He would kneel down and gently brush their expressionless faces with his callused hand and talk to them in a normal manner. As they were slowly waking from their unconscious state, he would inspect their shoulders and act as if he was searching for an object lodged between the shirt or blouse and skin of the dancer. He would eventually remove shiny, black pieces of rock—obsidian—and place them in his twin bandolier bags.

"That is what they use: bullets," said Grandmother.


On the long drive back to the States, I found it hard to discount the ritual we had witnessed. For Alan, though, there was pleasure in sneaking up and jabbing my shoulders with dry, sharp twigs. I played the shooting game with him despite Grandmother's repeated objections, and I was fascinated by the prospect of shiny, black bullets—talons—that couldn't be seen, tumbling end over end in a flurry of sparks. At each roadside stop we reenacted the stick-shooting. The black talons flew from four rotating sticks and impaled themselves in the necks, shoulders, and spinal column of the Red Swan carriers.

William must have sensed my curiosity, for before we got back to the Settlement, he inquired if I harbored any intentions of becoming a member.

I must have nodded

Many years after the pilgrimage to Horned Serpent Lake, I found myself in an earthlodge at sundown, beating the hand drum with a loop-tipped drumstick. The Red Swan Society songs, we were told by William, had to be memorized and sung in the right manner. Furthermore, they could be learned only through frequent attendance of ceremonies. I knew then that no matter how much I beseeched the Holy Grandfather to guide me as He had done with my father and William, it wouldn't happen. At least not right away.

Because of this religious deficiency I sometimes wonder whether a stray obsidian bullet grazed my heart that morning in Canada at the "stick-shooting" ceremony. Instead of empowering me, the ricochet talon ripped me apart from responsibility.

When William Listener passed away six years ago, he took with him many songs and prayers of the Red Swans. A human-shaped presence consisting of hundreds of tiny lights evidently emerged from the intensive care unit and floated down the hallway of the Heijen Medical Center. These lights were said to be all the songs that only he knew, the total embodiment of religion leaving, for there was nothing around here for them anymore.

I knew this, and so what was I to do?

# A Softball Game That Was More than Epic

In the summer of 1969, on the playgrounds of Weeping Willow Elementary, I found myself engaged in a rather laborious game of softball with children and several teenagers who had congregated from the various neighborhoods. Comprised of an even mix of boys and girls from opposite parts of the Black Eagle Child Settlement, it soon became a competition between the "uphillers" and the "downhillers."

Although I was slightly older than most who were playing that afternoon, I was feeling energetic for a seventeen-year-old. By then I had barely struggled past eleventh grade at Why Cheer High School, and the only thing that mattered was the immediate present.

On this particular day, around two o'clock, I walked slowly up to home plate, swinging a crude homemade bat. Above, there wasn't a cloud to be seen and the blue sky had a certain limitless height. Thoughts of school were temporarily far away, and around younger-aged people I was feeling less inhibited about my batting and fielding skills. Meaning they weren't exceptional. Beginning from Weeping Willow's playgrounds and even inside its gymnasium, spherical objects that were either hit with a wooden club or bounced on a polished basketball court never struck me as being vital. The only complication was, since everyone else was playing these tiring, sweat-producing games, I had to take part and make like it was fun and meaningful. Otherwise, had I chosen to mope somewhere in a cor-

ner and act uninterested, they might have sent me to the mental institute in Independence, Iowa. So, to a point, I gave spherical objects
my best.

As I gripped the bat that was split and nailed together in several
places, I thought that it would be ecstasy not to dribble or bunt the
goddamned ball anymore. In fact, I was quite bemused by it all until
it dawned on me that I had one more year of physical education classes
at Why Cheer High School. Ever since mandatory group showers at
Weeping Willow, I loathed undressing in front of others and washing my body. I could tolerate sports activities, but when they always
concluded with nudity, it nearly pushed me over the line. In retrospect I know it had nothing to do with a fear of seeing penises or
subconsciously comparing the size of mine with those of other Indians or whites. No, nothing of the sort; being naked in a semipublic
setting was just unnatural.

Like the time I was about seven, standing stark naked in a metal
tub with my younger brother Alan. Even though we were in the cool
shade of a massive eight-parted maple tree, I was uncomfortable being
scrubbed with a washcloth and soap by a doting mother. No one was
around, but I still felt we could be observed from the gravel road by
people in cars or those walking. And that other time when I was
fording the Iowa River by the tribal fairgrounds with Grandmother
and the Water Runner cousins: I was told to strip my clothes and
carry them above my head. The three sisters, on the other hand,
merely folded up the bottom of their dresses to their upper thighs,
slipping them under the elastic of their underwear. There I was, slosh-
ing around in the swift current, nearly tripping from embarrassment,
and shivering with cold, retracted testicles and a profoundly embarrassed "Corn Mush." To this day I think Grandmother made me strip
for the benefit of her curious granddaughters. Maybe? Or was it for
my own safety, that I probably stood a better chance at survival minus
my apparel if I tripped due to my clumsiness?

Nakedness at night, Grandmother later taught, was the ultimate
defense against sorcery and unexplained phenomena. "When you
make your stand, chew the witch-counteracting medicines and spit-
spray yourself with it, covering your entire naked body. In particular
the arms and limbs, your heart and head. Walk right up to the entity

that has been sent and demand it show itself in person, making a strong verbal challenge. In its realm, due to your nakedness, you will also be invisible. . . ."


. . . Just when I looked up from home plate and realized who was pitching the softball, I had already unleashed a furious swing that sent the weather-hardened softball whistling toward a delicate young girl by the name of Selene Buffalo Husband. All the players gasped as the softball shot straight past her extended gloved hand and into her stomach with a loud skin slap.

Before, I hadn't really taken notice of her, that she had tied a large bowlike knot with her front shirttails, exposing and highlighting her belly button. She was wearing a light red shirt and blue jeans that were cut above the knees. I had been so intent on playing that her presence had failed to register. Which was odd because years before I had had a number of erotic dreams about her. But, on that particular day, the bare skin of her beautiful stomach was the sole contact point. The petrified softball hit her quite hard. She maintained her composure for a good ten seconds before slowly doubling over. As she held her stomach with a gloved hand and propping herself up on one knee with the other hand, her head dropped and her knees buckled.

That's when I remembered who she was.

She had long shiny brown hair whose tips had been lightened to a brownish red tinge by long hours in the summer sun. The color was identical to that time I first saw her on the warm sidewalk outside of the Why Cheer Theater after the afternoon matinee. Unlike most Settlement girls her age, she had strikingly photogenic qualities. She was even more visually pronounced in bright daylight. Yet, even in the darkness of the movie theater years before, as she struggled to gain her vision sitting beside me, I secretly espied the beauty in her future. There was nothing sinister or "Kensey" Muscatine impure about that, except in old dreams that only embarrass me. The biggest difference between the dreams "Kensey" and I had was that I never acted upon them. "Some children are simply born beautiful," Grandmother had said once at Horned Serpent Lake, Canada, "and they will grow into beautiful young adults." Selene Buffalo Husband, as it turned out for me, was one of them.

On that summer day, all of the softball players, myself included, ran up to her after the audible belly impact. What I almost did was turn around and flee. Even my companions, Ted Facepaint and Pat Red Hat, who had been watching from the hillside in a green Oldsmobile, began scolding me loudly for hitting her. I made absolutely sure I was the last one getting to the pitcher's mound. I remember thinking: What am I going to do if she's seriously hurt? Had that been me, I continued, taking it in the gut—what a strong girl she must indeed be—I'd be writhing in pain like a decapitated snake over the bluish gray pebbles. I stood back and waited anxiously for the right moment. Once her own brothers questioned her and ascertained she was alright, I gathered enough courage to walk right up to her and ask a stupid question. "Are you OK?"

"Of course not, *ke bi ti,* plugged-up asshole!" she said in a firm Black Eagle Child tone, straightening herself up as if that's all she needed to recuperate. "You hit the ball too hard."

"I know," I answered sheepishly, looking away as she brushed off the dust imprint of the softball over her stomach.

"Why did you have to hit the ball hard?"

"I don't know," I said with a sigh, feeling guilty and made uneasy all of a sudden by her assertiveness and reprimand. Finally, once everyone began to disperse, I looked into her exquisite light brown eyes and became transfixed immediately by her youthful luminosity. Of that I graciously partook and imagined to near reality how her actual presence in an assignation would overpower my senses with pangs of incurable physical desire.

She was photogenically immaculate.

And me? For the first three minutes out of the shower, I perceived myself as perhaps at my most handsome state. In those rare, fleeting moments, with hair slicked down by comb, along with a limp Fu Manchu–style mustache and facial skin that was shrunken down to the bone with icy water, I was clearly a fan of myself. After that, the face unthawed, revealing my worst. In terms of posture, my shoulders were drooped low and almost even with my chest. At five feet, eight inches, I fought hard to make my 158-pound body presentable.

In the midafternoon sun, Selene, the butterfly enchantress, was stunning, to say the least, for an eleven-year-old. The red shirt she wore seemed to reflect off her suntanned skin. Below her eyes was a fine sprinkling of freckles. She returned my gaze and smiled coyly before saying what she wanted to say all along and deservedly so.

"You're too old to be playing, anyway."

"You're right again," I said.

That was all it took to abruptly conclude what had otherwise been an enjoyable afternoon. We stood there, looking at each other while the bikes were jerked noisily from the dusty racks. The children who had accompanied their older siblings were being herded from the creaky playground rides toward the gravel road. In small clusters the uphillers went uphill, and likewise for the downhillers. Everyone would take up the whole road, knowing the Settlement automobile traffic was next to nil.

As I started to trudge toward my companions in the green Oldsmobile parked under the water tower on the hill, Selene, as a matter of coincidence, ended up walking in bouncy stride beside me. She had chosen to take another route home, a shortcut through the woods and the new residential area known as Candlestick Park. Her move puzzled me. I had just drilled a fossilized projectile into her gut, and now she was next to me. It caught me totally off guard.

"Where are you going?" I asked, turning my full gaze to her.

"Where I live, stupid," she answered with a faint smile.

"Shall I walk you home?" I asked. "Do you need someone to watch you?"

"Somebody to watch me? No. But you can walk me home."

"Really?"

"Yes. If you're not afraid."

"I better not. Your parents might beat me up."

"They wouldn't."

To this day, I don't know what made me ask to walk her home. The words came out without the slightest hesitation. We walked a good ways up the hill, making small talk and going past the water tower and the Oldsmobile before I stopped and bid her good-bye. She chided me for being afraid to stay with her past Candlestick Park. "Yo-ur neigh-bor-hood," she said with what seemed overemphasized lip movements. I liked it; she was arresting. Underneath it all, though, I was uncomfortable at the prospect that my "paper cocoon" fate would one day envelop her as well.

As Selene walked through the wooded pathway with several butterflies following her, however, I couldn't stop looking at her. Her shoulders were wide and her long-legged walk was as graceful as slow-motion film footage of an ocean wave. After she looked back at me once more, she ran her fingers through her long, light brown hair. I locked my eyes on her and imagined what she might look like in several years. "You have a fan forever, Selene," I whispered into the flower-scented wind that had just flown around her halfway up the pathway. Before reaching the open meadow of the housing complex where my family lived, Selene was spotlighted by the intermittent rays of the sun in the way the wing of a turning airborne eagle shines high above in bright daylight over the Black Eagle Child Settlement. . . .

When I got back to the green Oldsmobile with Pat Red Hat and Ted Facepaint, they looked at me with smirks on their faces, like I had committed a felonious crime. My bedazzlement over Selene Buffalo Husband probably showed on my face, until the odor of cigarettes and stale alcohol stains came to me.

"Come on, goddamnit! She's just a little girl, a friend!" I protested, knowing that was all it took to exacerbate the situation.

"Well, well, Jesus! You've . . . you've talked about her long . . . long enough," said Ted, nearly snorting.

"How many years now? Two or three?" joined Pat.

They were right. In drunken binges I loosened up to the point where I had mentioned how precocious her beauty was. Rare was the moment I professed my admiration for anyone. Which was why my friends thought they were on to something, comparing me to the likes of "Kensey." They were wrong, though.

"Your 'little girlfriend,' what'd she say?" asked Pat through a pair of thick, Roy Orbison–type sunglasses. Since the spaceship encounter at Liquid Lake, he wore them also at night. Sometimes they became so grungy, we took them off out of compassion and cleaned them when he passed out. Ted and I sometimes thought Pat detested soap from his "mouth-washing" days. When I reached through the car window for a can of Schlitz beer, I could see myself still as a reflection in his sunglasses. Pat began pounding his massive clenched fist on the steering wheel, demanding to know what exchange took place. It was all an act, of course, but the effects were dramatic. I could hear the vibrations from the hits all the way from the steering column to the rear axle. "Come on, you fuckhead, tell us!" he cried.

"She didn't say much," I said, hoping that would be the end of it. But it wasn't. They sat still and then began chuckling in an *oh-she-didn't-say-much* mockery.

"Bo . . . bo-shit," said Ted from the front passenger's seat. "We saw you. R-r-really looking at her . . . her stomach. You didn't care about her injury, man."

"Hey, I was scared when the softball hit her. Alright? She took it real good, you know."

Pat turned the steering wheel and released it, smearing the green grass onto the front bald tires. He looked at me through the sunglasses and began talking. "Yeah, but when she saw you coming, she got better, it seemed like. Real quick like."

"Yeah, yeah. And . . . and you guys seemed to forget about who else was there," contributed Ted. "No-o-obody else in the who-o-ole wo-o-rld kinda thing."

After that, there wasn't much I could do to keep from cracking up at Ted's observations. I got into the backseat of the Olds, closed my tired eyes, and held my breath in preparation for a drink.

We were still there well after sundown. In multitudes the crickets sang to us, as did the mosquitoes when they were not bloating themselves with our blood. Their small whines signaled their victory. They ascended to the skies, Grandmother had said, to have a ceremonial feast.

We were bloated, too, with Schlitz and Leinenkugel's beer. The cooler, including the car's trunk, was full of beer we had stolen the night previous in downtown Why Cheer. At closing time we walked into the Spur Stadium, a redneck tavern, and staged a fight. While Pat was twirling a pool stick like a martial arts expert and running after Ted, I strolled to the mammoth refrigerator and began taking cases of beer out to the Olds. The local rednecks and wanna-be motorcycle gang from the skidrow "Perk-o-Dan" (Percodan), Zhevschtick ("Shitstick"), and Mirven families didn't interfere with the fight as long as it was an Indian-on-Indian assault. The manager called the police but the police didn't care either. In fact, they requested a blow-by-blow account over the telephone of the "fat poolstick-wielding Indian" versus "running skinny Indian" escapade. That's how we got most of our booze. Either that or direct break-ins.

Pat, who was a state champion heavyweight wrestler, was a good performer. He knew about angles and how crunching body sounds could be made by simply stomping the floor while the punches or kicks were being delivered. First influenced by professional wrestling programs from Chicago that he watched on television at the Settlement's Barber Shop and Pool Hall, Pat wasn't anyone to mess around with.

I once sparred with his behemoth grandfather, Mr. Dugan Red Hat, who was a retired professional wrestler and bare-knuckle fighter. Clayton Carlson Facepaint, a Black Eagle Child war hero, was a skilled deliverer of knockout blows and finger pinches; Mr. Red Hat was noted for touring twenty years with the Greater American Midwest All Star Wrestling Confederacy. Everyone knew about his travels overseas to the country "down under," as he'd say: Australia. Not many, it was reported, remained standing in the ring. People gambled at the bare-knuckle fisticuffs he hosted and participated in as an undefeated champ.

When Mr. Red Hat challenged me to "a gentlemen's match," all I was doing that day was retrieving two buckets of water from the pump in old man Jim Percy's yard. Inside the bare circle of tan dust where a Star-Medicine ceremony had taken place the night previous, I tightened the shoe laces on the ragged boxing gloves with my teeth and looked across the makeshift ring constructed of twigs and baling twine. I remembered seeing Mr. Red Hat. For two days, unlike the other people who had come and gone in the cars or on foot, he was restless. Which was strange because he was also the first and last person there. The legendary grappler didn't stay for the actual mushroom ingestion ceremonies themselves, but he was there whenever food was being served. Three times on schedule.

High atop this hill, next to Jim Percy's two-story house, the doings were held inside the canvas tipi. Beginning at the tail end of sundown on a Saturday, when the lone drum first echoed over the valley, Mr. Red Hat was sliding down the steep path to the gravel road. From behind the mailbox post he pulled out a brown paper bag. After looking around he took a drink from the bag and disappeared around the bend of Wolf Alley, a notorious hangout for local winos and disenchanted beings.

Following the opening drum roll, the long, drawn-out singing of a single man descended from the night. From then on, there was drumming and music. Different voices singing different songs. From the bedroom window of Grandmother's house, we could see the orange triangle of the tipi on the hilltop flickering with sparks as the campfire was stoked. The next day, on a Sunday, everyone filed out of the tipi, spoke, and chatted until the morning food of meats, sweets, frybread, coffee, and Kool-Aid was served. By midafternoon, after the noon meal, most of the cars and their passengers had left. Except Mr. Red Hat. He and old man Jim sat on the wooden bench in the shade, drinking coffee. At seven o'clock the next morning, as I went after buckets of pumpwater, they were still sitting there. They didn't say much. Maybe this was why Mr. Red Hat brought the boxing gloves out that first time, to cure the utter silence.

"And in this cor-r-r-ner, ladies and gentlemen, we have Ed-d-d-gar Pr-r-r-i-in-ci-pal Bear!" he yelled out with giant cupped hands to old man Jim and the others as we walked over to the smooth earthen ground where the tipi had stood. "Representing the Black Eagle Child American Legion Hall Boxing Club out of Why Cheer, Iowa. Zero fight history. Let's give Prince Bear a round-o-plause!"

Mr. Red Hat's command of the English language was superb. His voice sounded like a radio. After he announced himself, we squared off. At first, before we stepped on the ground sculptures within the tipi circle, we skipped or jumped over them. But when the contest got heated, the four small ash mounds got scattered. I had always looked upon the configuration as a spectacular toy, and I always left it untouched. Encircling the mounds were a series of rect-angular imprints of sacred mats.

Initially, I didn't understand why I had agreed to fight an aged adult who looked like a majestic Northern Plains chief. All that was missing was his long, trailing war bonnet. Yet I ended up taking his challenge seriously, whereas Mr. Red Hat was mildly inebriated and having "a jolly good time." He had a Buster Crabbe–like hairdo that reminded me of a wood duck's head; it was cropped close to the skin along the front and behind the ears. At the grassy sides of the tipi circle, our audience barked, whined, and scratched the ground. From the large, flat wooden bench, old man Jim and the left-behinds chuck-led. We had our gloves raised high and both of us were consistently jabbing from afar and missing. We shuffled over what Mr. Red Hat said were the "Three-Stars-in-a-Row" and the "Star That Is a God." "Ain't that right, Jim?" he'd yell while looking toward the shade of the apple tree.

"*E a i,* yes!" old man Jim would confirm. "*Na a wi, mi ka ti ko!* Now fight!"

Curiosity awakened, I looked down at the elaborate ground sculptures only to be a target for a good wide-fisted uppercut. Since the gloves were tattered and soft, my head turned upward. I found myself staring at the blue sky while falling backward in short, choppy heel steps before hitting the powdered dust.

"Stay down, son," Mr. Red Hat advised as he began a panting eight count. But I was determined to stick it out and stood up. The fight proceeded. When we accidentally landed blows to one another we were surprised.

That was my rude introduction to the legacy of the punching and grappling Red Hat family. Every other Monday morning for two summers while retrieving the cool pumpwater for Grandmother I would be challenged by Pat's grandfather. . . .


Upon learning of the Spur Stadium caper and the cache that we absconded with, we were soon joined by a bevy of thirsty friends. Pat and Ted reenacted the staged fight over the moonlit hillside and got good laughs out of it. Buzzing into the summer moonlit night, I was warm-faced. Selene Buffalo Husband enveloped me with heart-stirring thoughts. Nothing was as important as Selene in the "who-o-ole wo-o-rld," as Ted had concisely put it.

"You know, Ted," I later said, "I wouldn't be surprised if I went out with Selene one of these nights. Somewhere years down the line. Holy, she impresses me!"

"That's what I thought," he said. "Once you've told yourself that it will happen, then what you wish will transpire."

"Transpire? Where'd you get that stuff, man? Anyway, Selene surprised the hell out of me. Especially when she teased me for being afraid to walk her through the neighborhood."

"What harm could have come from it?"

"None, I guess. Maybe I was afraid of my intentions being misconstrued."

"Hey, where did you get that word, Ed? Mis-screwed? I don't get it."

"It's misconstrued. Meaning somebody might have thought I was up to no good. A wrong interpretation. 'Corn Mush' himself aiming for the moon business."

"In broad daylight? What could happen? Bo-o-o-shi-i-it!"

"Good point," I said. Maybe I should have accompanied her, I thought, at least through the housing complex. Hell, she would have teased me even more for being afraid to be seen with her in front of my parents' house. Or hers, I went on thinking.

Selene Buffalo Husband, in those few minutes, uncovered forever my frailties. Her biting comments, along with her youthful radiance, would stick with me for years to come like a long hard drive up center field. In my mind a dozen times over I beheld her presence and easily relived those moments we shared. I could will the thousand multicolored dots that floated and clustered behind my closed eyes to assemble, making that day at Weeping Willow repeat itself. . . .


That night when the ice melted in the cooler and the booze got warm, I ditched plans on getting "mizzed," miserably drunk. It had been a hangoverish but exciting afternoon to begin with, and there wasn't anything left of the weekend. Like a huge bowling ball, the highlights had rumbled through the checkered Mirolike alley of my totality, exiting with a deafening crash. The mock fight downtown and seeing Selene Buffalo Husband face-to-face was all that could possibly happen.

That was the thought going in.

From the dashboard-lit interior of the Oldsmobile, the reception on the radio was astounding. I really wasn't paying attention to what Pat and Ted were discussing. It didn't matter; I was emotionally numb. The DJ from Little Rock, Arkansas, introduced the band called Smith, reminding me of Luciano Bearchild's girlfriend, Angela Holiday, singing like that at the Lonesomest Valley.

*It's not the way you smile that touched my heart*
*It's not the way you kiss that tears me apart.*

I recalled the day's uneventful but typical start.

There was a miz-warmth over my face when I plopped my body to bed. It was three o'clock in the morning, two hours before my parents awoke to get ready for the Brown-Spotted and Black-Bobtailed Bear clan ceremonies. By sunrise my parents, Tony and Clotelde, had put in their false teeth, showered, and eaten a hefty breakfast of fried side pork, eggs, steamed frybread, and coffee. I woke up briefly when they began chatting and then arguing about the previous day's events. Their bickering signified that the day-long activity of prayer, song, and ritual was stressful. When the argument escalated I tugged the covers over my head.

Waking up shortly past noon, I went outside and discovered the weather was splendid. The warm breeze swept through the nearby pine trees of Candlestick Park, and the leaves of the tall corn rustled in my parents' well-kept garden. On the roof of the cookshack three Siamese cats were sunning themselves; in the shade of the light blue house a group of mongrel dogs greeted me by closing and opening their eyes in contentment. I knelt over the water faucet and drenched the top of my neck with cool, scintillating water. Tony, Clotelde, Alan, Dan, and the girls had all gone their ways. It was a feast day, the first earthlodge observance for the harvested crops and the imminent arrival of autumn. . . .

\*    \*    \*

At the precise moment when I was overcome by guilt for not being with them, the Oldsmobile took a hit: a volley of walnuts rattled the roof. We all got out and looked up into the trees. We were somewhat frightened until a group of boys began to chuckle. Perched above us as dark, hunched figures, they resembled vultures on a snowy day at rest.

"What the hell do you punks want?" demanded Pat angrily. He slammed the car door hard, rocking the entire frame.

"We want to tell you guys something," said one of them, as he slid down hurriedly over the rough bark. In a dark T-shirt, ragged blue jeans, and tennis shoes, with long, scraggly hair tied into a ponytail, the short boy with a jutting jaw stepped forward. "My name is Little Big Man," he said.

"I'm a big man, period," answered Pat, "and what are you going to do about that?"

The boy trotted to the incline and pointed down toward the front of Weeping Willow Elementary. "Down there—"

"This better be good, you little green pea shitball!"

"Hey, cool it . . . okay? We saw some guys lip-locking."

"With some girls?"

"Not even, Steven," said Little Big Man. "They're weirdos."

"Ah, c'mon!" shouted Pat.

Little Big Man followed us to the car and persisted until he convinced us to have a look-see. We crouched low within the tree shadows, skirting the center-stage action. From behind a row of bushes that lined the front of the school we spied on two unidentified males engaged in a rigorous clasp of arms and legs, with a third male standing close by, panting.

"Dragonflies," whispered Pat, "mating with their mouths."

"You guys want a disgusting picture of this?" asked Little Big Man in an imperious tone.

"Sure, why not?" answered Pat, nudging us.

"That'll cost you money, mister!"

"How much?"

"A twelve-pack of Leinenkugel's long necks and a pack of cigs."

"The cigs okay; the booze is gone."

With that, Little Big Man, who named himself after a novel

excerpt in *Playboy* magazine, dashed swiftly across the driveway of Weeping Willow. Next, he got on his stomach and crawled across the lawn. We waited and watched. The photograph was timed perfectly. In the camera's skyrocket flash, the mascara outlines of three heterosexual fireflies—Horatio, "Grubby," and "Kensey"— were immortalized.

# The First Dimension
# of Skunk

*It is the middle of October*
*and frosted leaves*
*continue to introduce*
*their descent as season*
*and self-commentary.*
*On the ground yellow-jacket*
*bees burrow themselves*
*into the windfall apples.*
*On the house the empty body shells*
*of locusts begin to rattle with*
*the plastic window covering*
*torn loose the night previous*
*in the first sudden gusts of wind.*
*South of the highway bridge*
*two extinct otters are seen*
*by Selene's father while*
*setting traps.*
*"Mates swimming;*
*streamlined and playing*
*games along the Iowa River."*
*In the midst of change*
*all it takes is one anachronism,*
*one otter whistle.*

For us, it began with the healthy-
looking salamander who stopped our car.
So last night we stood in the cold
moonlight waiting for the black
coyote. No animal darted
from tree to tree, encircling us.
There was a time in an orange grove
next to the San Gabriel Mountains
when I was surrounded by nervous
coyotes who were aware
of the differences
between thunder
and an earth tremor.
Selene motioned for me to stand
still, and the moonlit foothills
of Claremont disappeared.
An owl began to laugh.
I remained quiet and obliged
her gesture not to mimic its laugh,
for fear we might accidently trigger
the supernatural deity it possesses
to break this barrier—
and once again find ourselves
observing a ball of fire
rise from an abandoned garden
which separates into four fireflies
who appear like four distant jets
coming into formation
momentarily
before changing into one intense
strobe light,
pulsating inside an apple tree,
impervious to hollow-point bullets,
admissions of poverty and car lights.

We stood without response
and other disconnected thoughts came.
From the overwhelming sound

*of vehicles and farm machinery,*
*together with the putrid odor*
*of a beef slaughterhouse,*
*such anticipation*
*seemed inappropriate.*
*Whoever constructed*
*the two railroad tracks*
*and highways through Indian land*
*must have planned and known*
*that we would be reminded daily*
*of what is certainty.*
*In my dream the metal*
*bridge plays an essential part*
*and subsequent end of what*
*was intended to occur.*
*I would speak to the heavy*
*glass jar, telling it*
*the paper bullet*
*was useless underwater.*

*Three days ago, in the teeth*
*of Curly and Girl, a skunk*
*was held firmly and shook*
*until lifeless.*
*The first evening*
*we hear its final death call.*
*At the same hour the second night*
*we hear it again. The third night-*
*sound is more brave and deliberate;*
*it waits to blend with the horn*
*of an oncoming Northwestern train,*
*forcing us to step backward,*
*taking random shots at objects*
*crashing through the brush.*

*We have a theory that Destiny*
*was intercepted, that the Executioner*
*ran elsewhere for appeasement.*

*We also think the skunk's*
*companion returned on these nights*
*to mourn a loved one,*
*but all had to be deleted,*
*leaving us more confused.*
*Yesterday, we examined the dead*
*skunk and were surprised to find it*
*three times less the size I first*
*saw it with Mr. D.*
*My parents offered an explanation.*
*"A parrot or a pelican on their*
*migratory route."*
*With our surroundings*
*at someone else's disposal,*
*all we have are the embers*
*and sparks from our woodstove*
*and chimney: the fragrance*
*to thwart the supernatural.*

From *The Invisible Musician* by Ray A. Young Bear, Holy Cow! Press.

# The Incorporeal Hand

The loss of William Listener in 1980 wasn't fully felt until the Red
Swan successors took over as the main communicators in the first
spring following his untimely passing. Among the leaders was my
father, Tony Bearchild. Their overreliance on William endangered
ceremonial-related memory, faith, and tenacity. Those hypothetical
situations William once offered in his sermons about our fate as an
Earthlodge clan were now real.

In the smoky din of the earthlodge, he would bemoan how we
had fallen short of spiritual obligation by not abiding by the Well-
Known Twin Brother's teachings. As with everything, there was blame
to be placed. Himself excluded.

"They cannot even converge as a group; they have lost everything to time and disregard. Now, is that what we want? Our personal downfall will result through our own ignorance and the reckless
actions of thoughtless others if we permit it."

The next day my father, Tony, would pick up the topic. "The
responsibilities are incredibly difficult. Sometimes it is a challenge
to do as he has done. He certainly instructs us well, utilizing a vast
array of approaches, but one regrets not recording on audiotape the
many songs and prayers he knows, songs that have been with us since
the Beginning. . . ."

*    *    *

The Red Swan songs that once flowed out of William's exceptional repertoire like a clear, fast-running creek were no more, "a living songbook" closed. What my father and the other successors were able to remember was quickly transferred by pen to paper. Unfortunately, the tribal notation of music was insufficient; yet much of what couldn't be conveyed thus—the pauses in voice, rattle, and drum— was documented through singing rehearsals.

Although William was convinced during his later years of the advantages of an audiotape recording machine, especially with hard-to-learn-and-memorize songs, no one had the courage to propose a record-ing session. For the longest time he hadn't permitted it. Asking a spiritual leader to relinquish in one sitting the elaborate sacredness of a series of god-given songs acquired and amassed since childhood from his father and grandfather was contrary to the precept of "learning through diligent attendance." The presence of God that was sought and achieved within the smoky earthlodge could not be present in a Sony or Panasonic tape recorder. It was a contradiction to communi-cate the greatest message onto a thin strip of plastic. It wasn't a last resort. He felt the religious continuity he had vigorously espoused was far from being lost.

It was my father, though, who brought up on occasion the igno-rance that was imbibed through modernity itself. Hence, disenchant-ment with tribal ceremonies and ways. Knowledgeable in another people's language, William was no doubt receptive to social change, but he was also of the opinion that indulging in the Outside World's offerings, be they education, alcoholism, drugs, or whatever, offered only short-lived pleasure. Once the infatuation ceased, we would understand that the only way to prepare for the Black Eagle Child Afterlife was through the Principal Religion.

It was during the final year of my "infatuation" with academia that Selene Buffalo Husband and I came home one November day and learned that William had become comatose after a long bout with a cancerous illness.

We accompanied my parents and Grandmother when they went

to his bedside at the Heijen Medical Center in Sherifftown. By the deep, peaceful expression on William's face, I felt he would never wake from his rest. The years since our trip to Canada had taken their toll. With one arm amputated and a hip bone "in degeneration," he had been confined to a wheelchair.

Grandmother, unafraid, walked up to William and brushed away the white tufts of hair from his forehead and spoke to him as if he were awake.

"*A kwi ma ke ko no tta wi ya ni-to ki wa ni-ki sko.* Nothing will happen to you when you wake, Ki sko."

She spoke softly to William as if she were his mother; she also addressed him with the name given to all Black Eagle Child first-borns, *ki sko.* Listening to Grandmother's pleas for William to awaken, I felt the welling of sadness inside me. In a tribal society that was historically burdened with obstacles, suppression of emotion became an art form. To cry over the departed was to inflict misery upon their "shadows." In death there was a deep-rooted fear that personal grief could bridge the world of the real and the nonreal. Whatever our affliction—physical pain, bereavement, sheer loneliness, or embarrassment—being ostentatious was not part of our demeanor.

The more Grandmother assured William with touches and words, the more I wished and prayed for his recovery. Yet there was an underlying feeling that he would not be bothered anymore by our ignorance and ineptness. Us mortals. He had done all that was humanly possible to instill in us the means to emulate his accomplishments as a carrier of the Red Swan Society.

On the evening of Thanksgiving in 1979, a week after our hospital bedside visit with William Listener, Selene and I were preparing to eat the day's bountiful leftovers in my parent's kitchen when something mysterious inside a large, grease-spotted grocery bag began to shake by itself.

We froze and looked at the bag that sat in the middle of the cluttered table. From inside the bag we had taken almost the last of the frybread, leaving a flattened piece or two. We knew there was nothing in there that could make it shake that much. Mice, three or four of them, were a possibility. Or birds. When the bag started up again, it began to inflate and deflate itself as if it were breathing and then worked itself into a frenzy until the palpable shape of something took over.

And then just as abruptly as it began, there was quiet. We sat still and were gradually overtaken with a nightmarish terror that we were about to experience a paranormal occurrence. The bag shaking was only the establishment of a presence. The chatter of the television and the conversation between family members in the living room began fading away, and the kitchen table along with the floor beneath brought a bloating effect, an intumescence of concrete substance.

Next to the bowl of red Jell-O and marshmallows, the fire-singed squirrel legs and flour dumplings looked trite and cold as the presence displayed its power again. The grease-spotted grocery bag shook once more. This time we could see the shape of a fist, striking out from within. Open-mouthed, we were stunned by the furious motions it made. Regardless of how hard the phantom fist hit the paper bag, it couldn't break through. The sound—like empty popcorn bags being blown up, sealed, and exploded under the foot—was hard on our ears.

Years before, in a university housing complex, we had heard and seen plastic trash bags topple over by themselves and then inflate and deflate. The noise made by these visitations stuck with us for days. When these events escalated to all-out animation, we were baffled. We later figured out that our ghostly kindred were probably annoyed by how much food we were throwing away, and were reminding us they needed to be fed also. In Black Eagle Child tradition, a dish should not be left with its contents uneaten or unfinished; everything given or taken should be eaten. Food is treated with respect and not as an object at one's disposal. When we started setting aside portions of our meals, offering sacred tobacco, alcohol, a lit cigarette, and a short prayer that included the enunciation of their names—at least those we could remember on either side of the family—the trash bags stopped breathing.

Selene and I ascertained that, aside from our being punished for disposing of edible food, our infrequent participation in religious gatherings attracted the wandering spirits of our departed relatives. To show us their displeasure in our lifestyle and forgetfulness, trash bags were crushed. Actually, it was my choice—not Selene's—to cover every square inch of my small-framed body with parchment, glued, resembling Robert De Niro in the movie *Brazil* as he attracts masses of swirling paper trash off the street until he is suffocated. Selene, in her trust and faith, hung me like a piñata from the ceiling and prodded me with a stick to spin and dry, communicating with me through a copper umbilical tube. Hoping to show humility, I became literally what Ted Facepaint used to call my "paper wall from clan responsibility."

We were already familiar with animate trash bags. This manifestation of the incorporeal hand in the grocery bag shouldn't have surprised us; yet we were on the verge of emotional devastation.

The hand, we felt, wanted terribly to get out or tell us something that was pressing. To be trapped in a bag that once held the fried delicacy of bread must have been agony for some lonesome spirit. But I later thought: What if the hand was sending a signal of distress, a warning? What if Thanksgiving was only a rude irony? It was clear that the trapped hand didn't arrive as an idle knocking on the door or the slight lingering odor of flowers beside the bed in the early hours before sunrise. It had chosen instead to single us out in the house of my parents at the peaceful close of a holiday. It had done so by scaring us senseless.

After the fourth manifestation, and when the struggling and the hitting ceased, I slowly rose from my chair and reached over to open the grocery bag. Except for a few flattened pieces of frybread there was nothing inside. Empty.

In a state of numbness we walked to the living room and informed my mother and father what had happened. They were bewildered. My mother believed us right away, but the skeptical nature of my father kept him indifferent. The fact it took place in his kitchen was hard to take. It was only when Clotelde said that it could be my father's comatose brother's spirit did he think something could be wrong.

He went out to the cookshack and brought back the ashes in a cast-iron skillet—the same one used to make the frybread. The kitchen was then purified with the smoke of the cedar bough.

Maybe that was the last time William Listener was with Selene and myself. Maybe that was his way of letting us know he was fighting what ailed him. But he died several months later without ever waking up from the coma. . . .

# Part
# Three

# The Perils of Being a
# Black Hummingbird

Rose Grassleggings was the only woman ever chosen from the tribe to stand with the men who sang the Black Hummingbird Society warrior songs. Her vocal accompaniment was a trademark of sorts, something people would recall for years and years. Her presence imbued the songs with a wailing female emanation. What was discerned in her incredible voice, it was said, was the encumbrance of being a woman. She could sound like a bereaved mother weeping unrestrained in the hills after sundown, or she could sound like a grandmother who was singing for all the present and forthcoming Black Eagle Child generations. . . .

During the summer in which the Black Hummingbirds were taking their vows of subservience, the initiates came to her porch, leaving four red stones on a freshly woven reed mat. Aged and shiny in a patina made by centuries of ceremonial upkeep—which "overnight" non-Indian tribal art scholars will pay thousands of dollars for, knowing they can quadruple their return upon selling them—the invitation stones resembled Easter eggs made of catlinite or pipestone. Upon them were epigraphs written in French and Black Eagle Child. Parallel to the stones themselves was an antique French rapier with a beaded scabbard that was decorated with the spotted heads and tail feathers of two small indistinguishable birds of prey.

Ordinarily, invitations were extended to men, preferably those with combat, hunting, or singing and songmaking experience. Because of Rose's extraordinary healing skills, the Black Hummingbirds made an exception. They knew she would honor them by returning these sacred materials, her gesture of acceptance. The community was dependent on her invaluable services. In addition to her traditional doctoring, she had the burden of performing the "shadow-releasing" ceremony for most deceased tribal members. She cleared the way and opened doors to the Hereafter.

Long ago, under the tutelage of a prominent medicine woman named Jane Ribbon, Rose Grassleggings accepted the awesome responsibility of healing. It didn't happen right away, though. But it should have because Jane was a close relative. For Rose, adulthood wasn't as easy as childhood. Romping along the shores of the two rivers with her renowned pearl-diving Many Nickel sisters was far from the debilitating existence she had had as a woman.

Were it not for her association with Jane Ribbon, Rose could not have gotten through a succession of failed marriages, children with different fathers, and episodic bouts with alcoholism, obesity, and abuse. Jane was the one person to whom Rose crawled in misery. Oftentimes she woke up on her porch. From Jane she learned how to heal herself with medicinal plants; from her mother's aunt Sophie she learned words spoken to the dearly departed, words that strengthened one's own existence.

For the Black Eagle Childs, time was an adversary. In the past and up through the present it sandblasted the stone pictograph of our bird aegis to an unidentifiable object, leaving a remnant that only the blessed, like Rose, could read and understand. As the elders passed away, one by one, including Jane Ribbon, those people who had last been close to the elders were seen differently. Rose eventually attained status as a keeper of importance. In spite of her original credibility problems, tribal members realized she had acquired vast healing and "shadow-releasing" knowledge. Even if it was on a piecemeal basis. The elders rationalized that Rose's instability personified the very plight of the keepers themselves, that unstable roads were an intrinsic part of living.

For years these healing and "shadow-releasing" practices remained within the Ribbon family, but when the remaining Many
Nickel sisters careened off the spiritual road, Rose Grassleggings was
stuck with an enormous obligation. Fearing that she would ultimately
fail her mentors Jane and Sophia Ribbon, Rose made a number of
wrong choices. It wasn't until the birth of her hermaphrodite daughter named Brook that Rose's association with Jane deepened. The
Holy Grandfather had asked her to heal people and send them on
through to the doors of the Afterlife, but He had also asked her to
suffer, to experience unimaginable torment.

"Long ago we either lost or mishandled the gift of healing," said the
Black Hummingbirds delegation after they knocked on her door. Their
combined, syncopated voices came through the door, and the brass
hinges squeaked along and vibrated. In the air was the fragrant aroma
of the autumn leaves of walnut and red oak trees.

"With fewer and fewer Earthlodge clan worshippers, we are
making rules that are less strict," they said in a short spiel.

That was the main pitch. They were inviting her to become a
member of the elite and much-feared Black Hummingbirds.

"*Ka tti-ni ni we na-tte we ske?* Why, is that all there is?" she asked,
wondering whether she should turn on the porch lights.

"*E a i,* yes!" they said.

"*A kwi-ma ma ka tti-ni na wa tti-na ka mo we kwi ni?* Will you
not sing first?"

"*A kwi,* no!"

And that was it. She heard a clatter of footsteps, the shutting of
metal doors, and the 4 × 4 truck engines rumbling to life, along with
several motorcycles.

It didn't take much deliberation. She sent word by messenger
that she had accepted their invitation.

The next day a person arrived to advise and instruct her on what
to expect.

"There are eight persons in all who stand up throughout the
elaborate day-long ritual," she was told. "The clans themselves sit

outside of the earthlodge ten to fifteen feet away and quietly observe, careful not to disturb or interact with the worshippers."

The four wall panels, the corners, of the elongated octagon-shaped structure were removed for people to see what was happening inside.

She was already aware of these factors.

At the juncture where the day was divided into four parts—pre-dawn, morning, noon, and sundown—the Black Hummingbirds took turns singing the songs in groups of two, two singers per wall panel opening, while the other six prayed or partook of the boiled goose meat sprinkled with the sacred black-feathered hummingbird's heart.

"You don't seem to see anyone," said Rose in a low voice to Ted Facepaint in the corridor of the Black Eagle Child Recreational Center. "The songs blur everything out. Focus is accorded to the music, the drumbeats and where they are placed, the speed and tempo. And the eating is essential, too. Not only are you the cook, singer, and partaker of the sacred concoction, you are also the dancer. As for the observers on the outside, you know they are there. For the purpose itself, though, they don't really matter."

Ted didn't know how to take being asked to participate as a last-minute replacement. It was sheer coincidence that the eighth person was part of a Iowa National Guard contingent sent to the Persian Gulf.

"But what if I forget the songs?" Ted asked. "There might be too many. To boot, I've never done anything outside the Well-Off Man Church."

Rose shifted her poundage inside her large Hawaiian print smock and smiled. "Ted, we know this. Which means we can help you, carry you. The observers won't even see, hear, or know. It will all come together smoothly."

Her detailed explanation of the ceremony sounded academic—point by point, step A to step C.

Ted shook his head in apprehension and spoke.

"Even with your help, Rose, there would be nervousness. Errors. I'd screw it up and make a fool of myself in front of everyone."

That's about how the soft but poignant conversation went. I caught only part of it as I walked up to them. The rest was masked by the echoing shouts and screams coming from the gymnasium where local Girl Scouts played volleyball.

My eavesdropping wasn't intentional that winter 1989 night.

Since it was rare even to see Ted, much less to talk to him, I sometimes think that maybe I didn't really want to hear what Rose said to him. Strange, that's how I first hooked up with Ted: not wanting to hear what was said to him. During our first years at Weeping Willow I rescued him. Encircled by an onslaught of older, strong-armed students who were making fun of his speech impediment, Ted cowered and trembled. Feeling sorry for him I struggled past the crowd, shouting as my grandmother would have, "Leave him alone! He isn't doing anything to you!" My brashness didn't work; I was blindsided with a straight palm to the temple and shoved toward him.

"Can you understand him?" the angry crowd asked, as I sought to regain my balance with small outstretched arms and twisted legs. "He can't even talk right!" someone shouted in my ear before being pushed. "Now get in there and protect him! Speak for the wordless snake!"

With sparks revolving within my sight, I screamed, "*Leave me alone*, he is saying to you! *I haven't done anything!*" Someone backed off and the rest followed. The crowd then converged on someone else down the sidewalk.

Ted Facepaint looked at me through his messed-up hair and tried to express his gratitude. What he missed saying, I made up in my head. From then on, throughout Weeping Willow Elementary, we were virtually inseparable. My reasons for befriending him were fundamental. Hardly anyone liked him or spoke to him. Ted was a loner, a contrarian—like myself.

After that schoolground incident, Ted became a regular visitor to our home. Alan found his speech problems amusing. He even named him "Three-Speed" after a fancy English bicycle. Grandmother said she already knew him from cooking for his family's doings on weekends through the Well-Off Man Church. Which also happened to be the unusual oblong-shaped house where Ted lived with his aunt, Louise Stabs Back, in an area known as Whiskey Corners Road.

From about ten feet away, out of courtesy, I announced myself. Startled, Rose backed away fast and nudged Ted on his left shoulder with her huge, puffy hand. In remembering, I didn't like how the fingers and palm were evenly spread over the physical mass of who was and still is my closest friend. Sorcerers or would-be spellcasters employed this conspicuous maneuver: walking up from behind people and greeting them by touch. It was so obvious and outwardly evil to me, for rarely did we as a tribe or family resort to physical groping.

But weakened by modernity, we were vulnerable. Entrapment was easy. A touch was a touch. Few of us knew this wasn't the case.

In infancy I was told of an elderly visitor, a neighbor, who in essence raked my newborn skin with her long, crooked fingernails. It had actually been a gentle stroke of the knuckles, but my face broke out in a rash the next day, and while the applied medicines cured it, some pockmarks remain near the jawline. This was part of the reason why Grandmother gave me the stone-knife necklace, pointing outward, repelling spells. In my first few days of life I was already a target in the supernatural shooting gallery.

*Wearing the shroud of the stone-knife, this is what the sorcerer sees of me: Painted over the top half of my face is the color of yellow. These words are then spoken to the disguise-wearing visitor: "Whoever you are, whatever your purpose, you will stop this travesty. Go back and tell the one who sent you your medicine has failed to get hold of us. You will also tell that person how the shot was reversed and how the projectile embedded itself in your heart and that you decomposed willingly at earth's first light."*

Ted stood in a half-slouching pose. Within the chaotic din of the girl's volleyball game—Rolling Head Valley versus Stone House Bullheads—he had been listening very carefully to Rose.

If I had only intervened earlier, risking perhaps my own life or those of my immediate family, he might still be alive. I'm not saying Rose Grassleggings is responsible or anything, you see. I just think Ted was a target all along. And the shooters were many. From different directions for different purposes. At any time, anywhere, akin to Dorothy Black Heron and her lovely sister, the One Most Afraid, we are all susceptible.

Disguised as a circus, the supernatural shooting gallery would attract our earthly shadows to a festive gathering of ordinary humans and nonordinary beings. Lulled by the showlike atmosphere, we would be caught off guard. Like Ted Facepaint, we would knowingly allow death in the form of a fat Hyena to circle the booth where we sit, listening to the one-piece country and western band called Mike & Mike in the Dutch descendant village of Hellendoorn. We would watch the Unworthy Hyena of Nothing, with its lower jaw hanging heavy by a mouth darkened and stuffed with cheap chewing tobacco, attempt to speak in the yellow foreign air.

The biggest difference between us, as it has always been since that late evening in 1970 at the Marion, Iowa, train depot, would be the stone knife that Grandmother gave me, the one I wore inside the locket necklace before my travel westward.

Since then, aside from navigating Selene Buffalo Husband and myself over the Black Eagle Child Ocean, deflecting adversity, the stone knife has on occasion sparked before us like flint and iron. By doing this, it reminds us of its omnipresence.

On the Night of the Hyenai, however, during Ted Facepaint's last visit, the sparks reversed themselves: they came out from his sad eyes in spiraling miniature bullets of light. Halfway across the room they faded. After he presented us with a six-pack of Michelob beer, we never saw Ted alive again. That next morning, wondering what the spiraling eye lights meant, I opened the locket and discovered the stone knife had split itself four ways. At the same moment that I separated a single piece for Ted, my brother Alan drove up the driveway in his Dodge truck, bringing the tragic news. "Something's wrong with Three-Speed." That's when I decided to wrap the stone remnant in leather and take it to the funeral home. When we changed Ted into his traditional regalia, I affixed the small bundle with a safety pin under the lapel of his ceremonial shirt; I placed it as close as I could to his gentle sleeping heart.

# The Deformed
# Pearl Diver

There were thin, white strips of clouds that held motionless against the blue summer sky. High atop a cottonwood tree, three insects buzzed noisily together in their rendition of a sun-burning-skin song. Through the high grass and shrubs somewhere along the edge of the Iowa River, there rose the mirthful sounds of human conversation and laughter. These were the oblivious targets, walking humans. The insects sang, accompanying each other; one would start, the lead, and sing the loudest and longest skin-burning song; and the other two, at separate points, would join in, staying a pitch softer than the lead and stopping just before the end.

Upon hearing this, the blue-and-white-colored kingfisher rattled the humid air with its own dissonant cry, warning any of its kind nearby. Everyone present froze and waited. In an attempt to listen, the kingfisher leaned forward with tail feathers high and peered into the bend. The insects stopped their music, too. But there was only calmness. And the only movement detected was among the few butter-flies crossing the open stretch into the dense woodlands on black-and-yellow fluttering wings.

As the human voices came up through the trees, the insect's skin-burning songs picked up again. The sun's rays were being directed downward to the skin of the unsuspecting humans.

*"Darken them, darken them, for being so bold as to walk in the sun's fiery light,"* sang the insects.

The kingfisher's eyes followed the music and cried its warning for the last time. Nearby, a heron leapt clumsily into flight from a weeping willow tree and flew south along the winding path of the river. Below, the heron could see the flickering shadows of the many footprints made on the glaring bone white beach of sand.

Through the thick forests of the Black Eagle Child Settlement, the ever-present sun reflected and broke into a thousand shimmering pieces as a group of giggling children and their guide waded into the dark green water with bare feet. They stood still for a moment and listened. Among the children themselves arms were pointed, heads nodded, and questions quietly asked. Including an adult female, there were three girls and two boys. The boys, about seven and nine years old, furtively looked up and down the length of the large crescent-shaped beach before whisking their clothes off. The girls, as they had been taught, chose to keep their dresses on. Yet, as the woman took her bag to the bushes to change, the girls secretly took turns stealing looks at the skinny buttocks and penises of their brother and cousin. It wasn't so much the idea of viewing a male private part as it was a chance to see each other make a "broken face, *ba na tti na ko si wa*" expression while looking at something they weren't supposed to.

The woman observed them gawking as she was changing into a fancy and modern bathing suit. Flailing her arms and grunting, she scolded them for being capricious and informed them of the king-fisher who sat on a tan branch of a half-submerged tree in the hazy distance.

*"Ki a tti me ko wa-ke i na-wi ske no.* That bird will tell on you."

The young people and the kingfisher watched each other as the woman walked out from the willow saplings, wearing a black bath-ing suit that had a small fancy skirt trimmed with yellow lace. From her bag she pulled a large oval mirror and looked at her spurious self while the children went to their designated spots in the river. This was the only place where the woman felt secure. There was privacy. From her share of the pearl-hunting proceeds she ordered modern clothes from a catalog. The earrings glittered as the "Deformed Pearl Diver" positioned herself over the deepest but most lucrative pool.

In the cloud-streaked clouds above, the black-and-yellow-winged butterflies hovered in place over Half Moon Beach. With their sparkling wings they danced hypnotically to the skin-burning insects' litany. Suddenly, as the woman waded into the pool, she stopped. There, with the cool river water rippling against her knees, she removed her sunglasses, shielded her eyes from the glaring sun, and peered into the dense, serene surroundings. Sensing an instantaneous change would occur, she walked back out onto the hot sand and placed a large veil hat on her head.

From a faraway cottonwood perch the heron brushed branches and leaves aside to observe. Like a World War I Sopwith Camel biplane the kingfisher buzzed the beach twice and strafed the area on its return run with a blaring staccato shrill. From the air traffic observatory post the skin-burning insects, *e te si ke a ki,* confirmed a manifestation was imminent, and their music was amplified by conches that were inadvertently abandoned by migrating pelicans. The spiral-shaped seashells wedged in old, hollow trees resonated like the sound of the trumpets once employed by Triton, the inferior sea god, half-man, half-fish; and the music's intonation changed from a message of direction to that of paranormal warning.

Not knowing what else to do, one of the girls who was waist-deep in the river froze when she found herself standing atop a sleek creature. Each movement made urged the submerged creature to inch forward. She took off the shoulder bag of clams, tossed them to the closest diver, and waved to the shore, until the woman in the bathing suit inquired what was the matter. Through sign language the girl calmly asked if human-sized fish existed. The woman signaled back: *Mi ya na me kwa-ye to ki. Me ke ki ne ta ye to ki?* It must be catfish. A large one maybe? The girl's fearful situation persisted. Her companion divers, including the heron and the kingfisher, watched helplessly as the girl drifted downriver. She instinctively stretched out her arms, attaining balance before being flung into the air. In an instant a black-whiskered seal exploded to the surface of the quiet, green river, barking in vigorous protest as it flash-swam through the exposed roots of the massive maple trees.

Knowing seals were considered bad luck, the pearl-diving expedition participants jumped out of the waters running. In a close pack, like ancient clan runners, they ran back through thick forest. The sound of their bare feet slapping against the dried mud of the winding riverside paths made ground-level roosting birds screech and flutter.

Still protective, the woman in her stylish bathing suit grunted and groaned in a frenzy to keep up with the young pearl divers' full-pitch run. Born with a face that appeared to have been viciously ripped in half down the middle and then sloppily sewn back together with a dull knife and rope, the woman had seen her rapturous tormentor, the mystical animal who caused her facial deformity and speech-hearing impediment. "The Well-Known Twin Brother had no regard whatsoever for making her nose and mouth properly aligned," she recalled her aunt saying. Throughout her life the woman's deformed face, along with a stumpy tongue and a set of partially missing ears, made children scatter like mice. They squirmed and cried at an unimaginable hideousness under her large, veiled hats. The fact was, the only people privileged to see her disassembled Picassolike visage were close relatives. "It is no coincidence she laughs like a festive circus seal," the woman's aunt speculated, imitating her guttural sounds. "No wonder children hide."

The watery belly flop landing stunned the girl who had been bucked off by the seal like a rodeo bull rider. Atop a seal's back one moment, swallowing fish-ridden river water the next, and leading the way along the mud-hardened river path was all she remembered of the pearl-diving excursion as she shivered uncontrollably at home. To her aunt she described her frightening encounter. Beside her, in a small shovel of coals, a clump of cedar twigs crackled under an eagle wing fan. After the blue cedar smoke was directed over her body and head, she gave an engrossing account of how she rode for a short distance on the seal's back. She thought it had purposely humped its back to lift her higher out of the water. Once she vaguely realized she was running on land, she said, the seal sounded like it was right behind her, barking! When she looked back and saw it was their chaperone and companion in the stylish bathing suit, making those scary noises, she blacked out. After being cleansed with cedar smoke, another girl picked up on their encounter and detailed how they crashed through the thickets and rushed recklessly over the Indian Dam. There, as they were midway across the dam, white fishermen agitated the situation. "Jesus! Hey, you girls, run from that damned monster behind you! Run! Jesus! *Run! Run!*" they had yelled out. Along with their own piercing screams and the cascading man-made waterfalls, the fishermen's shouts of concern for their safety height-ened into a chaotic din. The aunt asked what the white men called it. "Dam Monster," she was told by the sobbing girls.

The woman in the provocative bathing suit stood near the crack-ling cedar. Long before her worldly emergence she was punished. The aunt walked over to the trunk, pulled out a movable eagle wing, and attached it to her left arm. Controlled by a mechanical contraption held in the right hand, the pulleys and small wires creaked as the spotted eagle wing was stretched out, mimicking flight.

Thus on a summer afternoon amid the insects' song—*Darken them, darken them, for being so bold as to walk in the fiery sun's light*—the erroneous christening of a seal occurred.


Rose Many Nickel was eight that year in 1938 when they met up with a seal on Half Moon Beach that went on to become known within the family as "Dam Monster." The name came about as a result of a major misunderstanding between the white fishermen and them. Sure, she was there on Half Moon Beach with her sisters, including her brother and cousin under the care of Jane Ribbon, their mute and facially deformed chaperone. In fact, they participated in the whole affair, but there was no monster to speak of.

In the "Local Comical Events" section of the *Why Cheer News-Herald,* one of the fishermen reported "the seal woman waddled out of the water, grew legs and arms, and began chasing after the Indian girls." In the "Local Crimes and Jail Sentences" section, the fisher-men were arrested that same night for intoxication, but the story of their seal woman sighting was received as a joke.

As the years dragged on and as the story became more far-fetched and embarrassing, Rose disassociated herself from the whole affair.

In doing so, she was denying her own initiation as a premiere medicine woman. To the closest relatives and friends, however, she said they had been diving for clams in an area where summers previous the family had done well. Except on this occasion a seal, whether real or imagined, sacred or evil, chose to pop to the river's surface, glistening under the sun in its sleek blackness. . . .


The Many Nickel family resided near the riverbottoms of the Iowa and Swanroot Rivers. The father, Nelson Many Nickel, was the most famous pearl diver in eastern Iowa; he also happened to be an Indian. Accordingly, his six daughters were taught to dive for clams early on. It was a way of living. The Many Nickel name on strings of pearls was highly sought after. Pearls for necklaces and clamshell buttons were traded for household materials, like nails, boards, pots, pans, and food, as well as school clothes.

As the daughters got older, however, the father was compelled to stay home and clean the pearls. It wasn't respectful to see the bodies of his partially clothed daughters on their pearl-diving excursions. Between the parents it was agreed that when wet blouses began to cling to their growing breasts, a female chaperone would accompany them. The mother, Esther Many Nickel, with other things to do, like cooking, sewing, and selling beadwork sometimes on old Lincoln Highway 30, called upon her mother's relative, Jane Ribbon, to guide and watch the girls.

Jane Ribbon was a facially deformed mute and a recluse. She was quite trustworthy, though she rarely ventured out into the tribal community or anywhere else. Except for her elderly caretaker's immediate family, no one knew how to communicate with her, much less look at her without being intimidated. It took years of practice to accomplish either task. During their summers as girls, Esther and Jane went on pearl-diving and fishing excursions. Whenever they met people on the paths, both whites and Indians would stand to the side, look away in respect and fear, and let them pass. Esther and her elderly aunt never thought of Jane as "Encumbrance." Instead they accepted her presence as a blessing from the Well-Known Twin Brother.

"That's why she can swim and dive like a muskrat," they would say with hand gestures, comparing her to the one who dove into the ocean and retrieved a pawful of mud for the Well-Known Twin Brother, the mud that shaped the Second Earth.

"The muskrat is a hideous thing to look at," Jane would signal angrily from the corner of the herb- and hat-cluttered room.

"That's all, though," they would return, emphasizing a muskrat could not watch and cook for babies as well as she could. Nor could a muskrat sew floral designs in appliqué and get high prices from white collectors.

In an effort to make the public at ease with her, and her with herself, they mail-ordered the latest hat styles of the season from C. M. Marshall's catalog. But Jane Ribbon preferred to stay in the dimness of Aunt Sophia's old home.

It wasn't productive arguing in sign language with a muskrat-resenting mute obsessed by her own misfortune. It was frustrating to stand in the shadows in a flurry of arm and hand gestures. If Jane looked away, the meaningless arms flailed. Sometimes Esther's elderly aunt ended up hitting herself accidentally, and she would hold her poked eye and weep.


For the Many Nickel family, Jane Ribbon was a lifetime friend and companion. In fact, she frequently baby-sat the girls while their parents hunted for pearls. They all learned to communicate with her in sign language developed by their wise, elderly aunt Sophia, who foresaw physical abuse and starvation for Jane were she to be institutionalized. They unanimously concurred Jane wasn't crazy. Her features merely took getting used to, but not if one knew her from infancy. Although public-shy, Jane was unusually fashion-conscious. In fact, Jane introduced hints of Western civilization to the girls through her impressive mail-order catalogs. In the dank half-lit corner of her room, Jane modeled clothes. Enthralled with her presence in shiny red high heels and frilly skirts, they were "mute-sensitized" long before schooling at Weeping Willow Elementary. Jane, of course, graciously declined any suggestion to pose in full daylight.

# Mystery-Solving
# Sherlock Holmes
# That She Was

Rose Grassleggings began having dreams that a shadow, or "soul," was trapped between the two sets of sliding glass doors at the Heijen Medical Center in Sherifftown, Iowa. There were four large doors that opened and closed automatically at the presence of human beings who arrived and left like insects en masse. She understood the mechanics of a large hospital, conserving its air conditioning in summer and its heat in winter. The self-monitoring doors served their purpose well.

She also knew—through newspapers read, maybe—that they were gifts from two prominent Dutch families with a legacy in the gravel and truck radiator businesses. The doors were installed in posthumous honor of beloved relatives. Kinetic tombstones with names embedded in bronze plaques interacted with people twenty-four hours a day. Constructed from silver metal and large sheets of tinted glass, these doors had a simple function; through electrical vision they opened and closed for people.

While Rose Grassleggings saw them as architectural reminders of our short lives as human beings, our impermanence, the public saw them as a welcome convenience. Beyond that, no one thought about them much. Only two families—the benefactors themselves— knew about the philanthropy. No one read the bronze plaques; Sherifftown citizens didn't care about that kind of "uppity" stuff. All

they wanted the Dutch founders of the Heijen Medical Center—
namely, Ans Visser and Fleming Joop—to do was open and close.

How would you thank them, anyway? Rose asked herself. Yellow and red tulips in wooden shoes? Dutch Friesland tobacco and
Grolsch beer?

As the dreams progressed, Rose nearly became confused.

How could a shadow, or "soul," get hopelessly stuck in the air
space between the two sets of sliding glass doors?

Before long, and with the diligent help of neighbors, relatives,
and prayers, she learned Ted Facepaint, a tribal member, had been
pronounced dead between the two sets of glass doors of the hospital.
Officially. Which was a violation of an old but stringent agreement
between tribe and state: *"It shall be understood by all residents of Tama
County and other surrounding counties that no person other than a
Black Eagle Child priest shall formally address and pronounce a fellow
tribal member deceased."* It had always been taught that shortly after
the moment of death, any word spoken to the deceased by anyone
would liberate their shadows anywhere. Even between the doors at
the Heijen Medical Center.

As the dreams began to unfold, like a puzzle, Rose saw herself
in the glass-framed edifice: She stepped into the electric eye and
opened the glass doors to commune with an invisible shadow. If everything went according to plan—this would be the first among her
deeds—the ghost of a green parrot would escort the shadow to celes-
tial freedom. Literally.

Upon waking, Rose Grassleggings assessed that this task wasn't
monumental, and embarrassment to self was minimal. Ted Facepaint's relatives would have to "go out on a hunting expedition" for
an exotic bird. Its sacrifice would be next, causing a commotion.
Eventually she would be manhandled by hospital security and taken
into custody. The cost was small in return for a shadow's eternal
comfort. Wasn't it? Rose asked herself. Who would enjoy being
a tortured "soul," reliving an unwanted body-leaving moment over
and over, like a stuck record on an old Sears record player? And
could denial of this death and others have wide-reaching universal
complications?

"Why . . . yes, yes. Certainly," she whispered as the dream demonstrated where to hold the exotic bird, how the leather hood was tightened around its feathered neck, and the words said to implore the shadow to watch for another "arrival." The glass doors were also crucial, for contained therein was the voice of Dr. Plees, the special coroner of Tama County. She learned he happened to be leaving the hospital when Ted Facepaint was brought through the front entrance. When the paramedics told the special coroner the victim was Indian, a necro-crime was perpetrated. Dr. Plees, a former tribal doctor with a hidden agenda, hated himself for speaking the despicable Black Eagle Child language. But sometimes it came in handy, as it did in the case of Ted Facepaint. Rose knew for certain what happened. Dr. Plees bowed over the sheet-covered body, genuflected and made an upside-down cross sign, and said in a sarcastic tone: "I pronounce you dead to the world, Mr. . . . what's a good Indian name?" Caught up in the strangeness, the paramedics had kept still until he answered himself. "I'm telling you now, A ni kwa-ne ni wa, Man Squirrel! Officially. *Ka ta na na tti to ki ka ni!* May you never wake again! Now let's go inside and get the damn thing over with; I won't have to do this tomorrow." And he didn't.

Everything the dreams explained thereafter was crucial. Observed from all angles—sometimes with a mirror or simply in reverse—the stories were ceremonies. Luckily, mystery-solving Sherlock Holmes that Rose was, the messages revealed themselves with the aid of pencil and paper. Hasty drawings were done on Safeway grocery bags. Arranged in chronologic order, the brown paper drawings were kept in her fully beaded purse. She pulled them out like playing cards and rehearsed exactly the way the Deformed Pearl Diver, Jane Ribbon, her mentor, had taught.

The reenactment of these dreams was important: The large green parrot, for instance, would be asphyxiated within the glass structure. It was also known that the "shadow-releasing" rite worked stronger with an audience. The latter, she methodically adduced, wouldn't be difficult, for visitor traffic at Heijen Medical was constant. On the downside, being arrested for disorderly conduct and cruelty to exotic birds wasn't good. Yet she was driven by a haunting feeling of despair that went beyond the norm. She wouldn't mind sitting in a police squad car. Handcuffed. She could even tolerate hospital security imitating squawks the limp parrot made before it was thrown to them.

But that was only the beginning. For a moment, as the leather "suffocating" hood was unraveled from the parrot, the hospital security would shudder at the ghastly sight of a small human face before the compressed feathers ruffled back into shape. Half shadow, half bird. That's what she was after.

In the guise of mockery the special coroner had knowingly liberated Ted Facepaint's shadow by reciting the words—in Indian. In death, too, according to Black Eagle Child beliefs, there was a need for some guidance even if it didn't lead to anything. In a dimension without a physical sense, akin to a quick, premature birth, Ted's bereft shadow leapt out upon the instruction "not to wake," only to find itself encased in glass and part of a kinetic memorial.

Long before Dr. Plees hated Indians, he studied their customs, language, and "heathenish practices" with avid interest. As an educated person he felt obligated to learn the inner workings of a Woodlands-based tribal society. More so with a lucrative health services contract at stake. Treating ailments of the Black Eagle Child Nation was secondary to the thrill of gaining insights into their ancient worldviews. Ideologically spawned by the greatest sin of Western civilization—that which seeks, connivingly befriends, steals, and then destroys—Dr. Plees made what he couldn't possibly know through books his first priority. Another people's intimate ways. Who could have foreseen the following upon his interfacing with the Black Eagle Child community?

- When the needle of the ethnologic compass levitated upward, shattering the glass face with such force that "fecal matter hit the propeller" (as whites by colloquial habit are wont to say), the cardinal points became clouded, and then he became disoriented.
- When the Tribal Council canceled his health services contract, with the state medical board's blessing, the white communities of Why Cheer and Gladwood rallied behind him, urging him to burn "Indian books" and attend church.

- When the town's white businessmen called relatives from surrounding counties, sick people made thirty-mile round-trips—some driving themselves—to express disgust with his public firing and asked him to be their doctor.

- When his dejection allowed the seed of bigotry to be planted, there materialized a five-year membership to the exclusive Indian Acres Country Club and a second job, issuing certificates of death to the local populace.

Initially, the special coroner believed his position was created out of sympathy. Later, though, he learned the county's Social Statistics Department had diverted federal funds intended for the tribe to local banks. As a result, a five-year backlog on Indian deaths and other program matters existed. However, it also made possible a new Chevy Blazer, complete with federal/state jurisdiction over the Black Eagle Child Settlement. The Blazer rolled over the thoroughfares of tribal land—anytime, anywhere—for the wrong reasons.

As a new member in a white anti-Indian community, Dr. Plees soon took special delight in learning that hefty interests helped sponsor the annual Twintowns rodeo and agricultural fair. Indian money was operating and public relations money for the Twintowns Chamber of Commerce. If federal agents ever planned an audit, he was told, "there was enough there" to cover anything—close to two million dollars. Twice a month the country club had live music, risqué men stuff, and free alcohol. Moreover, twice a month the wives held luncheons, flower-arranging sessions, and fashion shows—cosponsored by the Why Cheer Preservation Club—with "real models" from Ames, Cedar Falls, and Winterset. Twice a year the members selected Why Cheer High School students—four males and two females, "preferably white and smart"—for college scholarships. Once a year the club's exclusive Indian Acres Open drew golf amateurs from as far away as Dubuque and Council Bluffs to vie for the five three-thousand-dollar awards.

The Black Eagle Child Nation unknowingly paid all expenses, including tips for the caddies. But there was one thing the country club patrons couldn't take away, and it bothered the hell out of them: "The Black Eagle Child Field Days and Chautauqua." Every August for eight decades white visitors crowded to watch the powwow, take part in pretty-baby and gardening contests and footraces, and enjoy parade music by the All-BEC Indian brass band. Its four-day success was measured by how many miles the automobiles were backed up on old Lincoln Highway 30.

The country club's campaign to outdo this extravagant affair failed. Even with embezzled money! The rodeo and the hay-cutting exhibition with antique machinery attracted sparse audiences. This devastated the annual Pork Queens. They would bob their bonnets in sobbing spells inside the two or three registered floats of the rodeo parade.

But even in defeat theft continued.

Quick to capitalize on our celebration, the country club members took turns manning donation posts at the intersections of Highways 30 and 63. With aqua-colored buckets and gaudy cowboy outfits, they begged for pocket change. No one questioned if a charity organization called "Shetland Pony Rides for the Disadvantaged and Crippled Children of the Appalachian Mountains" really existed. After giving wrong directions to the Indian powwow, the rodeo clowns handed out suckers to visitors who willingly "gave" at the four-way stop signs.

A terrible lesson was learned: The fact that a new doctor took over a well-established clinic and its tribal health services contract didn't necessarily mean all was well. Not even if he spoke Black Eagle Child fluently. Dr. Plees, the trustworthy doctor who had ministered to the tribe for years, began to crumble. Why? No one knew. Infidelity? A likelihood. Combat-associated flashbacks? Depending. Untimely incestuous urges? Who knows when and where medical incompetence begins and ends?

In any case, on the basis of growing complaints and charges, a tribal referendum vote fired Dr. Plees. The news media portrayed the dispute as "a simple misunderstanding." In a show of support, a splinter group, the Indian War Veterans, held a chicken and boiled corn dinner dance for their honorary legionnaire, Dr. Plees. It was a flop, but a bevy of reporters took photographs: Here stood the honoree in a Northern Plains war bonnet, shaking hands with the Mad Soldier brothers—their real surname—inside the BEC American Legion Hall. That's all the conservative *Central Plains Register* wanted. Sensationalism was SOP at the state's biggest newspaper. An editorial even questioned if "outsiders" or "educated but radical-minded goons" were behind the mess. The press was, therefore, disappointed that there were no wild-eyed protestors brandishing placards with seething epithets.

In fact, it proved to be a downright boring dinner dance. None of the Settlement drum groups who otherwise sang "at the drop of a dime" showed up. The Rocky Raccoon Singers, a noted Black Eagle Child singer and his scuzzy backups, were nowhere to be seen. They could usually be hired for food and seventy-five dollars. Rocky Raccoon—his legal name, based on a Beatles tune—wasn't all there, but his music was tolerable. If the tape recordings were slowed down, someone said, you could actually hear and understand his word-songs. The rest, sadly, vanished in his falsetto style of singing and horse neighs. No songs of honor were sung, the leg bells didn't ring, and the emcee, "Mongol, the Texaco Man" (Rocky's uncle), didn't have to do his crocodile tears routine. Instead, the grandchildren of the veterans sat in their beaded and sequined regalias listening to the amplified music of Elvis Presley and small, annoying speeches.

To the doctor, these were "the heroic exception, the golden warriors" who saw the carnage of foreign battlefields and came home "with the American flag still in hand." This statement drew the loudest commotion of the night, a smattering of mumbled affirmation from the Indian veterans. With cameras poised, the press could not discern who did the soft war whoop.

"The remainder, though, Dr. Plees," inquired the newspaper reporters, "are they your enemies?"

"I don't understand your question," replied the doctor.

"It's obvious the Indian War Veterans respect your impeccable combat record, but how do the rest of them feel, the Tribal Council and those who voted against you?"

"These are fine Indians. Generally. You fret none; I haven't lost anything."

\*    \*    \*

We were, however, accountable for the loss of his folksinging daughter's San Francisco Bay Area apartment. As he telescopically adjusted the crosshairs of his stethoscope on the frail walls of the Earthlodge clans, he orchestrated his necro-trickery. Devastating high-caliber control. The proverbial silver bullet tumbled in its illuminated trajectory path, splintering upon impact inside the bark and reed panels of traditional dwellings. Impalpable pieces of silver shrapnel swirled inside and clogged the mouths of priests in worship.

Since "shadow-releasing" priests, like Rose Grassleggings, were a pestilence, he entertained the fire and ambulance crews with parodies of their rituals. It was silly, but when news of his sacrilegious antics reached the Earthlodge clans, he was considered "the devil." Which was odd because the concept of the Antichrist was not Indian. A belief in a dark, evil side was shared with Christianty, but we do not believe that evil is embodied in a single man. With Dr. Plees, an exception was made.

At crime scenes with Indian families present, the coroner, along with the police and paramedics, respectfully awaited the clan priests. If he was first on the scene and short on patience, however, he took the cherry-lit stage by blaspheming the most sacred of all tribal customs. The lifeless victims were shadow-released. Afterward, he whisked them to the clinic. There, it was rumored he crossed his scalpels before performing unauthorized autopsies on the "Bela Lugosis of the world."

But what made him notorious were accounts that internal body parts were missing. Hollow bodies seen through telltale stitches. Whole stomachs mysteriously disappeared. Especially during the winter season. The coroner knew no clan priest would dare disturb what he had already violated. If Indian families cried foul play, he always disagreed and backed his protests up with information that only a forensic pathologist could provide. No one knew. Through shoddy examinations he summarily dismissed all suspicious wounds and doubts.

Black Eagle Childs, you see, respected—in a fearful way—their dearly departed. When their blood was spilled, for instance, a safe distance was maintained; it was thought that tangible evil used pools of blood as portals through which the legs of innocent passersby were tripped and grabbed.

*  *  *

Rose Grassleggings concluded emphatically that the coroner was the source of most apparitions. Her dreams said so. Each sequence would begin with a team of doctors standing around the cold, bruised body that she figured was Facepaint's. She paid special attention to the minor details of the scenery. On occasion, the room wasn't the same one she purified. There were subtle differences in color, smell, light, and dimension, and everywhere a wanton disregard for humanness resonated. English was spoken and biting comments were addressed to the deceased, who lay naked except for the white towel that covered the crotch area.

Ignoring their harsh conversation, she would sprinkle dry roots of the clusterberry followed by granulated cedar pines over hot embers. This she had already performed in real life. First woman-root and then man-root fell onto the hot toy shovel and crackled. Sparks darted and gathered to make a blue fire. Above the small, smoldering flame she used an eagle-wing fan, along with her hissing breath, to direct the smoke over the body, feet first. Purification for travel to the Hereafter. What she had failed to detect was the coroner's vile presence: he stood in the haze of the emergency room, presiding. Several times she recalled telling this horrid little man that Facepaint's face conveyed anger, not contentment brought by suicide nor the fear expressed from a fatal car accident.

She wondered why the coroner was there that day. Counting sick Indians? Had he dashed in and out of their rooms, reading charts? She thought it was part of the job requirement, unavoidable red tape. Indian families through outdated constitutional bylaws had to have a certificate of death before funeral funds were disbursed by the Tribal Council. There was absolutely no way around that obstacle. Before the inception of the tribal gambling enterprise, two thousand dollars "for grief" was a pretty heavy affair.

Rose Grassleggings and Dr. Plees had already met three times. She was there at the behest of mourning families. "Do they really care? Do they have the metabolism to mourn?" she overheard him say. "Or is it just the two grand?" She recalled it was necessary to ask for a moment of privacy. With the doctors gone, she took out the buffalo horn from under her sweaters and uncapped it. Inside, smoldering faintly, was the hot coal that lit the way for the wayward. She comically equated the coal with the Olympic flame from Greece, and it was known by that euphemism. Families relied upon her to say whether an autopsy was required or not.

On the occasions that she went against the coroner's word, his hatred raged like an ocean of boiling lava. Vessels containing Indian shadows had little chance to set voyage. All for a mediocre nightclub-singing daughter in San Francisco; all for a thirty-five-thousand-dollar-a-year apartment on Fisherman's Wharf once financed by the Black Eagle Child Nation.

In the stillness that followed her dreams, she was aware a lot had happened at the Heijen Medical Center. The kindred spirit of Ted Facepaint was unwilling to accept its sliding door destiny. For several months she would lie in bed, wondering why all the negative forces convened on the sharpened end of a screwdriver, the crude weapon used to riddle Facepaint's upper torso with puncture wounds. During these quiet hours in which the refrigerator hummed and the gas heater turned itself on in response to the cold, she envisioned the patterns made by the puncture wounds. Even before Ted's body had been washed by the Facepaint family, she could see pictures had been drawn.

Was this the artistry of Dr. Plees? An extra stab to the human canvas for morbidity? Was this the main reason why the precursory examination was deliberately botched?

Was it just coincidence that one picture resembled three owls in flight with fully extended wings while another—on the right arm—looked like the sacred, astronomical icon of the Well-Off Man Church, the Three-Stars-in-a-Row?

Obviously, sorcery came into play at some point, as did the bigotry of the law enforcement and judicial agencies of Tama County. It had been like this for ages. Among the white farmers and city folk there was a consensus that Black Eagle Child Indians "had no claim to being any kind of race." Sometimes, especially through the art of human-on-human mutilation, it was hard not to agree.

But there were other factors to consider, like the assistant county attorney, Peter Beech, who boasted about "holding the federal crime laboratory boys by their blond fuzzy balls." If there was indeed an

Antichrist among the whites, "Peter Bitch," as he was known by Indians, had to be the Antihuman. Attired in grungy blue jeans, smelly sneakers, and sky blue ties with pink curled-pigtail designs, he remained dog-loyal to his superiors and downplayed anything that had to do with their Indian neighbors. "Mighty friendly bunch they are and law-abi-i-i-ding," he would chortle at the end of televised press conferences. "Reason why the feds stay out. No crime whatsoever!"

And so whenever an Indian-on-Indian crime occurred, there was unbridled glee within the Bohemian communities of Why Cheer and Gladwood. The town councils, along with their Protestant backbones, delighted in the exchange of blood and gore. Reporters with gruesome photographs that were still curled from drying met with the police and fire departments to share additional details that might have been overlooked by the camera. Like the vivid color of a tongue that had remained with the decapitated torso. Sometimes when their own townspeople took credit for "Duo-skin-cides" (double suicides of redskins), afternoon outings with hogshead cheese on rye bread, "Old Country" pastries, and iced Kool-Aid were made. With ladies from the Why Cheer Preservation Club decked out in old-fashioned parasols and men in suspenders and large straw hats, there was agreement how befitting it was for heathens to make the railroad tracks their pillow.

"Here! Here!" they were known to yell as they cautiously walked down the tracks balancing their picnic baskets. From the hazy hilltop of O'Ryan's Cemetery, the Indian gravehole diggers said their hats and parasols looked like black crows, hopping angrily from carrion to carrion, as if there wasn't enough "refreshments" to go around.


As the bluish gray moonlight came through the cracks of the curtains and onto her carpeted bedroom, Rose Grassleggings, Black Eagle Child's premiere medicine woman, convinced herself winter was a lonely season to begin with. There was no denying that, not even for the few who *saw* what others couldn't possibly see. She was no exception.

Encumbrance appeared. Regardless of the many people she healed to unparalleled physical renewal, she was constantly being tested in the most devious ways. These dreams, plus the one that lived with her as a nightmarish daughter, were two recurring examples.

The Journey of Encumbrance was explained to her this way by the "Deformed Pearl Diver": *"The Principal Father, for whatever reason, made a pact long ago with the Sinister Deity. It was a truce of sorts; a tenuous abatement in the war among supernatural deities. Already destroyed was the First Earth, and death became a permanent reality for one of his sons, the Lesser-Known Twin Brother. And so it came to be that just as there is kindness, there is outright evil. In a way, we are an ongoing test, for embodied within is all that is needed to properly look after ourselves. . . ."*

The gift of life had therefore been *given,* but during moments when we digressed to unnatural states, we had someone sinister to thank. More and more, the winter acted like a ghost train, picking up the shadows of relatives. How ironic, too, Rose Grassleggings thought, that the snow symbolized the Well-Known Twin Brother's return to earth. This was one of the very first animistic concepts taught to tribal youth. In the form of snow *He* watched everyone, scrutinizing their conduct, and judging whether or not they were responsible.

# Pipestar, Medicine Man
# Extraordinaire

Junior Pipestar, medicine man extraordinaire, sat upright on the undisturbed edge of a Ramada Inn hotel bed. He looked over to the large reddish curtains and motioned to his assistant where minute spots of daylight could be seen on the carpeted floor. In one sweeping motion the young, thin girl stood up and quietly pulled down the cords. Any hint of light and all city traffic sounds beyond the brass curtain rods were shut out by two large, beautiful star quilts that hung on six giant safety pins.

Things might have worked more smoothly, I sometimes reflect, had it not been for the RCA color television. This juxtaposition of natural and supernatural realities seemed awkward. Of course, if the RCA had been turned on deliberately, with the volume set very low, I can see its usefulness—to serve as a buffer for newcomers to an incomprehensible feat. Yet, from another perspective, the RCA was no different from the Kellogg's Corn Flakes that sat on the food tray. The cereal box bore a Kansas City Chiefs football player with a gaudy-looking grin. Further postmodern incongruity. Another annoyance.

As soon as we had entered the room, our eyes fought the intermittent darkness. With our backs to the RCA and the window, Junior Pipestar, twenty-first-century medicine man, sat on the bed, facing us, with a Bic cigarette lighter in one hand and a crudely fashioned cigarette in another. If a sense of utter respect has anything at all to do with being intimidated by a nonordinary human being, especially someone who could see, hear, and conjure what normal people couldn't, then we were quite fearful. According to Rose Grassleggings, this medicine man could commune with ghosts that reached through the floor.

Near the feet of my parents, Tony and Clotelde Bearchild, were four bundles of dry goods and miscellaneous gifts. With the cotton ropes untied, there were eight wool blankets from the Amana Colonies, sixteen cans of Iowa-produced ham, four fifths of Four Roses liquor and thirty hundred-dollar bills dangling from a wreathlike arrangement of cottonwood willows. This was the stipulated payment for not being put on the six-to-eight-month waiting list. We had been graciously accorded twenty minutes.

On behalf of the bereaved Facepaint family my parents and I were there that day in Minneapolis; after driving all morning from central Iowa on Interstate 35 we barely made the appointment due to Super Bowl traffic. Not only were we compelled by the recent loss of a close friend, their son and brother, there was ample reason to suspect another factor was involved. That which is known as murder.

Entangled in the complex, tragic story, however, were the Tama County authorities. As a matter of practice, law enforcement departments viewed most Indian deaths as "alcohol-related suicides" or "more unfortunate accidents." Investigating allegations of Indian-on-Indian crime was minimal, if anything. It was departmental policy to let Indians kill themselves. In some instances it seemed to work. Killers remained free—in a tribal community of fifteen hundred residents—to kill again. And they did. Ted Facepaint, in this case, was a victim twice over.

For over 130 years, the Tama County authorities believed we'd eventually decimate ourselves. Through his growing dependence on alcohol, Ted Facepaint fraternized with most of the area sociopaths —white or Indian. Ever since the Facepaint family broke off from the Well-Off Man Church, a twenty-year sobriety period collapsed under the weight of old acquaintances who possessed Thunderbird wine–soaked livers. Households that revere this toxic bird have children who are apt to become chronic abusers as adults. Which is to say that Ted Facepaint, at forty, was under the influence; he was well beyond the limit.

And so when reports circulated he had been beaten savagely on the Settlement thoroughfares prior to the vehicular mishap, the Facepaint family—with infamous intoxication arrest records—knew they weren't exempt from Tama County's departmental policy of noninvolvement. Fearing retaliation from these authorities if they asked more questions than usual, the Facepaints asked us to meet Junior Pipestar in Minneapolis and handle matters from there.

Renowned throughout Indian country, "Mr. Pipestar"—as we were advised to address him in the parlor of the hotel suite—could provide psychic insights. A day's journey on our part and up-front money for the medicine man's services were required: three thousand dollars, preselected gifts, and other gratuities.

Perhaps the television was a necessary distraction to make people more amenable to the drastic switching of dimensions. *"Even here there was seduction,"* I would record in my journal. *"A painful but calculated nip to the metaphorical newcomer ear by the master of paranormal wizardry. And who could deny the tangibility of surreal cereal ads and the prospect of a long-lost friendship renewed?"*

Through past experiences with hallucinogenic mushrooms, including encounters with ghosts, UFOs, and sorcerers, I was fascinated with theories of how these nightmarish, reality-altering states might have worked. One theory dealt with the vulnerability of the human mind and character. Essentially, without preparation or understanding of powerful, unseen influences, a person was exposed—becoming a "target," if you will. Ignorance made vulnerable people legitimate "targets" within a clan system. If a clan leader, for example, had an impenetrable defense, it was alright to disable or eliminate his or her innocent relatives. It made no difference who, infant or elder. No sexual discrimination for sorcerers. The trick, of course, depended upon the skills of the "shooter."

"When something wrong starts, don't pay it any attention," my grandmother once noted. There was no word for a supernatural manifestation, but I understood what she meant. As the sunlight came through the west window of her small, yellow house, she spoke into the silver grille of the Sony tape recorder: "In order to counteract it, don't dwell upon it. Any thought relinquished weakens the self." During her discourse on the protective quality of trees, a few strands of her ninety-year-old hair loosened, emitting a white, treelike effect against the shadows of the hallway. As the Sony whirred, capturing her words, I thought she stood like the trees that smothered the hillside clear down to the sandy edges of the nearby creek. Overwhelmed, I felt she was the earth herself—Grandmother Earth, that is—because her words of insight encompassed everything.

Ada Principal Bear, my maternal grandmother, believed the small, spring-fed creek that ran beside her yellow house reflected the importance of water for all humankind. There was a tenuousness, first and foremost, in our relationship to the water we drank and the air we breathed. But there was more. Using the base of an empty but hot iron skillet, she said the sparks that crisscrossed the surface symbolized global warfares taking place at that very moment somewhere. Without radio, newspapers, or the English language, she knew flag wars were integral to being alive. If the sparks were many in a day, we sat on the porch and waited for nightfall. The Northern Lights would appear as she had predicted, a distant war gone out of control. Below the glittering stars, the deities would show themselves briefly before mouthing the urgent details about the war's origins and its casualties in numbers. With this tenuousness in mind, there was never assumption in our meager existence, for most had been predetermined. What mattered the most was spirituality and a lifelong undertaking for acceptance to the Black Eagle Child Hereafter.

The geography around her home was an ever-shrinking microcosm of a greater Black Eagle Child world steeped in mythological and spiritual interdependence. Sparse green grass surrounded this disarming site. Embedded along the hillsides were moss-covered boulders that served as messengers to the lesser and greater deities. Under the tin roof of the cookshack was the sacred fire, another messenger. From hanging chains or atop iron grills, food was prepared in blackened kettles for family, the dead, soldiers, humankind, and the Creator alike. Inside, old coon dogs sometimes warmed themselves beside the sleeping embers. Even the dogs were spoken to and did as instructed: to detect unusual things in the night and alarm others, like chicken, geese, or people. Beside the whiskey-soaked ashes and the half-smoked cigarettes—for deceased grandparents who once partook of the same—was an overturned skillet that covered portions of sweets, meats, and fruits from the family table. These portions—if the coon dogs didn't get them—were invisibly sent. The cleansing smoke of the fire, like Grandmother's shroud of words, swirled over the garden, forest, rivers, insects, birds, fish, clouds, rain, stars, and all life-forms, including the deities contained therein.

The trees and the dogs watched her and she watched them in return. Imbued with compassion, she had the same effect on others. I knew that. Essentially, protective elements protected her—in more ways than one. When I was a child who insisted on walking to Why Cheer, she made branches furiously whip about on windless nights, erasing my movie plans. On another occasion, at sundown, we walked into the thickets and came upon a small clearing where the skeletal structure of a miniature lodge unraveled its leather ties and stood up as an oblong formation of willow saplings. I knew that whatever she said was true, for everything under her care and tutelage responded accordingly to her love and kindness.


My grandmother also elaborated on how to evade a supernatural manifestation: "Keep on as you have been doing, and there's a chance it will disappear. When it retreats, speak to it in a spiteful, scolding manner. 'Whoever and whatever you are,' you will say, 'I pray your own wrongdoing turns itself upon you, for you are not wanted here tonight. There is no need for you here; go home and let illness impale itself upon you and fester. . . .'"

It was easy to envision willpower, the evil persuasion, mixed with ancient secrets and medicines, transforming into a luminescent protoplasmic state that floated four to five feet off the ground. Upon command this compact mass acted like a trespasser within the frail, unsuspecting minds that were either awake or asleep. Paranoia, paralysis, and wicked intent, acting as one, disabled the rational mind in the surrealistic huff of a nocturnal Bearlike breath. Information like this was taught indirectly; it was never addressed to me. The Sony tape recorder in this regard was truly priceless.

In the blue-gray, flickering haze of the RCA, we sat utterly still and listened to eerie sounds that were coming through the walls of the Ramada Inn. We thought we heard what sounded like small children playing in the street below. Suddenly, we could hear an adult, a female, sobbing in some kind of marital fear. Raised amid theories on supernaturalism and having witnessed a few events myself, I had yet to meet a person, a human—a former acquaintance at that—who could conjure unfathomable, nonphysical occurrences. I was impressed by this formidable display of reality-altering.

From Pipestar's callused fingers the bulky cigarette emitted long swirling rolls of bluish smoke. His gray eyes squinted coyly at first and then closed as he puffed three to four times in a row with a sense of urgency. He looked discerningly into the blue swirls and began talking in a near whisper. "There's three of them. They're the main ones and—"

Before he could finish, the teenage girl physically interjected with an extended arm, "Mr. Pipestar, you should flick the ashes."

The ashes were then flicked into her cupped palms. The teenager sat back in the chair and transferred the precious ashes into a small leather pouch wrapped around her muscular neck.

My parents stared at the rings of smoke made by Pipestar's expertly controlled exhales of breath.

*"Hypnotic donuts, magic ones,"* I noted in the journal. *"Junior, Jesus Christ, was that you?"*

The cigarette glowed and it crackled loudly through the thick leaves of the Dutch Friesland tobacco. Its blue smoke rings remained stationary and then swirled, stopping midpoint only to pick up in the same speed, encompassing the small tan room.

We saw embedded in the mist what looked like a montage of images and we found ourselves engaged in a game we did as children, looking for faces in clouds. There wasn't much to spring from, but the smoke, moving and constantly being divided by differing air currents, suspended itself in four-to-six-inch interval layers. Upon inhaling it, we smelled the comforting redolence of cedar rather than harsh tobacco. Which was disconcerting.

Here, in the divided fog, we began to experience what Junior Pipestar was noted for. The way the RCA simulated the flashes of a strobe light juxtaposed the objects and people within, their pain, induced a realm that had already been there, an imbrication—a fish scale, the superimposing of previous occurrences, the unseen doors we unknowingly open and pass through each day, night.

We saw how the entire earth, below and above ground, was very much like a graveyard, with the invisible shells of former human existence reacting like massive sails in the wind, and for some reason we stumble into them.

When we could no longer see Pipestar's face and upper torso, his hand, embodying what seemed its own consciousness, levitated from his left knee. This manifestation, a disconnecting human limb, was eons beyond the art of Japanese puppetry.

Either the smoke is thick enough to make the hand appear detached, I whimsically thought, or . . . it has actually been sliced in order to orchestrate this extraordinary trip backward with the *ne a bi a,* a person who can see, to the exact moment of death.

And this was Junior Pipestar's ancient gift, conjuring the past. This was the gift of navigation that kept his traditional healing services in high demand. He possessed knowledge of which plants and trees grew from the earth and their curing traits, and they became his supernatural allies.

I remembered earlier how Pipestar had met us over coffee and apple pie à la mode to explain what was to take place, "the process." "We are like minute pieces of dust afloat inside this dark earthlodge where daylight enters invisibly and slices the blackness," he said, while demonstrating manually with the blinds. He closed and opened them, controlling the entry of sunlight before taking a fork to the ice cream.

"While that which is us is largely unseen as well, it is the meeting, this joining of unseen light and our tumbling life that reflects, revealing a defined presence in the murky subterranean air."

Pipestar's ghost-hand provided the port into this reality-altering dimension; it could travel freely within and make the past relive itself. The hand, as we had been told, literally wore the suit of Pipestar's hand. A limb with bone structure and living tissue is borrowed, like a garment for a few minutes as it reaches out from an intangible world.

As the suited hand gestured, it reminded me in a comical but troublesome manner of a ventriloquism act, the kind supernatural deities—I could only imagine—would perform for one another. It was vaudevillian in essence, but the distortion of dimension actually began there, in humor. A mental cushion was first established for the newcomer. Regardless of how incredible the events appeared, it served as a self-administered anesthetic to the subconscious. Strangely, mine dealt with television personalities.

As my own surreal retrospection began, I saw how humans and nonhumans entertained one another, whether in life or death or somewhere between. The one aspect that provided a semblance of sanity was the association of Pipestar's ghost-hand to the detached hand called Thing of the 1960s television show *The Addams Family.* Novelties that I grew up with became part of the transference to past events, turning an aberration into a comedy. *"No wonder Americans are so fucked up,"* I wrote. *"Think of all the things that could arise from this abnormal fascination with death. Morbid scrutiny turned backward and inside out. No privacy or resolution for a society bound for mass suicide . . ."*

Scattered over the landscape were discarded shells of the once-living. Their sails caught the wind for centuries. There were so many ghosts overlapping other ghosts that everything became a retrospection. Drifting without direction over the vast plains in multitudes, we became a reenactment of their stories. Up close they were said to resemble fluffs from a cottonwood tree on a windy day. This was where preplanning for humankind took place. Here nothing was important or unimportant. Amid the floating dust the cottonwood fluff was accidentally struck by a beam of daylight, as Pipestar had said, setting off a faint glimmer inside the Ramada Inn.

Force-fed to believe there's a constructive answer to everything, I foolishly adduced that what I had just witnessed was something easily explainable. Throwing false voices to a grotesque wooden puppet wasn't all that was there, however. Minute bits of rationality had been dissected and left to twist and dry in turbulent provocations. Undeniably, the master voice-thrower spoke the hand's words. The voice began as a faint fluttering, like a small desperate bird getting caught behind the window curtains, but as it changed into the distant rumbling of an approaching thunderstorm, I envisioned being in a cabin on precarious stilts overlooking a mountainous valley that was about to shake.

As the storm got closer, reverberating in a low monotonous drone, the normal audiological senses were splintered. The higher the buzzing became, the more spherical the spatial proportions of the hotel room scene—where I was really at.

The carpet inflated, along with the desk and table lamps. The furniture took the same route as well by forcing air into its wooden lungs. The separate pieces of furniture began to breathe, expanding in the corners like wary, snarling animals. Underneath our feet, the earth did the exact opposite: It deflated, became brittle, and cracked into a thousand pieces of iciclelike formations. We slid into a nightmarish vortex of perceptual change.

All this from airborne cigarette smoke? I questioned, as thick billows of fog seeped through the tiny cracks where the floor merged structurally with the four walls. I attempted again to analyze this methodical destruction of reasoning: *"The montage of all those people who had lived, for instance, were in actuality our own mortality, an awkward depiction thereof, theatrical in substance but nonetheless a metamorphosis, a glint of the existential mirror in the woods. We would ferret out tragedy, mete it out randomly, along with the predictable suffering, the beauty, its love, and wonder. We remained answerless in a question-filled iridescent sky. . . .*

*That's who we were. Unskilled pilots through an unplanned existence. We were hopelessly imprisoned, the progeny of lost shadows. We were also in dire need of federal-funded psychologists who specialized in tribal-related despondency and dysfunction.*

*Prisoners of earth. POEs . . ."*

When Pipestar's ghost-hand began indicating places where each participant stood on that 1989 night when the Hyena brothers celebrated Mardi Gras, Howdy Dowdy, Morticia, and Gomez dissipated in the predawn fog. The silhouettes of trees on the tribal fairgrounds came into view, replacing the hotel room walls. The hand was careful not to point directly to the people present. Through him, with the crooked cigarette as our guide, we were verbally transported to the actual scene of the crime. The words were painful at the slightest mention of Ted, the vivid descriptions of the fight he had put up and lost to the attackers who were attired . . . in women's clothing.

A cool and nearly imperceptible breeze entered the room and touched our skin. An affirmation.

"Others were there but they had little or no part," spoke Pipestar in a matter-of-fact tone. "They're all afraid of being implicated for being there. Their secret is akin to having an alcoholic's urge to use a railtrack for a pillow. But these three were the instigators, and they were also the most vulnerable—being hopped up on drugs, smoke, and alcohol."

Along with my parents I anchored myself to each word transmitted and held on tenaciously, for this meeting could be reported only once. Reality and nonreality, for our own psychological safety, was switched to on and off sequences like a rare electrical implement. An internal mechanism could shut it off as soon as imbalance was attained. Japanese puppetry brought it back. In these places I saw how it might be possible to formulate human figures and their actions through the fluctuating airborne smoke.

"But there's also a fourth," continued Pipestar. "While this one didn't actually touch Facepaint, he was responsible in leading him out to the tribal fairgrounds and setting him up with the other three. Which is just as bad . . . There's something wrong here, though. Something frightening, the potential for harm . . . because he is mentally unstable, yet he interacts with people. Normally. That makes him dangerous—being wounded and exposed. He is not an Indian among you, he is mixed. In not being what he could have been, he lashes out at those who are. Like he did to Facepaint. In any case, the three young men were indeed 'used, *a wa te ni*,' by both human and nonhuman sources. Messages were implanted during their drug and alcohol-weakened states of consciousness. When talons of this caliber interlock, no one has a chance. But there's more to this and I'll explain. Do you have any questions?"

My parents, perhaps wishing to slow down the emotionally charged meeting, inquired about the three owls who appeared in our yards at dusk to casually stroll across the lawn. They also inquired about the owl that divided itself into three golf ball–sized lights. These lights then chased them before shooting upward and freezing in a star's place.

"These three are night-enemies. They saw how drunk these three young men were and took over their minds, instructing them in their hour of weakness on what they should do, which was to inflict intense bodily harm or commit murder. But there was a precedent; we know it was delivered in the guise of another event. It gave the appearance of revenge, but it was basically evil taking advantage of evil. Twicefold. But it took lots of serious planning, for the opportunity was seen years ago."

# One Bucket
# of Twenty Moons

**Junior Pipestar:**
Near the tenth winter of my early existence—"120 moons exactly," as
my grandmother had calculated and translated—I found myself
stripped down to my underwear beside the rocky bank of the Cedar
River. In the cold subzero weather I shivered uncontrollably as my
body parts seemed to contract into the skeletal hollow of rib cage and
chapped hips. My elbows melted to my skin and became stumpy arms,
and I stood contorted.

(Today when I envision this scene, I see myself as a hieroglyph
of a eunuch in attendance of some maniacal but enchanting Egyp-
tian queen who desires entertainment. Someone named Nefertiti or
Cleopatra, whom I saw depicted and read about in encyclopedias—
the masterpiece portrait bust of "Nef" and, of course, "Cleo," whore
to Julius C.)

Across the river, Bruiser and Hundo—a husky and a young pit
bull—ran beside the frost-covered forest with craned necks and
pointed ears, trotting and sometimes breaking into a prance. Their
black paws broke through the coarse snow, reminding me of show
horses with stiffened manes. When a fox squirrel broke from a tree,
a chase ensued over the railroad tracks. In a frozen submissive state
I couldn't stop the squirrel-chasing.

Slightly bent over, I stood and balanced myself as the polar land-scape reverberated. There were barks followed by echoes, and then there was only the northern wind. Bruiser and Hundo could have been taken in sacrifice to the North to plead my case. They were fine, majestic animals—one like a silent wolf and the other a two-headed beast—with clouds of their frenetic breathing punctuating their small-game hunt.

Didn't ancient Egyptians entomb pets of the deceased? To hon-orably serve as protectors of their masters even in death? Yes? Well, with some tribes it's the same—to a certain extent. But not as lavish as, let's say, an Asian warlord who is buried with a regiment of statue warriors and their weaponry. With so little to be thankful for in my childhood, I don't know how I would have said it to my grandfather: What if bad luck strikes and I die? Would Bruiser and Hundo be entombed with me?

"Do you think plastic flowers over graves mean anything?" Grandfather might have snapped. "They're attractive reminders, but dead people can't eat synthetic petals and stems." The joke referred to whites divorcing themselves from their kindred ghosts, not feed-ing them specially cooked food. Their favorite sweets, meats, drink, and tobacco. Remiss mortuary customs and such. There was retri-bution of sorts. Manifestations of the anger of the dead and forgot-ten souls merged into tornadoes, destroying their farms and cities. Elsewhere the ground shook and split open, avalanches slid down mountainsides, and thundershowers bombarded a rain-soaked val-ley until a river of mud swallowed people and made them part of the landscape's horizon.


In the skylit haze of a December Iowa morning, I mentally recited a song that had been taught to me by Joseph All Stars, my half-blind grandfather. It was a Song of Necessity to beseech spiritual aid dur-ing my chest-high wade across the open part of the river. Over the summer the family dove for clams here. In a different season, with floating, massive slabs of ice, the shallow stretch of river was impos-ing. Each chunk of ice represented obstacles—natural and unnatu-ral adversities—I would later meet.

As strong gusts of wind drove flecks of biting snow into my exposed skin, I almost shouted out the first crucial verses of the song. But I shout-withheld and cringed in remembrance of how glasslike shavings from sawed clamshells felt when they became lodged in the sweaty pores. I looked to the gray North where work was being done on a Supernatural Clamshell and wondered: If fine grains of snow can sting this much, what will become of me helplessly wedged between jagged, protruding pieces of ice? Razors were lightly tapped over the tender limbs of girls in first menses, but this was crazy. Later, half-dollar-sized shells, the ones I helped sand to shape, would be placed over my wounds and blessed as future ornamentation.

The stinging snow continued to layer until I pictured the snowflakes changing into knives, inverted icicles, impaling themselves to my torso in barbed increments.

(Actually, I didn't know which was less threatening: a crystal porcupine rolling away like a tumbleweed before splintering beyond recognition or a block of ice containing a missing half-Indian boy in off-white underwear. To imagine what could have happened . . . that's just dandy! The local press would have salivated while developing the negative, getting aroused by the pungent smell of hypo and other things.)

The maple tree saplings along the sandy beach of the Cedar River clattered, as did the clenched jaws with my small teeth in between. Under my breath, the words formulated in anticipation of the half-submerged icy walk:

> *A ke tti ki wa ni-e ne bwa ka wa ni-we tti na na na to na ni:*
> *Wi to ka wi ka ba-ni ba ma te se wa ni? Ta ka mi a tto ke wa ni?*

> For the reason you are old and wise is the reason I ask:
> Would you permit life for me? If I wade across?

The year was 1960. My grandfather, Joseph All Stars, wearing his best old German Amana wool blanket, moccasins with mink fur lining, buckskin leather leggings, a fire engine red breechcloth, and an otter-hide turban, sat in relative comfort and warmth near an uprooted cottonwood tree that had been set ablaze. As the fire crackled and hissed, he pointed to my bare feet with an antique medieval French sword. In a stuttering melodic tune he reminded me of the second verse.

*Sing the first four verses*
*when your feet are*
*underwater.*
*Shortly after touch the water.*

With the blade pointed next to my hands, he chanted further in a soft fractured tone:

*Sing the next set when*
*the river comes up to your elbows.*
*But when the river is up to*
*your neck—*
*this is extremely important now—*
*change the words.*
*Slightly.*
*Everything depends*
*on how*
*you do this.*
*Keep your thoughts clear*
*of disturbances. Let the dogs hunt;*
*they are helping you*
*by not distracting you, feeling sorry*
*for you.*
*They know you*
*have to sing in this fashion,*
*grandson:*

*"For the reason they are old and wise is the reason I ask them:*
*Will you permit life? If I come across?"*

I remembered the third and fourth verses—changing the "they" to "we" and "them" to "you"—had to be sung during the actual crossing and midpoint in the river itself. To intone these word-songs, he emphatically urged, would push back the icy river from the physically compressed heart.

The medieval French sword was chimed against the rock-strewn sand.

> *Do you understand*
> *everything that you are supposed*
> *to do?*
> *The songs' sequences?*
> *It is imperative that*
> *you do.*

During the whole Passage of Necessity I wasn't permitted to communicate verbally; one had to reserve strength for the ultimate plea, Grandfather All Stars had reminded, that of life itself.

To indicate I clearly understood, I waved my arm twice between his limited field of vision and the shiny surface of a sword blade, named "side one" in jest. The sword's mirrorlike sheen was the only light source capable of penetrating his marble blue diseased eyes. The opposite, "side two," was left unpolished and used in extreme sunlit conditions only.

Momentarily blocking the sword's blade light, sending a quick shadow onto my grandfather's weathered face, let him know you were about. He preferred that type of greeting as opposed to voices or intrusive touches to the wrist. For people who rarely touched one another except in marriage and child-rearing, touching was not customary, necessary, or welcome. Caring in essence was not the sum of hands or arms wrapped around a relative, or wet lips upon lips. Affection had to do simply with being there as part of a family.

My presence was known by two quick hand waves near the shiny blade middle. Custom dictated he instruct in a singing voice, a skill that took a lifetime to acquire and perfect; Grandfather All Stars was characteristically reserved and didn't expend energy by inquiring in song who was signaling. He could talk normally, though, and he could hear fine. Especially by nightfall, once the sword's hilt clicked against the engraved scabbard.

* * *

In a brief spell of awareness as an infant, I heard my strange cousin, Denton, refer to Grandfather as a "meter of spiritual devotion." I memorized the English words for some reason and didn't know what they meant until my grandmother noted the glass-covered device affixed to the side of our house that measured electrical usage. Under Grandfather's scrutiny our piety was constantly being judged through our physical emanations. Considering the irreverence exhibited by Denton, I wasn't surprised by his comment. For Denton there was nothing to measure.

Whenever the yellow utilities truck from Rural Power Cooperative drove up the farm driveway thereafter, I associated its company logos—a cartoon of a smiling lightbulb-headed man with a lightning-bolt body—with faith, and mused how a displaced Canadian Indian family in the wretched hinterlands of the American Midwest lost it all. . . .


As my thin, fragile body began marking the Cedar River's depth— first the feet and then my hands, elbows, and neck—I sang the appropriate verses in the midst of indescribable cold, and the soles of my feet felt like they were being scorched by the hot coals of an underwater fire. Eventually forced to start swimming by deep, unexpected drop-offs, I gasped and lunged forward, somehow maneuvering myself between giant wedges of ice. The flames of the icy fire rose in conspiracy and slashed prescient pictures on my arms, legs, hips, and rib cage. With punctured skin and coagulated blood, my bare chest became an instant perforated shirt.

(During this agony I envisioned Grandmother sitting calmly on the bed with her daughter Emma, tapping the straight razor like a telegraph key over her bare back. It was a bloodletting code known only to the Supernatural Clam, that of the Shining Red Shell Woman.)

Once, when a pack of ice got in my way, I lunged on top, hopped to numb feet, and ran the length, diving headfirst without caution. As I surfaced, even with Grandfather's encouraging shouts behind me, I became disoriented and couldn't breathe properly; I began emitting heaving sounds like a child does when a cry can't be stopped.

When the final set of verses came up, I took several inhales of air mixed with slush and called for help (dialing frantically, no doubt, for Aphrodite, born from sea foam, protector of seafarers: 1–800–GOD-DESS). I wept and swam forward like that mythical frog deity—the Invisible Musician, the frog from those old stories who skimmed over the summer swamp grass in its flight from the green, French-speaking eagle—until my legs felt something solid, holding me up, something that felt like a carved slab of stone. . . .

In 1920, as a young night-enemy disciple—an endeavor he attributed to naïveté—Grandfather All Stars climbed onto the roof of a bark-covered longhouse one evening to observe and spy on an adversary. He explained that in thinking the sorceress was crippled, he believed he could make a lot of commotion. She probably won't bother to inspect the noise, he had foolishly assured himself. Under this assumption he shimmied over to the smoke portal and looked down into the interior illuminated by the open cooking fire. Silhouetted against the red-hot wood ashes was a stone knife. He said there was a flicker, a movement: a hand had tossed a lethal combination of antiwitchcraft medicines over the stone knife. He knew exactly what he had come up against. Green birch leaves that had a dusty coating, fine twig roots of the female and male clusterberry, along with pieces of woolen lint—a reinforcing agent—shot up as smoke and singed his inquiring eyes.

In recounting this story he would grab his eyes and lean over in pain.

"The last thing I saw was the lame sorceress's weapon silhouetted over the iron grill, the intense fire being fanned by a crow's wing. Before I had a chance to jump free, the antiwitchcraft smoke blew out from the longhouse and cauterized the delicate tissue of my eyes. The sorceress laughed like an insane owl as I slid off and plummeted to the ground. Sadly, there was no antidote."

It was a strange turn of events: The same knife-shaped stone that deprived him of sight made a French medieval sword surface one day from between two intertwined box elder trees as he was led by rope by his niece to the river to wash clothes. Its silver glint pierced his morose, embittered mind. In descriptive, haunting sentences he told how the trees subtly ground into one another, making human-sounding whispers, *"Eh-e-e-s-s-h-h-e-e-eh! A yo he i, ne si me! Ayo! Over here, my little brother! Here!"*

*"Ha-i! We ko ne tta-ne ta we ne ta me kwi.* Ha-i! What is it that you want?" Grandfather All Stars cried out, jerking back the rope and nearly dislocating several bones from his niece's delicate shoulders.

The box elder trees creaked in the wind and spoke again.

*"Ke ke te ma ke ne me ko ki-tti na we ne ma tti ki-ki tti me ba te si tti ki.* Your (deceased) relatives feel sorry toward you. *Ne ta no ka ne ko be na-ni bwe to na ki-ma ni-ke tti-ma te si.* They asked that we bring you this long knife. *A se ni-ma te si-ke ne tti wa na ji e kwi-tte na-ma ni-bi ya be ko wi ki-a kwi.* The stone knife destroyed you but this metal one will not."

And like muscles under stress that help ease a thorn from its wound, the sword emerged at the precise moment he determined his suicide was preferable to hand-scrubbing unseen clothes. Helplessness of self and dependence on others gone. It was amid this sublime contemplation that a silver light pulsated and the tree deities spoke. There was sincerity in their words, Grandfather would pontificate, and the flowing Cedar River sounds nearby corroborated that the sword was a god-given implement. He dropped the laundry sack, asked his niece for food and supplies, and spent the next few days carving out the antique sword from the milky red twisting lines of the box elder grains.

As I reminisce about that particular wintry day, I am convinced the knife-shaped stone that stole Grandfather All Stars's eyesight arose from its watery grave and floated directly below my dog-paddling feet until I made contact and stood up, balancing like an ancient Hawaiian on a sacred slab of stone, a surfstone. In the singular block of daylight that came through the static clouds—a synthesis of science and destiny—I was propelled past the reef-crashing waves. Within that particular beam of daylight the dust particles of our lives collected into a definable, corporeal shape. There were pale seabirds who flew just above the watery explosion, following the contour of the tropical landscape sculpted by the bird deity eons ago. Nearby, sleek black fish were navigating toward the islands, zigzagging through the rocky narrows.

It happened like that. The river surfing business. My journey began with small, colorful dreams that foretold. They didn't mean much initially, but when I started telling my parents and relatives what I thought would happen, predicting events became easy. A radiance would envelop my face when "the knowing of exactly what will happen" unfolded. It was a talent that I fought against, however. In the end my resistance was useless. Suffering was a prevalent factor in anything, like the river-surfing incident. Fording a river of ice was a minuscule achievement, however, compared to dreaming: the dream of the white and yellow convertible that rounded a Claer street sideways on two wheels and the one about the soldier who threatened to injure himself under the Cedar River bridge invaded my senses. They clubbed me senseless in adolescent sleep. Two passengers, except the driver, died in the convertible and the lonesome soldier died under a bridge in Germany.

"Indians and alcohol in unfamiliar places, if this were a mathematical equation, equals incongruity," Denton, my strange cousin, used to say. "Like catfish bloated with dead shad in the springtime, it was fuckin' bound to happen. Piss on the naysayers if they don't believe you, Junior!"

Edgar Bearchild used to preface and summarize stories by saying: *Ma ni tta-i ni-e na ska ki-a ji mo ni.* In this direction does the story fall." Bearchild used this phrase to an obsessive degree for everything. I later realized this statement freed the narrator from any information presented. *In this direction* being the disclaimer for words spoken in perhaps an unfavorable context, *does the story fall* being inevitability. History, or rather centuries of political subjugation, made Bearchild and the rest a careful lot. Black Eagle Child Indians were hard to befriend; yet they were honest and forthright. . . . Now where am I going with this? Was Bearchild's quote applicable here?

In this direction does the story fall:

The angry wind of December blew down upon the ice-crackling river, causing the water to churn and boil until the frothy waves became larger and larger, crashing resoundingly into the shallow shoreline. The maple saplings clattered against each other and bewildered crows crashed into the treetops in their flight from a wind of fear. Clouds of breath expelled changed into crystal tumbleweeds that rolled away, only to shatter over the beach in pieces. Decorated in bleeding clamshells and covered with layers of glazed ice, I rolled after the crystal tumbleweeds in a semiconscious state. (I was, you could say, mummified. Cryogenics.)

At the precise moment that the squirrel-chasing dogs howled, the stone surfboard whisked me away from the dangerous breakers. Guided by the faint, flashing light from Grandfather's sword the surfboard skipped across the treacherous river while melting sheets of ice slid off my arms and legs. The white sun that came through the gray overcast clouds bounced off "side one" of the French medieval sword and marked a singular hot spot on the opposite side of the river where I was catapulted.

# The Meaning behind Hawaiian Punch

Considering Ted Facepaint had stopped visiting my family altogether, he was still a good friend. Nonetheless I avoided mourning Facepaint's loss. There was simply too much to do in terms of establishing a credible and unbiased investigation. Ted's family were binge-drinking like they had never done. None of them, especially his aunt and uncle, Louise Stabs Back and Clayton Carlson Facepaint, were fit to contradict the findings of the special coroner, the county attorney, and "Barney Fife," the county sheriff.

This is where I voluntarily stepped in as the unofficial Facepaint family counsel. That much at least I owed Ted. Whatever action I could muster would come from my mediocre notoriety as a writer. He had encouraged me often enough to use my writing abilities for just causes, criticizing me when he thought I was using my writing "as a paper wall from clan responsibility." Now that my occupation was working on his behalf, it seemed awkward, requesting Ted's guidance.

But it happened.

It began the day after the wake, shortly before the funeral, while I stood spellbound in front of the bathroom mirror. "Ted, my friend," I whispered solemnly into the steamed reflection in the oval mirror. "Do you want me to get involved in the investigation of your murder?" At that precise moment, Selene, my wife, was on the telephone with her younger sister, Evelyn, who was seeking advice from their brother, Octavius Buffalo Husband, who was in the living room portion of their mobile home. In a voice that sounded remarkably similar to Ted's, Octavius said, "Yes, but this has to be done right away." I was stunned, hearing a response to my rhetorical question from the unknown beyond. When I reached out to clear an opening on the steamed mirror with my nervous hand, I heard him again. It was as if he were standing within me, looking at me woefully from behind my own eyes. His voice picked up and then fell back to its real owner. "They've gone this far. Things ain't gonna change because there's a new school." That incisive comment by Octavius jolted me back to reality.

Nevertheless, enlightened by this nonordinary but affirmative message, I started the process by contacting Senator Dan Frazier, the Republican farmer. For years he sent form letters congratulating my "valuable artistic contributions to America as a native Iowan—and a Poet." But his "helping hand" to the various law enforcement agencies involved turned out to be bureaucratic brush-offs. Ditto with the Federal Bureau of Investigation. If you're a prominent Iowa politician's intoxicated teenage daughter who snuffed two people on a highway, folks around us said, paperwork for a lenient sentence would be pushed and passed. If you're an Indian who happens to be a published author from a county of bigots, claiming "Murder! Not an unfortunate accident!" there will be—

That's how it all started. I theorized that Ted's miniature catlinite pipe became lonesome for its owner and began transmitting distress signals through a steamed reflection in the bathroom mirror and a timely corresponding voice. Ted's shadow began homing in, or it tried to. Knowing we would soon meet with buyers from the Minneapolis Institute of Art, Ted had brought it to our home after working on it for a year. The intricately carved slab pipe had the distinction of fitting perfectly in the palm of anyone's hand, large or small. The style was reminiscent of ancient mound-builder art. Since the dog effigy pipe was still technically Ted's personal property, I contemplated, it must have transformed into a beacon, slicing through unearthly barriers with its mournful cry. Inside Selene's jewelry box, the pipe had been wrapped in a reddish brown cloth with yellow figures representing Cambodian divinities. As Ted's ghostly shadow visited the houses of those who might have openly wept for him, the beacon must have "locked on" to something the moment I walked into the bathroom.


Disappointed with Senator Frazier and increasingly flustered by the special coroner's persistent claims that the facial and body wounds came from the automobile impact alone, I urinated thick red blood one week later. In the same bathroom at home. I guess that's when the emotional trauma of Ted's violent end hit me. It seemed incredible that Facepaint could die from "being unrestrained by a seat belt and landing repeatedly on the knobless gear shift, which punctured his ribs and chest." More so when new accounts gradually surfaced that he had been pursued and then rammed off old Lincoln Highway 30 after being assaulted by the three Hyena brothers. Although no names were given, this violent scenario was divulged a month later in Minneapolis by Junior Pipestar, the medicine man. To first be stabbed repeatedly by sharpened screwdrivers and then chased en route to the Heijen Medical Center was aggressive by any standard. Ted was found near the community of Suntour by a tribal member on his way to work at the Sherifftown pork processing plant. On the frozen portion of what was otherwise a soft, sandy hill, the front seat of the 1956 Ford with the Arbie's Pig Feeds logos became Ted's final bed. In broad daylight not one Suntour citizen had bothered to stop and see if anyone was in the smoldering wreckage on the outskirts of town.

But we knew the reason why: Indians are viewed as inferior beings. According to the adage employed locally, better to let an Indian die than permit its regeneration. This attitude is a carryover from early colonists who authorized the killing and excoriation—skinning—of any Indian males above the age of ten for bounty.

"Even when we dress better and are more clean in terms of hygiene, we are dirty by virtue of skin color," Mr. Mateechna, the janitor, used to say as he herded us into the biweekly showers at Weeping Willow Elementary. "So do your best to surpass them, but always be aware they can shoot you from a very long distance. An act of cowardice, but you die anyway."

Mr. Mateechna would smack his lips against the Juicy Fruit gum before prodding us with a stiff bristle brush, indicating areas we needed to lather and scrub. We obeyed and listened earnestly. "White culture—its wicked otherness—is like a father and son rapist team, and we are a teenage victim who has somehow survived a night of torture, sodomy, and three unsuccessful attempts on our life: a drowning where we have untied the ropes turns to a beating with a tire iron as we emerge from the debris-filled river, gagging and spitting out mud, and when we fall back, bullets ricochet off our skull and into the water."

This is what was conveyed as we stood listening under the soapy showers. We were said to smell different, moldlike, and we had the diet and mating habits of a crippled but vicious animal. Further, and there was eyewitness testimony, Indian mothers openly "tongue-lapped their mutts" upon their birth and their nipples were communally shared by the litter.

When the Why Cheer ambulance and fire crews finally arrived at Facepaint's accident site, the tribal casino–donated "Mega Jaws of Life" were late. For amusement purposes only, the hydraulic-driven mechanical teeth pried open the door that bore the roller-skating pig.

Making the case more difficult were the Hyena brothers' relatives, who corroborated hour by hour their whereabouts that night. "He was home, like the others, sleeping," said one relative of the accused half brother. Another family member in an abrasive alcoholic tone said, "Nobody went anywhere that night, except to the Bingo Hall, but we all came home. Together. He won three hundred dollars at bingo, yah-ha-ha-heh-heh!" Another relative of one of the accused—the main suspect—reported that their "good boy visited Mexican in-laws in Des Moines, drank with them, got mizzed."

These false statements, along with the sheriff's hasty, noncomprehensive interviews, stalled the investigation. Until that night, many in the tribe had let the brothers' cross-dressing abnormalities slide. In hearing about the predatorial nature of the crime the community was appalled. More so when the accused Hi-na brothers had established what seemed to be indisputable alibis. Finding their weapons became a compulsive obsession. For the Facepaints, for us. We knew who the killers were, but there was an abysmal lack of incriminating evidence. At hours when we would be inconspicuous, risking danger, we searched areas where they might have fought, struggled, leaving behind particles of clothing or hair, or any clues. It was the one factor that postponed my bereavement, finding items that could tie the Hi-na brothers to the location. But the blood in the urine business, as aforementioned, changed all that.

*Life drained.*
*Life unresolved.*
*A child is made*
*back into what*
*it once was:*
*a replica, liquid*
*in form, weary*
*and torn.*

*With toad-*
*like fingers*
*braced against*
*the foggy mirror,*
*a reflection that is*
*        not human*
*queries if something*
*that is gone can ever*
*come back.*

Selene almost got into a crying scene at the tribal health clinic when the toilet stool turned Hawaiian Punch red after I filled the specimen jar and was unable to stop the flow. Of course, I shouldn't have wimp-shouted out for help; I went into a state of panic. After all I had been through at the Heijen Medical Center and the funeral home where we dressed Facepaint in traditional regalia, I didn't think I could get sick. Internally. From the red-splattered walls of the bowl and the seat cover, I wondered what could be so shredded apart in my body organs. My thoughts petrified.

Later, with her pudgy Caucasian face near the specimen jar, the tribal health clinic nurse asked in a breath smelling of mustard, rye bread, and bologna if I had been unfaithful to Selene. From there the soap opera bolted into a full gallop. If it wasn't unqualified tribal employees—some with sexual abuse records—giving over-the-counter medical assessments, it was the physicians and the nurses themselves who got into an authoritarian prance, trampling whatever bureaucratic trust we had to bits. Of course, maybe the question of fidelity was pertinent, but the way it was articulated was completely tasteless and bizarre.

In any event, I asked the nurse rather sternly, "Just what in the fuck does this have to do with this bloody fruit juice?" Selene moved next to me and lightly touched the inside of my elbow. Through her tear-reddened eyes she pleaded that I settle down.

The nurse ignored the profanity in my question and skipped over to the laboratory like she was—excuse me, weight-conscious people—one of the gargantuan dancing hippos in Walt Disney's *Fantasia*. When albino-complexioned cellulite protruded through her blouse, Claude Youthman's quote about hefty women dawned. It was inappropriate and offensive. But considering the nurse's insinuation, I found my creativity operating like a popcorn machine. Rambling but pertinent items suddenly revealed themselves at just the right temperature over the flame, popping open in the sizzling lid-covered sausage grease: Before Claude Youthman's infamous cantaloupe attack on state dignitaries, for which he served prison time, he suggested that large women whose "blouse buttons were stretched to the max" could "sexually and anatomically vacuum" a man in bed better than bespeckled toothpick types. His commentaries were unbelievable and thought-provoking. But Pat "Dirty" Red Hat—all 290 pounds–plus—preferred Twiggy-type Settlement women. Red Hat, in turn, theorized that Youthman languished in infantile depravity, a mother hang-up, associating Jell-O-y breasts with pillows, food, and other such stuff.

"Follow me to the laboratory-y-y, plee-e-e-z-z-zeee," sang the hippo nurse while issuing furtive looks as if I were guilty of sexual indiscretion. Selene became even more distraught. Numb and insulted, we followed her anyway. "The laboratory" consisted of a single microscope, three quart-sized plastic bottles of alcohol, used tongue depressors and gauze, and a small refrigerator next to the two chrome faucets of a rusty countertop sink.

With her enormous belly propped on the wet countertop, the nurse adjusted the eyepiece of the antique microscope and musically remarked, "Wee-e-e-e are not-t-t-t go-o-o-ing to overlook any possi-i-i-billi-i-ity! Isn't that right, Dr. Wright?"

"Well, about your suspicions of infidelity, hell no," I promptly returned, with eyes fixated on the doctor's noncommittal gray eyes.

We turned again to the hippo nurse who was still craning her sparsely haired neck over the microscope. "Why that's re-e-e-ass-s-s-suri-i-ing!" she retorted as she synchronously tapped the glass slides together with her six stubby hippo fingers. The last taps made my teeth grind into the jawbone. I wanted to ask sarcastically if she'd like a real punch.

And these were the people who bungled the handling of Ted's body, I later complained to Selene on our way out. Dr. Wright, "Goofy," sent Ted's body to the Sherifftown hospital where Dr. Plees eventually saw it by coincidence inside the glass doors. Dr. Wright averted blame by admitting "a grave nontypical error had been made." He also mentioned hearing reports that Dr. Plees, special coroner, genuflected and made an upside-down cross sign over Ted's sheet-covered body before telling Ted in Black Eagle Child to vacate the human body. "Well, go home then, Man Squirrel," he was said to have instructed at the Heijen Medical Center entrance.

In traditional belief, Ted's shadow was instantly catapulted from his body into an adjoining nonhuman realm. There, it awaited his shadow's ceremonial transference to the Afterlife. Since Ted's family were former Star-Medicine eaters, a gratuitous effort was made to include these precautionary arrangements, but it wasn't enough.

A collision of values and prejudices was inevitable.

The former Star-Medicine eaters distrusted traditional mortuary customs; the special coroner was on a vindictive wavelength; and Dr. Wright, who replaced Dr. Plees for our Indian health care, kept up the calamitous atmosphere. The aged widower did the minimal

amount of work as required by whatever guidelines the tribal administration had instituted. Everyone who had been a patient of his knew
he was a screwup. Behind the drawn curtain Dr. Wright imposed the
same kind of sickness on others that plagued "Kensey" Muscatine,
former Tribal Council chair and now a convicted sex offender.

But there was no recourse. We could either pay for our own
medical care or go through Dr. Wright. Even with the tribal gambling enterprise, no one could yet afford a second, specialized medical opinion. The sick would therefore wait until it was too late,
knowing Dr. Wright would have failed in his diagnosis to begin with.
To keep costs down, he proclaimed the tribal health clinic as "the
disease stopping point." When he wasn't fondling teenage breasts,
rolling around someone's testicles without purpose, or inserting his
gloveless, long-fingernailed fingers in undesirable areas, the doctor
thought he had a cure for most New World diseases.

Regarding the belated discovery of Ted's lifeless, car-encapsulated
body in Suntour, the doctor was reprimanded for not contacting the
Facepaint family for instructions as to whether a "shadow-releasing"
ritual was to be done first, along with an autopsy. The way it turned
out, Dr. Plees pounced upon Ted as he lay breathless on the ambulance stretcher, committing sacrilege through Black Eagle Child words
spoken without even lifting the bloodstained sheet, then saying "a
cursory autopsy was performed."

It was pettiness on all levels.

On the exterior it had the makings of a holy war: anarchist-
wielding-a-torch-of-justice-for-a-deceased-friend versus the Earthlodge
clan/Tribal Council. In spite of the cheap political power playing and
maneuvering, the Outside World was undoubtedly present, but it was
inconsequential in the overall spectrum of the nonordinary forces at
work. Since the Facepaints were former Star-Medicine eaters, and I
was an outspoken critic of a hobblelegged tribal government, there
were vendettas that needed attending to.

Horatio, "Grubby," and "Kensey" long resented the involvement
of Ted and me in the episode during which a photograph was taken
by a boy named "Little Big Man" in the summer of 1969. Due to this
picture, Ted Facepaint, Pat "Dirty" Red Hat, and myself became their
enemies. With their lips interlocked and salivating, Horatio and

"Grubby" tried to swallow each other like giant bullfrogs in a fight-to-the-death-for-the-harem ritual. Beside them, "Kensey" was play-ing "pocket pool" and cheerleading. Their explanation about the event was that it was a club initiation based on the practices of notorious motorcycle gangs. Making things appear cool was the quick impreg-nation of Elvia Plain Brown Bear, Horatio's older sister, by "Grubby."

Although we alluded to the photograph, we never showed it to anyone. But now, twenty years later—through Ted Facepaint's death, then the Tribal Council's failure to support a proper investigation and the exhumation of the body for what would have been a first and only autopsy—resentment for the famous "Little Big Man Shoots Dragon-flies" escapade was still apparent. The tribal health clinic, under the auspices of the Tribal Council, supported the actions of Tama County law enforcement officers and the coroner with regard to Ted's death. Many parties seemed oblivious to Indian-on-Indian crime. It appeared the whole tribe was implicated as coconspirators.

Along the wooded, sheltering hills of the Black Eagle Child Settlement the prophetic warnings from the wiser elders resounded. Those who knew and heard prayed quietly with their families; and those who didn't give a turd, ate it.

Anyway, the Hawaiian Punch incident at the tribal clinic and the steps taken to circumvent and resolve Ted's exhumation issue made me think of Dr. Plees. In particular, about who he was, the good and bad things he had done while in service to the tribe, and, most im-portant, what he had become in the past ten years.

These transmuted thoughts, beyond astronomical, also steered me to a question that had been festering in the subconscious for a decade: When would the literary canoe on which I so fiercely paddled upstream capsize from the boney weight of indecision, alcohol abuse, mild drugs, and general aimlessness?

After a stint at the University of Iowa, where I experienced cam-pus claustrophobia for the academic year 1972–1973, I published a chapbook of poetry through the South Dakota Fine Arts Press. Dr. Plees, through a government-sponsored research grant on tribal health needs, was one of the first people in Tama County to buy a copy. For him, in those first years home from Southeast Asia, the Black Eagle Child Settlement was a healing ground. After two years away, he returned to our community in 1975.

For me, back then, the Settlement signified emotional instability: Struggling to breathe and addicted to short-range solutions, I drifted from one campus to another. Although home was only an hour away, it felt as if I had entered the Twilight Zone, an unexpected stopover in a village called Suicidal Phase. Postcards from "Ed Parallel Yellow" were sent back to the Settlement from the University of Iowa and Grinnell College. On them were listed all the "ology"-suffixed courses the alter ego proudly had taken. I might have sent one to Dr. Plees himself.

Whenever I reminisce about that period today, I jokingly equate myself with Diane Chambers, the bartender character from the TV sitcom Cheers. Like her, I was a professional student. It was embarrassing; I later ended up dragging Selene along for stints at the University of Northern Iowa and Iowa State University. Having failed at the most important lifelong goal, education, I withdrew into the earth-island's underwing, stretching two Maecenus grants as far as possible. During my tenth year of living with Selene, most of which had been underwritten financially through her beadwork, I sought Dr. Plees's help. By then his personality had dramatically changed. My verse likewise; I was writing "new stuff."

With his John Lennon–type wire-rim glasses balanced over a small pointed nose that held a conspicuous bouquet of blond nose hairs, Dr. Plees was curious about what I had written—in particular, anything about BEC and Twintowns. He intimated that since this was "home" for his family, it would be good to know my perspective, even if it was "make-believe." I didn't buy it, though; he knew the Black Eagle Child slants inside out. I visualized him commenting at length on my work, translating some of the cryptic passages, over cheese, crackers, and wine at the Indian Acres country club.

"Oh, I'm sure it's fictional, but everything in art has a foundation."

"Not my art," I said. "Not when it's the suspected source of my headaches, fatigue, and anxiety."

"Maybe your inability to structure your themes on what is currently at your disposal is doing this?"

"Is that a question?"

Resembling a giant rat, he came at me with his tongue depressor and nearly tripped. His demeanor was shifty and impulsive, reminding me of some weird composite character from *Alice in Wonderland*.

"I was wondering," he questioned, "was your last collection of verse ever reviewed?"

"Yeah," I answered.

"May I ask where?"

"No problem. In most literary periodicals. Magazines you probably haven't heard of."

He rounded the examining table with his stumpy legs and stuck a lighted probe into my ear. I winced in pain and jerked away.

"Hey, geez!" I protested. "Aren't you going to ask what's wrong with me?"

"You know, people read your work and they talk about it."

"That's what books are for, Doctor."

"Correct. But when books misportray or give a single version of events, it isn't fair."

"That's why we have freedom of speech, Doctor."

In his white smock he took a step backward, took a good look, and smirked.

"You have a mouth, don't you?"

"Listen, Doc, I'm in a jam and—"

"Do you ever unhinge your mouth and let the internalized bitterness ooze out, boy?"

"Hey, look, being a writer is bad enough."

"Anyone with a smart-ass attitude should suffer. The source of the affliction should be lanced."

"Oh, incidentally, that's what I'm here for. That's what you get paid for. I'm suffering. It feels like a concrete bridge is sitting on my chest and it's about to crash through."

"That can be fixed, son," he said. "A proper lancing to the jugular."

That's how we last interfaced. He supposedly wrote out a prescription for antidepressants. Whatever it was, if I think about it now, my hands sweat profusely. Thank God for the invisible stone knife, the one Grandmother gave me to wear before the train ride to Southern California in 1970. Similar to an antibugging device, the spike-tip stone warns me of ill intention or malice. Enclosed in a brass locket and strung on a short leather string that was secured with a safety pin to the inside of my shirt, the charm didn't react kindly to Dr. Plees. In my doubt-afflicted state I ingested the pharmaceutical concoctions until I recalled word for word what Grandmother had said on that train depot platform: "This past spring as the swamp buds were on the verge of poking through dead leaves and weeds, I found this stone knife and prayed for it. Take it with you; it will protect you. In each adversity you encounter—whether or not you are aware of it—it will point like an invisible knife in front of you."

I reached the conclusion that Dr. Plees had intentionally over-prescribed, that the pills might be harmful to me, and by extension to others. In my father's sweat lodge and under a blanket of stars, I rid myself of the toxins. Besieged with twisted meditations, I saved the pills and the plastic container they came in. Inside and folded up were two notes, one with Jake Sacred Hammer–like instructions: "these, along with insurmountable indecision and academia, will be determined as the cause of my insanity. please keep my body away from dr. plees. advise selene I love her still and to feed the dogs."

And the other a poem:

*Parallel Yellow could move strange*
*bullet-shaped lumps from*
*one arm to the other*
*travelling under*
*the skin of his*
*chicken pox-*
*scarred back*
*The conical lumps made*
*tiny squeaking*
*noises convincing*
*skeptics that an*
*extraterrestrial*
*had surgically implanted*
*two metallic tracking*

*devices*
*in his lower spine*
*and left gonad*
*shrinking*
*expanding*
*in accordance*
*to telepathic*
*messages sent*
*Twice he saw*
*them overlap*
*popping through*
*leaving the acrid*
*aroma of carpet*
*cleaner and a trail*
*of blue smoke*
*Dime-sized*
*the UFOs*
*roared like*
*Caterpillar engines*
*as they sped over*
*the Red-Hatted*
*Grandfather's Valley*
*of Mushrooms*

# The Ramada Inn

That doesn't seem like long ago. Imprinted still are mental pictures of events and the capricious manner in which they unfolded. Ted's loss didn't engulf me until I had had my bitter fill of county law enforcement agencies. I learned even the most insignificant detail, like the lettering on a can of oranges or the graphic minutiae of a kitchen tablecloth, languished in this hideous timeless state, the gradual realization of a traumatic loss.

Maybe that's why recollections seem vivid and nearby.

Upon receiving news at home that Ted had been killed in a vehicular accident, I took a shower to clear my senses. There, in the steamed reflection of the bathroom mirror, I asked whether he required my involvement. And when Selene's brother, Octavius Buffalo Husband, replied in the other room, sounding amazingly like Ted, I took it as a paranormal signpost. Thrust upon a catlinite surfboard that was hydroplaning over unearthly waves, I pulled down the navigator's goggles and crouched low behind the watchdog effigy masthead before rationality returned. But the fact of the matter was, and this is how revelations conceal themselves through coincidence, Octavius—at that very second—was giving advice through Selene who was on the telephone with their younger sister. He thought it was best to "pull her kids" from an ineffective bilingual/bicultural curriculum.

A week afterward, under duress, I donated Hawaiian Punch at
the tribal health clinic. A month later I was traveling on behalf of
the Facepaint family to Minneapolis to meet with Junior Pipestar. I
remember being in that motel room with my parents. It was on a
Superbowl day, and I was perspiring heavily between the fingers. In
the blue flickering light of the RCA television set, Pipestar's teenage
apprentice was unraveling the bundles of dry goods and purifying
them with cedar bough smoke: a small cord of muscles below the
thigh bone began to shake. Regardless of the fact that it was also a
long-awaited reunion, there was every reason to believe the realms of
perception would somehow be altered. As with everything imperfect,
revelation would arrive in a bungling "Keystone Cops" manner. Sure
enough, at the height of the psychic inquisition there was a disturbing blast of humor at the thought of grown men, the infamous "Hyena brothers" wearing dresses and masks. Is there such a thing as a
comedy-riddled death? I asked. Or is this all a delusion precipitated
by mourning postponed? Why this sarcastic urge to smile back at the
Kansas City Chiefs football player, another insignificant detail, on
the surreal cereal box ad? Whatever the origin of these thoughts I
quickly shook myself free of them, blaming the purported fathers
of the Hyenai. Even when they were told their children had non-
Indian features at birth, they signed the paternity and enrollment
papers. As a result, the cross-dressing Hyenai were considered legitimate members of tribal citizenry in the eyes of Black Eagle Child
government.


Late in their life the Hyena brothers, a.k.a. Mathylde "Patty Jo"
Hi-na's sons, were urged by Brook Grassleggings, the photogenic hermaphrodite, to stop fighting their effeminate desires. The brothers
found solace in Brook but they misinterpreted her messages. They
took her sympathy as a blessing to victimize those who didn't understand the full ramifications of their enigmatic sexual discovery.
    A group of Settlement winos known for their homegrown intel-
lect once theorized these "mixed-bloods" were so paranoid, thanks
to their illegal bloodline, that other personae took over. Especially
when they gathered into a mangy pack, downing gallons of Mad Dog

20/20 and popping "speed." The winos predicted a flesh-taking transgression was in the offing. With their translucent marble eyes reflecting in the car headlights of all-night parties, lectured Dr. Crockston, they'll subdue anyone who hints at their biological shortcomings. Documented full-bloods, especially those they had had run-ins with, like Ted Facepaint, became priority targets for their wrath.

Sketches of their shape-shifting were drawn on shoebox lids by wino-artists and passed around for all to study. The Hyenai were graphically depicted in werewolflike transformations by Professor Crockston and his graduate assistant, Dean Afraid, the daytime robber of the only Italian-owned grocery store in Why Cheer.

The shoebox lid sketches thumbtacked to the door held back little: Their bladders bloated up like balloons and grew from within, distorting and enlarging their exterior appearances until the predominant feature was a froth-speckled sneer that had yellow teeth protruding through grape-colored nostrils.

The winos, under the guidance of Professor Crockston, were never far from being correct. Amid the picturesque crown of hills, the Black Eagle Child people were surrounded with the pounding waves of an invisible ocean called eventuality. Not only did lives occasionally lose their footing and tumble headfirst into the surf, but personalities were ostensibly altered. Brook Grassleggings, as a prime example, single-handedly made Junior Pipestar go on a religious quest twenty-one years ago. While Brook wasn't quite a woman, biologically speaking, she/it convinced Pipestar to become an apprentice to Jack Frost, a legendary Canadian Indian medicine man. Abstinence, of course, was a requisite, as were sobriety and an unwavering diligence to learn paranormal skills.

But on occasion I would ruminate that if Pipestar's life had been predetermined all along, then a womanless devotion to God was inevitable. In other words, it would have evolved eventually, but who would have figured that it would happen prematurely and under compromising conditions?

The most embarrassing thing that could happen back then was being pushed by a clan priest down a rocky hill for being a belligerent drunk inside the ceremonial earthlodge. But not for Junior Pipestar. For him, the world vanished the night he met an Indian equivalent of "Lauren Bacall." Possessing a rock-stippled face that would remind tribal members one had attended a feast under the influence was a minuscule burden compared to Pipestar's misfortune.

Ted Facepaint and I, as it turned out, were indirectly involved in that encounter. Yet Pipestar never attributed blame to anyone other than himself. Nor was he angry. And how could he be? Too much happened from one reckless, isolated decision. His. Like a shiny plump fish he swam willingly toward the long beak of a calculating, androgynous heron. The "Brook person" in spurious minxlike mannerisms retreated into the shadows with a lit cigarette in its lipsticked mouth. The motions of a harmless firefly were imitated, and unsuspecting passersby, like Pipestar, mistook it for such.

In making the arrangements for our meeting with Pipestar, his young apprentice specified over the telephone that it would be impossible for him to visit the Black Eagle Child Settlement because of his schedule. But Minneapolis was fine. *"The Ramada Inn where crime-conjuring phantasms were part of the accommodations,"* I later recorded in my journals.

There, in the cafeteria, Pipestar explained: "The past is always near. It is as near as the presence of someone sleeping beside you in bed when you know you are alone. Memory has a breath. In the strangest hour it decides to leap atop your chest to breathe in syncopation with you. Conjoined, so to speak. Inseparable and mimicking. And then you recall—in every sensory detail."

We did, on different levels.

It was 1968. A humid summer night with a couple of cases of Leinenkugel's long-neck beers. We were all on a hunt, like honorable American presidents, in a divining rod kind of pose, organ-led and not heedful of the rapacious flame that raged within and warmed the recesses of our bellies. Facepaint and I were there being hosts to Junior Pipestar and his sister Charlotte. Because of our careless adolescence, Brook Grassleggings, a young and attractive half woman and half man, was able to hoodwink Pipestar into a near-sexual encounter. Captivated by Brook's husky but enticing "Lauren Bacall" voice and a slim physical stature to match, Pipestar had been lured away by a giggling group of cigarette-desperate girls. Someone who was courteous, accommodating, and curious was all Brook needed to initiate the public embarrassment that would make Pipestar split Tama County forever.

Originally, Facepaint and I commiserated with his despair, but we also advised him that people would forget about what happened at the old Grassleggings log cabin. He argued he had survived "the shenanigans of a deviate and gunfire from the county sheriff, some deputies, and assorted vigilantes." No one will care, we pleaded. "I was the one who was there with Brook," he protested. "Factor that into the dreadful equation." It was true. How could anyone who only seconds before was caressing a firm nubile breast in one hand and the shocking male protuberance of Brook in another survive after coming to under a volley of bullets and photographers' flashbulbs?

The last discussion before Pipestar's exodus ended in hysterics.

"Jesus Christ!" he cried. "Just put yourself in my place. Would you even go anywhere and show your bloody face?"

For the sake of argument we nodded yes but later concurred in secret it would be difficult to live an event like that down. From any perspective. The photograph taken of him in underwear after being roused by the posse, however, made the incriminating maple sugar pie calcify. No Houdini, not even in resurrection, could escape the award-winning newspaper photograph with a caption that read: "A BUCK BUCK NAKED." With mud-stained arms raised up to the night-sky as if in homage or surrender, Junior—hoodwinked by an oddity—participated unwillingly in his own despicable representation. This near-sexual encounter compelled Junior Pipestar to bid his Claer, Iowa, family members adieu and hitchhike northward to Canada in search of identity. Most forgot about him, as Facepaint and I predicted. In a way, everyone became an infinite part of the process, of moving on, forgetting.

Today, in the strangest irony of all, we were insignificant next to what Junior Pipestar had become under the tutelage of Jack Frost, the legendary medicine man of Horned Serpent Lake. We, those living and deceased, were dependent upon their supernatural seeing powers.

In the company of saviors, to whom and to what do you humbly give thanks? Unbridled lust, maybe? A pack of Camel cigarettes? Three thousand American dollars?

# What Held the
# Night's Attention

*The following audiotape recording was sent from Pinelodge Lake, Canada,
in April 1990. It was addressed "To the Friends and Family of Ted Facepaint." In a mixture of English and the ancient dialect of the Ontario
tribe, a language that he vowed to speak one day, Junior Pipestar, medicine man, discussed new findings about the murder of Ted Facepaint.*

*We were instructed by letter to seal the ceremonial room in the
oblong-shaped house also known as the Well-Off Man Church from
daylight and purify it. Sitting in the darkness on new folded blankets
and pillows brought to mind that it had been nearly twenty-five years
since Ted and I attended the first of what would be four Star-Medicine-
chewing ceremonies. A quarter of a century had passed.*

*By flashlight Clayton Carlson Facepaint, Ted's elderly war hero
uncle, the one invited to fly bombing missions with the RAF, turned on
the Panasonic tape recorder. In the background there were the unavoidable sounds of furniture being moved, the brushing of clothes from people
walking by, a crackling fire, along with a drum and a rattle being jostled
about. When Junior Pipestar cleared his throat to speak, we listened,
and everything else thereafter became silent. . . .*

Na ka-me ko-ne bya no ta kwa-ki ka ne na na-en ne ba a ni. *Again
our friend has come to me in my sleep.* Ma ni tta e no we tti: ba ki-me
ko-na ko ta ki to-e ba wi-ka ski-na kwa wa ni. A kwi ke-e i ki-na ta

wi-ko ta ki a ki ni-tti na e ma ki. Ne te ba na wa ki-be ki. Tte na-wa ba ta mo wa sa-ke te na-we ne a-ta na ki i kwe ni. *This is what he said: "I am greatly distressed at not being able to leave (this earth). And I also do not want to cause the same distress for my relatives. I care for them greatly. But they should look for whoever planned to assail me."*

Ki ye wa ki-o no ke na ni-ki wa na te se ni wa ni-i ya ma-o ta kwi-ma-e o wi ki ye kwi. *His shadow is still confused over there where you live.* Ki ye wa ki-me ko-ki wa na to se wa-wa ni na wi. *He is still roaming in a confused state everywhere.* Ma ni tta-ma ni-e tti-ne no ta ma ni: Ko tti-e se mi e ko-kwe ni-i yo-ne a bi-i kwe wa ni-tte na-a kwi-ka sko be ne na tti ni-ni be ki sa na ni tti-o no ka nwa wa ni. *This is the way I understand this situation: A medicine woman tried to help him before but she couldn't facilitate the release of his shadow.* I ni tta-we tti-bya tti-na wi i tti. *That is why he is visiting with me.*

*Since I have started helping him and yourselves, his relatives and people who care about him still, I have looked into the red-hot center of the Fire. I have also looked into the frozen part of Ice. It wasn't easy. There were—and still are—many forces with different agendas at work, and they all seemed to converge within the minds of three deranged men at the same time.*

*Through the benevolent Supernaturals I was shown the items you seek: what these people used to attack him, the sharp-pointed instruments. We know what happened; we saw them together through the element of Smoke and the Hand-ally.*

*That I will eventually speak of, go over, but first I want to tell you what else came to me: There were other people present that night when the assault was unleashed. They did nothing, but they watched as the person was being surrounded. These people believe they cannot say anything, for fear of criminal implication. They are correct. What they don't know is that within four years of the time of our friend's departure, the cavernous Window into the Earth will reveal two of them ending themselves. One will use the railroad tracks for a pillow; the second will shoot himself in the temple. The third, a woman, will set fire to her car and open the door to insanity; and the fourth will drink himself into a wheelchair and a heart attack. This is what happens when one harbors a terrible secret. What they could have prevented has returned, causing them to lose control.*

As for the three deranged men, their own families will experience difficulties. This will happen because the relatives have corroborated the stories of their whereabouts and innocence. The grief they have caused to others makes a complete unforgiving circle. A baby will die in its crib; a girlfriend will be stricken with a pernicious disease; a sober brother will drive inexplicably into a stone bridge; a father will attempt suicide and later succeed; an alcoholic sister will be found frozen and unidentified in a faraway city; and a host of other maladies will ensue, all in the name and memory of . . .

As soon as the circle of grief has made its rounds among the three brothers' families, the sharp-pointed instruments and the blood-splattered female apparel they used and wore will be found in a baseball diamond near the tribal fairgrounds. Along with an assortment of animal bones that the brothers thought possessed power, the weapons and the masks will be stored in an antique tin suitcase wrapped in a star quilt and plastic.

These items should not be feared. More important, they should not be turned over right away to the local white-skinned authorities, for they bear nothing but contempt for Indians. Proving them wrong with this case, which they considered "an unfortunate accident," should make others in your community suspect that far more crimes may yet be uncovered. The greater authorities should not be trusted either, for they— by virtue of the fact they are white—are in agreement with the locals. Before they expunge everything you have investigated and submitted to date, make sure the items are safe, untouched, and hidden. Eventually a situation will make itself available for you to relinquish the evidence to the proper people.

Only then, at the end of the four years aforementioned, will the non-ending darkness the three brothers encountered seek another host or hosts. The three cackling owls will launch themselves from the ledge of their spent lives. Only then will the three brothers' minds be uncluttered and vulnerable to retribution. In its own way an impermeable vengeance is already sculpting itself from the shadows of their own relatives.

This I leave in your thoughts: Be assured that your friend and relative will soon find solace that will enable his tormented shadow to fly as he has already dreamed, propelling himself from the glass doors in the form of a majestic bird whose color is that of the red dawn.

*Be assured also that what we have wanted for him, what we have prayed for, will thus occur.*

*This song, upon the discovery and retrieval of the tin suitcase, should be sung.*

*From the place where there is Fire*
*from the place where there is Ice*
*together have we gathered*
*wanting to know what it was*
*that held the night's attention*

*From the place there is Smoke*
*from the place where a Hand signals*
*together we have dreamed*
*wanting to know what it was*
*that held the night's attention*

*Only then will his journey to the Afterlife begin. For him, within the Grandfather World, it will take four short days. For us, here on earth, it will take four long years. Only then will this journey be whole. For him, for everyone.*

# Part
# Four

# The Lonesomest Valley

Luciano Bearchild, my first cousin who wore black pinstriped, hand-tailored suits, white silk scaves, Italian shoes, and perforated fingerless gloves, used to say, "Ah, bo-*shit, neigh*-bor!" to our futures. He would acquiesce to change by tightening his bow tie and shuffling across the concrete floor like James Brown. In addition to dancing like the famous black entertainer, he was addicted to "soul" music. He made uncultivated Indians like me cultivated.

Luciano Bearchild was unlike any other Indian I had met in my lifetime. Even now, near the year 2000, there's no one who can compare to the futuristic genius he was. Attired in an ironed white shirt and black slacks, he was spellbinding. His tribal language skills approached archaic perfection. In order to say some words they had to be enunciated or sung within a certain story. That took extraordinary memory, as well as agile tongue-to-palate collaboration!

If an honorary doctorate had been given to Luciano for simply being an exemplary, circumspect Indian, it would have shared wall space with Elizabeth Taylor and World War II German military memorabilia. He lived alone among these cherished collections. The most prominent—once the heavy log cabin door was closed—was a huge color poster of Rommel, the Desert Fox.

North Africa? I would ask, and later be sorry for the question. Where is this place?

He explained at length, using charts and photographs, to no avail.

What else was there?

Nailed to the door, above the German commander, was a hand-carved book rack. Books behind glass were imposing for us illiterates. Luciano, man, he opened the dustfree pages and read from them! At twenty-five he knew about the Outside World—Plato, Michelangelo, Degas, Gertrude Stein, Ernest Hemingway, and F. Scott Fitzgerald. There were cameras, new and antique, encased in illuminated curio cabinets; copies of *Life* and the *Saturday Evening Post* were scattered everywhere within the museumlike labyrinth of his log cabin.

Raised by the wisest Bearchild elders of the Settlement, Luciano knew more than most Indians twice his age. The immediate family saw this as a blessing, but other people saw intellect as a curse.

Luciano swam to fearful and unexpected places: he could sing you to the Black Eagle Child Afterlife, where questions on religious faith are asked. Unassisted, he'd do this for you, and the next day he'd attend a Navaho Indian anthropology lecture at Grinnell College, a twenty-minute drive south to a foreign country.

He dazzled the denizens of Tama County—white and Indian alike—from high atop the trapeze, hanging under the big-top tent, unafraid of gravity. His accomplishments would have made any Bohemian farmer envious, but among them he was feared for different, turtle-snapping reasons. Among Indians he was despised for being too cunning and prosperous.

And why is that? you ask.

Keep this in mind: To have every facet of life work to one's advantage was seen not as the glorious result of unbounded determination but as the workings of evil. This was—and even today is—the tribal community's mind-set. Illiteracy was shared. Poverty was blood-ingrained, and like the harmony that held the clans together, having little was inherited. Anything that tore through the delicate netting was regrettable, like suicidal Indians or those who chose urban relocation, coming home for their own funerals. What a pity! was whispered through cupped hands to respectful, listening ears. A life misled was lamented over sweet rolls and coffee, but Luciano's success with money and white women was deemed unnatural.

Suffering and bad luck were shared. Equally—like commodity surplus foods. Luciano's fortune benefited his immediate family and himself. Movies, picnics, fishing trips, and long-distance travel—stuff we were aware of—just didn't happen in our lives. That's when a rumor circulated that the new dark green Ford Fairlane in his yard came from flesh-taking secrets, the kind only sorcerers coveted. Witchcraft.

The family scoffed. "Since your critics cannot have money or white girlfriends, they now want your automobile. Wealth, in any shape, can have that dopey effect. The more you make them chatter, the greater their envy is. Believe us." Jealousy was thus perceived as admiration that had transmogrified, gone astray. Underneath acrimonious innuendo there was praise.

Although I struggled to understand how this reversal could work, the wild rumors continued. For seven years the dark green Ford remained the newest car on the Settlement. Those who were baffled by Luciano's success became obsessed with theories he was not of this earth. How and why else? they were heard muttering among themselves.

"O, I don't know about this *not*-of-this-*earth*-bo-*shit*," Luciano would say to messages I was asked to personally deliver. With a gentle tug on his goatee and a sharp, upward smile that made him squint as if the sun had hit his eyes, he wondered why he was the subject of so much attention. But when these messages became "paper bullets"—a sorcerer's seemingly innocuous method of sending a spell—the smile was replaced by an intense look of worry. And I was the barrel through which adoration spun out of control, tumbling end over end, chipping away at the scaled sleekness of a fish who was unlike any other I was to meet in my lifetime.

*Since then I haven't delivered messages to anyone. . . . I do not speak for anyone other than myself and the Six Grandfathers.*

Amazingly, after Luciano's mysterious disappearance, many spoke of him in respectful terms. Those who had been jealous enough to become enemies recanted statements he had been an extraterrestrial all along and took part in the search for him. There was a sudden realization among the disbelievers and hypocrites that Luciano, because of his precociousness, suffered the same tragedy as the Lesser-Known Twin Brother, the one who was double-crossed by his own relative in order so that a spark, the essence of life, might flicker occasionally in the murky cosmic earthlodge. . . .

Before he vanished on an errand for earthlodge elders, taking prayers, tobacco, and offerings of food and gifts to the silver metallic UFO that had crash-landed above Liquid Lake, Luciano was blessed manyfold. In fishing he excelled, catching and releasing prehistoric-looking fish we didn't know existed. In addition to being the fastest sharpshooter of a .22 caliber bolt-action rifle, he was inventive at hunting. With the shoulder stock shortened to rest across the top of his chest, he cradled the rifle with one inward-bent arm that was wrapped in a triangular-shaped braided leather sling. In this contorted sharpshooting configuration, where the rifle acted like a natural appendage, his free hand chambered the rounds while the thumb squeezed off the shots in blinding succession.

Fox squirrels that scattered in all directions rarely escaped his deadly accuracy. Ditto for his trapping skills: muskrats, mink, fox, and beaver saw his steel traps as the doors to their underground homes.

Some disbelieving people circulated rumors he possessed a medicine, a charm that mesmerized the animals.


"*Ki wi te me-ma wi na ta a bye ya ni?* Would you like to go with me on a trap run?" Luciano would ask from the porch-lit doorstep in his rubber hipboots.

"*Wi tte we no. Na bi ma i ni-ki o tto ni ya e me.* Go along. At least you will have money," Clotelde and Tony, my parents, pretended to encourage.

The money was good for half a night of lugging bags of dead animals. It was disarmingly simple: With flashlights strapped to our heads we sloshed through the swamps and unclamped the strangled fur-bearing bodies. They never put up a fight, but they became very heavy. That was it, we *collected* them. Like gifts.

After the rivers and swamps froze over, he switched to hunting and spearfishing. Both farmers and Indians placed prepaid orders for illegal white-tailed deer and catfish meat. This is how he supported himself—with mythical animal-attracting charms. In one season of lugging I had enough money for a small typewriter from Ben Franklin's, my first. I typed until my eyes hurt. I didn't mind the large kindergarten-looking print, but the low-watt lightbulb in my room was the fuel for future neurologic ailments caused by the literary profession.

On any weekend night at the Why Cheer Pool Hall, Luciano Bear-child arrived by cab. What we saw in movies and could only fanta-size about, he radiated in living, breathing color. He made the doldrums of midwestern Americana bearable. Tolerable.

With cue sticks in their hands still, city folk and Indians would edge to the large picture windows and take visual pleasure as Luciano's door was opened by Joe Gadger, the taxi driver. Luciano would come out and take a big stretch, shaking his long legs and getting the pressed creases of his slacks back. Physically, he was slim and tall with a bronzelike complexion, high cheekbones, slanted eyes, a wide muscular back, and pouting lips. Spectacular handsomeness.

If he arrived during a furious snowstorm, he wasn't bothered. In fact, he made a big production of putting on his black topcoat with assistance from Joe. Luciano was the only person who "tipped" in Tama County. A five-dollar bill on top of the dollar-and-a-half ride into town and back was incredible for the sixties. When my parents first said he "tipped," I took it to mean he fell over.

The pool games and the barroom chatter ceased.

From behind the dingy picture window, we observed a "one-take scene." As the taxi pulled away from view, Luciano would jump-start our collective fantasies by adjusting the frayed ends of the silk scarf and walking forward through the icy sludge in long strides.

"Just look at the dapper guy," said the farmers with specks of beer foam still drying on their face stubble. "He is one helluva dresser!"

"Yeah, and for an Indian at that!" the farmers' wives responded, straightening their hair.

"That's my first cousin," I would say to whoever stood beside me at the picture window, but no one ever acknowledged me. Yet I desperately sought to claim him. Over the grungy floor and amid the stench of beer and cigarette smoke, his angelic presence made everyone realize there was beauty in being human. The filth of our everyday lives, thick and visible, dissipated in the springlike breeze that swirled around him.

Incapacitated by his bewildering cologne, Man-Sent, the farmers' wives couldn't wait for their husbands to overdose on the beer soup special. The instant they did, the women raced to caress a face that came only in fantasy.

With breasts jutting out from chests of all sizes, the women would brush his back as he sat on a barstool. Luciano referred to them as a "flock of luscious skin-pockets." Before plopping coins into the jukebox machine, he'd raise one fuzzy eyebrow and smirk sardonically. "They want to entice me—after closing time—with electric nipples."

This area of adulthood would have remained indecipherable had he not compared his admirers to luggage. There were "bags," and there were "purses." As he danced with these women to the music of Tommy Dorsey, I sat and tried to determine which was which, not knowing what mattered, what didn't. He described their physical differences. His preferences. I imagined to no avail as he spun them around like Fred Astaire.

Among Luciano's flames there was Angela, a wavy-black-haired, unmarried Caucasian beauty. She was bewitching with her flirtatious smiles and touches. Angela and her brother, Chris, came from somewhere in the East. Maybe Pennsylvania or West Virginia.

In a red, hooded cape and black riding boots, Angela's entrance was just as dramatic as Luciano's. "Here comes Little Red Riding Hood and her Wolf brother!" whispered the grubby patrons. They were called "gypsies," and there was "too much contact between them" for brother and sister. Chris would indeed curl his arm around her thin waist and lead her by the wrist. Like ice-skaters, they were almost inseparable.

"Did you do that to your sister?" one set of farmers asked.

"Shi-i-i-it, I don't think so," replied a couple of others who became caught up scratching the deepest recesses of their buttocks.

"If I had a sister that looked like her," surmised one of the first set, "my hands would be elsewhere. Why, I'd carry her around, spin her, and show her off that way."

"Yeah, once you wash your goddamned nugget-digging fingers, you asinine prospectors!" the wives wisecracked.

Their lewd comments flustered me, but I remember how refreshing Angela's wavy hair smelled as she leaned over to whisper a message for Luciano. The crusty-eyed farmers awoke and salivated. A few loose strands of her perfumed hair would fall and catch on the moisture of my lips and eyes. Holding me, Angela—in her red hood still—would remove each one delicately while crooning over me, a lost, unfortunate puppy. In one dramatic movement she swayed and tossed her long hair out of the hood. Leaning over again she whispered into my ear, "Tell Luciano if he dances any closer to that big-breasted woman, he'll suffocate."

Without fail I would shut my eyes, and the vibrations of her sweet voice electrified my quivering puberty-ridden face.

As Luciano walked toward the picture window, we superimposed our reflections over his presence and wondered how we looked to others. Decrepit and pathetic perhaps. We were not fashion-conscious or pretty, and we certainly didn't carry around a wad of twenty-dollar bills. Most of the patrons, including myself as a high school student, wouldn't know the sensation of a hand-tailored suit from Neihardt's Executive Club of Des Moines for a long, long time.

The very first time I heard him say "hand-tailored" in response to my question about the suit, I thought he said Andy Taylor. You know, Opie Taylor's dad? Of the Andy Griffith television show? He laughed for an hour until he felt guilty and sent me to the small Italian grocery store for Chesterfield cigarettes and almonds to go with the two Bloody Marys he always started and ended the evening with.

The Gadger taxi kept its appointment at closing time. We would all pile in—Luciano, with Angela holding his arm, and Chris, her obsessive brother, clinging to *her* arm, and me following with three twelve-packs of Schlitz beer and potato chips. At the Settlement we'd transfer into the dark green Ford and check out the local party spots. Leaving these, we'd head for the smooth country roads and cruise them till daybreak, talking, laughing, and crying about the vast solitude of geography.

When the party was over, as I got out of the Ford, Angela would jump out of the front seat and either plant a kiss on my cheek or hug me hard. Before Chris had a chance to get out of the car, to sit beside his irresistible sister, I would slam the car door shut.

"*Neigh*-bor! *Hey*-y-y Thanks! With a capital *T*!" Luciano would say with a firm hand clasp.

I would go home drunk, staggering through the hybrid-corn fields, feeling good about the twenty-dollar tip next to the perfumed, folded handkerchief that Angela had placed in the back pocket of my blue jeans. There was also assurance that sometime during the week Angela, standing naked in front of me and poised over the red cape, would grind her soft, hairy groin against my dream of copulation—in Luciano's cabin—with a nervous and jealous Chris pacing nearby.

The dream of a standing, hip-grinding Angela, I can now say, was the concoction of Pat "Dirty" Red Hat, the elementary school scholar who imparted to us the purpose of male organs and ambulatory sex.

We—Ted, Horatio, "Kensey," "Grubby," and I—knew the details. The vivid moonlight. A skirt hoisted past the belly button and discarded balloons containing pools of "chicken soup." We were there unnoticed, hanging upside down from the intersecting beams under a bridge. We drooled as an overweight bat, *a sa mi-e na kwi ta-bi tta ka ni ne kwe*, named Pat gave a play-by-play account of a sexual assignation. His sister's. The lovers "whirled" over the sand standing up.

"It's also called *rock and roll*," said Luciano. "It's black slang for *screwing*."

"Self-explanatory music!" chimed Angela from the side somewhere. She sang out again. "Wake up, Edgar! For Christ's sake. The subject is mu-u-u-sic and the *What's My Line?* mystery guest has signed in!"

I looked upward at a blurry figure, trying desperately to connect her cheery voice with her fragrant face and body. Finally, after a drink of ice water, my misty head vanished. That was my lesson on binge drinking by the Why Cheer railway crossing. With her demure face and heart-topped mouth, Angela stood before the Wurlitzer jukebox that lit her up in yellow Degas-esque color. Inserting mass amounts of coinage, we made sure no one else was accorded a chance to select the music of the night.

"Hey, T. S. Bearchild, you hear me?" Angela called out. "What do ya wanna hear?"

From the booth behind us a drunk neighbor woman pretended to defend me, crying out, "Yeah, he hears you! Ed wants Johnny Cash! Johnny Cash! *Ke te nay-ke bi ti!* I said, plugged butt!"

I quickly snapped out of my drunken stupor, wanting to avoid a confrontation between the women. Not only was Angela an angel, she was mouthy.

"Rock and roll," I said in an extraloud yawn, hoping to drown out the antagonistic patron. The Zombies in the jukebox were winding down with "She's Not There."

"OK, OK, Roger Miller then, 'King of the Road,'" interjected the drunk neighbor woman in a rude tone. "The selection number is FU2!"

"I prefer rock and roll!" I repeated in a half shout as the Zombies lamented someone's voice being "soft and cool, her eyes were clear and bright . . . but it's too late to say you're sorry, how would I know, why should I care?"

At the song's end, while the jukebox was buzzing and clicking for the next selection, Luciano and Angela howled like a couple of coon hounds. "Ditto! Ditto! *Dit-to-*o-o-o! Ed-gr-r-r. But there's always room for . . ." With that, they took to the dance floor in a flash, jitterbugging to the Andrews Sisters' tune "The Bugle Boy of Company B."

In the booth behind us the neighbor woman whispered slurred aspersions. "What'd Angie bitch s-s-ay? Dildoo? Dil-do? Se-see. That's what I told ya."

If it wasn't the downtown rednecks complaining about the brother and sister gypsies, it was someone from the Sett. There was nothing more sickening than a tribal member doing a redneck routine. Our people, at least those who had renounced Black Eagle Child citizenry, mimicked the whites. Enraptured with their pedantics, they got into I hate-those-devilish-gypsies schtick in a split second.

Through them, we could sense how the evening would progress. Later on, at some desolate roadside of the Sett, our own friends and relatives would echo the Indian redneck's animosity. "What's wrong with you guyses?" they'd fume in Black Eagle Child from the safety of their locked, interior-lit cars. "Aren't you bothered their own people talk about them?"

It was strange that Angela and her brother were classified by Indians as whites and not as gypsies. Nevertheless, they were perceived as an incestuous dragonfly duo: a major negativity with arms and legs—and wings. "Remember what the whites said," we were advised at the onset, "everywhere they fly, they fornicate."

"The fact of the matter is," Luciano would respond an hour later, once we were far away from everyone, "we don't give a skunk shit what they say in town." He'd adjust the rearview mirror of the Ford Fairlane, looking for me. "Is that right? Edgar. Edgar!" I'd nod in agreement, knowing he'd spot the reflection of my glasses. "Else how could I tell you about the tantalizing softness of a female's palm? Angela here will verify it is a softness greater than a raccoon's paw."

"Ah, why don't you shove it, clown!" Angela would snap without fail.

The analogies between his successful fur-trapping business and his love life amused me—to a point. Otherwise, this is where the traditional prodigy stumbled and fell from his naïve corniness. In the tribal domain where animism and supernaturalism prevailed, he was not off kilter. He knew the appropriate "shadow-releasing" words to recite if someone suddenly passed away. Critical, spontaneous wording. With women, and in particular, Angela, he clamored like a three-year-old orphaned child seeking unadulterated affection.

"No, thanks, ma'am," he'd say right on cue, "this clown shove nothing."

From the front seat Angela would interrupt his philosophical discourse. Every weekend. "Ed-gr-r-r-r, man, tell your pal here to cease and desist with the wildlife metaphors. It's so uncouth!" Raising her palm in defiance to Luciano's impassive face, she would say, "Luji, look for yourself. It's me. Not a goddamned creature of the forest, OK? Impale that with a nail to your cranium, too."

Luciano Bearchild, exhibiting a rarely revealed side of his character, would look hurt. Raccoon analogies were good for a chuckle, and that was it. For as much as he knew of the invisible machinations of another, nonworldly dimension, something we could never fathom, this separation of knowledge, of cultures, gnawed at him. It would eventually topple him. On our trapping excursions, if he saw a monolithic maple tree beside a river whose roots were exposed in the air and underwater, providing refuge for winged and finned creatures, he'd walk up to it proudly in his squeaky rubber hip boots and say, "That's me, helping everyone."

When he related this story to Angela for the first time, she was unimpressed and sarcastic. "Big deal. If you're so helpful, Luji, make the whites and Indians quit being so hostile to us."

"I might be able to," Luciano replied, before he leapt onto another encounter story with nature. "In my dreams a family of beavers approached me." We awaited the remedy to society's illness that never came.

"What do beavers have to do with hostility?" queried Angela.

"Maybe nothing, but listen," he said. "They visited with me several times and they spoke normally as you and I are doing. My vocal cords were paralyzed but I spoke to them with my thoughts. I know it's not right, I pleaded, killing them and their families sometimes. But without them I'd starve. I told them that." For Angela the dreams of the beaver family were annoying; for me they symbolized the unmerciful toppling of a monolithic maple tree, the one that Luciano most admired.

Around the winsome Angela Holiday, either you had to be a lover of music or you had to act as if you were at least aware who the major recording artists were. Luciano, aside from his flawless looks and pockets that were brimming with green wonder, qualified as a soul music aficionado. Her penchant for all kinds of jukebox music grew on me, a simple groupie. Country and western music became, as she described it, "tolerable and even admirable." Around closing time, with the bar and the ever-present jukebox to ourselves, she'd sing along note for note with Patsy Cline or Fontella Bass.

It was no different in Luciano's car.

From the second she was in the front seat of the Ford Fairlane, the radio was flicked on to blaring proportions. Tapping her long dark purple fingernails on the dashboard, her zestful I-want-to-be-a-nightclub-singer-in-Chicago energy elevated our merriment to astronomical heights.

On Friday and Saturday night, at one of the Why Cheer taverns, Angela gained more insight into the future through a beer-stained jukebox than she had from life all week. Highly influenced by "little signposts"—like a bluejay feather landing near her laced high-heeled boots or a drunk speaking to her in midsentence as if she were a close relative—she changed her mood largely in accordance with whatever "forces" were present. She believed in and understood "the unseen world," but not Luciano's lifestyle. For our own selfish reasons, we kept babbling drunks out of hearing range and made careful jukebox selections.

"Glenn Miller and the Andrew Sisters make me think of old film footage of the war," she once commented when old farmer couples overtook the jukebox when we weren't looking. All night thereafter and right up until daybreak, we had to share or compose "war stories." Luciano, being a genuine World War II buff and souvenir collector, lectured tirelessly on history-swaying battles. He also spoke about Glenn Miller, the big-band leader from Clarinda, Iowa, who disappeared mysteriously in flight over Europe in 1942. If we left a tavern playing country and western songs, like Marty Robbins or Jim Reeves, the night had a cowboyish undertone. If the lyrics had a hint of sadness, we'd eventually reach point zero of morbidity, dredging the necro-pits for skeletons and victims of murder. Barry McGuire's "Eve of Destruction," for example, would set this off.

Knowing how Angela tended to overreact in her "signpost" readings, Luciano made me feed the jukeboxes mass coinage as if they were hungry sharks. "As long as our influence is there," Luciano would say, "we'll make things smooth for Angie."

Racing over the desolate flatlands toward the quickening dawn, the Ford Fairlane rumbled like an experimental rocket car, leaving behind a large cloud of dust that settled as chalky film over the corn tassels and leaves beside the gravel road. Red-tailed hawks and crows didn't even have time to take flight from their posts; they hopped and flexed their startled wings. Inside the windswept vehicle we peered out of the open windows with twisted eyelashes. Hearing nothing but the radio and the incessant pinging of rocks under the front and rear fender, we saw the pastures and livestock passing by in blurs.

As monotonous as the southern roads were, we'd cruise over them, trying to get lost and making a game out of it. We got drunk instead, and we always knew where we were. There were miles and miles of track for the experimental rocket car; we'd reach speeds of ninety miles per hour on loose gravel.

Once the car engine and KIOA radio station were finally turned off on the ridge leading into the Lonesomest Valley, we'd sit still until the skin on our stretched faces relaxed back into shape, until the gritty taste of dust from our lips blended into our mouths. Like tuning forks our bodies would patiently calm down as we waited for the morning haze to set over the valley.

Angela Holiday looked sensational at six o'clock in the morning with puffy eyelids and smeared eyeliner. She would stumble out and head for the highest dirt bluff. "Spirits who live here, please forgive this womanly intrusion!" she'd cry out. The only ones who responded were the chickadee birds who trotted up the few shade trees like tiny windup toys, chirping loudly.

Situated on a massive humpback hill on the south side of the Black Eagle Child Settlement and hidden among taller hills, the dead-end road had natural acoustics suitable to Angela's a capella free-verse style of singing. There was just enough echoing for her to subtly change voice pitches and pause, making the land respond like an instrument. Many mornings were spent sleeping, sobering up, or closing the festive cruise with Angela's music.

This is what I recall from our last night together before Luciano Bearchild's disappearance on the hills above Liquid Lake:

*Luciano, behind his World War II pilot's sunglasses, studied Angela closely as she went through the preparatory motions for the Lonesomest Valley amphitheater—in the front seat. After gulping down Schlitz beer, Luciano pursed his lips and hissed, "It has-s-s to do with becoming s-s-some kind of nightclub s-s-singer." Angela began stomp-*

ing her boots slowly on the car floor in percussion syncopation with a
song that only she heard. She then pantomimed holding an imaginary
microphone. Holding it steady between her pale hands, she clutched
the mike over her small but erect breasts. To the left and then right her
head would weave, keeping in time with these rhythms that only she
heard. With her glacier green, watery eyes quivering and her faint red
lips poised to go on stage, she pretended to reach backward, groping for
more microphone cord and tugging. I could almost see the entangled
cord on the floor; I swiftly moved my feet out of the way. With her right
arm extended, holding the microphone, her upper torso trembled. And
then she let loose the song from the Zombies, in a strong voice, articu-
lating the words:

> Well no one told me about her
> the way she lied
> Well no one told me about her
> how many people cried . . .

When a few loose strands of Angela's black wavy hair became sunlit, her trancelike facial expressions in the rearview mirror were outlined with small, fiery explosions. Like a brittle, unconscious dragonfly
I collapsed onto the rubber mat on the floor.

Still handsome in his white shirt and oiled-down hair, Luciano
began his evaluation. "All this, she says, all this yodeling and prancing
around is rehearsal. I'm supposed to tell her what I think, what needs
improving, et cetera. As if I'm the etiquette director at Motown Records!
Shit, what do I know?"

With his fingerless leather gloves he gripped the steering wheel
tightly and bitched some more. "She hates my talks on nature. She
knows I'm limited to James Brown and German Field Marshal Rommel
knowledge-wise . . ."

Something caught his eye near the fence by the pasture. He rolled
down the window and pointed at first to the jittery birds and then to
Angela as she opened a barbed-wire gate. ". . . And those vertical-walking
chickadees, those over there by the trees, are announcing that a Pre-
Raphaelite angel within the vicinity is about to reach her monthly cycle
. . . Maybe her? Who else?"

Looking at Angela as she teeter-tottered over a mound of dirt curiously brought to mind the menstruation hut my mother used to have beside the small two-room unpainted house. As children, my brother Alan and I would sneak inside the forbidden space whenever Grandmother wasn't looking. Other times we would cup our hands to our chest like homeless people, asking for a delicious morsel of her fried canned food—Spam and Vienna sausages.

Angela's extemporized wailing always left me hungry.

Before beginning its test run home, Luciano's Ford Fairlane rumbled and smoked like a land rocket vehicle. After the Ford got to a proper speed over the expansive salt flats, it made a fiery arc upward to the constellations, using a passing railroad boxcar as a means of propulsion. "Showing off . . ."

# The Blackbird Swarms
# My Loneliness
# Summoned

In the fall of 1972, while fishing for game fish beneath the swells of the Indian Dam, Ted Facepaint turned to me and said, "Ed, have you ever thought about death?"

"No, not lately," I answered, wondering if the question was linked to the fall of Jim Morrison of the Doors the year previous. Believing we once met the celebrated rock-and-roll singer/composer in person on a Southern California mountainside, we deified him. Convinced we had unknowingly translated a Star-Medicine song, which was then rearranged and released by the Doors as the haunting Top 40 song "Riders on the Storm," we felt a mixture of guilt and pleasure. For a few glorious months, before word reached us Jim Morrison had died in Paris, we bragged about our roles as translators and source of inspiration for the stolen song. Ted took the news badly, just as my younger brother Alan was stunned by the death of Jimi Hendrix. For me, a leather-clad musician/poet hero had fallen.

By habit, and maybe because of our mythical meeting we called "the Night of Jim," we jokingly spoke of celebrities on a first-name basis. Part of this stemmed from our older relatives who met and had photographs taken with Pancho Villa, Joe Louis, and Bonnie and Clyde. Seriously. Jim Morrison, for us, was the one. The only complication being, he was a song thief. Allegedly—with all due respect. Or could it be one hell of a coincidence!

But did Jim Morrison make me dwell on death? Hardly.

The fact was, death was distant. Ever since the accidental shooting of Skip Water Runner, a cousin, during my childhood, the subject was virtually nonexistent at the family supper table. Losing Luciano Bearchild in the hills directly above us, I contemplated, was in many respects a rehearsal for all the relatives and friends I would eventually be deprived of.

"Other than my grandfather," I continued on the subject, trying to remember, "no one has really died in my family." And then several flashbacks blipped on the cerebral screen. Blood seeping through sterile gauze bandages wrapped around lifeless bodies. The cold wintry wind and the hard ice-encrusted ground of O'Ryan's Cemetery. An absent mother. The smoke from the fire intended to keep the grave diggers warm zipping by. Grandmother pointing each person out, some having just visited us the day previous, and others who died in their sleep while we were there. She whispered their names and what might have happened. Serious vehicular accidents, suicides, or savage beatings. For others, those who were older, there were long, exhausting vigils in kerosene-lit kitchens. Outside was the sound of either winter howling or summertime crickets.

"That's not what I'm asking," Ted responded in a laughing tone.

"Well, there really isn't any reason to think about it," I returned, a bit startled. On the occasions when I was exposed to the morose topic through my grandmother's acquaintances, I didn't like it. On top of that, I was vaguely aware I had accompanied her on visits that may have been deathwatches. Grandmother had been summoned to administer traditional medicines and to soothe the frail minds of terminally ill people.

Chances were, Mother was out with my father then. Absent. Hence, the reason Grandmother and I were doctoring late at night and well into daybreak. They were probably cruising the farm roads somewhere. The color photographs I once saw of Mother in a yellow bathing suit on the shore of Liquid Lake may correspond with this particular time period. Like the funerals back then, her four to five poses left me feeling indifferent.

After feeling a couple of shakes, Ted reeled in his line to check on the hook. There wasn't anything there except for the split shot and sinker.

"It's gotta be northern pike," I said excitedly.

"Does your family ever discuss death?" Ted asked while motioning for a chub fish. I stuck my hand into the bait bucket and brought out a feisty one, which was then hooked through the tail and tossed gingerly back out into the river's current.

"No, hardly," I said, and then made a correction. "Well, maybe Grandmother. But not a lot. Why?"

Before answering, Ted drew more line out, adding slack, until the hooked chub dropped into a whirlpool and settled. "I'm just wondering," he said, while bracing the pole against a Y-shaped stick that was impaled on the muddy bank. "You know, I just wonder. I mean what kind of funeral will I have? A traditional one or a pan-Indian type? The Well-Off Man Church doesn't believe in shadows of the departed. Speaking to them special words and stuff."

Ted's line picked up, slowly drifted with the current, and then stopped. "Somebody's there again," he said in an extrasoft voice that was punctuated with two short inhales. "That's where the game fish will most likely be, waiting at the base of the drop-off points to feed."

"Wouldn't you want someone to release your shadow?" I asked.

"Yeah, but if my parents—should I die before them, I mean—decide against it, I'd have little choice. Right?"

"Yeah, but what if you told them your preferences now. Just in case."

"Just in case what?"

"Your hypothetical demise, *ke bi ti*, plugged rear."

"Hey, isn't that what Selene Lovely Buffalo called you? Wait. Think someone's pulling." Ted gently tugged the line, bouncing the bait and sinker off the bottom and back into the current. "Well, that's been bugging me," he continued. "If I bought the Maggie tomorrow, let's say, my parents wouldn't permit anyone like Rose Grassleggings to come close to my body. Shadow-eaters they call them. So it's really not up—"

In midsentence Ted whipped up the thick fishing pole from the wooden brace and set the hook. The pole bent forward in his arms and a run ensued. Ted followed the caught fish along the shallow banks, releasing some line for slack.

"I gotta let him swim to the middle!" he said loudly.

"What's this 'gotta' business?" I asked sarcastically as I walked behind the action. "You got no choice."

Before the fish went north toward the dam, it swam up to the top of the rapids and made a jolting turn. There was a large boil of water after the huge tail of the northern pike flashed. Ted and I couldn't believe the enormity of the fish we had long stalked. For over ten years we had had the distinction of hooking it five times and being provided with ten to twelve minutes of heart-pounding exhilaration. He ran parallel with it past the sandbar and up to the dirt cliffs that encircled the dam itself. From the falls the fine watery mist floated toward us, coating our sweaty skin with the enveloping smell of fish and moss. Ted shielded his eyes from the glaring reflection of the sun in the water. He began yelling again, reporting. "Shit, he's too fucking big! Ah, man, he's diving to the deep part! Toward the wire snags underneath!"

"Start bringing that line back!" I shouted. "Hurry!"

The thick fiberglass fishing pole that was rigged with twenty-pound test line and wire leader was on the edge of splitting. That's all Ted needed, a fiberglass explosion in his face.


It had been five months since our infamous return from college in Southern California. Ted hitchhiked and got into some adventuresome trouble, while I got lucky and wrangled a jet ride home through a poetry reading in Minnesota. There were differences, you could say, in how we each got home to the Black Eagle Child Settlement. I flew and Ted . . . Well, long story. The major point was, no one paid me to commit a crime along the way. Whereas Ted financed his trip through a purposely botched murder in Wyndam, Utah. Things would have been cool but he was later trounced by a couple of roadside hippie thugs. That's the way we tumbled out of academic orbit. Permanently. We were content knowing we had each given it a try—and failed. We stayed apart for the summer, trying to figure out the next move in our dysfunctional post-teenage college dropout years. By then I was a student at the University of Iowa, studying my favorite subjects, poetry writing and art. Ted was still partying excessively.

It was hard being a college student and going home on weekends. Vice versa for Ted not possessing "a goal." Mine wasn't firm but it occupied my interests. All week I attended mass lectures on Postimpressionism and snuck into art classrooms to create my own etchings; I hated the still-life assignments. In terms of poetry, college was a downer. I quit one class where the distinguished prof was flicking his cigarette ashes over the sample manuscripts. Believe it or not, that's how it was determined who would go and stay—whose samples had the most burn-throughs. Fortunately, I bypassed that procedure by telling the workshop prof that my work had been published in the Seneca Review, next to his, the year before. After a night of barhopping, I questioned if anyone had the background knowledge of my tribe to see that mythical complexities superseded line structure and rhythm. The next day I ascended the marble steps and opted for a general creative writing class. On Fridays leaving campus had a pattern: I'd stop off at the Airliner Tavern for a bottle of Heineken. On the minijukebox—the kind mounted on the wall of the booth—I'd select Peggy Lee's "Is That All There Is?" Next, I'd walk to the Greyhound Bus Depot across the street and buy the $4.10 ticket for the ride home with Sylvia Plath's unread book tucked under my arm. At Why Cheer I'd stop off at Bender's and call Joe Gadger's Taxi. Anyway, Ted would be there among the hard-core winos. If he didn't blank out, this is where we made plans to go fishing at the Indian Dam. . . .


In small, mincing steps, Ted traced the river's earthen edge with his tennis-shoed feet and reeled in the taut line with quick, circular motions. The legendary northern pike was at least three feet long, looking like a torpedo. Its sleek body shot toward the Indian Dam's deepest channel, going past the submerged baling-wire entanglement.

"Just doing something like this," said Ted, pointing to the sun-baked edge, "could kill me." The roots on the high riverbank were exposed and the swirling current constantly claimed small and large chunks of dirt, weakening the edge to a dangerous point. Suddenly, the thick fiberglass pole and the attached line began to strum to the movements of the strong fish.

"Hi-e! quit rambling," I implored. "Catch the goddamn thing!"

"I can't. Something's not right."

"What do you mean?"

All the while the fishing line began to stretch and tighten.

"Those dreams that I'm having, of leaving for no place specific, to never come back, bother me."

"We all have them," I said, "and this isn't the time to talk about them."

On the other side of the river a crowd of white curious fishermen began to collect, chatting and keeping parallel with us as we walked upriver. From deep inside the forest of brightly colored fall leaves, a thousand blackbirds began to exit, darkening the popular area.

"Bo-shit, man!" protested Ted. "Those kinda dreams ain't normal. I keep having them like . . . like as many birds there are here." He pointed upward to the treetop branches that were flickering with blackbird shadows and then to the ground where they seemed to emerge like wasps. Their nonstop chirping din even drowned out the sound of the waterfalls cascading over the Indian Dam.

"No, that's the truth," I returned. "Look, figure it out. Your dreams are far-fetched to begin with and—"

"Hey, I wouldn't call getting dressed for directionless travel far-fetched."

He was right, and the blackbirds knew this. On a bullshit spiel I posited that dreams had multimeanings. "That's where interpreters come in as people who can single out factors that are most prevalent," I said.

"That's where I come from, Ed. You nitwit."

"Oh yeah," I said, remembering what the Facepaint family's role was in the early tribal encampment days. They painted dreams for people. His dreams and my travels came from a common inter-dimensional plain.

It occurred to me right then and there that we admittedly were not as perceptive as our forebears, but there was room in the realm of possibility for the argument that our talents were inherent. The rest depended on commitment, which neither of us had much of. As for Ted adopting the stance he was credible as an alcoholic interpreter, it was ludicrous.

Death talk on the banks of the Indian Dam made me think of Luciano Bearchild, who had similar dreams. Shortly after his disappearance, I came to view journeys, trips, or vacations as rehearsals for one's actual demise. What possible justification could there be in leaving home? Luciano often questioned. The more journeys I took, the more I increased the likelihood of never returning. In other words, being in school out in California was equivalent to near death. Ted's wine-induced recurring dreams were probably no different. I neglected to interject subtly that heavy boozing, along with a lack of sleep and food, was not good.

Before we ever got to discussing his overall condition, he'd bring up the California "blast." To regale as he did was infectious. The flip side was, our partying led to academic indolence. Ted didn't think of it that way. "Be glad it happened," he'd opine before immersing himself in wild tales. Among the many things that happened, Ted was bemused by the Jim Morrison encounter. "Meeting him must have been a malfunction in the Creator's plans," I'd say, to which he agreed. Few on the Settlement could accuse the Doors of plagiarism. Upon our return from the West Coast, though, it got us into an unlikeable situation. When the word-stealing event circulated, Ted and I were interrogated on a roadside by the Well-Off Man Church elders. We emphatically denied being responsible. This was the first time I realized that Grandmother's warnings about the inherent power of word was true. Through the car window the elders recounted verbatim the story they'd heard, beginning with how we had waited for the rainstorm to come over the San Gabriel Mountains before we pounded the octagon-shaped hand drum. This is what you were said to have said, we were told. The connection was indisputable. Indeed, the first verse of the Star-Medicine song did begin with the simulated sounds of falling rain and the crack of lightning, exactly the way it was done in the prelude to the Doors song "Riders on the Storm," with the words set to the same music but in a slightly upbeat pace:

Ke me tto e me na na-e se mi e na kwa-bye to se wa-mi ye ki
*Our Grandfather who helps us walks toward us on the road*
Ma ni tta-e tti te e ji: ni ta na bwi a wa ki-ma ma ke a ki-ni wa
    kwa wa ji
*His thoughts are: I will await these toads to leave, go away*
*Therefore you will let your children pray*
Ki wi to ka wa ba tta-ke ta be no e ma wa ki-ni ma ma to mo wa
    tti
*If you let the savior arrive*
wi to ka ye kwi-ni bya tti
*the total number of your family he will help*
e ta tti ye kwi-ki a se mi e ko wa
*Grandfather Savior . . . on the road*

The truth of the whole affair was, in our collective altered states
the cardinal tenet escaped. We were unable to refrain from providing detailed words of Black Eagle Child Star-Medicine songs to the
*wa be ski na me ska tti ki,* white-complexioned people. Instead of being
backed up by the Angels of Circumspection, we had treated our
uninvited but esteemed guest to translated insights, which he then
scribbled into a notebook. Next, undoubtedly, we imagined, came
the studio recording sessions where the Red-Hatted Grandfather was
portrayed as an evil impersonator.

    That same year, through the Doors, the sacred song was released
as "Riders on the Storm" on radios across America, Europe, and the
entire universe. . . .


As Ted looked out over the Indian Dam, he held the bent fishing pole
against the blackbird-decorated panorama of water, land, and sky.
The tempestuous fish beneath shook and twitched its head, causing
the monofilament line to vibrate. It was a sign that it was settling
down to the riverbottom and holding still.

    From Jim Morrison to Luciano Bearchild the train of thought
switched: Long before Luciano's alleged abduction by UFOs at Liquid Lake, he sat and lectured heartily in his dingy log cabin on dream

symbolism. "Edgar, to travel is to have your earthly departure simulated," he imparted, "the summoning of thee by the Holy Grandfather of All to act out the grand finale." Luciano communicated that Carson Two Red Foot defined it best when he compared death to "the return of all memory." But Luciano, much like Ted Facepaint, despised the repetitive dreams he was having, those that had him taking great measures to go somewhere, though he didn't really know where. After devoting himself to religion, making preparations to join all those people who had come before him in the Grandfather World, he found his mission elusive. With head slightly angled to the slabwood floor that was sprinkled with cigarette tobacco, Luciano's discourse on the positive and negative of dreams was informative. "A small distraught child's late afternoon dream can be a funnel," he'd say, "through which the ill-minded spirits travel and become troublesome." Mindful parents or caretakers, like mine, forbade children to sleep during this period. Those who didn't, according to Luciano's teachings, unknowingly invited a mass gathering of noisy blackbirds. They clogged the trees with their presence, weighing them down like wet snow from a chaotic, sight-impairing blizzard. It was believed the restless conscience-ridden shadows of suicide victims sat on their shiny wings, as well as the shadows of those who were not properly sent on to the Grandfather World by their negligent relatives. The blackbirds in swarms would encircle the house where the disturbed child slept. Deprived of care and mistreated as a tiny, fragile human being, the child, with undiscerning eyes, would find the blackbirds appealing.

In my own grandfather's passing, Grandmother used to recall the blackbird swarms my loneliness summoned. They darkened the small wooded valley where we resided. In thinking of these symbols I wondered what our specific life purposes were. Through my poems and the travels that resulted therein, was I on a metaphorical quest for my grandfather? Had I been rehearsing my own departure through the transport of writing all along? There was no greater being than what flowed from the tips of my fingers. My worship was for the writing instrument—the pencil, pen, and keyboard—and not what the fragile all-pervasive shadow needed.

"In the end," Luciano used to observe, "the only one that matters is the all-inclusive you, dying alone." He inculcated the idea that being away from home, whether in reality or dream, was similar to death. My writings thus evolved into Luciano-based themes of leaving, returning, and forgetfulness. In an era when tribal literature was fashionable I went around—in my so-called death rehearsals—saying there was no such thing as American Indian literature, that the only thing vaguely resembling tribal literature was religious and therefore inaccessible. What does that leave you? "Assimilates," as Pat Red Hat used to say. Victims of linguistic atrophy expressing themselves in a language not theirs.

As the large northern pike fish whipped its tail fin toward the depths of the Indian Dam, Ted's fiberglass pole gave in and cracked. A kingfisher who had previously strafed a lingering flock of blackbirds with its staccato cry swerved from the gunshotlike sound. Everyone winced at the near catch and watched as the busted line flew back to the rod tip, growing limp. On the other side of the river, the white fishermen clenched their fists and threw them down in disappointment, cussing. Exasperated, Ted and I sighed our profanities. Above us, near the Sand Hill lookout point, the red and yellow leaves that were caught in a breeze became indistinguishable from the swirling butterflies.

# To See as Far as the
# Grandfather World

*The photograph. On this particular March day*
*in 1961, Theodore Facepaint, who was nine*
*years old, agreed to do a parody. With hand*
*balanced on hip and the left leg slightly*
*in front of the right, my newly found friend*
*positioned himself on Sand Hill before turning*
*to face the hazy afternoon sun. This was a pose*
*we had become familiar with:*
                              *the caricature*
*of a proud American Indian, looking out*
*toward the vast prairie expanse, with one hand*
*shielding the bronze eyes. When I projected*
*the image of the color 35 mm slide onto*
*the wall last week I remembered the sense*
*of mirth in which it was taken. Yet somewhere*
*slightly north of where we were clowning around,*
*Grandmother was uprooting medicinal roots*
                     *from the sandy soil*
*and placing them inside her flower-patterned*
*apron pockets to thaw out.*

*Twenty-nine years later, if I look long enough,*
*existential symbols are almost detectable.*

*The direction of the fiery sun in descent, for example,*
*is considered the Black Eagle Child Hereafter.*
*Could I be seeing too much? Past the west*
*and into the Grandfather World? Twice*
                    *I've caught myself asking:*
*Was Ted's pose portentous? When I look*
*closely at the background of the Indian Dam*
*below—the horizontal line of water that runs*
*through the trees and behind Ted—I also know*
*that Liquid Lake with its boxcar-hopping*
                    *lights is nearby.*
*For Ted and his Well-Off Man Church,*
*the comets landed on the crescent-shaped*
*beach and lined themselves up for a ritualistic*
*presentation. For Jane Ribbon, a mute healer,*
*a seal haunted this area. But further upriver*
*is where the ancient deer hunter was offered*
*immortality by three goddesses. While*
*the latter story of our geographic genesis*
*is fragmented, obscuring and revealing*
*itself as a verisimilitude, it is important.*
*Ted and I often debated what we would*
*have done had we been whisked through*
*a mystical doorway to a subterranean enclave.*
*Ted, unlike the ancient hunter who turned*
*down paradise, would have accepted—*
*and the tribe never would have flexed*
*its newborn spotted wings. In the hunter's*
*denial we were thus assigned as Keepers*
*of Importance. But the question being asked*
*today is, Have we kept anything?*

*Our history, like the earth with its*
*abundant medicines, Grandmother used*
*to say, is infused with ethereality. Yet in*
*the same breath she'd openly exclaim*
*that with modernity comes a cultural toll.*

*In me, in Ted, and everyone.*
*Stories then, like people, are subject to change.*
*More so under adverse conditions. They*
*are also indicators of our faithfulness. Since*
*the goddesses' doorway was sealed shut by*
                    *our own transgressions,*
*Grandmother espoused that unbounded*
*youth would render tribal language*
*and religion inept, that each lavish*
*novelty brought into our homes would*
*make us weaker until there was nothing.*
                    *No lexicon. No tenets.*
*Zero divine intervention. She was also*
*attuned to the fact that for generations*
*our grandparents had wept unexpectedly*
*for those of us caught in the blinding*
*stars of the future.*

*Mythology, in any tribal-oriented society,*
*is a crucial element. Without it, all else*
*is jeopardized with becoming untrue. While*
*the acreages beneath Ted's feet and mine*
*offered relative comfort back then,*
*we are probably more accountable now*
                    *to ourselves—and others.*
*Prophecy decrees it. Most fabled among*
*the warnings is the one that forecasts*
*the advent of our land-keeping failures.*
*Many felt this began last summer when*
*a whirlwind abruptly ended a tribal*
*celebration. From the north in the shape*
*of an angry seagull it swept up dust,*
*corn leaves, and assorted debris,*
*as it headed toward the audacious*
*"income-generating architecture,"*
*the gambling hall. At the last second*
*the whirlwind changed direction, going*

*toward the tribal recreation complex.*
*Imperiled, the people within the circus tent-*
*like structure could only watch as the panels*
*flapped crazily. A week later, my father said*
*the destruction was attributable to the gambling*
*hall, which was the actual point of weakness*
*of the tribe itself.*

*Which is to say the hill where a bronze-eyed*
*Ted once stood is under threat of impermanence.*
*By allowing people who were not created*
*by the Holy Grandfather to lead us we may*
*cease to own what Ted saw on that long-ago day.*
*From Rolling Head Valley to Runner's Bluff*
           *and over the two rivers*
*our hold is gradually being unfastened by*
*false leaders. They have forgotten that their*
*own grandparents arrived here under a Sacred*
*Chieftain. This geography is theirs nonetheless,*
*and it shall be as long as the first gifts given*
*are intact. In spite of everything that we are*
*not, this crown of hills resembles lone islands*
*amid an ocean of corn, soybean fields,*
*and low-lying fog. Invisibly clustered on*
*the Black Eagle Child Settlement's slopes*
*are the remaining Earthlodge clans.*
           *The western edge of this*
*woodland terrain overlooks the southern*
*lowlands of the Iowa and Swanroot Rivers,*
*while the eastern edge splits widely into several*
*valleys, where the Settlement's main road winds*
*through. It is on this road where Ted and I walked.*
*It is on this road where Ted met a pack*
*of predators.*

*Along the color slide's paper edge the year*
*1961 is imprinted. Ted and I were fourth*

graders at *Weeping Willow Elementary.*
Nine years later, in *1970*, a passenger train
took us to Southern California for college.
It proved to be a lonely place where winter
                     appeared high atop
the San Gabriel Mountains on clear days.
Spanish-influenced building styles, upper-middle-
class proclivities, and the arid climate had a subtle
asphyxiating effect. Instead of chopping firewood
          for father's nonexistent blizzard,
I began my evenings in Frary Dining Hall
where Orozco's giant mural with erased privates
called Prometheus loomed above. My supper
would consist of tamales and cold shrimp salad
instead of boiled squirrel with flour dumplings.
Through mountain forest fires the Santa Ana
winds showered the campus with sparks and ashes.
In a wide valley where a smoke- and smog-darkened
night came early, the family album possessed its
own shimmery light. Pages were turned. A visual
record of family and childhood friends. Time.
          Ted and I transforming,
separating. During the first Christmas break
in which we headed back to the Black Eagle
Child Settlement, Ted froze me in celluloid:
against a backdrop of snow-laden pine trees
a former self wears a windswept topcoat,
Levi bell-bottoms, cowboy boots, and tinted
glasses. Ted and I, like statues, are held
captive in photographic moments.
          As the earth spins, however,
the concrete mold disintegrates,
exposing the vulnerable wire
foundation of who we are not.

# The Night of Jim

Right up to 1982, fourteen years ago, like a couple of wide-eyed, captive elementary school students, Ted Facepaint and I would wait for the reverberations of Doors music to enshroud us in nostalgia, along with selections of Creedence Clearwater, Carole King, Chicago, John Mayall, Jethro Tull, Jefferson Airplane, Led Zeppelin, and Santana. We saluted Jim Morrison, legendary singer, composer, and poet, with Miller's High Life beer and a joint of righteous homegrown on occasion. While many from my fortyish age set can relate to the music—though not so much the character—of the noted American rock-and-roll band called the Doors, there are few in Iowa who can actually recall spending an evening before an earthquake with its lead singer, the "Lizard King" icon of the flower child era.

As far-fetched as it may seem, with the exception of the characters involved, the following story actually happened:

When Ted Facepaint and I were college students we found ourselves partying with Jim Morrison—or at least someone who resembled him—in a doorless mountainside cabin that was situated right over the San Andreas Fault. Facepaint often reflected that "this must have been at the pinnacle of Jim's illustrious but tragic career." Ever since the tombstone door was closed in Paris over the musician, a rare and unexpected visit from Ted Facepaint couldn't pass without playing the audiocassette tape of *The Doors Collected Hits.*

Selene Buffalo Husband, my wife, who was grateful that I had a visitor at all, forced herself to sit with the Settlement's oldest hippies before excusing herself to go after her sister, the "Woman from Hengelo," down the road. It worked. Both of them would slap us back to Paula Abdul and Michael Bolton reality. To understand the enormity of the contribution to the history of American rock and roll we thought we made, and to not be credited, gnawed away at our rural complacency.

In our get-togethers we'd describe the San Andreas Fault as nature's version of the famous sidewalk vent that blew Marilyn Monroe's skirt upward. The main difference was, the earth-breaking crevice couldn't delight us with a view of the breathtaking anatomy of a sexually charged female. When the layers of rock beneath the mountains could not stand the subtle shifts of the Pacific Ocean, the energy released had no alternative but to become an unknowing accomplice in the taking of human life.

And we were there, doped-up silly and unable to distinguish night from day in an abandoned mountainside cabin on stilts.

Shooting forth from Grandmother Earth that morning were unseen bullets, awesome aftershocks that caused the untimely collapse of a freeway on a carload of commuters on their way to Los Angeles. Other bullets unleashed violent rock slides on school playgrounds. In one episode a slide raked an unsuspecting mother and her eight-month-old child into the froth-filled ocean.

For weeks afterward, whenever we heard of "the famous one" that rocked the Richter scale, Marilyn Monroe ceased being the source of male adoration. The subterranean shifting of the West Coast made us realize how insignificant we were in the greater scheme of things.

Back then there was rarely, if ever, any occasion to weigh seriously the ramifications of one's own life-related decisions. But being on a mountainside at the wrong bone-jarring time crystalized for us the perception that we as humanity were indeed infantile. Being reminded of our powerless ways was, in an odd way, beneficial. Earth gave, earth took.

For me it went a little bit further than that: I got myself into those predicaments due to my own dangerous immaturity. In short,

I shouldn't have been partying with some hooligans in an unfamiliar area. Clotelde, my mother, had specifically warned me through letters. Sometimes, in the acting out of denial, it seems as if I were absorbed in a Star-Medicine-induced dream. Academia was there but in the flutter of an eyelid I was miles high in a fluid noncommittal state of consciousness.

That's how much being far away affected me.


On that particular Southern California mountainside, loneliness took a tangible form: With my eyes still closed I woke up to the familiar but atrocious sound of buzzing flies, o tte wa ki. They reminded me instantly of summer mornings past when the oily colored flies congregated on the screen door of my grandmother's small yellow house, the one that had been converted from a chicken coop for three hundred dollars.

The flies would gather in blotches every day in the cool of the morning before the scorching sun came over the wooded hill. The brilliant unrelenting rays would make conditions miserably hot and sweaty. The flies made things worse, of course.

Drifting in and out of REM, I thought I was actually home for a few seconds. There was the faint humming of insects that seemed to echo from within the cornfield, and from the treetops came the cacophony of a skin-burning song. The drone entered my ears and it rung like a telephone wire that had been grazed by a sling-propelled rock. I listened and visualized. Four horizontal gray lines slit and divided the woodlands. As the pieces peeled away and wrapped themselves around me I became aware of where I was, the sound I heard.

That was the very humming that originated from Grandmother Earth and her inhabitants. Grasshoppers flitted into the flower-scented breeze, crisscrossing the lawn and garden. The bees followed whatever moved and the house wasps hung upside down. Above, crows and vultures, along with an occasional red-tailed hawk, went their ways in search of food. By midday, ants, spiders, and box elder bugs warmed themselves on the yellow-aged knots of sunlit lumber. By sundown the pensive crickets were ready to join the locusts and tree frogs with their hypnotic shrilling.

Here, I recalled what Grandmother said about the oily colored flies amassed on the screen door. All it would take would be one plump fly on the nose of Ma kwi ne tti, Bear Paw, to make him a keen-nosed hunter. It would be unsightly, squishing one on his snout to ensure exceptional hunting services. The honor that came with a belt full of dangling squirrels was hard to resist, however. A minimum of three squirrels had to be shot for a meal on the table. Their ages were important with regard to meat texture. If they weren't up in their years, it was certainly worth the firemaking. Once they were properly singed, they were degutted, cut into quarter pieces, and then rinsed, along with the squirrel's head. Several hours in a boiling pot of water, lid partially closed, made the charred pieces of sinewy meat tender. Then the final ingredient of cornmeal was added.

As I sailed over the plains of half dream, half sleep, President John F. Kennedy unexpectedly came to mind. . . . On the day he was assassinated in Dallas, my uncle Winston Principal Bear and his sidekick, Dwayne Afraid, emerged from the forest of orange leaves with ten squirrels apiece. The small game was slated to make the main dishes for a family-sized ghost—*remembering people no longer here*—feast. But no one would have the luxury of eating boiled squirrel brains, a Black Eagle Child delicacy. Not with perfect head shots. This skillful practice, Winston taught, eliminated the chance of a wounded squirrel returning home high atop the inaccessible cottonwood trees and dying inside a hollow tree next to his mate. I dreamt that the president of the United States was one of the unfortunate fox squirrels back then. On that day in Texas, I asked myself, were his last meditations centered on home, family, or politics? Or were his thoughts totally absent at that precise second?

In a twisted tangent, did it fucking matter?

*In jerky, squirrellike gestures the president leapt forward from the cab of the limousine, and the excess skin on his autumn-fattened sides expanded into a parachute, guiding him upward instead and away from the range of the Carcano rifle. From a nearby thorn tree a single insect stole sound away from the lesser insects in the humid summer air. Attired in a grooved black shell, the large Lee Harvey Oswald insect hoarded the precious wind, grass, bird, animal, children, and cloud music. It*

*hunched protectively over the Carcano. When the presidential motor-
cade appeared, the insect opened its white-tipped transparent wings as
a prelude to the deafening raspy cry that a more intense sun ray, a darkening skin agent, was about to be thrown out. This was the insect's assignment, to burn skin. E te si ke a was its name. And somewhere within
was the fingertip-sized piece of obsidian, zipping along in accordance
to the calculated trajectory path. Standing next to the projected point
of impact were the green cornstalks that would soon be saturated with
the bloody aftermath.*

I remembered watching the grainy black-and-white television
footage of the slain president's horse-drawn casket clacking down the
street. Standing in attention next to the widow-immaculate Jacqueline
was the well-dressed child who saluted his father.

People for one reason or another always leave each other behind, Grandmother taught. Recklessly they entrust to others the care
of all humankind. Recklessly. As her grandson of twelve years I questioned if we could manage world affairs without the Squirrel King
named John.

As I reviewed the solemn procession again, an inscrutable question sprung out of the mishmash: Did Jacqueline, the first lady, wear
perfume that day? What kind? By custom, I thought, Black Eagle
Child women left themselves free of beautifying ointments until the
mourning period is over. Was the perfume on her delicate wrist bone
releasing its wondrous beguiling scent amid the calamity?

Another question, circling back to home, formulated: What did
Grandmother cook this morning? Having no desire to see what I suspected might be there instead, I dream-tricked myself into a home-
style entrée of sticky rice and beef, golden brown frybread, maple
syrup, and cool, green tea. For now it was pleasant, this nostalgic
stimulation of the senses. I could put up with flies for one academics-
free day, away from the valley where classes on philosophy and American literature awaited.

Growing more convinced I was on a familiar threshold, I permitted the daylight to crack the shells of my eyes open on the rusty
rim of an iron skillet. Drained of spirit, hungover, and paranoid, I
found myself in an old, abandoned cabin that was perched on stilts

overlooking a mountainside in Southern California. The prospect of Grandmother's cool green tea dissipated in the yellowish haze of the smog that hung below the midmorning sun, and the only thing that mattered was my endangered life.

As I stood up on nimble legs, the cabin seemed to respond by swaying. Something creaked from beneath and I held still, waiting to see if it was an aftershock—or just me. Structurally, the cabin wasn't safe. Even a minor cramp of my left buttock could trigger a hazardous quiver. With legs and arms extended, I stood still. Looking down, I saw where the cabin had been ripped in half and thrown back together; the splintered edges of the wooden frames overlapped, pinning some sleeping bags and blankets. I pictured Jane Ribbon's facial deformity, what the Creator had done, ripping it up on purpose and piecing it back together with rope; I pictured Rose Grass-leggings riding the waves on a black whiskered seal surfboard over the Iowa River. Stretching my arms farther out for equilibrium, I pictured Mr. Mateechna, the school janitor, bowing to a blank wall of the Well-Off Man Church as he felt the first mind-altering effects of the Star-Medicine mushroom as "a horrendous cramp of the buttock." In this panorama of recollection, lo and behold, my left buttock began twitching!

Not wishing to plunge earthward with a bad hangover, I leaned over slowly to gather my blankets into a loose bundle. It was a mistake. When I caught a glimpse of the ground below through a large crack on the cabin floor, nausea settled in. I had every intention to stumble forward to the open window and throw up, but the hot, dry wind made my body fluids evaporate before I got there. It caused the eyeballs to shrivel up. Whatever anatomical moisture there was hardened. I doubled over, oinked like a piglet, and wobbled on my bell-bottomed hocks. Racked with intestinal muscle spasms, I clutched my belly as the sickly fumes of alcohol filtered up my throat, shimmying its loose particles into my nose. Through the cabin's gray floor I saw white, jagged boulders below and even the shimmering tops of pine trees. The boulders resembled thick, deadly onions made of rough concrete, sticking out from a green hillside. On weak legs and with a mouth that failed to produce saliva, I stuck my head out the window. Eventually, vertical blanketlike patches of stripes overtook my field of vision within the cabin's interior, creating the effect of distant rain. The exception was, these were miniaturized and pulsating less than ten feet away. From across the room the small clouds quietly flashed, reminding me of the thunderstorm I saw as a boy at Horned Serpent Lake, Canada. Before the sound of falling rain began, lightning shot through the cabin floor. The booming thunder traveled across the rocky landscape in the voice of a mortal, Alfred Potato, a well-known musician and war veteran.

When the abandoned cabin on stilts began to tremble and weave on the mountainside, my throat began to fossilize and my lungs palpitated to the emergency of body fluid depletion. Without vital lubricants asphyxiation of self was imminent. Instantly there was melancholia and unconsciousness. . . .

In my thoughts was automatically recorded the poetry of what would be a largely unnoticed death:

*Grandfather of the Grandfather World*
*thus was the reason you taught*
*our old people to weep*
*at the oddest*
*inopportune moments*
*In our naïveté*
*we never knew they openly*
*mourned and in advance*
*of the turmoil that we*
*your youth*
*would undergo*
*We the future generations*
*the unsuspecting*
*and subjugated grandchildren*
*who will never know*
*our rightful home*
*why we even*
*exist*

As soon as I heard what sounded like the ringing of glass, I came to. Groping, I felt nothing. Outside, the flies were silent. . . . Gone was the Lee Harvey Oswald insect whose skin-burning song transported the fingertip-size piece of obsidian from the window of the

Dallas book depository, blowing the Fox Squirrel King's brain to smithereens . . . in the limousine, in Jacqueline's hands. I remembered the miniature thundercloud's rain and swallowing whatever had collected. It wasn't much but it jump-started the system; I took a breath, stood erect, and made my way gingerly across the dangerous floor in short, deliberate shuffles. Once I was up against the wall, standing over unseen log beams, I nearly gasped and shuddered at what could have transpired; I was grateful the invisible, swirling sentinels kept me from rolling down the treacherous mountainside.

In the adjoining room my companions began to snore louder and in unison. Along with the stifling rock-heated air, the smell of stale alcohol was emitted from deep somewhere within the human bellies. Fermentation continued. The putrid odor of Chianti and Brew 101 beer remained like a rude, uninvited visitor. Looking out across the pine-filled valley, I took note of the reddish brown haze—the sweet but toxic exhale of Los Angeles—ascending through the trees of Mount Baldy.

During days when the smog came to a standstill over the quaint town of Claremont and the Claremont Colleges, it hid the lovely snow on the mountaintop. Because of its geographical location and shape, Mount Baldy served as a "dead-end" alley for the Pacific Ocean. Its swift winds whisked the potent industrial and mass traffic emissions all along the thirty-mile stretch from downtown L.A. The only trouble was, the industrial stench became lodged at the base of the mountain and its unfortunate populace. Below, the red-eyed and raw-throated citizens adjusted uncomfortably to a valley that experienced night an hour or two early.

Today's smog level, I thought, would surely be reported as an alert. Elderly citizens with respiratory ailments would be advised to stay home. It was ludicrous to issue these warnings when breathing alone meant inhaling the same unavoidable shit. I then made my way to the moldy table and sat down for a Marlboro cigarette, braintalking still:

*Instead of being ejected from the cockpit of the meteorological craft, parachuting to safety on iridescent butterfly wings, I would drop from the cabin like a buffalo calf ejected out of its standing mother's womb.*

*There's nothing more depressing than a Suicidal Phase Village hang-over. World squalor on a day-to-day basis embeds itself and crystalizes over my malnourished and jaundiced tissue. A wobbly legged pursuit ensues for the buffalo mother's cool but elusive shadow. . . .*

That's when I began recalling sketchy details of the previous night's events. Foremost was the earth tremor, the Initial Messenger, and the chilly, Wandering Spirit, coyote cries that prompted everyone to pray. I also remembered the person who knocked at the doorless cabin, claiming to be Jim Morrison of the Doors.

"Now that you guys know who I am, may I join you?" he asked.

I wondered why a black-leather-clad, bedazzling hippie would want to translate into English word for word the Star-Medicine song Ted and I were singing on the octagon-shaped hand drum.

"May I ask also what the song is called?" he asked. "What? 'Riders on the Storm'? Cool, man. Real cool."

But later when the hippie started to sing along, the mountainside began to rumble. Impressed with what we thought we had produced, we drunkenly egged one another to participate more. Say this, say that. Pass the wine and the smoke. Soon an unholy reverberation shook from deep within the base of the mountain, and its tremor coursed through our delicate bones, making us scream.

That's how it all started.

I concluded no one chose to wake up right away that morning due to profound embarrassment. A crying face, after all, is imprinted stronger than a drunken face, which smiles and laughs. Except for the wild-eyed Jim Morrison look-alike, we had all wept like three-year-olds dreaming of monstrous serpents, and we clung to each other as tightly as we did to our mothers. In the deafening din of an earthquake, Jim Morrison sank into the corner and blended perfectly into the candlelit room.

As I puffed the Marlboro cigarette, thinking through currents of fear, I felt horrible for having helped Ted Facepaint provide "Jim" with an English translation of the Star-Medicine night-dividing song.

# The Milieu
# of Forgetfulness

Midway up Ridge Road, on the blacktop road now marked "SETTLE-MENT TRAFFIC ONLY," is where I first embraced the moonlit face of Selene Buffalo Husband. It was the summer of 1974. I was twenty-three and she was sixteen. Near the area known as "Doc's Driveway," where "the butterfly enchantress" and I held each other closely in romantic admiration, there are now new houses. Twenty-one years have passed; my love for Selene remains strong. Sometimes as we pass this area by car, I gaze at her secretly and marvel that the girl who captured my heart so long ago sits next to me as a beautiful woman. For young and old alike this place is no longer a party place, however. Lots of memories, good and bad, were made there. Today, from the benefits of the tribal gambling enterprise, new houses dot the hills to the north on newly bought tribal land.

There have been extensive changes—in our lives and that of the tribe.

Located less than a mile from "Doc's Driveway," over what used to be cornfields, is the Black Eagle Child Casino and Bingo Extrava-ganza. Because of the twenty-four-hour casino-related traffic, Ridge Road no longer intersects with Highway 30. What was formerly the northern Black Eagle Child Settlement entrance is now an elaborate highway mixmaster that orchestrates traffic toward and away from the casino.

To look at this place today in terms of people and geography is to realize things have been radically altered. Having endured cataclysmic misfortunes in the progress and resistance modes of a tribal society, we are about to be rolled down the hill physically, so to speak, by a greater nonhuman priest. We have been overswept by greed and hypocrisy. The land is a barometer of our own mortality.

A question therefore arises: In one's short lifetime how can geographical markers—such as gravel roads and whole countrysides—be razed and replaced by something as audacious as "income-generating architecture," complete with gigantic parking lots and sparkling neon-lit highway billboards? According to the most sagacious Earthlodge clan elders, we have entered a critical stage that is infused with apocalyptic themes. They are far from being wrong when vivid indicators sprout up around us.

In any other world where there "ain't a damn thing wrong" with capitalism, everything "would be cool." There, not only do the real remnant groups sell themselves but they relinquish their status as nations, jeopardizing ours in the process. Or so it has been argued. Convincingly. In the eyes of Big Brother they have the authority. In the eyes of their own particular Earthmaker—I'd wager as someone who disagrees 100 percent with this "we are one tribe" slogan—they must be a nightmare.

For an ancient Woodlands tribe like the Black Eagle Childs whose culture is still intact, these electronic highway billboards that bear the name *given* us by the Well-Known Twin Brother contradict the very practices of tribal isolationism. They are, in fact, foreboding. You wouldn't think so, however, by the long lines at the tribal center for bimonthly per capita checks. The Black Eagle Child gambling and recreational complex is more reflective of where we are going than who we are and were.

Change is either inescapable or controversial here.


Toward the latter part of summer 1990 a message that many tribal members thought originated from the Holy Grandfather came down from the dark gray central Iowa sky, using the exact path taken long ago by the aged but menacing Arbie's Pig Feeds Ford. In the guise of inclement weather the Holy Grandfather unraveled a rare whirlwind on land that was long heralded by the Earthlodge clans to be tornadofree. Although it couldn't quite be classified as a twister per se, it had the same heart-pounding effect.

On the northern tier of the Black Eagle Child Settlement the whirlwind swept down from the clouds "like a goddamned seagull," jumping Highway 30 and causing a semi-truck loaded with chicken eggs to jackknife into a ditch. After demolishing the monolithic neon-lit casino sign and a new utilities power substation, the scornful wind headed straight toward the Black Eagle Child Recreation Complex, where a tribal celebration was in progress. Amateur video captured the path the invisible force took, choosing its victims and their vehicles indiscriminately. The KRCG television crew that was there also documented the pandemonium from the press box before it collapsed. From under the debris the camera operator continued to film for the ten o'clock news. Blinded by the dust and electrical sparks, a "stretch" limousine collided with a BMW. Over the parking lots, casino security guards scattered about aimlessly looking for their posts that were no longer there. A charter bus that was loaded to the max was headed toward a soybean field. Inside were passengers who were oblivious to the fact they were driverless. No different from a jet-plane movie disaster, the bus driver had been sucked right out of the cab.

Upon reaching the recreation complex, where the Black Eagle Child Field Days and Chautauqua had been forced indoors, the whirlwind began rattling the aluminum panels of the circus tent–like structure. Huddling inside the giant skeletal framework were two thousand wide-eyed powwow goers and their families. As the panels flapped violently, the casino goers who had been asked to evacuate the gambling hall could see the powwow goers. They were running in circles and trying to determine which panel would stay open long enough for them to exit the controversial prefab building. Inside, it was later reported, it sounded like an abominable, hellish rattling of hail on a tin roof.

Elsewhere, the giant Chia Pet–type buffaloes who stood at the casino entrance were sandblasted into nothingness. The revolving floodlights that illuminated the night skies were lifted to the cloudy vortex and spun until the gear came down as a heap of crumpled stainless steel and shattered glass.

\* \* \*

As it traveled down Milkman Ridge, the whirlwind could have killed many people but instead it injured, leaving people scattered over the artificial turf gymnasium floor. Within minutes the earthlodge elders, along with the agnostics and the good-for-nothings, issued aspersions amid the eagle plumes and cotton candy that were still airborne. All the more reason, they ranted, to disenroll all known and suspected disbelievers and their mixed-blood cohorts. The dissenters, those who didn't have it their Burger King way politically, pounced upon the tragedy, crying, "There should have been a referendum!"

Selene and I were home when it happened, loading the PA system into the truck for the Young Lions, our singing and drumming group. We quickly ran to the safety of the trailer and soon freaked out on the trees as they bent halfway toward the rain-saturated yard. Next thing we knew, a caravan of powwow goers cruised by like a funeral procession.

Within a week a videotaped segment was broadcast nationally on NBC's "Eyewitness Extra." Horatio Plain Brown Bear III, a fourteen-year-old boy who volunteered to hold down the elaborate, modern big top made the front pages of the *Central Plains Register*. He was suspended twenty feet in the air, holding on to the cables and being lifted by an aluminum panel. Behind him a banner of the powwow's theme read "GOODWILL & HARMONY FOR YOUTH." This photograph was then picked up by the *New York* and *Los Angeles Times* Sunday newspapers. The London and Sydney newspapers reported that "Mongo, the Texaco Man," the powwow chairman who also served as an emcee, kept repeating, "Sing and say the Indian way," in a state of delirium.

With the world as audience at their punishment, the elders were devastated. Before, the tribal celebration had all the makings of a fantasy powwow—one hundred dollars a day just for dancing and fifty dollars for children under twelve. The organizers were an unlikely crew: veterans, some of whom had been kicked out of the service, and the tribal casino personnel. With financial backing from the casino's management firm, GSIA, Gambling Says It All, the celebration created community excitement. Famous dancers and singers arrived a week early, and the local hosts who made out as if they were

friends of the comely professionals were stuck with motel and restaurant tabs.

On that same day of the whirlwind, a young white woman who
had moved from southern Iowa to be within proximity of the casino
fatally shot herself due to meager gambling debts. Out in the country roads an old white man was robbed and beaten to death, "a random crime," with tire irons after winning at the casino. The deaths
of these two white people occurred for less than six hundred dollars.
(I asked: If the old white man and the girl hadn't come here to gamble,
wouldn't they still be alive? F. A. right!) Because the media toned
down the connection between the casino and crime, GSIA bought
lots of space and key time slots to advertise the Black Eagle Child
Field Days and Chautauqua: Five thousand dollars was offered to
adults in all dance categories—traditional men's and women's, men's
grass dance, jingle dress dance, men's fancy feather, and women's
fancy shawl.

But it wasn't to be.

The whirlwind hovered directly over the gambling hall before
slamming down on the powwow after Grand Entry and during the
introduction of the visiting dignitaries. A Native American Hollywood
actor who made an asshole of himself by admitting he couldn't "talk
Indian" started everything through his rendition of a Christian prayer
in sign language. The aftermath was a sad, shocking scene. "Mongo,"
in his Texaco service man outfit, emerged from a nearby cornfield
and staggered out on the giant big-top panels. On his head a crumpled
war bonnet. All around paramedics, stretchers, wailing ambulances,
and a severed microphone in his muddy and bruised hand. Under
what was once the big top's arena, the Rocky Raccoon Singers could
be seen in the video clips. In their zeal to be A-1 dependable, they
had remained steadfast in their chairs. Many remarked they were
stupid not to run. Trying to be cool guys, they were videotaped humming a song together while being cut out from the cables and basketball court partitions by the emergency crews with acetylene
torches. In graphic slow-motion "Eyewitness Extra" footage, an aluminum harpoon shot out from the skies, puncturing Rocky Raccoons'
concert bass drum, missing the singers by inches. The powwow music
disemboweled.

* * *

Rumor, like the whirlwind, spun out of control.

Blame the casino, decried the traditionalists.

Blame transgression and taboo, said the priests.

Blame the family who failed to isolate a girl in her initial menses, whispered the innocent women at the Gracious Senior Citizens' Center.

Shit, blame yourselves, countered the girls with maximum cosmetics plastered on their faces. Did she open the curtains, churning the winds with her fiery eyes? the tight skirts added sarcastically. Hey, old fogies, why don't you guyses blow a Trojan and float away, okay?

The cheap aromatic smell of the girls' perfume, "Bobbie Sex," mingled in an undesirable way with everyone's cigarette smoke and politics. All of the buffoons pointed to each other accusingly. Others double-barrel-fingered.

Ah, what the hell, blame youth, debated the old men playing cards. Blame woman for the downfall of man. Fists were pounded atop the green table. Cards flew and the coins chimed in agreement.

Hey, wait a minute . . . you guys aren't Pine Sol clean either! shouted their grandsons dressed in baggy clothes, baseball caps, and heel-lit tennis shoes.

Alright, you yellow-shitting punks, challenged the elderly combat veterans, you come here and say that!

A bold-faced high school Explorette Scout leader stepped between the two groups and gave her opinion: I blame the ignorant traditional dancer who carried another tribe's ceremonial staff into the arena. Blah, blah, blah.

Excuse me, interrupted the long-legged schoolteacher, but isn't he too fat to be dancing, anyway? And isn't his wife the one who does a stupid imitation of a Northern Plains woman's cry? And aren't you the Texaco Man's mistress?

How about you, teacher lady, aren't you the one who wraps long legs around men like an anaconda, making them fartsy, making them cry? the slobbering old men audibly whispered.

Hey, chuck that filth, alright? pleaded the atheist Indian artist, the one who was extricated from his moped with the "Jaws of Life" and charged with drunk driving.

Yeah, she's state-certified, said the ineffective tribal social services worker.

Hoping she wouldn't be seen, Grace Disgrace, the tribal grants writer, took advantage of the ruckus and excused herself to go take a crap, complaining she should have gone sooner.

Go on then, Ma, get out of here, she was told by the fifth executive director we had had in eight years, Scotty Disgrace, convicted embezzler and wife beater.

Blame taco salad, if anything, said the intellectuals as a sarcastic joke to Grace Disgrace's ill-timed exit.

In addition to the main Disgraces, you're all a disgrace, spoke the members of Weeping Willow School Board, who had just been canned by their employers, the Tribal Council.

What does *your* firing have to do with the whirlwind? asked the antischool buffoons. Have *you* gone bananas, in Lakota *zee-skopa*-ed? The Missooni Indian woman *you* hired got smashed at *your* Halloween party and assaulted her husband afterward on the intersection of Highways 30 and 63. Listen to a local newspaper quote. "Noted for her jingle dress dancing abilities and not her academic credentials, the lady subdued her pumpkin-masked mate with flying roundhouse kicks." Need we say more?

And it went on like that, day after day, constant bickering until foam from a dozen frothy mouths formed a slough. Whew! Pe-e-eeeooo! Whenever the controversy began to dry up in its own heat, the once-sympathetic elders renewed the attack. Backed by the Tribal Council —all of whom were suspected of embezzling casino cash—the elders presented their sons and grandsons as good examples. Role modelish. *Ish* is right. Ishi-bound. Everyone snickered. Like prosecuting lawyers in a high-profile criminal trial, the cynics outlined their case item by item. The council members and their records were reviewed. There were loopholes, inconsistencies, and outright hypocrisy.

"Kensey" Muscatine, the pedophile-horticulturalist and former Council chair, for instance, hoodwinked the clans into praying with him for a lenient sentence. Of course, he was assisted by a new generation of informants who had no qualms selling the Earthlodge clan gourds. Only a handful had the guts to leave but in so doing they set themselves up as targets.

These cronies are engaged in sacrilegious doings, said the cynics.

Those who left the "asking for a lenient jail sentence" feast were visited that night at their windows by exotic-sounding birdcalls that changed to loud, electrifying growls of a bearlike creature who stood upright in the moonlight, emitting sparks from its inquisitive snorts as it dropped on all fours and drove away in grinding, mechanical gear sounds.

Those who worship figurines supposedly symbolizing past warriors are fooling themselves, said the cynics. (It was believed the Black Hummingbird Society were sorcerers who replenished their own lives with other lives. Ancient Count Draculas, Jekyll and Hyde characters. Nighttime ceremonies in which arrows of light were seen ascending to the stars through the earthlodge portals scared everyone. Sorcery as religion, they said quietly among themselves.)

At televised community meetings, "Kensey" Muscatine condemned the fate of anyone who wasn't an earthlodge participant. The room temperature was ice cubish. Save yourselves for the good of the tribe! he urged.

Does that mean forcefully shoving a minor's face to your sweaty crotch as redemption? shouted the cynics. Is this why your daughter leaves home every summer because she can't stand your repulsive BO?

The curious onlookers and assorted good-for-nothings expressed whoas.

Forgiving relatives of "Kensey," from "Grubby's" and Horatio's side of the family, shouted back until the pedophile's wife, Devonshire Muscatine, keeled over, all 258 pounds of her, knocking over the television camera crews of KORN—Channel 9 Local Access News, ending the meeting.

Above them, the turbulent skies hovered. Devonshire, amazingly, was the only one to witness the revelation. A tiny lavender whirlwind descended into her hairy nostrils until the smell of gunpowder was exhaled, defusing her original opinions. Against her husband's wishes she forgave the cynics before she was on her cellulite-swollen ankles. She indicated it was "heavenly" that small ceremonies were being done by these families within the privacy of their homes. Belief in the Principal Religion was taught, she added.

But then so is immorality by some of the earthlodge and Tribal Council leaders, retorted Grace Disgrace, who was composed and rejuvenated upon her return from the can. In spite of their superior knowledge, she indicated in her closing remarks, some earthlodge leaders are charlatans!

Not far away, old men wept over disobedient sons. There were insinuations these sons witnessed the seduction of their aunts and sisters while their mothers snored on the floor nearby. Unwanted babies, not long ago, were smothered to assure family dignity. Retroactive fatherhood was inconceivable but it was done.

In the verbal aftermath of the whirlwind no one was right, no one was wrong. For centuries we had gone against the white-skinned people, sensing they carried with them earth's demise. Into them are we helplessly drawn today. The whirlwind, it was said, exemplified that very possibility.

# The Mask of Seeing

It would be good if my self-published book of verse, *The Mask of Seeing* (Hominy Creek Press, 1989), inspired Lorna Bearcap and Claude E. Youthman to write "The Weeping Willow Manifesto." Unbeknownst to the *Black Eagle Child Quarterly* editors, namely Billy "Cracker" Jack and his supervisors, the article was published in the spring 1990 issue. The mimeographed community newsletter that had published my poetry three decades ago became a glossy tabloid. Aimed at the casino-oriented market via "Big Money Winners" and trivial "Card Dealer of the Month" selections, the publication arm of the Tribal Council had a promotional slant. And so when "The Weeping Willow Manifesto" made it through the censors to a large readership, there were outcries and feelings of consternation from the tribal members.

In one way Bearcap and Youthman were the exception when it came to Black Eagle Child people. Distinguished in their knowledge of tribal culture and in their Earthlodge clan participation, they were also certified to teach in the state of Iowa. No small deed. They were nevertheless ostracized by the Tribal Council for being "educated." "These teachers can work," they stipulated to the Weeping Willow School Board, "with the understanding they remain free of political opinions, i.e., unnecessary editorializing in newsletters and general acts of subversion." No joke. Under these restrictive conditions Lorna

Bearcap and Claude Youthman postulated in "The Weeping Willow Manifesto" that there was a common enemy: "ourselves and our relatives."

Much of who we were and what we had become was reflected in the unacceptable curriculum of the school, which conformed to the greater society's restraints. The condemned building represented to Bearcap and Youthman "a wild-eyed creature ensnared in razor-sharp barbed wire. In its movements to free itself, the creature who didn't know better and would not rest became its own enemy." Instead of developing an institution of tribal learning, we prepared Black Eagle Child youth for an unpredictable and irresponsible tomorrow.

After an incident whereby the Plain Brown Bear family sent themselves and not the eighth-grade graduating class to Disney World, Bearcap and Youthman resigned in protest from Weeping Willow. Through fear of retribution no one else objected because the Plain Brown Bears and their Muscatine cousins sat on the Black Eagle Child Tribal Council, as well as the gambling, school, housing, recreation, culture, fine arts, and health boards. Resigning from the wretched school and secretly entering their article in the casino-backed *Black Eagle Child Quarterly* computers were admirable acts for Bearcap and Youthman. The only problem was, although we came from the same philosophical encampment, I was adamant in the belief that teachers and writers were different. You had to be either one or the other. They, in this case, were the other. They were bureaucrats in limbo, no authority to do anything. "If given a chance they'd perpetrate misdeeds themselves" was the opinion expressed by my Principal Bear uncles. Nevertheless, that did not prevent me from bubbling with glee when the following excerpt appeared in the *BECQ*:

> Behind the receptionist's desk of the BEC health clinic sits Abraham Plain Brown Bear, Weeping Willow Elementary School Board chair-for-life and alleged "lollipopper" of young boys and men. Through his father, an influential earthlodge leader, he wants you to think he's clean, repentant, and remorseful. But honestly, *ki nwa-e me to se ne ni wi ye ko,* you who are the people, are you comfortable that your medical records and physical condition are open to Abraham? Do you

care if he handles them, making photocopies in case you're a rival or an outspoken critic? Are you comfortable that he's urging youth to roll up their blue jeans up and over the ankles, showing the white socks? How would you like it if someone asked you to apply the eyebrow liner toothpick-thin, dark, and crooked—and you were a man? Abraham's records show he once got several boys intoxicated in a hotel room, tied them up, and took photographs of them in the nude. Asked by the judge why he shot photos from angles that made the subjects' hands and feet appear abnormally large, Abraham replied, "I like K. C. Zormon's lithographs, Your Honor. Mr. Zormon is a contemporary Indian pop artist." Without being asked, the all-white jury nodded they, too, hadn't heard of "Mr. Zormon." Why was the judge so preoccupied with bondage, camera angles, and the photo enlargements of the male minors? Why this blatant disrespect for their families and their privacy?

Why ponder this triviality? It's reality.

Black Eagle Child people, *to ki ko,* wake up! Seriously now.

The courthouse scene is no different from the current tribal administration.

Present at Abraham Plain Brown Bear's trial were Horatio Plain Brown Bear, the defendant's brother and secretary of the Tribal Council; Kensington "Kensey" Muscatine, the defendant's cousin; and Hayward "Grubby" Muscatine, the defendant's brother-in-law and Tribal Council treasurer: character witnesses.

On the stand "Kensey" attests to Abraham's "divergence on occasion" and dodges questions about his own problems. The prosecution states that as Why Cheer High School STU-JEPP (Students in Academic Jeopardy Program) counselor, "Mr. Muscatine molested disadvantaged white females, for which he was found guilty. He was thereby forced to resign as chair of the Black Eagle Child Tribal Council." "Kensey" explains he is going to be a "greenhouse horticulturist." "Grubby" Muscatine, brother-in-law of Abraham and Horatio Plain Brown Bear, confirms the horticulture grant is part of the Tribal

Council's rehabilitation program, not a reward. He does this while yelling. There is a fifteen-minute recess. "Grubby" apologizes for the outburst and fidgets with his long, silver braids that are wrapped in stiff strips of yellow leather. He is last seen leaving the courthouse with his wife, Elvia Plain Brown Bear-Muscatine, following closely behind. Funny how tall people look when they flee, someone was heard saying, their big tennis-shoed feet plopping loudly over the polished wooden floors.

What happened? people were saying also.

Did "Grubby" see a photo enlargement of himself as a youth gang member, based on motorcycle rider ideology, French-kissing Horatio Plain Brown Bear? Did the photo taken of a group of kids reveal more than a rebellious, cool, and sixtyish fad worshipper? And is that him peering from behind the hangers inside the proverbial closet? Is this why he staunchly supports Horatio and Abraham Plain Brown Bear? Was Elvia, the sister, the last conquest, the last sibling to be embraced . . . spreading . . . bending? Which was it? Who gives a _____? "Grubby," lip-locker and provider of bisexual acts among the Plain Brown Bears . . .

Billy "Cracker" Jack, *Black Eagle Child Quarterly* editor, almost lost his job. He found it necessary to make late-night visits, reminding Tribal Council members he had their signatures. In his long, dull gray Cadillac, "Cracker" Jack brought gambling to the Black Eagle Child Settlement at ten thousand dollars per vote from the seven-person tribal government. The people despised his gestapoliticking demeanor and "wise guy" connections. Without knowing a referendum had taken place, the tribe awoke one morning to televised press conferences we had voted unanimously for gambling. That was years ago. The houses "Cracker" Jack promised are slowly being built for relatives of whoever is in charge, and no one is a millionaire.

With a circulation of eighteen thousand copies, the *Black Eagle Child Quarterly* issue was an instant collector's item. Thanks to the blistering attack by Bearcap and Youthman. Lambasted as a leader of the corrupt Black Eagle Child gambling enterprise, "Cracker" Jack cruised the thoroughfares of the Settlement with his Batmobile late into the starlit night.


There was a plethora of unmet conditions in the offing that prevented me from joining forces with Bearcap and Youthman. Politically inspired diatribe intrigued me. It was hard resisting a visit to the houses of these exemplary visionaries. The fact was—and Bearcap and Youthman understood this—I had no allies other than the Six Grandfathers' Journals. But regardless of the chasm between writer and teacher, all three of us were saying the prophecies our grandparents most feared were here. It was little consolation, however, because a majority of the tribe, for lack of better words, "sucked eggs." To them *we* were the incongruity. Anyone who possessed a college degree or an honorary doctorate in letters—wrote books—could not be trusted. The Tribal Council stated that "the Settlement has no room for educated people; the casino was established primarily for the uneducated." In their tainted love/hate relationship with education, they raised the Weeping Willow Elementary tribal culture instructors'— their wives'—salaries to be comparable to those of state-certified teachers. My parents complained that since the school was operated by illiterates, they were jealous of my sister student-teaching at Weeping Willow.

As the uneducated leaders and their followers took the helm of the craft christened the Black Eagle Child Settlement, the Creator's whirlwind lifted the prefab big-top tent above and down upon the Black Eagle Child Field Days and Chautauqua crowd, injuring many.

It was useless.

The Tribal Council members didn't get the message, not even when the Creator, according to Professor Crockston, affixed the postal zip code and their tribal names to their letters: *Bo ki te ba, Me ma ka na tti ya ta, Mo tti ti ya ta, Wi ni ko ma ta-a be ji, Me ta na ki ti ya ta, Ka ske ti ta, koni Be mi te wi-ma ki ti ya ta, Why Cheer, Iowa 53229.* Hole-in-the-Head, Large-Testicled One, Dirty-Assed One, Constant Dirty-Nosed One, Entirely Naked One, Constipated One, and Lard Big-Butted One, Why Cheer, Iowa 53229.

It was rugged commentary but needed in a reclusive community where points were rarely made and understood.

The vortex of evil brought lovely female impersonators who did
blow jobs on old, unsuspecting white men and handsome male impersonators did the same on old, white ladies. White-on-white crime
—for the time being.

Disgusted beyond the point of control I contemplated trashing
the casino's Christmas display of Snow White and the Seven Dwarves
that lit up in neon letters "WISH U A MERRY X-MAS!" along the Highway
30 casino mixmaster. The dwarves alone were worth twelve thousand
dollars apiece. No one in the casino marketing department knew why
Snow White had been ordered for the Christmas holidays.

In my journals I wrote: *"If they (the tribe) could only wake up,
they'd realize they have no future as long as the Tribal Council is in
charge. It will be like before: At a critical juncture when everything we
represent and own—central Iowa realty—is under jeopardy of being lost,
only then will the tribe turn to the O ki ma, the Sacred Chieftains."*

To advance my argument, the *Central Plains Register* out of Des
Moines was helpful, publishing my essays on the deconstruction of
tribal government to eliminate corruption. In spite of the fact that I
was no shining example of a circumspect, half-assimilated tribal
member, my journalistic skills would keep me away from "the big
house." For Horatio, "Grubby," and "Kensey," there were federal
charges pending on gigoloism, embezzling, and racketeering.

As Grandmother forewarned, a certain evilness had set in. The
destiny of the tribe was determined by a grossly uneducated Tribal
Council whose members were easily swayed by Twintowns businesses
with projects that benefited only the whites and themselves—and not
the tribe per se. For the Tribal Council, the sudden influx of casino
cash was mind-boggling. They left government and state monies alone
because it could be traced. The truth was, some were no different
from their greedy grandfathers.

Beyond the money issue, there was the matter of the former
council chair, the pedophile-horticulturalist, "Kensey" Muscatine,
who reminded us that the potential of another Dorothy Black Heron
situation still lurked. The threat also existed in the personage of the

present council chair, Horatio Plain Brown Bear II, who spent most of his waking hours in court on a number of paternity suits. When he wasn't impregnating his two younger brothers' girlfriends, there were suspicions he was at his sister Elvia's house when she conveniently wasn't there, loin-locking to the extreme with "Grubby" Muscatine! The stories were vivid. Through the window they were allegedly seen: the round, obese frame of Horatio behind the bent-over frame of "Grubby," and both with cigarettes dangling from their mouths, discussing whether the soap actress Susan Lucci would ever win something for her acting. Whether this happened, no one really knew.

As for the women who incubated Horatio Plain Brown Bear's history-altering seed, it was reported they had settled out of court. The payment? Diamond earrings from a Beverly Hills jewelry magnate who opened a shop at the tribal casino complex. Forever silenced, these women who so desperately wanted their children to be medically proven as Horatio's and thus enrolled as Black Eagle Childs, receiving all the tribal benefits—an identity along with housing, health, education, and a casino per capita trust fund—disappointed everyone. Nine pairs of earrings worth thirty-five hundred dollars apiece were given to the Black Eagle Child and Why Cheer women, provided they drop their paternity suits. The tenth pair was given openly as a gift to the paramour brother-in-law, "Grubby." These were eventually seen being worn by "Grubby's" wife, Elvia, and her brother, the notorious "lollipopper of men and boys," a perennial Weeping Willow school board member.

It was depravity, a demented parallel universe, the kind that began an infamous Black Heron legacy.

The power that came with the indiscriminate signing of gambling enterprises consumed everyone. At the highest point of corruption, tribal members fought among themselves when they couldn't get access to the "cash cages" at the casino complex. Brandishing charms from a variety of hired guns, irreputable medicine men, those within arm's reach of the money, hid small bundles of animal bones and other spell-producing agents that couldn't be destroyed in the desktops of rivals or near surveillance cameras. If access was still denied, they'd scurry around with petitions about what the "other side" had done. It didn't matter who was in charge, they were all part of the same kleptocracy. Nevertheless we'd sign the petitions hoping someone had the intellectual wherewithal to realign our destiny.

We were wrong on all counts, however. There was never anything in our stories that told us to go that direction. By replacing the window of the Cosmic Earthlodge with aluminum paneling, we encouraged a sudden gust of wind to tear it apart, which made us cringe as the other elements gathered around us in force.

# My Summer of 2004

## Honorable Mention in Doetingham Junior High School's O'Toole Creative Writing Award

**MAYA MAE BEARCHILD:**
Mud-scooping duck in the leftover pools of rain, what did you feel when the slimy water serpent wound its wet body around your chapped leg and webbed foot, refusing to be your meal? And what were your thoughts when the white-chested, red-tailed hawk swept by like a Chinese Mig jet taking in its afterburn your throat, your life, and the half-alive prey?

Luciano Bearchild, I hear, was taken like that. Such was the story of the golden-bodied fish, exploring and living off "other tributaries" before the stars came after him. Encased in glass and stashed away in an antique trunk in the attic, we still have the fur military hat—the earmuffed one—Luciano cherished more than anything. Here's proof of an extraterrestrial abduction! he probably wanted to yell, Frisbeeing the Red Star symbol hat over the metallic strobe-lit body of the UFO until the search party came up the sandy hill from Liquid Lake, telling each other upon its discovery, "Hey-y-y, this is the one he was rarely without."

What a grotesque scene the trio made: the hawk, the mud-scooping duck, and the serpent, all clasping one another in the defiant blue sky, all entrapped by differing instincts. Their silhouettes twisted high above in the hazy midday sun. The red-tailed hawk barely made it over the towering pine trees. I looked at the grass-covered slough as its water collected around my bare feet. In rapt attention I stood, taking notes. As the victims struggled the hawk lost control. They spiraled downward until someone froze, regaining flight equilibrium.

Upside down crashed the Chinese Mig jet.

Inside out was Luciano's shadow, extracted by the silver spaceship, embedded in a sandy hill. A bloodless, clueless evanescence was instigated.

The macabre scene of a redtail carrying a duck who itself is carrying and fighting with a snake over lunch rights reminded me of mobile sculptures I made at school. Especially when they hung still in the erratic autumn wind, suspended over the reed-edged pond, for the ten to twelve seconds I counted.

A description of my next sculpture: Christmas tinsels spray-painted brownish yellow with lines of green; with the aid of an O'Connor model six-bladed fan the reeds will blow upward, fluttering vertically. Over the pond where no one swam or fished a giant circular sheet of Reynolds foil reson-undul-ates. Constructed from wire hangers, string, painted cardboard, rubber tubing, roadkill hawk feathers, and a duck call—all mechanized—"The Life Expectancy of a Duck and Not a Grebe," rotates near the skylight ceiling of the Weeping Willow Educational Complex. Under Plexiglas the meaning: *"The avant-garde kinetic sculpture with wings, metal serrated teeth, cables, and pulleys, all powered by a windmill, makes the gear-grinding music that is music to the inner fluffy ears of the three evil owls who bob their heads and necks in dance when death is imminent. I was thinking of the person my parents, Edgar and Selene Bearchild, sometimes talk about: Ted Facepaint. 'He is the one that died so that you may be,' I was told early on by my father, a troubled artist. 'From the Grandfather World, far away from our day-to-day struggle on these minute islands of ourselves,' my mother added, 'Ted, with the aid of my grandmother and your mother's mother and aunt, arranged it so that you may be here in their place.'"*

In any event, moving, descriptive sculptures—breezemakers—are my existential calling. She had known since fifth grade, they'll say, when she tied slices of bread on tree branches on subzero windy days for hungry birds that there was nothing aesthetic about a violent wind sculpture. "Cinque" the revolutionary gray cat got very chubby that year from birds that were knocked unconscious.

Which raises another question on aesthetic presentation: In what way could I depict the moment the snake and the duck shook simultaneously in an attempt to break free, causing the hawk's talons to break and shimmy through their rigamarole of bones, innards, scales, and leathery skin, canceling out any hope of being released? Hopelessly locked, the tips of the talons acted like fine, curled needles that clamped shut, impaling both victims, who saw an upside-down earth view before Black Heron consciousness waned.

What is the history, you query, of the Black Heron name?

(You scribbled "How does it fit into the story?" on the first draft of 9/23/04. It is a stat that in our lifetimes one in three of us will meet a murderer. The mud-scooping duck, the serpent, and the hawk incorporate this "Black Heron" metaphor.)

According to *Black Eagle Child*, my father's book, it began in 1890 with Tama County's cover-up of Dorothy Black Heron's murder. My great-great-great-grandfather's father went unpunished for the crime. Blackmailed by whites into signing a document that made him a federally recognized chieftain, my grandfather thrice over brought education into the tribe, including freedom for an ancestral criminal.

Next came the One Most Afraid. In 1894 she was born to Albert and Clarice Black Heron four years after the loss of their first daughter, Dorothy Black Heron. Because of her spellbinding beauty, the One Most Afraid, at fourteen, stole John Two Red Foot, a good provider to five children, from Martha Two Red Foot. In 1908 John Two Red Foot chose the young enchantress over his family responsibilities as a father.

(Per your request enclosed are the two stories of which I speak: "How We Delighted in Seeing the Fat" and "The Great Flood of the Iowa River" by Edgar Bearchild.)

According to Carson Two Red Foot, the oldest of the five abandoned siblings, their mother, fearing humiliation, took them on a hinterland odyssey. (Carson, for your edification, was my grandmother Ada Principal Bear's brother adopted by ceremony.)

In 1911, however, after the unprecedented flood of the Iowa River, which swept away their *wi ki ya bi*, or lodge, near the Amana Colonies, they were forced to return to Black Eagle Child. Unfortunately, due to their mother's inscrutable suspicions, Bent Tree, Carson's sister, committed suicide in 1913. Driven by new bouts of depression and guilt, their mother was fixated with the personage of the One Most Afraid.

In 1915, in another place entirely, the Pipestar family, along with three others, arrived from Pinelodge Lake, Canada, and took up residence as communal farmers near the township of Claer, Iowa. Four decades and five years later, a ten-year-old boy called Junior rode across the icy Cedar River on a stone surfboard guided by the reflection of his grandfather's French medieval sword.

My great-grandmother, Ada Principal Bear, offers a related narrative about the Two Red Foot family. In 1919, she states that her husband, Jack Principal Bear, as a young man, with the aid of a friend, captured a shawl-wearing sorceress on the first bridge, *ko ka i ka ni*, of the Settlement, holding her there until the morning light. Her identity unveiled, the well-respected woman physically deteriorated shortly thereafter.

And so it came to be that in 1920, when Carson's mother befriended the legless sorceress, a transaction was probably made for the One Most Afraid, herself a mother of two by then, to avenge Bent Tree's suicide. Never having had a chance to know other men-friends, the One Most Afraid was set up by the sister of a young man she took a liking to.

On a summer night, as she anxiously awaited her promising beau, three small floating lights nearby in the bushes shape-shifted. Three strangers thus approached from behind as she sat on a log and began clubbing her until she stopped moving at twenty-five years of age. Here, reminiscent of her older sister's death, there were suspects, but the authorities did very little.

My great-grandmother indicates that also in 1925 her family took the legless sorceress and her elderly companion into their home. Out of gratitude they eventually entrusted her with their powerful "seeing" medicines. The transference of these secrets caused anger. The closest relative of the feared duo by the name of Aunt Sophie, a "shadow-releaser" who had shunned them, promised retribution when she learned these "bone-affixed-to-limb-for-traveling" parfleches went to someone else.

Used for wrongful purposes, the medicines could make one invisible or airborne, and allow one to see at night. Used in the right way by making the sick well, the medicines prolonged one's existence, which was how they were used by my great-grandmother. Among them is the "stone knife," the one I now wear inside a brass locket necklace.

In the 1930s were born my grandparents, Clotelde and Tony Bearchild, who subsequently brought into this world an ochre, seal-eyed "word-collector" of Capulet and Montague descent by the name of Edgar Bearchild, upkeeper and maintainer of the Six Grandfathers' Journals who went on to fall in love with my mother, Selene Buffalo Husband, in 1973, thereby giving birth to me—after three miscarriages—in 1991, two years after and replacing ceremonially the place once occupied by Ted Facepaint . . . Ada Principal Bear . . . Pat "Dirty" Red Hat . . . Luciano Bearchild . . . William Listener . . . and my lovely grandmother, Lillian Buffalo Husband, and her ever-present sister, Alice, going back further to my other grandparents and their own grandparents on either side, *wa wi ta wi*. Especially the Sacred Chieftains, *O ki ma wa ki,* and the Holy Grandfather who arranged their rightful return as decision-makers of the Black Eagle Child Nation, proving that my father was simply a pessimist all along.

Verily, through the scattering of cigarette tobacco on the floor and through these ever-circling stories, I call upon all those before me, including Dorothy Black Heron and her younger sister, the One Most Afraid, to partake with me of this journey, reminding me every day how imperative it is to realign our destiny, to salvage these cherished but immutable islands of ourselves that tumble aimlessly among the blinding stars. . . .